I0763930

ISBN: 979-8-9919089-4-8

The Crystal

Parts 4-6

Part 4: The Politician

“Politics is too serious a matter to be left to the politicians”

Chapter 1

I lifted my hand and knocked on the wooden classroom door. Perhaps I should have felt suspense, or guilt, or even excitement, but I was mostly just tired. This was just another entry in my ongoing saga of being late to class. Specifically, late to this class. One thing was for sure, this would be the last time it ever happened.

I watched through the small window as the student seated nearest to the door stood and opened it. The door squeaked open and the uninterested student slouched back to his seat. When I entered, I walked into the intense glare of the teacher, Mr. Johnson, who spoke in his trademarked, monotone voice.

“Late again,” he scolded, “How many times does that make it?”

“Since it's the last day of school, I'd say that makes it the last,” I replied.

“You're lucky it's the last day or I wouldn't tolerate that kind of attitude,” Mr Johnson continued, having the faintest bit of annoyance in his inflection, “I can still bar you from walking across that stage tonight.”

My first thought was “I'd like to see you try”, but I decided to keep that to myself. I had to fight enough; I didn't want to do it here. These were my off hours.

“Sorry, sir,” I apologized.

Mr Johnson looked back at his text book, “Have a seat. We still have content to cover.”

“Weren't grades due three days ago?” I questioned, reflexively. I knew it didn't matter and wasn't worth bringing up, but the words just slipped out. I don't have much of a filter when I'm tired.

“Grades were due, but that does not mean I have to stop teaching,” he retorted.

I accepted defeat and took my seat next to Bailey in the back of the classroom. She gave me a disappointed and concerned glance. She knew exactly why I was late.

"Where were you this time?" she whispered as Mr. Johnson continued his lesson.

"Brazil," I replied groggily. My eyelids were so heavy I could hardly keep them open. I had been awake for over 24 hours now, and I knew I would have to be up for quite a few more with graduation tonight. I didn't get very much sleep lately.

"And why did you think you had to do that alone?" Bailey questioned.

"Because I could handle it," I answered, matter of factly.

It had been nearly eight months since the Battle of Broken Valley: the battle that secured the Ekklesia's spot in the war. Since then, there had been an unspoken ceasefire between The Organization and the Ekklesia. Both sides were taking time to recover and build their forces. That is, until three weeks ago, when one of the Ekklesia's weapons storehouses in Ecuador went up in flames. There were no witnesses and no survivors.

From there, similar attacks began to happen along the coast of Central and South America. I had been traveling back and forth trying to catch the illusive strike team. Though their attacks seemed random, ALI ran an algorithm and guessed the outpost they were going to attack next. Last night, I caught them in the act.

"In recent years, artificial gravity has been the highlight of modern science," Mr. Johnson lectured, "Scientists have found that highly energized, counter rotating mercury fields can create a bend in the fourth dimension. Mercury has this ability because..."

"Are you at least going to be at graduation tonight?" Bailey asked, obviously still dwelling upon our previous conversation.

"I wouldn't miss it," I whispered, "I've made sure of that."

"You better not," Bailey warned playfully, "This is our last bit of normal before we all jump back in." She paused sentimentally, "And you deserve this."

Her comments made me smile. I was so looking forward to tonight. We did deserve this. We'd fought hard for this. And everything was starting to pick back up again. This was our last night of being kids, before we went back to being soldiers.

"We do have a High Council meeting first," I informed her.

"It wasn't scheduled this morning," Bailey said.

"Well, I..."

"Please at least pretend to pay attention Mr. Sons," Mr. Johnson interrupted.

"Sorry sir," I replied, cutting my tired eyes in his direction.

"You're just like your father," Mr. Johnson complained.

"Thank you," I quipped. I really did take that as a compliment, though I knew he was referring to my father's misbehavior. "I'll tell you later," I mumbled to Bailey. She nodded her head in response.

Blake, who sat a few seats ahead of us next to Ana, turned around in his seat and made eye contact with me. He raised his eyebrows to tease me for getting in trouble.

I smiled and shook my head. He turned back around and once again began to pretend to listen to Mr. Johnson's lecture. Typically, I and all my friends would actually try to learn. I had made sure all of the classes we were taking were ones we would need on the battlefield: Chemistry, Physics, Mechanics, and Nursing. Today, it was safe to say all of our minds were elsewhere.

As I did my best not to fall asleep, I stared across the room and through the large window on the right hand wall. The sun was beaming through, illuminating the yellow film of pollen that clung to the glass. Through the window was the teacher parking lot and a planter housing a blooming cottonwood tree - the culprit of the pollen film.

Its purple clusters of flowers were bouncing in the late spring breeze. The large round leaves fluttered with each passing gust. It was a tall tree and its growing shadow shaded many of the cars in the lot. The sunlight that made it through the thick layer of foliage danced on the ground in ever changing patterns that reminded me of the patterns that would flow across my body when I used the power of my crystal.

It looked so peaceful. It looked normal. It looked like nothing had happened here. But it had. This section of land looked untouched, but much of Tullahoma would tell a very different story.

Many neighborhoods were just now beginning to rebuild after the battle that had taken place here less than a year ago. Scars from crashed fighters littered the landscape. Burned forests looked as though they hadn't even begun to recover. This thought made me think of just how miserably I and my friends had failed at being normal these past six months.

I had brought us back here with the intention of having a somewhat normal life again. In the beginning, I'd thought I could take a step back and have some time to myself. After all, The Organization had grown silent, and we needed time to grow our forces. I thought my friends and I could take six months to just be kids and jump right back in after graduation. It just didn't work that way.

We'd already seen battle, we knew there were people who needed us, and we were good at what we did. In fact, we were really good and getting better. That's part of the problem the council had with us stepping back. They said I was just prolonging the war. They wanted us to run missions as a team to cripple The Organization further while the rest of the Ekklesia grew in strength.

Unfortunately, I agreed with them. I just wanted it all to end, but my friends so enjoyed being away from it all. Of course they wanted to help and be involved, but they also wanted time off. Bailey and Blake were just glad to be kids again, while Ana and Alex were having their first taste of what it was like to be a kid instead of a weapon. So I took up the slack. It wasn't enough to please the council, but I didn't care.

I did my best to make it look like I didn't need my friends' help, so that they wouldn't question it when I made them stay behind. I never complained. I never asked for their help. I didn't even tell them when I was leaving or when I was coming back.

Admittedly, it had made me feel a bit isolated. There were days when I would be flying from a meeting, or surveying damage, or running a covert mission, that I would feel so alone. The only thing that made it worthwhile was coming back and seeing everyone together, enjoying life and each other.

When I was home, I spent most of the time with Bailey, trying my best to nurture the romantic side of our relationship. It had been hard to find time with Blake, or anyone else for that matter. Really, I didn't even spend that much time with Bailey.

I was actually glad that school was ending. I had looked forward to it in the beginning, but now I was run ragged. Plus, I had done this to be with my friends, but I actually saw them less than when we were fighting in the war together.

These recent attacks were timely in my opinion. The Ekklesia was stronger than it had ever been. My friends were more proficient in their abilities, and with my crystal no longer fragmented, I was more powerful than I had ever been. Plus, everyone in the whole Ekklesia was ready to get back to fighting: the council, the troops, my friends. We had rebuilt from the initial attacks, and we were ready to start tearing down The Organization.

"Does anyone know what the fourth dimension is?" Mr. Johnson asked. His question broke through my uninterested daydreaming.

No one answered, so he droned on, "Time. Time is the fourth dimension. Gravity is a bend in that fourth dimension of time. Some scientists suggest that because we can now tap into that dimension, we can bend the very fabric of space and time. Why might that be important?"

"Space travel," Someone answered. I looked and saw that it was a kid who was usually quiet. I guess the subject interested him.

Mr. Johnson's tired eyes lit up, and he looked up from his textbook for the first time since I had sat down. It was the most excitement I'd ever seen him have in a given moment (maybe even if you combined every other moment together).

"Yes. Yes, exactly," he said. His voice actually carried a hint of emotion. It was so out of the ordinary that it captured the whole class' attention. For the first time ever, heads raised and consciousness awakened within the students as they actually gave their attention to the lecture.

"Space travel!" Mr Johnson continued happily. "With all that has gone on, especially this past year, that prospect may seem far from your mind, but think about it," he paused for people to consider, "What has come about during this forsaken war that could lead to space travel?"

Mr. Johnson eagerly awaited another response. His eyes squinted with hope that another student would have the courage to speak. I did.

"Massive flying ships," I said, "They are pressurized and have life support systems. It wouldn't take much to make them space faring vessels." I knew this because the subject had been brought up in council meetings multiple times.

Mr. Johnsons' eyes grew wider than I knew they could open. The grin on his face grew into a cheesing smile.. "Yes," joy filled his voice, "And the chemistry surrounding each of those ships is astounding! Just in the engines alone-"

Ring!

The bell cut off perhaps the most interesting lecture Mr. Johnson had ever given. He cut his eyes angrily at the P.A. speaker in the ceiling. "And, um, the engines…" Mr. Johnson stumbled for his words, knowing he would never gain back the attention of the class.

The once interested students began packing their bags and standing up from their chairs. Their momentary fixation on Mr. Johnson's found emotion was engulfed by the looming graduation.

"They use plasma repulsor boosters that use hydrogen to…" he sighed, hung his head, and allowed his monotone inflection to return, "Oh, well, have a good summer everyone."

He slouched back to his desk as the students filed out. I actually felt bad for him. I guess years of no one answering his questions had taken its toll on him.

The class filed out of the room. I sluggishly gathered my things and made for the door as well. I was the only student left in the room.

My senses were so strong now that I rarely had to attempt to sense people's emotions. It sort of just happened. As I walked by Mr. Johnson's desk I sensed his disappointment, but not just that, he felt defeated. My compassion rose to meet it.

"They use Hydrogen because it isn't dense, and they can carry large amounts in a small space. The reactors cause the Hydrogen to undergo fusion and act as secondary power for the ships. They use anti gravity repulsors, powered by energised, counter rotating mercury to keep the ships in the air."

Mr. Johnson looked up and smiled. All his disappointment was snuffed out by a ray of hope. He wanted what everyone in the world wanted – purpose. He felt like he'd made a difference. "Have a good summer," he said affectionately.

"You too Mr. Johnson," I replied and walked out the door.

My friends were waiting for me in the hallway.

"So, how'd it go last night?" Ana asked.

"It was definitely interesting," I alluded, trying not to be too conspicuous with all the people bustling down the hallway.

"What's that supposed to mean?" Blake asked, "Did you get them?"

"I got most of them," I said, "But one got away. That's why we have a meeting with the High Council in thirty minutes."

"Hey, how'd the mission go?" Alex asked, walking up behind us and putting his arm on Blake's shoulder. He was oblivious to what had already been discussed.

"My people can't find him?" Ana asked, ignoring Alex.

"He's...Well, let's talk about this where there's less people" I suggested.

"Did I miss something?" Alex asked.

"Not really," I said, "I'll fill you all in on the way home.

The group agreed, and we made our way through the labyrinth of hallways, out into the parking lot. From there, we began walking toward our neighborhood.

"So, what happened?" Bailey asked once we were away from the crowd of students.

I honed into my senses to make sure there was no one else around. When I was sure we were safe to talk, I began my story.

"So, you guys know how we have a high council meeting in a few minutes?" I alluded.

"Yea..."

"Uh, huh."

"I got the notification at lunch."

"What about it?" Blake asked.

"Well, that was because of my mission," I explained, "We got the location of the raid right. We caught the strike team."

I paused just long enough to breathe. Which apparently meant I wasn't telling the story fast enough.

"So what's the problem then?" Alex asked.

"Well... I'm getting there," I continued, "The team was small, like we expected. They had some pretty advanced weapons, but nothing we couldn't handle. I didn't even think I was going to have to step in until… he showed up."

"Who's he?" Bailey asked. The whole group had stopped walking and leaned in to listen.

"Another crystal bearer."

Chapter 2

A flood of questions erupted from my friends.

"What were his powers?"

"How old was he?"

"Where did he go?"

"Did he beat you?"

"Guys. Guys!" I motioned for them to calm down, "I don't know very much. We didn't even really get the chance to fight."

I waited for someone to butt in, but everyone was now listening intently. "They came out of the forest thinking they were just going to hit and run like they'd been doing. When we engaged them, the bearer revealed himself. He has very explosive powers. He conjured some sort of fireball and flung it at the outpost. I blocked it, and when they saw me, they ran away. We pursued and caught everyone except the bearer."

"Did radar not pick anything up?" Ana asked. She knew that her people had the very best surveillance systems in the world. They could track anything. Well, almost anything.

"We detected an initial burst of energy," I explained. "We think he can use his powers to fly, but once he was airborne, we lost him completely."

"Do you think that's new stealth technology or a part of his powerset?" Bailey asked. Our little group had now formed a circle on the sidewalk.

"There's not a good way to know," I said, "but since the others didn't use it I'd say it's his powers."

"I knew you should have taken us with you," Bailey complained, "I could have flown after him."

"Being able to fly wasn't the problem," I countered, "He just got away from us."

"And how do you think that council is going to take that?" Blake asked.

"Probably the same way they take everything else I do lately," I shook my head and began walking again. We were only a few blocks away from the lake where all of our homes were.

As we finished our walk, our conversation drifted mostly toward the identity of the bearer and where his crystal would have come from. For centuries there seemed to be a consensus among those who knew about the stones that there were only five. However, in the past year that number grew by over half, and that was just the ones we knew about.

Before this, we all had some confidence in the fact that the only crystal bearers were on the side of the Ekklesia. Now, The Organization had a new bearer, and we could only pray that they didn't have more.

We arrived at my house and walked to the secret basement where my dad's old command center was. It had been completely remodeled since our first time here.

The entire system of tunnels had been given the pristine, seamless white coating that the halls of the mountain base had. The old control panels, once covered with buttons and knobs, were now one large screen.

The main control room, the one you first enter when walking into the complex, had a large round holo-table in the center. Here we could have meetings and view missions in 3D before ever setting foot there.

On the back wall was an elaborate rendition of the Ekklesia's flaming dove insignia, made from pure Unitum. It was placed there as a memorial for my father and had a plaque beside it commemorating his accomplishments.

From that main room, the hallways branched, leading to various other control rooms, armories, and barracks. Some even stretched along the bottom of the lake, which made for interesting views.

My friends and I entered the main control room and gathered around the holo-table. On the side, there was a green blinking light, indicating that the council was already waiting on us.

"Alright everyone, time to look professional," I said. My friends knew exactly what I meant and lowered their backpacks to the ground. All at once, we found our pucks and placed them on our chests.

When the puck had made contact, a white ring of light spread out from it. Simultaneously, a black mist swirled around us and created a black cloud around the table. As quickly as the mist had appeared, it solidified and formed to our bodies, creating our light grey bearer uniforms (All except for Blake and Alex; theirs was a darker shade). As the mist formed, the white line of light left behind our gear as it was teleported from the nearby armory.

I gave everyone a quick glance, took a deep breath, and pressed the green button on the side of the table. I used to walk into these meetings with the utmost confidence. Now, they filled me with anxiety. It seemed that no one on the council ever seemed to agree anymore, especially with me. It was always a fight. As if I didn't fight on the battlefield enough.

The lights in the room automatically dimmed and the bluish glow of the hologram filled the room. Projected above the table was each of our perspectives from where we would be sitting if we were physically at the meeting. Everyone's view was unique. I never understood how it did that.

Sitting across from me was General Raddick. He had grown to be my greatest ally on the council. Ironically, next to him was my greatest foe on the council: a grouchy, ambitious middle aged man, Captain Jeremiah Sparks. I didn't know it at the time, but he was the captain of my flagship at the Battle of Broken Valley. When one older member stepped down a few months ago, he claimed the spot. He made the first remark.

"Finally," he grumbled, "What is your mission report, Director?"

All eyes turned to me. I made eye contact with the General. He gave me a worried and annoyed look, urging me to behave myself. I did, for now anyway.

I still gave the captain an annoyed side-eye, but delivered my report without protest. I explained everything just as I had to my friends

"...And then, he dropped off the radar. We searched for hours with no luck, so I returned home."

"I'm not sure what good sending a crystal bearer does when all he does is sit back and watch," Captain Sparks remarked.

"Like I said," I countered, "The troops were handling it just fine until the other bearer arrived. If I had made myself known, we still wouldn't know about the bearer."

Besides Captain Sparks, everyone on the council was mulling over the information they had just received. A new crystal bearer was not welcomed news to say the least. I knew I had already answered any questions they could ask about the bearer. The next step was to come up with a counter move.

"We should put the entire Ekklesia on high alert," General Raddick suggested

"None of our forces are strong enough to fight off a crystal bearer," the man projected beside me said. He was the intelligence director.

"If we can at least get a hit on the radar, our team can engage him," Blake suggested.

"So you're finally brave enough to come out of hiding?" Captain Sparks insulted.

"I think these bearers have proven their bravery," General Raddick defended. I gave him a quick "thank you" glance and picked up.

"It's not a matter of being able to take him out," I said, "It's a matter of pinning him down. He's undoubtedly on the run now."

"Especially with his team captured," the intelligence director added, "He's likely trying to find a way back home, if he hasn't flown there himself already."

"The problem is that we don't have enough information to act," another officer pointed out.

"Then we don't" I suggested, "I say we give it time. We stay on high alert and see if we can catch a glimpse of him, maybe even measure his powers. He'll mess up eventually."

"How long until he does is the question," the medical chief said pessimistically.

"And how many of our outposts can he go through before he makes another mistake?" the weapons officer added.

"I don't see a better option," General Raddick said, "Useless anyone has a better idea?"

The group was silent. I could see Captain Sparks smoldering in his chair. I couldn't use my senses through the hologram, but I didn't need them. He was furious that he, in fact, didn't have a better idea.

"Then we will alert our officers of the issue, and report back here when we have something to report," the general said, "Meeting adjourned."

Everyone stood up from their seats and we all stepped back from the table so that our images would no longer be projected. I was ready to move on, but I overheard some chatter over the speaker. Some of the officers were still in range. I recognized Captain Sparks' complaining.

"Why that crystal came into the possession of that little brat I'll never understand."

This didn't bother me. I already knew how he felt about me. But what he said next cut me.

"I used to respect Daniel," he gritted, "Now, I think he got what he deserved."

My face turned red and my powers surged across my body. I spun back around to the table, my jaw clenched and finger pointed. Just as I was ready to scream, the table turned off.

"You!..." I looked wildly around the room. "Bring it back ALI!" I yelled, slamming my fist on the table. I still had enough sense about me to do that gently. There was no sense in breaking the table.

"I don't think that would be wise sir," his mist bubbled out from under the table, forming his round, slotted emblem in the center.

My hotheadedness quickly cooled, and I realized all my friends were staring at me.

"Dylan," Blake walked over compassionately.

"No," I held out my hand and turned away from him, "I just need to be alone."

I hastily walked out of the room and made for one of the long corridors.

I knew I shouldn't let the captain's words affect me like they did, but I couldn't help it. He found the right button to press. I didn't care what he thought about me or the way I did things. I cared what he thought about my father.

For better or worse, I felt his legacy was attached to mine. I had such admiration for my father. I had been trying since the day he died to honor him and his legacy. To hear someone speak ill of that legacy and blame me for their ill speech expounded on my greatest fear… and greatest regret.

I regretted not refusing to let him use the crystal. I regretted not running to him after the debris fell between us. I regretted my inexperience. I feared that I truly didn't have what it took to fight and win this war. I knew my dad did. Now, it was on me. And that was terrifying.

If something, anything, from the biggest blunder to the smallest mishap went wrong, that was on me. If anyone died, that was on me. If we lost, that was on me. No matter who stood in my way, no matter who made the final decision, it was ultimately on me. No matter what, everything was on me.

I wound through the seemingly never ending tunnels, passing by the med-bay, armories, control rooms for the cannons in Tullahoma, and finally arrived at a large glass panel. It looped over the ceiling and came down on the other side of me. The only part of this tunnel that wasn't glass was the white tile floor beneath me. Through the glass was a view of the lake bed.

The lake was spring fed, making the water extremely clear. I could see at least thirty feet out before it began to grow hazy. Giant boulders littered the ground, as did crashed fighters that had landed there during the Battle of Tullahoma. Algae covered their broken metal corpses. Schools of fish had made them their homes, choosing them over the boulders. They swam in and out of the various compartments of the sunken ships.

I stared out, remembering that battle. It was the only one where my father and I had fought alongside one another. The only lesson about my powers that I had received directly from him was during that battle, when he taught me to channel my energy through my staff. I placed my hand on the staff that was clipped to the back of my waste, remembering when he'd gifted it to me. I longed for Dad to still be here, teaching me now.

I was interrupted from my thinking by a blinking light on my wrist where my vanguard would be if I had my armor on. ALI's voice played from the speaker on my shoulder, "You're receiving a transmission from General Raddick."

"Put him through," I said emotionlessly, not looking away from my view through the window.

"Dylan," his voice played through the same speaker, "I'm sorry you had to hear what you heard."

"Better I hear it than people go on saying it behind my back," I sulked.

"Well, that's actually what I was calling about," the general alluded, "There are lots of things being said here behind your back."

"Why am I not surprised?" I rolled my eyes. I'll admit, I was feeling down. I tried so hard, and they never appreciated it.

"Well, sir, for what it's worth, it's not because you aren't doing a good job," his voice carried optimism, "Objectively, you really are doing a good job, but these men, people like Sparks, they don't see that."

"I thank you for your concern," I said, as passionately as I could, "But you should know by now that I don't care what men like him think."

"But you should know by now that you should," the general's voice took a more stern tone, "You aren't in this for the titles or the accolades. That's good, but even a reluctant leader can't stay out of the politics of leading."

His genuine concern made me feel bad for blowing him off initially. I felt like I was exiting my emotions, and now gave him my full attention. "What are you saying?" I asked.

"I'm saying that so far you've been a very good soldier despite… or because of your convictions," the general explained, "You've been The Soldier Who Wouldn't Kill. That won you the Ekklesia. But, if you want to keep it, you're going to have to become a politician as well."

"You want me to pander to Sparks?" I asked, "Lie to get my way? Doesn't really sound like me."

"That's not what I'm asking of you," the general replied, "I'm just saying you should consider playing to your strengths. Do good things, make good friends, and turn people against your enemies." He paused, "But then make sure everyone knows about it."

That was the kicker. I was not a public facing person. I liked to carry out both missions and meetings in private. I didn't want to be seen or applauded. "You had me until that last part," I halfway joked.

"I'm not saying make the change all at once," Raddick suggested as a bass swam by the glass, "Enjoy your graduation tonight, then bring your team back to the mountain base. Show everyone you're still in the fight. Then, go from there."

It was a good plan. The fight was ramping up anyway and it would be good to be back at the base. "Deal," I agreed, "I'll tell everyone to pack a bag after graduation tonight. Looks like we'll be going on a senior trip after all." I surprised myself with a chuckle.

General Radick chuckled back, "I'll see you soon, Director. –For the nations."

"For the nations," I recited. This had become the battle cry of the Ekklesia ever since I had used the words in my big speech on the flag ship. It had turned into a formal goodbye as well.

The general ended the call, and I began to walk back to the main command center. I felt more like myself again and was glad to have a plan. The general's pep talk had really given me a boost. Sometimes it felt like the whole Ekklesia was against me, but it only ever took one meaningful interaction like this one to remind me I still had many supporters, despite the haters that had climbed the ladder to make their annoying voices heard.

I soon reached the command center, and planned on going in search of my friends. However, as I passed through, the Ekklesia's emblem caught my eye again. Feeling sentimental, I walked over stood in front of the memorial. I looked at the plaque, next to the white metal dove.

"IN HONOR OF DANIEL SONS: FOUNDER OF THE EKKLESIA. MAY HIS VISION FOR A FREE WORLD GUIDE US INTO A BETTER FUTURE."

I stared at the words, admiring the legacy of my father until a hand was placed on my shoulder. I immediately knew who it was.

"You better now?" Bailey asked.

"Yea," I replied tenderly, "I just needed to cool off."

"I don't understand what his problem is," Bailey slid her hand around my waist and admired the Dove with me. I put my arm around her shoulder.

"He's just trying to get me out because he thinks he can take my spot," I observed.

"Dirty politicians," Bailey scowled.

"Guess it comes with the job," I shrugged, "You ready to graduate?"

"Ready or not, I'm about to," Bailey said sentimentally, "Actually, I'm glad I found you; we have to go or we're gonna be late. Blake's already home getting your things together for tonight."

"I didn't figure I would end up with that much stuff to get ready," I questioned. I used to have good grades, but everything had gone downhill when my dad died... the first time. I didn't play any sports or anything. I never won any competitions. I didn't think I would qualify for much more than a cap and gown.

"Of course you do!" Bailey grinned, "You have all kinds of metals and cords."

"For what?" I asked.

"Well, there's the saving the world medal, the cord for being Director of the Ekklesia, the sash for being a superhero."

"You've got to be kidding," I laughed.

"Of course not!" Bailey retorted cheerfully, "You deserve every single one of them."

"Whatever you say," I smiled.

We both turned and walked up the stairs, through the basement, up another set of stairs, and out the front door of the unassuming house. I hadn't even realized the sun was setting until I walked outside into the twilight.

The entrances for all of the soldiers and workers in the tunnels were elsewhere, so there wasn't a lot of commotion around the house. It didn't look any different from any of the other houses on the block. You'd never know there was anything special about it unless you knew.

Bailey and I hugged, then split up. She and her mom were staying across the road. I still lived with the Vales, a few houses down. I walked down the sidewalk, entered through the front door, and kicked off my shoes.

Walking in, on my right was the living room. Mr. James sat on the couch reading a book. "Well, there's the other graduate!" he exclaimed, putting the book face-down on the glass coffee table. "Sun's gettin' low. You better hurry if you're gonna make it on time."

"Yea, Bailey just sent me over here to get ready," I said as I made for the stairs, "Blake is supposed to have my stuff upstairs."

"I just saw him with it a second ago!" Mrs. Cassy yelled from the laundry room across the house. "By the way, GO DYLAN!"

I smiled and laughed as I walked up the stairs to my room at the end of the hallway. Blake's door was open. I peeked in as I passed. His gown and honors were draped across his bed, but he wasn't in there with it and neither was my stuff.

"Blake?" I called, trying to locate him.

"Here!" he called back as I walked into my room. If I had only waited a second to call, I would have found him. He was laying out my honors across my gown.

"What is all this?" I asked in amazement. Sitting on my bed were about four medals and seven cords, each one a different combination of colors. Across them was a purple sash.

"Looks like Bailey pulled some strings… or, heh, cords" Blake laughed.

I shook my head, sighing at his dad joke.

"You good after earlier?" Blake asked, walking up to me.

"Yea, it just got under my skin," I said.

"He had no right to say that," Blake scolded.

"Well, maybe not, but I haven't exactly been doing things that they see are productive," I replied, thinking back to my conversation with General Raddick.

"We've all done more for them than they'll ever be able to repay," Blake sighed.

"That's not why we do it," I pointed out.

"I know," Blake said, and I knew he knew. I also knew what he was getting at. They would have never stood a chance in this war if it wasn't for us – for me – and still some had the audacity to complain. "A thank you would be nice though," Blake sighed. He shook his head and then fixed his posture, "Anyway, are you ready for this?"

Blake walked toward the bathroom that connected our two rooms.

"Ready as I'll ever be," I joked, "Honesty, I am just kinda ready to be done."

"Honesty, me too," Blake said from the bathroom sink. His voice was soft, as if deep in thought. I knew he didn't just mean graduation. He meant all of this. The war. The Politics. The uncertainty.

That was all we said before we got ready. Dress code for the guys was a white button-up shirt and Khakis (not that anyone would see it under our robes).

I kept my puck in the back pocket of my pants. I didn't know why, but something told me to take it, just in case. The same thing must have been speaking to Blake because I saw him taking his as well.

I bundled up the gown and all of my accolades and was ready just a few minutes after Blake. Then, we both headed down the stairs together.

We didn't see our parents before we prepared to walk out the door. It was too late to look for them.

Just as my hand latched onto the door knob I heard a voice behind me, "I don't think so young man."

Mrs. Cassie and her husband were peeking out of the laundry room and were now walking toward us. "You're not getting out that easy," Mr. James joked, "Not with her around anyway." He nudged his wife.

She gave him a brief stink eye, but continued in her course. "Group hug!"

Blake and I both smiled. Our recent experiences had made us appreciate what would have once made us cringe. Now more than ever I loved the cringy, sappy moments between us.

"Don't forget me!" Kinsie called from the top of the stairs. She hopped down, skipping most of the steps, and slammed herself into the group hug.

Everyone giggled and let go.

"Now, if you can't see me in the stands, just know, I'm the one screaming the loudest," Mrs. Cassie said.

"She means crying the loudest," Mr. James teased.

"Only if his sobs don't overpower mine," Mrs. Cassie countered. The two put their arms around one another, and Mrs. Cassie began to cry. It started out as a couple tears, but quickly turned into what we called a "boo-hoo".

"Oh, look, there she goes," Mr. James pulled her into an embrace, "You two get outta here. I'll try to fix her before we leave."

"It... won't...work," Mrs. Cassie sobbed.

"Why's mommy crying?" Kinsie asked.

"Love you guys!" Blake said, reaching around me for the door.

"We'll see you in a few minutes!" I said, "Love y'all."

And with that, Blake and I scurried out the door, into the light of the streetlamps. Ana and Bailey were already waiting on us at the end of our sidewalk and Alex was walking toward us from his house.

As the group merged our excited conversations broke out.

"I've never been to an American graduation before," Ana said.

"Me either," Alex added humorously, though it was true.

"They aren't particularly exciting unless you're in it," I said.

"They aren't particularly exciting if you are," Blake corrected.

"Yea, probably true," I agreed.

"Nonsense!" Bailey said, taking my hand, "This is gonna be the best night of the year!"

"I like your confidence," I said.

"Have some faith," Bailey encouraged.

We walked toward the school, and I couldn't help but feel how normal this was. It was like nothing bad had ever happened, like there was no war. Then, I felt guilty because I knew that the rest of the world didn't have this opportunity. In fact, this wasn't normal anymore.

This was fake - a facade. It was a creation I had made. And honestly, I had made it to hide. General Raddick was right. It was time for me to be a politician. I loved this, and I would enjoy it tonight, but it was time for it to end. It was time to grow up.

We entered the lunchroom and met with the rest of the kids in our class. Everyone was zipping up their gowns and hanging their honors around their neck. We did the same.

We joked through the endless formalities and were finally instructed to line up on the football field. The order separated me from all of my friends except Blake (since we now shared the same last name). Two lines formed next to one another in alphabetical order.

I looked into the stands. I couldn't make out anyone I knew through the sea of parents and relatives. I could have used my powers to locate my family, but I chose to just be normal for one more night. I would do it just like everyone else.

The alma mater began to play. A hush fell over the outdoor stadium, and one of the guidance counselors began to direct us forward, one by one.

Blake was ahead of me and gave me a proud glance as the counselor called him forward, then me. We were directed to our chairs on the football field, in front of a rickety, makeshift stage. We were so far away, we couldn't even hardly see the people sitting on it. This was the only downside of carrying the Vale's name.

Bailey, Alex, and Ana were all sitting on the same row, all the way at the front of the class. There were about thirty rows between us. Soon after Blake and I took our seats, the alma mater stopped playing and the Principal took his place at the podium.

Blake was right, it was boring. The microphone switched hands from speaker to speaker, all of which cried. The echo was so bad by the time the sound reached Blake and I, neither of us had a clue what they were saying.

Then, finally, the music began again. The Principal returned to the mic and began to read off the names of those in the first row, then the second, and so on. Each graduate was given time to walk across the stage and have their moment. But that meant Blake and I were just stuck waiting.

We were given a brief moment of excitement when our friends' names were called, but there was a long gap between us and them.

"So, does having superpowers do anything to make this less boring?" Blake asked. He often liked to ask about my powers, but this time he did so humorously.

"No amount of superpowers could make this less boring," I sighed.

After an eternity, the row in front of us finished and our row was directed to make their way to the stage. "Finally!" Blake and I said at the same time.

We walked up and claimed our spot in line. I was actually nervous. I didn't know why. I didn't like to be in front of all these people, but I certainly wasn't scared of them. None of them were even trying to kill me. Still, something about the moment captured my emotions.

My nervousness capped when Blake's name was called. I clapped, but my face turned pale. I knew I was next. Blake pranced across the stage and received his diploma.

"Dylan Isaac Sons - Vale"

Like magic, my nervousness turned to joy when my name was called. I felt like I was floating as I made my way up the wobbly stairs onto the stage. I was grinning from ear to ear as the cords and medals dangled from around my neck, and I stretched out my hand to take my diploma from the principal.

Just as I had taken hold of it, something caught my attention. A feeling of something approaching. I almost ignored it, but then I saw flicker of light out of the corner of my eye.

I broke my eye contact with the principal and looked to the sky where I had seen it. There, off in the distance, a fiery streak was cutting its way through the night. I had seen it once before. It was the new crystal bearer.

Chapter 3

The principal gave me a confused look and tried pulling me in for a handshake (the predetermined moment for the photographer to take our picture). I didn't give in and instead shoved my diploma back into the hand he was extending for me to shake.

"I'm gonna need you to hold onto this for me," I said, just as I sensed a fiery blast of energy coming toward me.

It moved extremely fast, much faster than any bearer's energy I had come into contact with. Bailey's powers being the only exception. I spun around and held up my left arm. From it, I formed a shield in front of both me and the principal. It expanded just enough to protect us from the blast when the orange fireball exploded across the surface.

I sensed two more on the way, and conjured my own blasts to intercept them before they reached the crowd of students between me and the other bearer.

My purple energy flew across the sky and met the orange over the middle of the football field. The two exploded, but the blast was high enough that no one was harmed. Screams came from the crowd.

"ALI, suit up!" I commanded, and I conjured two concussive blasts to project myself out onto the football field.

I lunged forward and leapt from the platform, using the power from the blasts to get away from the people in front of me. As I flew through the air, a white light spread over my robe and honors, teleporting them elsewhere. Underneath, my white bearer uniform had already appeared, my gear teleporting in before I ever hit the ground.

I sensed two more blasts coming, and rolled as I hit the ground to get out of their way. I had landed about ten feet from the nearest student's chair. The first fireball exploded on the ground next to me. I was able to get one knee under me, and I raised a shield just in time to intercept another.

The grass around me was now black and scorched as I raised up to assess the situation. The bearer was still a few hundred yards out.

Everyone in the stadium had only been witnessing this for a few seconds, and already, they were in an uproar. Screams of terror came from every direction. Babies and small children cried, and fathers were scooping up their families preparing to run. The graduates were stampeding off the field.

I saw people running toward me and instantly knew that they were my friends. Everyone already had their suits on (I guess that voice told everyone to bring their puck). The only one I locked eyes with was Bailey, but it only lasted a brief moment. We both sensed the next blasts coming, but this time, they were aimed at the crowds. Without talking, we both knew the plan.

I summoned my crystal from the puck on my chest, to my right hand. I focused as much energy as I could through the crystal. A purple beam of energy shot out from it. It traveled about one hundred yards into the air before spreading out into a domed shield. It was moving quickly, but the bearer and his fiery energy were moving faster.

The blasts ducked just beneath the edge of the shield as it made its way to the ground. Bailey conjured her own white energy bolts to intercept them. The fire erupted over the stands, but she had stopped it just in time.

The edge of the purple energy field was now about halfway to the ground and moving fast, but the bearer himself was closing in. He had dove down and was now soaring just above the ground. He was going to make it under the shield.

"Bailey, give me a boost!" I yelled across the field.

She turned and formed a beam of energy between the two of us. I held out my left hand and the white energy crashed into it. From there it mingled with my own almost instantly spread across the shield. It was now moving faster, but it was still going to be close.

Ana, seeing what was happening. Conjured her own magenta energy and blasted it toward our attacker. Magenta tendrils clawed their way across the ground before propping up a shield that made up the difference between mine and the ground.

The gap was closed and the bearer was forced to pull up. My shield finally connected with the ground as the bearer skimmed across the surface. I couldn't actually see him though. He was completely engulfed in flames and looked like nothing more than a fiery streak as his energy trailed behind him.

He zoomed around the shield, blasting it with orange fireballs as he went. He was probing it for weaknesses. I knew he wouldn't find any though.

The purple crystal floated just above my palm, its own energy orbiting around it in flat, swirling ribbons. Bailey had stopped feeding it extra energy and now the beam shooting up from it was its own vibrant purple color. Little streams of energy separated from the main beam near the pinnacle of the domed shield, that cast a soft purple light over everything under it. The shield itself was a translucent purple, that stretched around the entire football field and the stands on either side. Everyone was safe under it.

My friends ran over and formed a huddle around me to make a plan.

"Is this the guy?" Blake asked. He was the first to reach me, but the others were close behind.

"Yes!" I said, being careful not to break my concentration on the shield. The fire bearer was still probing it, flying from one side to the other. "Where's our family?"

"They're huddled under the press box," Blake said.

I could breathe a sligh sigh of relief. They had picked a spot that I could easily protect if I had to.

"We've got to get these people out of here," Bailey said when she reached me. I could hardly hear her over all the commotion.

I acknowledged her with a glance, but didn't say anything, because she'd already given me an idea. I held out my free hand and summoned the microphone from the podium on the stage - or what was left of it.

The blasts of energy I had used, caused the stage to collapse and the podium lay in two pieces out in front of it. I didn't see any of the administration that had once been on it, but I could check on them later.

"I need everyone to stay calm," I commanded into the microphone. No one listened. People were running in every direction either trying to find a way out, or trying to run from the ever changing location of the Bearer above us.

"Everyone! We can help you, but you have to listen!" I pleaded. I doubted anyone could even hear me.

"Well, that's not working," I said, looking back at my friends.

"Clearly," Blake added.

"Any other ideas?" I asked. Just then, I sensed something changing outside the shield. I jerked my head in that direction and my friends looked with me.

The bearer had found one place on the shield and was hovering above it. He was shooting a continuous blast of energy at the shield, focusing all the energy into one spot. He was projecting a beam directly from his crystal. The flames radiated out from the impact and I could sense the shield thinning. I directed as much energy to that one spot as I could without losing the rest of the shield.

"We're gonna need something fast!" I said, "I can take him one on one if you guys can get the people out of here."

"ALI, where's our armor and jet packs?" Blake asked.

"Three minutes out," ALI said over the coms.

"Three minutes we don't have," I said, knowing the bearer could break through at any moment.

"I can take him," Bailey suggested, "I can fly and push him out from the people. Dylan, you can intercept any stray shots, while Blake, Ana, and Alex get everyone out of here."

"Bailey, I can take him," I insisted. I didn't want her to fight a new bearer that we knew nothing about.

"I'm sure you can, but so can I, and I can fly. You would have to fight him too close to these people."

I knew she was right. I ground my teeth. I didn't like it, but I could feel the energy of the bearer beginning to slip through. "Fine. Go!" I commanded, and everyone jumped into action.

Blake and Ana ran toward the crowd on the home side. Blake sprinted for the stands to get all of our families. Alex made for the visitor side to help usher those people out. All of the people were now pressed around the perimeter of the shield. As soon as it was lifted they would run. My friends needed to be there to guide them away from the fight.

Bailey's white energy engulfed her body, concentrating at her hands. She ran for a few steps, then lifted into the air. At the last second, I released the shield, simultaneously shooting a powerful beam of energy from my crystal.

The purple blast passed Bailey and crashed into the bearer just as the shield in front of him dissipated. He was launched out into the blackness of the night sky. Bailey followed up my attack with her own white bolt of energy, pushing him further away.

I watched from the ground as the two soared toward each other. They came together about 500 yards from the football field and began fighting. I couldn't really see what was happening and at that distance, my senses weren't very keen. All I could do was wait. She just had to hold him off for a few minutes. But in a fight, that would feel like hours.

Stray blasts came from both of them. Most entirely missed the people Alex, Ana, and Blake were directing off the field, but a few, of both Bailey's and the unknown bearer's would have taken out large swaths of the people if I hadn't shielded them from it.

I watched on still. Bailey was taking some hard hits, "You holding up, Bailey?" I asked over the coms.

"Yea," she replied, clearly out of breath, "He's good though."

“ALI, status report,” I requested, as I shot a blast of my own energy to intercept a fireball headed for the parking lot.

“Armor and packs are just over a minute out,” he informed.

We were halfway there. “How are Bailey’s stats?”

“Heart rate and blood pressure are elevated. Energy flow is mostly even. She has a mild abrasion on her left abdomen.” He informed.

“This is too early for her to be taking damage,” I worried. I wanted to help, but I couldn’t shoot any energy her way without risking hitting her by accident. They were too far away and moving too fast.

“These people are crazy!” Alex said over the coms.

As he spoke, I noticed a bright magenta glow coming from behind the stands. I couldn’t make out what was going on. I didn’t have to wait long to find out.

“People here are getting trampled,” Ana said.

“We need backup and medics,” Blake requested.

“Already on it, sir,” ALI said, “I’ve got a transport on the way with troops as well as a medical carrier. They’re four minutes away.”

“ALI,” I added, “Go ahead and scramble every fighter we have. Get them to surround the area. If he gets away again, we need someone to see him before he falls off the radar.”

“Yes, sir” he said.

As soon as I finished, I caught a glimpse of something shimmering in the sky to my left. It was our armor!

The convoy of Unitum metal split up to travel to its owners. “Bailey, armor’s here!” I informed her. She would need to get some distance between her and the bearer before the armor got to her.

My armor finally reached me. I held out my arms. The vanguards reached me first. They secured themselves on my forearms. The rest of the armor arrived all at once. Tassets, shin guards, breastplate, and pauldrons all went to their assigned places, and the light grey fabric molded over the top of them, concealing the metal. Finally, the jetpack secured itself to my back.

The blue, pulsating flame ignited and without hesitation, I blasted off the ground. I used my concussive blasts to propel me faster than the jetpack could accelerate. I zipped past Bailey, who was just receiving her armor and collided with the bearer that was a few yards away from her.

There was a mighty, booming crack as our bodies, and energies collided. He was thrown backward, and I could instantly tell that I was stronger than he was. That didn't mean he wouldn't put up a good fight.

He conjured multiple blasts, but I conjured my own to meet each one, all the while moving closer to him. I soared through the lingering purple and orange energies and summoned my energy to my fists.

When I reached him, I tried to punch him, but he swerved, and blasted me in the shoulder. I was knocked down a bit. The bearer came down to meet me and delivered another blow to my chest. Since he moved with his own power and not a jetpack, he was much more maneuverable than I was.

I was kicked back. He positioned himself to blast me again, but I held my arms in an "X" across my chest, forming a shield just big enough to block the shot.

I pushed forward through the blast and shot my own energy at him. He dodged again, and lunged forward, flying directly into my chest. He pushed me backward. I knew I was moving toward the ground - fast.

He held my wrists with his flaming hands. I couldn't see any of what was under the flames, but I could see the fiery silhouette of his body. We scuffled for a moment before a blinding white glow and a loud *CRACK* filled the air. The bearer was knocked off of me.

I knew it was Bailey, but I couldn't focus on what she was doing. I was falling and had to correct my trajectory.

I stabilized myself, getting vertical again, but my momentum was still pushing me downward. I got my hands at my sides, and summoned a concussive blast from each. The blast came just a few feet above the ground. I landed hard on my feet. I instantly summoned the blasts again, launching myself into the air and back into the fight.

Bailey and the bearer were now in a scuffle, both traveling further into the sky. Now that he was occupied, I saw my opportunity. "Keep him busy," I told Bailey over the coms.

"Let me," there was a pause as Bailey countered an attack, "get right on that."

I flew upwards, getting a good vantage point above them. I reached around to the staff that was on the back of my utility belt. I took it and thrust it out to my side. The two ends extended and released a small blue blast of energy from each end. I allowed my energy to flow over the weapon. Swirling, purple patterns covered the staff. I held it out in front of me and began to concentrate the energy around it as I took aim.

"You think he can take it?" I asked ALI.

"I would hold back just a bit, sir," ALI suggested.

"Twenty five percent sound about right?"

"I believe so, sir."

"Good," I now spoke over the coms, "Bailey, look out."

She immediately obeyed, and launched herself away from the bearer. He pursued, not realizing my position. I pushed energy through the staff, forming a concentrated beam that tore through the air, almost instantly making contact with the orange dot I had targeted.

He was swatted to the ground like a fly. The beam pushed him into the dirt. Just to make sure I'd completed the job, I pushed him along the ground for a ways, making a deep scar on the landscape. I finally let up on the barrage of energy and flew toward his impact crater. As I flew, I quickly noticed that he was still glowing.

Wanting him to be very unconscious, I gave my staff a twist, changing out the repulser on the back for a tiny engine. The staff rocketed out of my hand and made contact with the bearer's chest. A blue shockwave spread out from the impact, but I could see he was still barely conscious. So I summoned the staff back to my hand and thrust it at him again. It made contact, released its shockwave, and returned to my hand. This time, his orange glow faded.

I landed on the ground next to him, and Bailey landed beside me. I got ready to jab him again, but it looked like he was out now. Bailey and I leaned over him.

This was the first good look we'd gotten of him. He wore an Organization uniform, no different from that of any other soldier. It was solid black and held only an atom sword around the waste. Typically there would be a plasma gun as well, but I suppose he didn't really have a need for one.

He wore a helmet. Again, there was no difference between it and the standard issue for The Organization. The only thing that stood out at all was the glowing orange crystal on his chest.

It was pointed on both ends, just like every other one I'd seen, but this one was different. It wasn't shiny or opaque like the other crystals. It was much more solid looking, more like a rock than a crystal. It still radiated light like the others. Now that I was close to it, I could tell that it was a bit more of a red-orange, than a bright orange. I guess the flames were just brighter than the energy itself.

"Is he out?" I asked ALI.

He didn't have to reply. I saw the bearer move his hand slightly, trying to fight through the symptoms of being struck by the staff. I thrust my staff into his chest again. The blue shockwave spread over his body and pushed him deeper into the crater he was laying in. His body went limp.

"He is now," ALI said.

"Good," I said, "Now, let's see if we can figure out who he is."

I knelt down beside him and felt around on his collar for the release button that controlled his helmet. I found it, and upon pressing it, his helmet retracted. This revealed the scared face of a young man (likely younger than me, but it was hard to tell).

The scars on his face were disturbing. They swirled and flowed in the patterns that the crystals' energy often created. There wasn't a single spot on his face that was spared. He didn't have any hair, instead, the same raised patterns traveled over his bald scalp. The patterns actually reminded me of the scare I wore on my chest - the one I received when I got my powers from the crystal. However, this was on a whole other level.

"Poor thing!" Bailey said empathetically.

"He's just a kid," I sighed, "What is it with The Organization always going after kids?"

"They're the most impressionable," ALI answered.

I wasn't really looking for an answer, but ALI was right. They were trying to raise up a generation that was loyal to them. All it would take was the indoctrination of the next generation, my generation, to erase any memory of the truth.

I pressed a button on my left vanguard that released a nanochip from a slit on the side of the armor. I took the tiny chip in my right hand and placed it on the ring the bearer's helmet had created around his neck. It dissolved into the metal.

"See what you can find out, ALI," I requested.

It wasn't long before ALI's voice gave me a reply, "His name is Lucas, but that's about all I can gather," ALI informed me, "There are no stats, no age, no point of origin, no coms. He's completely dark."

"Is there anything on him we could trace?" Bailey asked, remembering how we had traced a spy a few months ago back to his home base by analyzing the model of phaser he used.

"There is nothing unique about him other than the crystal and what appears to be a dampening device for his powers," ALI replied.

"What's a dampening device?" I asked.

"He appears to have some sort of device that helps curve the damaging effects of his powers," ALI explained, "It releases a type of energy I've never seen before. I can't get any good readings here. I imagine it keeps whatever caused this scarring from happening again."

"We need to get him to a lab," I suggested.

"That might be more difficult than you're thinking," ALI said vaguely.

"Why?" I questioned, "We know how to sedate him."

"That's not the problem," ALI replied, "The device is damaged."

"What does that mean?" Bailey asked, looking at the boy from over my shoulder.

"I can't be sure," ALI said, "However, according to these readings, he could begin to burn up from the inside or...explode"

"Explode?" Bailey and I said at the same time.

"I've never seen anything like this," ALI replied, "I can't be sure what will happen."

As we debated this, I heard the roar of engines in the distance. I looked up to see two transports, both sporting the Ekklesia insignia. One was as a grey troop transport, and the other was a white medical carrier. They both had the same boxy body shape, but the medical carrier was more heavily armored and had no weapons, while the troop transport had two large guns mounted to the bottom. They both landed on the football field (which was still smoldering from the attack).

"We still need to move him," I said, "There's got to be some place we could keep him without him posing a threat to anyone."

"There is a radiation containment facility at the Mountain base," ALI said, "It was made to experiment on the crystals. It could contain him, but it's getting him there that's the problem."

"No it's not," I offered, "I can ride with him on a transport. We'll keep him sedated, and I could contain any explosion with my own powers."

"Dylan, you don't know that," Bailey scolded, "You and everyone else on that transport could go down with him."

"That's why it'll just be me. ALI can fly," I planned.

"That's dangerous," Bailey warned.

"I've survived worse," I countered, "ALI, call in another transport."

"Yes, sir."

Bailey frowned at me. Usually, it was me protesting her doing dangerous stuff. I guess I was just getting a taste of my own medicine. I opened my mouth to say something comforting, but Blake's voice cut me off.

"Did you get him?" he asked.

"Yep," I replied, "You take care of business down there?"

"We got everyone calmed down and troops are directing traffic out of the parking lot," he informed.

"We're treating injuries on the field," Alex added.

"How many are hurt?" Bailey asked.

"Looks like about twenty with real stuff, broken bones or whatever," Alex guessed, "Then, there's a whole slew of people that just think they're hurt. I think everyone's gonna be fine though."

"Good to hear," I said. I knew the stampede could have caused a lot more damage than that, even deaths. I was relieved to hear that there were none. “If everything’s under control, do yall wanna come meet our new friend?”

“He flipped sides that easily?” Alex questioned.

“Well, I don’t mean he’s actually our friend,” I laughed.

“Oh.”

“Yea!” Blake said excitedly, “Ana and I are on our way.”

“Yea, I’m coming too,” Alex added.

I watched them all fly in with their jetpacks. They landed graciously, and walked over. We formed a small huddle around the unconscious boy.

“He’s so young,” Ana pointed out.

“What happened to him?” Blake questioned, noticing the scars.

I sensed the overwhelming empathy coming from our little group. Even though he was on the opposing side and wanted us all dead, we knew what he had been through - at least to a point.

Young and naive, ripped up by the roots and flung into a war that he didn’t deserve to be a part of. Scared by a power he couldn’t comprehend. Given powers he could never hope to fully understand. Just a kid trying to survive.

“How old is he?” Alex asked. I sensed the most emotion coming from him. He knew more than any of us what this boy was going through.

“From what I can tell, he's about 15,” ALI said.

We all shook our heads in silence, as if to honor what the young man had been through. Then, I spoke, filling them in on everything we had learned and what my plan was.

“You guys can take a separate transport and meet me there,” I suggested.

"You're sure you can handle it?" Blake asked.

"Of course," I said. I was mostly sure.

"No he's not," Bailey said. Sometimes I forgot she could read minds, especially mine.

"No fair," I smirked. "I really am mostly sure. This guy's just an unknown."

"Looks to me like you can handle him alright," Blake commented.

"Your transports are on the way," ALI informed us.

"I can't believe it's been six months since we were at the mountain base," Blake said nostalgically.

I tried to be mindful of my thoughts, but I knew Bailey was sensing my discomfort toward returning. She didn't say anything though.

I knew they already knew a lot, but I would have to have a talk with them later about being careful about what they said and who they talked to. I had avoided the base so long that I didn't know who was my ally and who was my political enemy.

It was so strange to me that we could all have the same goal in mind and be so divided on how to achieve it. Divided to the point that we attacked each other. Though no one would be trying to kill us there (except maybe this bearer), we would have to be politically careful.

"I love the views," Ana said.

"You don't get those where you come from?" Alex asked.

"We have beautiful views," she defended, "They are just both beautiful in different ways."

I had been to El Dorado once. Ana and her people called it "Kab'ah K'uhul". It means "the hidden city", but carries a more sacred tone. It was probably the most beautiful place I had ever seen. Though, perhaps since Ana had grown up there, she felt that same way about our mountain base. Maybe it was the change of scenery that made it beautiful. Indeed, the views from the mountain base were perhaps its best feature.

"Maybe Dylan will let me go there one day," Blake sighed playfully. He was being serious though.

"Take that up with Ana," I replied, "I wanted to let you go, it was her council that denied you."

"I have no sway over what the elders do," Ana defended, "I did try to get him through."

"What are they going to do when we get married?" Blake asked. He said it lightheartedly, but Ana turned serious.

"Probably kick me out too," she frowned.

Her society had very strict rules and norms, and falling in love with an outsider probably broke every single one of them. I couldn't believe they even let me in. The only reason they did is because their governing council wanted to interview me before they gave their allegiance to our cause. They did formally join the Ekklesia that day, but it was probably the most intimidating experience of my life. They are very powerful and very strict.

The gloomy end of our conversation lifted when our two transports arrived. We were sitting in an open field next to the football stadium. It was the part of the school property where they held events like field day and occasionally they painted it to be a soccer field.

The transports cautiously landed about thirty feet away from us. I called over the coms for one of the medics to make their way to us with some sedatives. While we waited, I informed the pilots of what we were about to do.

The one that flew my ship was to ride with the others to the base. There would be plenty of room on board. They accepted my assignments, and I told my friends to go ahead and load up so that they could be waiting for me in the hangar when I arrived.

We grouped up to say or brief goodbyes. “Alex, you sure you don’t wanna go?” I asked, “I could really use another ally up there.”

“I’m sure,” he replied, “I think I’m just going to stay retired.”

“I don’t blame you,” I said, “You’ve earned it.”

He stretched out his hand, and we shared a firm handshake, but then I pulled him into a hug. I knew he wasn’t much of a hugger, but he needed it every once in a while, and I wasn't going to be seeing him for a while.

“The rest of you, I’ll see you at the base,” I announced.

Ana turned and walked toward the transport. I sensed no hesitation or anxiety from Blake. He trusted everything would be just fine. But Bailey stayed back a bit longer.

“I can sense what you're thinking,” she said in my ear.

“What am I thinking?” I asked.

“You’re thinking that I’m worried for nothing,” she read.

“You are,” I replied.

“Well, you worry for nothing about me all the time,” she pointed out, “I’m allowed to do the same.”

We pulled away and smiled at each other. “Wrap it up, lovebirds!” Blake called from the door up the transport, “We’ve got a schedule to keep.”

Bailey and I laughed. She turned to walk to the transport, and I turned to the medic that was approaching us. “Be careful!” Bailey commanded.

“I’m always careful,” I promised.

Blake coached her into the ship while I held my hand out to the medic. She shook it. Then, we began discussing the plan and how much sedative it would take to get him there, accounting for the quick recovery his crystal would theoretically grant him.

The average person would have been out after the first blast from a staff. Since it took three to knock him out, we could use that as a gauge to see how many times he would need the sedative on the flight.

"I really need to be on the flight to monitor him," the medic said. She was tall for a woman, a bit taller than me. She was very assertive and matter-of-fact. "If you overdose him, he may lose his subconscious control over the crystal.

"If that happens?" I inquired.

"In theory…Boom"

I bit my lip and shook my head, "And if he doesn't get enough?" I asked.

"Boom"

"And even if I possibly give him the right amount?"

"Possibly… Boom."

"Good to know," I said falsely confident. I was glad Bailey wasn't here for this conversation. Their transport was now lifting off, leaving only mine parked in the field. The wind from the thrusters blew the tall grass and our hair as it jetted off into the night sky.

"You can't come on the flight," I told the medic, "I can only confidently protect myself in the event of," I tried to think of the most sensitive word, "...Boom"

"I'll show you how to administer the sedative," she said, walking over to the unconscious bearer.

She knelt down and pulled a syringe from her pocket. It had a cap over the needle that she bit off and spit onto the ground. "You'll need to find a vein," she said, "The easiest is probably the jugular with a case like this."

She gently tilted his head to the side. “Oh my, he has a soaring fever,” she said.

“I think it’s probably normal for him,” I smirked. I wasn’t thinking that she probably hadn’t observed his power set.

“Anyway,” she continued, confused by my statement, “You can feel his heartbeat here.”

She grabbed my hand and yanked me down next to her, placing my finger on Lucas’ neck. His skin was warm, and I could feel the slow beating of his heart.

“Feel that?” she asked.

I nodded.

“Take the needle and slide it at a 45° angle into the skin. The angle gives you a better chance of hitting the vein.” She took the needle and pushed it into his neck. “Then, slowly inject the sedative.” She pushed in the medicine and then slipped out the needle.

“Oh, my!” she exclaimed. The part of the needle that had been inside the boy was glowing red hot.

“Well, I’d say he does have a fever,” I joked casually. Truly, nothing surprised me anymore.

The medic looked at me with a pale and confused face. I only smiled and thanked her. She reluctantly gave me four more syringes loaded with the same sedative she had just injected.

“You will, um, need to do that every time his heart rate gets over 60 bpm, but don't let it get below 40,” she recited stunned. “Can you monitor that on the ship?”

“Yes,” I said, “You’re a good teacher. Thank you.”

“Yes sir…” she said and walked off in a confused daze.

I placed the syringes in a small zippered bag on my waste and then scooped up the bearer into my arms. “Let’s go for a little ride, Lucas,” I said.

The door of the transport was open. I stepped over the ledge and gently placed the motionless boy in the center of the floor. ALI closed the door behind me. I walked to the cockpit and took a seat in the pilot's chair.

“ALI, display his heart rate on my vanguard,” I requested.

Without answering, a tiny screen on my left vanguard lit up with a pixelated display. The nano chip I had used would allow ALI to hijack the functions of his suit. Heartrate, I knew, was one of those functions. It was currently resting at 52 bpm.

“Thank’s, ALI” I said.

“Of course, sir.”

The various buttons on the control screen began to change as ALI began to pilot the ship. The heads-up display on the windshield displayed our rising altitude and increasing speed.

As we took off, we circled around the school for a moment, per my request. I looked at the damage. There was a line of people on the football field waiting to receive medical attention. All of the once elegant and festive decorations were either burned, trampled, or turned over.

There were multiple groups of people standing in circles, likely discussing what had happened and the failure of the Ekklesia to prevent an attack this far inland.

I noticed that one of the stray fireballs had taken out the stands of the baseball field on the opposite end of the school. I had probably deemed it as not a threat during the heat of the battle.

Another had landed in the teacher parking lot. There would have been no one there, but I noticed something burning on the ground. It was the cottonwood tree that had once grown there. It would have been insignificant if I hadn’t been looking into that very spot a few hours before.

The whole sight made my heart ache. I had tried so hard to protect this little slice of my world and now it had been attacked twice. This was too much. They'd gone too far. It was time for this war to end.

No more hiding. No more normal. No more waiting. It was time to take the fight to The Organization.

Chapter 4

The flight wasn't a very long one, only about thirty minutes, but it gave me some much needed time to think. I had been drifting through the last few months. Nothing had really happened, so I had allowed the current of life to flow around me without realizing how far downstream it had swept me.

I was about to walk into this base, the base that I ran, a stranger. The very people that had given me their trust last year, were now questioning that decision. Perhaps rightfully so.

I needed a plan. I had to plant my feet and fight the current. But how?

I knew Lucas would be unlikely to give me information. They trusted him with black ops. There was no way he would flip sides easily. Still, we could learn valuable information about his powers, and while he was in custody, that was one less crystal bearer we had to worry about. Hopefully, he was the only one we had to worry about.

It was clear his target was El Dorado. Likely not trying to overthrow it (their team wasn't big enough), but maybe just trying to find it. The destroyed outposts were probably just a front and a bonus as they cut their way through South America. It wasn't such a bad idea.

Our entire operation relied on our two main bases: the Mountain base and El Dorado. There were no other well equipped military bases for us to occupy. We had outfitted many of them with new defences, but none were strong enough to hold off a full scale assault against The Organization. We ran everything out of those bases. If they ever got both of them, we could be crushed. That made me think, maybe it worked the same way for them.

Sure, they had tons of secret bases and hide outs, but they couldn't have anything very big. When the world didn't know about them, they wouldn't have been able to hide a huge base, especially without the stealth technology of Ana's people. That means they probably ran everything out of one top secret base somewhere in the world, similar to Montana base - something hidden away in a mountain valley or a tundra. Something small enough to not be seen and official enough to look like a government secret. They wouldn't be able to risk having too many of those, because they would have started to look suspicious. If we could find their capital we could cripple them. That is, if we could take it down.

We'd done it before. Maybe that was a fluke, but I would be willing to bet we could do it again. That would be the plan. Find the capitol. They already had one player out of the game. I was certain I could convince the council to go along with it.

Lucas began to stir. I was so deep in thought that I probably wouldn't have noticed it, but my vanguard's screen began to blink red, indicating an increase in his heart rate.

I stood up from my seat in the pilot's chair and walked to the cargo hold. Lucas still lay where I'd sat him, but I instantly noticed something was wrong. He was slowly rocking from side to side. That was already a feat with all the sedatives running through him. But more than that, little bits of orange light were beginning to zip up and down his body.

"ALI, how's he looking?" I asked, pulling one of the syringes from the bag on my waistband.

"Not great," ALI said, "The device that was keeping his power under control seems to be malfunctioning."

"So, are we looking at a *'Boom'* type situation or…?" I readied the syringe in my right hand and prepared to use my powers, calling just a bit of energy to my left hand.

"No, I don't believe it's that bad yet, but it is causing him discomfort."

"More sedative?"

"Let's do a half dose," ALI suggested.

I walked over to the boy and knelt down. I administered the medicine just as the medic had shown me and waited for the needle to cool. As I did, a question came to my mind.

"How did that random medic know about treating a crystal bearer?" I asked.

"She wasn't a random medic," ALI answered, "She was from El Dorado. She was trained to be able to help Ana if she ever needed it, but when you all came to Tullahoma, Ana's people thought it would be best for her to take a residence there."

"And how do you know about this and not me?" I asked mistrustingly.

"Sir, If every little thing that goes on in The Ekklesia were run by you first, you wouldn't have time for anything," ALI concluded, "It's called delegation."

He had a point, but this only made me worry about all the other things I didn't know. ALI must have realized this. I'm sure my facial expression gave it away.

"I promise you, I run all of the important things by you first," ALI assured me, "And, unlike you, every little thing that goes on in the Ekklesia can be run by me first. I know everything, so you only have to ask."

I didn't know if that was reassuring or worrisome, but I just decided to let it go. Through the windshield, I could see a lone mountain, rising tall above the others and the yellow shield surrounding it, glowing in the darkness: The Mountain base.

The needle had cooled, so I zipped it up in the pouch on my side and then walked to the front of the transport. The base wasn't particularly busy, but it was far from dormant.

Various hanger doors were open, the light from inside shining out into the night. Far above the shield, I could see the lights of two flag ships keeping watch over the hive. Various models of fighters flew in 'V' shaped patterns patrolling valleys. Ahead of us, I could just make out a little speck flying toward an open hangar bay. It had to be the transport my friends were on.

"ALI, call a meeting with the High Council first thing in the morning," I commanded.

"That's not much notice," he advised.

"They'll be there"

As we flew in, I stared out into Broken Valley. The debris from the battle fought there had not yet been reclaimed by nature. The heaps of metal reflected the gentle moonlight. Where you could still see the mountain side, the ground was scorched and bare.

Really, it wasn't just one valley that we called "Broken Valley". It was a whole section of the mountain range. The mountains rose and fell, and a steel bridge stretched between each peak, creating one contentious path across the center of the battlefield.

The bridge was constructed in such a way that no supports reached the ground. It was wider on the ends that connected it to the mountain and skinny in the center.

The ship turned, taking the memorial out of view. A slit had opened in the shield to allow us to pass through. We were now passing over the crashed Organizating ship I had seen when I first crashed here, as we descended toward our hangar. The hangar was about halfway up the side of the mountain and faced the lake at its base.

I heard the engines' hum change to a lower tone as they powered down for the landing. As we entered into the light of the hangar, I stood up and joined Lucas once again.

The doors of the transport opened, and we glided into the bay. I could see my friends waiting for me on the ground. I watched the wind from the engines blowing their hair, and I hopped out of the ship.

I hit the ground a bit harder than I intended, but I landed it without falling. I gave it my best superhero pose (which was really just me genuinely steadying myself) and greeted my friends.

Bailey reached me first, followed closely by Blake and Ana as the transport's landing feet folded out onto the ground behind us. The engine powered down completely now and Bailey spoke.

"How was the ride?" she asked.

“Uneventful,” I answered, “But we should probably hurry up and get him to that containment room so it doesn’t become eventful.”

“See,” Blake spread out his hands in my direction, “I told you he wouldn’t blow up!”

Bailey gave him a smirk and a side eye, then looked back at me. I smiled. Then, I turned back to the transport.

I leaned over into the hold of the ship and pulled out the sedated bearer. He was still out cold, but he squirmed in clear discomfort as I took him into my arms.

“ALI, where is this facility,” I asked as my friends created a small huddle.

“Someone is on their way to take you there now,” ALI answered.

As he spoke, I spied someone walking out into the hangar. They would have been hard to miss since we were the only people in the hangar. Well, besides the security detail along the walls.

“Look at that,” Ana said, pointing at Lucas. She was pointing out the little tinges of energy racing up and down his body. They were sporadic and made a quiet hissing noise as they moved across the fabric of his suit.

“It's just his energy,” I said, not understanding why she seemed so shocked.

“Yes, but look what it's doing,” she expanded.

I looked closer and realized that it was leaving a trail of singed material behind it. Since the suit was black, it was hard to see.

“Poor thing,” Bailey said.

“You think it's hurting him?” Blake questioned, “I mean, wasn’t he a literal ball of fire an hour ago?”

"It looks like it hurts," Ana said.

"He does seem uncomfortable," I added, "But our energy can be pretty hot sometimes, and it doesn't bother us."

"That's only when we concentrate it," Bailey said, "Maybe his starts out hot."

We didn't have much time to continue our discussion because the man ALI sent had reached us. He wore a normal Ekklesia uniform and a white patch on his shoulder, just above his Ekklesia dove, where his national flag would have gone. This indicated that he started out in the Ekklesia before we adopted all the other nations.

"This must be our new bearer," the man said. He saluted casually as he reached us. He was in his thirties and seemed kind.

"Delivered straight to your doorstep," I adaged, "Do you know where he's supposed to go?"

"I do," he answered, "I'm private Coby Wales. I'm here to take you there."

"Lead the way," I said as I adjusted the boy's weight to a better position to carry.

I let the soldier go in front of us and my friends flanked me. We didn't say much as we traveled down the various halls and elevators. None of us were very good at small talk besides Blake. It would have been awkward without him there.

By the time we had reached the correct level of the base, we had learned this soldier's whole life story. He was an American, born and raised in Los Angeles. He joined Ekklesia after The Organization destroyed his neighborhood, using gang violence as a front. He never figured out what they were after there, but when he became involved, he found out about both sides, something that most people never did. He chose ours.

He lost most of his family to the crime wave started by The Organization. Sadly, he lost his remaining sister when L.A. was bombed last year when The Organization attempted its takeover. It was one of the cities that we couldn't save along with Denver, Portland, Phoenix and a few other cities out west. He did have a spouse and a new baby boy that he was very proud to have. They were the reason he kept fighting.

Just when we probably couldn't have learned anything else about Coby, we reached a hallway different from the rest. It was a long corridor, white like the rest of the base, but rather than branching hallways or normal doors, this section was lined with a series of vaults. Each was a round grey door, sunken into a cut out section of the wall. Each had components that were outlined in blue, notches, handles, and cutouts. I didn't know what purpose they served.

Beside each vault door was a small panel. Each had a screen and numbers as well as an I.D. scanner. Cody walked us down the hallway a bit and stopped in front of the fourth vault door. He entered a code on the panel, swiped a card and then placed his hand on the same panel. A green line of light moved from top to bottom, scanning his hand print. When it was done, the whole panel turned green and components began to move within the door.

I actually knew what this place was. My father had left me books, folders, and files full of his secrets. They were entrusted to only me. ALI couldn't even access some of them. I hadn't made it through many, but I had read about his research labs. This was exactly what he had described.

The door continued to clank as it slid open. "They keep this place locked up pretty tight since the old director..." Cody stopped his exposition when he realized who he was talking to.

"It's okay, Cody," I smiled at him to assure him he had not overstepped.

He was, at the very least, embarrassed. He continued silently into the vault, which, despite having a vault door, wasn't a vault at all. It was a lab.

We entered a large room with various lab stations and control panels around the wall. On the far side of the room was a wall with a glass panel in the center. Through the glass was a similar sized room. It was fitted with equipment such as long robot arms, lasers, and other things that I didn't recognize. In the center of the room was a chair. I did recognize it.

It was the same kind of chair I'd been held in when I was first captured by The Organization. It clearly didn't belong there. They must have brought it in from somewhere just for him. I didn't like that they just had one of those sitting around. We didn't torture people. Did we?

As my friends and I were taking it all in, a man in a lab coat walked up from one of the work stations. He was an older man, probably in his sixties. He had salt and pepper hair that was slicked straight back and a thick, well kept mustache to match.

He held out his hand, "I'm Dr. Hopkins," he said. "You must be Dylan."

I nodded. I would have shaken his hand, but my hands were full. He realized this and laughed, "Of course," he clasped his hands together and gestured toward the other room, "You can sit him in there."

"We won't be using that chair on him," I said, demandingly.

"Oh, of course we won't use it in any nefarious way," he scrunched his eyebrows together as if he were offended, but I sensed insincerity, "It's just the only thing we have strong enough to restrain him."

"It didn't work on me," I remembered.

"Well, this is a different chair," Dr. Hopkins said.

I didn't like it, but I didn't see a better choice. We couldn't keep him sedated forever, and when he woke up, he needed to be contained. I conceded and followed the doctor to another door like the one we had entered through. It opened to the other room, and I placed Lucas in the chair. The doctor bound his hands and feet. I only watched.

What would he think when he woke up? This looked just like something The Organization would torture someone in. The glass was even tinted so that he couldn't see his captors. I looked around the room, imagining what his first moments would be like.

I noticed at the back of the room a grey metal circle, about two feet in diameter, in the center of the back wall. “What’s that?” I asked, pointing. The Doctor finished his work and looked.

“That is a vent that allows us to release excess energy from a crystal we are experimenting on,” Dr. Hopkins said, “Rather than the energy bursting through the wall and killing us, we can vent it out of the mountain side.”

“Could he escape through there?” I asked.

“If he weren’t bound to the chair and someone opened it for him, I suppose he could,” he smartly admitted, “But he can’t get out of the chair. It's the strongest one ever made.”

We walked out of the room and joined my friends and Cody. I exchanged a worried look with Blake. I could sense his unease. We were the only ones in the room that had experienced those chairs. It wasn’t something either of us would want to put this boy through.

“So, you're only using the chair to restrain him, right?” Blake asked.

“That’s the only thing he’s going to do with it,” I answered for the doctor, “Or else he’ll find himself in prison for war crimes.” I looked straight into the eyes of the doctor when I spoke, being careful to sense his every emotion. I was sure Bailey would look deeper.

He was mostly full of enjoyment. If there was anything else, it was buried too deep, “I already told you that was all I would use it for,” he insisted.

“I just wanted to be on the same page,” I clarified. In reality it was more of a warning. There was no sense in fighting The Organization if we were going to become them in the process. Unfortunately, I feared that line was thin anyway.

“One more thing,” Dr. Hopkins said, “What is my objective in studying him? Is there something you are looking for?”

"I want you to learn everything you can," I said, "We especially need to know how the dampening device he's wearing works so that we can fix it. ALI can give you more specifics."

"Ah, I see," the doctor thought for a moment, "I believe I can do that, but it would be nice to have some information on your powers to compare as a baseline,"

"No," I said bluntly, "Those are top secret."

"Are you aware of my security clearance?" the doctor looked offended, "I know you are new, but I am the chief scientist here. I'm shocked that I don't sit on your high council, but aside from that, there is no secret of your powers that your father kept from me. I already have those readings. I was simply asking for a wider range of data."

I stared at the doctor, then turned around to my friends. Blake was clearly leaving it up to me as he always did. Ana shook her head 'no'. I knew her people would look down on her if she allowed us to gather any information on their crystal.

I looked at Bailey last. I noticed her crystal above her chest glowing a bit brighter and her irises were bright white with her energy. Her voice appeared in my head, "Just be careful".

I shook my head and turned back to Dr. Hopkins, "I'll let you look at mine and Bailey's data, but it goes on an encrypted file and ALI will either approve or disapprove what you ask for."

"Not very trusting, are you?" the doctor sighed.

"Not really," I smirked, "Comes with the job."

I saluted the doctor and then requested that Cody escort us back to the barracks. Once we were back to a section of the base that I knew, I sent Cody away and we walked the rest of the way on our own.

"You don't think he'll do anything to that boy, do you?" I asked the group as we walked.

"No," Bailey said, "He's on our side, and your father must have trusted him."

"The only problem is, they may not trust me," I sighed, "I'm not my father."

"I think you're letting Sparks get to you," Blake consoled, "He's not the majority; he's just really loud."

"I hope you're right," I said. We were reaching our quarters. The base was low on Barracks since we'd had so many people enlist. Blake and I would share a room, and the girls would share a room. We stood outside our doors and continued our talk.

"Ana, what do you think?" I asked. I knew she would look at things very differently than Blake and Bailey.

"I think..." she paused, not to gather her words, but to decide if she should say them, "I think that here you people here are very different from the people back home. In Kab'ah K'uhul we are one people. The greatest can trust the least and the least can trust the greatest. We are strong because we know each other. We are family. But we don't accept others.

Here you accept everyone, but you struggle to trust the people you accept. I don't understand this."

"I don't understand it either, Ana" I frowned and looked at the ground.

"You make up for it though," Ana continued, "You're compassionate and united behind a cause. It's beautiful. But fragile."

"We'll just have to be careful not to break it then," Blake added optimistically.

And with that, we entered our rooms and prepared for sleep. We wouldn't get much tonight so we would have to make the best of it. I put my puck, armor, and gear in its proper place (a specially made cabinet built into the wall) and lay down.

I wanted to take a shower, but I was exhausted. Blake couldn't sleep without one, so he went to the bathroom. My mind tried to think about graduation and the plan for tomorrow, but I was quickly overwhelmed by sleep.

***

The morning went by in a flash. I woke up with just enough time to take a quick shower. I was in and out before the water could even warm up. I threw on my suit and armor and met up with my friends in the hallway.

Now that everyone was awake, the base felt crowded. There was a steady stream of traffic going both directions down the hall. It felt like changing classes at school.

All of the soldiers were on their way to train. This base is where we kept not only the finest soldiers the Ekklesia had to offer, it was also where we trained the new recruits. The best of the best weren't just tasked with field missions, they were training the next generation.

We made our way through the crowd to the War Room. This was one of the rare occasions where my allies were the first people to arrive. General Raddick was the only one already there. We gave each other a proper salute, and I gave him a firm handshake.

"Good to see all my friends made it here in one piece," the general said.

"Good to see you kept the base in one piece," Blake joked.

"Well, I assure you, it was not an easy task," Raddick laughed, "Especially with people like," his eyes grew dim as someone walked in behind us. "Well...you know," he smiled.

Captain Sparks was walking in, along with his two friends on the council. One was over Aviation, and the other was over our Naval fleet, currently patrolling the coasts. Not the most powerful positions by any means, but their votes counted the same as everyone else's. This was supposed to be an advisory council for me, but it had formed into a governing council. That was probably my fault though.

"Well, nice of you to finally show up to one of these things," Captain Sparks insulted.

I wanted to bark something back, but I remembered General Raddick's advice, "I figured since I was making you get up early I should probably come."

I said it as nice as I could, but every one of my friends curled their nose at the man. I'd forgotten to talk to them about politics. Honestly, I was probably the only one that really needed to worry about my image. Maybe it wouldn't be so bad if they just said what I was already thinking.

Captain Sparks was confused by my kindness, and rather than respond, he just chose to take his seat. The room quickly filled. We all took our seats, and when the small talk died down, I began to speak to the group.

"Thank you everyone for being here so early," I greeted. There wasn't a single smile among the group. Maybe an early meeting wasn't the best idea. "I wanted to get a jump on things. As you all may or may not know, my time in Tullahoma is at an end for now."

My friends were all clearly shocked by this. I guess I'd forgotten to tell them that too. "We are the strongest we've ever been. We've rebuilt what we can for now, and our territory has been properly reinforced. I think its high time to begin shifting gears to a new task."

"And what is that?" the intelligence director asked.

"The stalemate with The Organization is clearly coming to an end. The attacks by the new bearer prove that," I answered, "It's time to start taking the fight to them."

"Clearly you've overlooked the constant fighting on our border in Alaska and the Pacific," Captain Sparks barked.

"No, I haven't," I replied boldly, "Those are only minor scuffles when they happen. The Organization and the Ekklesi\a can't coexist. The goal of one is to eliminate the other. If we keep letting them grow, they will outpace us and take us over. Now is the time to press them."

"We haven't pressed because they have made their borders too secure," the intelligence director said, "When we try to, they respond too quickly and with too great of force to gain any territory."

"That's because we've been focusing on territory encroachment," I explained, "That's not the way The Organization has been fighting, and I think we should take notes."

"Now he wants us to be like The Organization!" Sparks blurted out.

"Let the director speak," General Raddick barked back.

"What I was saying was, I think they are using a good strategy," I did my best not to let my anger through. Bailey was clearly not doing the same. She was scowling at Sparks. "They are looking for our capital bases. We knew that if they ever took out one or both, we would be crippled. I think finding and destroying their capital would do the same to them."

"They have far more long standing bases than we do to be able to recover," the aviation director said.

"But I'm willing to bet they have at least one other crystal there," I said, "Plus, if we take a capitol, they'll have to reallocate. That'll take time that we can use to weaken them further."

"Usually taking the capitol is the last step of a war," the weapons director pointed out.

"I think it's a good strategy,' the Naval chief said. He received a hate filled look from Sparks.

"It's better than just trying to gain land a little bit at a time," Blake added.

"We just have to find the capital first," I said. I looked at the intelligence director, "How could we do that?"

"Well..." he paused for a moment. I could sense he was nervous, which was rare for a council member. "There is one person on this base who knows exactly where it is, but he'll only speak to you."

"What? Who?" I asked, but I immediately answered my own question. The blood rushed away from my face, and my legs grew weak. "No," I said under my breath. Anyone by him. I looked around the table. Everyone's eyes were fixed on me. I looked at General Raddick. He mouthed a word to me, "Politics."

"Of course," I said to the group, "I think now is as good a time as ever."

"Then, you'll meet with him and report back to the council before we vote on your strategy?" General Raddick asked.

"I think that sounds like a very good plan," I agreed. My voice was shaking. I had to fix that. I took a breath, "In the meantime, you all be discussing this and start working out the details."

Everyone stood at once and saluted. Then, they began to talk with one another about the discussion. I probably should have tried to "Politick", but I only had one thing on my mind. I had to get this over with.

"Blake, Bailey, come with me, please," I said as calmly as possible. We walked out of the room; I was practically dragging them. I didn't mean to leave Ana, but I was sure she could handle herself.

I marched down the hallway. "ALI."

"Sir."

"Call ahead to the brig," I requested, "Tell them to prepare for my arrival. I'm going to need a meeting with Darren Flyhe."

Chapter 5

We walked down the hallway and entered an elevator that would take us into the heart of the base. The cells were on the lowest floor to snuff out any hope of escape for our prisoners. We didn't have many, but the ones we had were top tier threats to the Ekklesia.

When the door of the elevator closed, I took a moment to breathe. I couldn't figure out why I'd been so worked up. I mean, there were the obvious reasons, but those shouldn't be bothering me now. I dealt with those things nearly eight months ago. Traveling down this elevator was like traveling into the past. The closer we got to Darren, the more my buried emotions flared.

Bailey and Blake didn't say anything for a few minutes. They just waited for me to speak first. Bailey could read my mind with her powers, and Blake could do the same from being with me for so many years. There wasn't really anything to be said.

The elevator moved fast, but the ride still took a few minutes. It finally reached the basement, and the door opened. The three of us walked out. I was walking briskly. My friends matched my pace, flanking me on either side.

There was a long corridor between the elevator and the brig. It was lined with explosives that we could set off to collapse the tunnel and seal the prisoners in if they tried to escape.

This long hallway was rounded, a half circle, the flat side being the floor. It created a dome similar to the tunnels back home, only these were grey steel. There was no attempt to make it look fancy. One long cylindrical light ran down the length of the tunnel. At the end, there was a vault door, exactly like the ones we'd seen in the lab.

We reached the door, and I turned back to my friends. I had been conjuring up a plan while we walked. It was simple. I wanted to be quick. I knew Darren had a way of getting in our heads, mine especially. I didn't want to give him the chance.

"Okay," I started, "I'm going to do the talking. I'll ask him what we want to know." I looked at Bailey, "When he doesn't give it to us, I need you to do your mind reading thing on him." I looked at Blake now, "You're there for back-up." He placed his hand on the staff strapped to his waste and nodded.

Just as I finished talking, the circular vault door began to clank as the various locking mechanisms began to release. The door then rolled open, moving totally out of the way of the passage and disappearing between the walls. Standing on the other side was a particularly intimidating man.

He wore a black uniform: like the other Ekklesia uniforms, but black. I didn't recognize the flag on his arm, but it looked middle eastern, and so did he. He had tan skin and thick, curly black hair. He had a close cut beard that was nearly as thick as the hair on his head. He was tall, broad shouldered, and very muscular. The perfect prison guard.

I saluted him and introduced myself, "I'm Dylan Vale."

"Yes," he said in a low gravelly voice. He had a thick Arabic accent, "Word of you even makes it down here – Believe it or not." He placed his palm on his chest, "I am Benjamin"

He had to search hard for his words. He must have only recently learned English. He escorted us into a lobby of sorts. Really, it was just a big empty room with a single rectangular steel door and another control panel. He typed in a code and then we entered the real prison. It was just another long hall with doors lining each side. Each door had a control panel beside it.

There was an armed guard of two men, their helmets covering their faces, in front of the first cell on the left. They wore the same uniform as Benjamin.

"We just moved him up here for you," Benjamin said, gesturing to the cell. He walked over to the control panel and typed in a code.

I didn't say anything. I only waited as my anticipation grew. I had no idea how I would feel when I saw the face of The Parasite. I didn't currently feel anger or hurt. I was only nervous: nervous for what he would say and nervous for how I would react. I feared reliving those memories.

I noticed the other doors we had walked through automatically closing behind us. Darren's door slid open. Blake, Bailey and I walked over and stood in the doorway. Blake still had his hand on his staff , and Bailey's crystal grew a bit brighter as she prepared to use it.

Finally, the door had cleared from the entrance, revealing a skinny, scruffy looking man sitting on a metal bench in the center of the empty room. He wore a white jumpsuit. His brown hair was long and unbrushed. He also had a scraggly beard that stuck out this way and that. Every emotion I'd felt faded to pity.

Was this really the man that had ruined my life? How could this be the formidable opponent I'd faced last year? This man may have taken a lot of valuable things and people from me, but I couldn't help but see that I had taken everything from him. I was the victor. And it showed.

A genuine smile spread across what was visible of Darren's face when he saw us. His eyes beamed as he moved his bangs out from in front of them. I sensed happiness, and it caught me off guard. It must have done the same to my friends because we all just stood there staring at him.

"Dylan!" Darren exclaimed, not standing up, but stretching his hands out toward us, "It's been so long. How are you doing?"

Despite all the heightened senses I had, I still couldn't tell if he was being genuine, had gone insane, or was playing one of his games.

"Good." I stared, puzzled. I shook my head. *'Stick to the plan,'* I told myself. "We're just here to ask you a few questions."

"Don't you want to hear what I have to say?" Darren asked. He sounded offended and his joy faded, "I've been asking to speak with you for so long. I thought you'd finally come to listen."

"Umm, sorry," I apologized, I did kind of feel bad, "We're here on business. I need to ask you some questions."

Darren stared at me. I tried hard, but I couldn't sense anything. No emotion. No intention. His mind was either blank, or he was blocking me somehow. I turned slightly to the right to look at Bailey. Her eyebrows were scrunched, and she was glaring at Darren. She was trying to read him too.

I took a few steps into the room and then began my questions in my most official tone, "How many bearers are there?" I asked. I figured I would start with a test question to see if he was going to give me anything. If he did answer the question, that would be helpful too.

"Total?" he asked. I was almost certain he was putting on an act now.

"Working for The Organization," I clarified, hoping he would have his fun and then answer.

"Have you encountered another?" he asked.

"That's classified," I answered.

"Well, all things come at a cost," Darren said. His voice took on a semblance of his stronger self, but quickly retired to a feeble tone, "Can't you give me something to think about? It's so boring down here. Who am I going to tell anyway?"

"We just captured a bearer that can conjure flames," Blake said from behind me. I turned to look at him. The plan was for me to do everything, but I guess this wouldn't hurt.

"He speaks!" Darren exclaimed. I realized this might have been the first time Blake and Darren had spoken to one another. He addressed Blake, not me, "The Boy's name is Lucas."

"We knew that already," I said.

"Then, I assume you know his sister?" Daren questioned.

This was news. I thought we might be getting somewhere. "He has a sister?"

"Yes," Darren smiled a sly smile, "You don't know her?"

I only stared back at him because I knew he knew the answer.

"And he hasn't burned up yet?"

"No," I said. I tried to make it seem like the boy was perfectly healthy.

"Then, I'm sure you'll meet her soon enough," Darren alluded.

I could guess by now that she was a bearer and her energy was likely the same as the strange energy coming from Lucas' dampener. This information wasn't that helpful, but now we knew there were two bearers. I didn't want to press too much, so I asked my real question.

"Where is the capital of The Organization?"

"Now that's a question that will cost you a great deal more for the answer," Darren said, almost sounding like his old self again, but he still had a tinge of crazy in his inflection.

"Name it," I said.

"My freedom,"

"Not a chance," I laughed, "Maybe you really have gone crazy."

"And who's fault would that be?" Darren raised his voice and started to stand up. Blake drew his staff. Bailey and I called the energy from our crystals. Darren stood in a half stand for a moment, composed himself, and sat back down on his bench.

"I was thinking something along the lines of a nice hot meal, but I guess we'll just pull it out of you," I called the energy across my body and sent it across the room to Daren. I caused it to flow over him, binding his body with thin rings composed the same way I'd make a shield. I lifted him from his seat and slowly pulled him towards me. He didn't say a word. He only looked down his nose like the whole thing was beneath him. The act was up. The old Parasite was back.

I held him a few feet away from us and pulled him down to eye level. I folded his legs up so that he still wasn't touching the ground. Bailey, seeing it was her time, walked between us. Her arms were covered in the white energy that flowed from her crystal. Her eyes glowed white. She looked Darren in the eyes, and placed her two middle fingers on either of his temples. The white energy flowed from her and onto his head where Bailey pushed it gently through his thoughts.

She stared into him and asked, "Where is your capital?"

He stared back with his same snotty glare.

"Where is your capital," she asked again. She needed him to consciously recall the thought to retrieve it. Otherwise, there were too many thoughts for her to dig through. Usually, just asking the question was enough for her to find the answer if the subject did indeed know it.

I watched from behind as the two locked themselves in a battle of wills. I actually worried who was stronger. That worry grew when I saw Bailey tremble a bit. It was subtle, but I caught it. She did too and responded by flattening her palms over the sides of Darren's head. She pulled more energy from the crystal as she tried to bend his mind to her will.

Darren's glare turned into a hate-filled scowl. I could see his jaw clenching and teeth grinding as the white energy flowed across his face. Then, across his body. I didn't catch what was going on until it was too late. A bolt of energy came from Darren's body. A white flash filled the room.

I was blown back into the hallway and landed between the two soldiers guarding the door. I sprang up just as the two soldiers stormed into the room. A blue flash lit up the corridor, and I saw Darren slam into the back wall of the cell.

Blake's staff was extended. He was still braced from jabbing The Parasite. Bailey lay on her back on the floor. The two soldiers were pointing their guns at Darren who was on all fours across the room. I sensed them about to pull the trigger.

"Don't shoot!" I yelled. We still needed him.

He was trying to stand up, so I used my energy to slam him against the wall again. I held him there, just as I had been holding him before and rushed over to Bailey. Blake had already knelt down next to her. I got down on my knees on the opposite side.

"Are you hurt?" I asked, lifting her head into my arms.

"No, I'm good," she groaned, "It was my own energy. He just knocked me down."

I stood up, relieved. "Blake, get her out of here," I commanded.

He helped her up, and they started out of the room. I turned back to The Parasite who I still had pinned against the wall. As soon as Bailey and Blake were out, I let him fall to the floor. The soldiers still stood ready for a fight, their weapons pointed at Darren.

The Parasite steadied himself on one knee and spit blood from his mouth. Even after what had just happened (which I didn't fully understand) all I could think about was how weak he was.

"I should have known this was a mistake," I mumbled. I looked to the guard on my right. "Take him back to his cell."

I turned to walk out of the room, but Darren called after me, "It doesn't matter where the capitol is, win or lose, Ekklesia or Organization, none of it matters," he yelled.

I was going to just keep walking, but what he said next caught my attention, "It's all an experiment. No matter who wins, the Overseers will claim the Earth as their prize."

I turned back to him. My pity was beginning to turn to annoyance, "And why should I believe a word you say?" I probed.

He knew he had my attention, so he began his monologue, one that I think he'd intended to give since he first heard I was coming, "Remember that dream you had last year?"

Now I scowled. The memory wasn't a pleasant one. The Parasite had hijacked my mind and made me see horrible things.

"I didn't send it," he said, "I only opened you up to the visions that tortured me for years," the old Darren was definitely back now.

"The stones, three of them, have a strange affinity for time... and *YOU* for some reason. I'm sure you've noticed it. Your girlfriend probably has too." He used girlfriend as a derogatory term. His insults couldn't disinterest me now though.

"Sensing things just before they happen, discovering new abilities as though they're instinct. Sound familiar?" Darren leaned in, "Look at you, you know it's true. It's not instinct. You live life feeling like you've lived it before, and it all started the day you picked up that crystal."

He was eerily right. Everything he said, if it was a lie, felt like the truth. He'd been in my head before, and he was trying to psych me out now. I was done.

"Where's the capital, Darren?" I asked impatiently.

"You'll find it," he prophesied, "But it won't matter unless you prepare for the Overseers."

I was done with his tricks. He was lying. He had to be. I didn't want to hear any more. I turned and walked out the door, but he called out after me again, "I've seen your victory," I stopped and he continued, "And I see, in your victory, a grave defeat."

"You're no prophet," I snapped, swirling back around to face him.

"And you're no saint," He said sharply.

I felt my face turn red. If he was trying to get under my skin and in my head, he had succeeded. I briskly walked out of the cell where Binjamin opened the doors for me to get out of the prison. Bailey and Blake were waiting for me outside. Thankfully, Bailey looked to be back to normal.

My emotions had settled by the time I had reached them. I was mostly just disappointed that I had expected anything different from what had happened. The man was a leech. He had always succeeded at draining the life and joy straight out of me. Somehow, he knew exactly how to do it.

"Everything okay?" Bailey asked.

"I feel like I should be asking you that," I smiled. She smiled back, but the look that followed insisted that I give her an answer. I was about to do that, but just as I made the first syllable, ALI interrupted.

"Sir, it's urgent," ALI warned.

"What's urgent?" I asked.

"The boy, Lucas, his device quit working. He's burning up."

The three of us exchanged frantic glances. Then, all at once, we sprinted down the hallway to the elevator. Blake was the last one in. Once we were in, we anxiously waited as the elevator crawled up through the bedrock. This gave ALI just enough time to explain.

"The doctor was researching why Lucas needed the device. He had your father's research that discussed the genetic mutation that allows you to wield the crystals' energy. Well, it's not a mutation, it's a trait. Dylan, yours is pure. You absorb 100% of your crystal's energy. Bailey's is 68%, Ana's is 94%. Blake, surprisingly, yours is 89%. For reference. Most of the population is under 0.3%."

The elevator door opened. Thankfully, the research floor wasn't much higher up than the brig. ALI talked as we ran to the open vault door.

"Lucas' is 80%, but his radiation is so hot, he burns up if he doesn't have the negative energy from the device."

"His sister's energy," I connected, as we ran into the lab.

The room was lit by the orange flames coming from the room Lucas was in. I could just make out the silhouette of the chair and Lucas though the inferno. The doctor stood at a workstation, wildly pressing buttons.

"I'm trying to vent out the energy, but there's just too much," Dr. Hopkins lamented.

A horrifying scream came from the other side of the glass. I couldn't imagine how loud it had to be for us to hear it out here. I racked my brain for any ideas on what to do. I could only think of one. He needed his sister, and he was the only one that knew where to find her.

"The council's gonna kill me," I mumbled. I pointed to the door. "Everyone out!" I commanded, "ALI, seal the door."

"What are you going to do?" the doctor asked.

"I'm going to save his life."

No one argued and quickly evacuated the room. I nodded my head and my helmet formed. I summoned my energy across my entire body. Its purple streams flowed from the crystal. Another terrible scream broke through the soundproof room. I looked back to make sure ALI had sealed me in the lab. I didn't want the flames to escape and turn our mountain into a volcano.

When I saw that the vault was closed I commanded ALI to open the door to Lucas. I braced myself as the door slid open. The instant there was a crack in the door, the orange energy erupted out into the lab. I held out my hands and formed a shield. The explosion pushed me backward, but I remained upright.

The energy swirled around me and my light grey suit, though it tried to heal itself, began to char. My visor tinted to protect my eyes from the light of the inferno. I started sweating. I pushed against the torrent of orange flames and finally made it into the room with Lucas.

His agonizing screams and moans surrounded me as much as the energy did. My heart pounded. My body was heating up even more as sweat poured down my face. It was like Hell on Earth.

Both my energy and my suit were failing to protect me from the furnace. I was burning up. Finally, after pushing my way to the center of the room, I reached our prisoner.

I nearly wanted to puke realizing what we had done to him. He was being tortured here, in this chair, in a far worse way than anything we could create with our own technology. I spied the binders on his hands and ankles which were glowing red hot. In anger and disgust, I ripped them off.

As soon as he was free, he flew out of his chair. He grabbed my shoulders and slammed me against the tinted glass panel. All the while, he was still screaming in torment.

"Lucas!" I yelled over the sound of the furnace, "You're free. Find your sister. There's a vent behind you." I tried to point, " Leave! Go!"

I couldn't see his face. It was completely consumed by the energy, but I could feel when he let me go, and not long after that, the flames subsided.

I took a breath, retracted my helmet, and slid down against the wall I had been thrown against. "ALI," I said, "Get one of Ana's stealth ships to follow him. Maybe he'll take us to the capitol."

Chapter 6

I sat there, leaning against the glass panel for a while. I wasn't hurt, but I didn't realize until now how much energy it had taken to protect myself from the flames. I was out of breath.

ALI must have let everyone know that I was done, because Blake and Bailey came barreling into the lab.

"Are you okay?" Bailey asked, kneeling down beside me. Blake stood behind her.

She sounded panicked. This confused me because I had never considered this to be life or death, for me anyway. We had certainly been through worse.

"Yeah, I'm fine," I said. Blake stretched out his hand. I took it, and he pulled me up off the ground.

"You look a little… well done," Blake joked.

It took me a second to realize what he meant. Then, I realized why Bailey seemed so concerned. My suit, once light grey, was a charred mix of grey and black. Some places had burned all the way through and my skin was visible. The coating of material that usually formed over my armor was gone, exposing the shiny white metal. Everything was gone off my hands and the top of my shoulders where the bearer had grabbed. The skin was exposed, but it didn't feel burned.

"Let's get you cleaned up," Bailey suggested, putting her hand on my shoulder.

I agreed silently, and we walked out of the lab, into the control room. Dr. Hopkins and Cody were waiting here for us. Cody looked concerned, but Dr. Hopkins was angry.

"You let him go?" he complained.

"Not much you can learn from him if he's dead," I jabbed.

"He had a crystal strapped to his chest!" The doctor almost yelled, "One we'd never even seen before at that!"

Just then, a siren started to blare, and a red light began to flash on the soot covered wall. I could see them flashing in the hallway as well. Then, a voice played over the intercom, "All soldiers to your battle stations. We are under attack."

Everyone looked up at the speaker, then at me. I didn't look at anyone. I just ran out of the room. I needed to get to the surface. I sprinted down the hall and ripped open the door to the elevator. I jumped in, ignited my jetpack, and flew up the shaft.

Attack? Surely the boy wouldn't be stupid enough to attack the base in his condition. Unless his meltdown was an act. No, that couldn't be true, his screams were too real. Unless he was a really good actor.

I finally reached the top of the shaft (thankfully the elevator was under me). I pried open the doors and shot outside. I was at the very top of the mountain where Bailey and I had first found my father. There was a view in every direction, and I didn't have to look long to see what was going on.

Fighters were launching from nearly every hangar on the side of the mountain. The turrets that dotted the mountainside had opened fire. All of this commotion was directed at an orange dot, bouncing along the edge of the shield like a bug caught in a jar.

Our own yellow blasts of energy were exploding against the inside of the shield as Lucas did his best to dodge. Coming up behind him were about seven "U" shaped fighters (which I finally discovered were called Stingrays).

"ALI," I called, "Connect me to the base coms."

"Done, sir"

"Stand down!" I commanded, knowing the whole base could now hear me, "Stop your assault. Everyone stand down! Open section 22 of the shield. We are letting him escape."

The Stingrays pulled up and turrets stopped firing.

"Do not open that shield," Captain Sparks quickly demanded.

"This is Supreme Director Dylan Vale. I said,
Open - the - shield," I demanded, making my order clear.

A thin slice of the shield dissipated on the western end of the base and Lucas finally flew out. "ALI, where's that stealth ship?"

"Already trailing him," ALI said.

The Doradin stealth craft were tic-tac shaped and black. No engines or weapons were visible, and they could move at incredible speeds. When they flew, they could also use a cloaking device that made them invisible to all types of radar and the naked eye. The only way they were detectable was through lidar. These type ships were how Ana's people were able to gather information about the world while staying safely tucked away and hidden.

I watched until Lucas was out of sight, which wasn't that long at all. Then, I just leaned against the bunker that housed the elevator. The trees were cleared from the top of the base because of the shield. The view was incredible. I had come up here many times just to get away.

The honeysuckles bloomed this time of year. Their succulent scent drifted up from the forest below in a gentle breeze that blew up from the valley. The skies were clear, but tinted yellow by the shield. Above that, the two flagships that had been there the night before still kept watch.

I watched the Stingrays circle the base, and finally land in a hanger. I started to go back in, but when I thought about facing the council, I decided to just sit up here in the quiet. I needed to gather my thoughts.

Face the council. What a joke! This was my council, my father's council. They are supposed to work for me. How did it become this way?

I was playing so many angles, it was hard to keep track. I knew I had to save Lucas. That decision was made in the heat of the moment.

Literally. But I had quickly thrown together a deeper plan than that to convince the council I made the right decision.

Why was I having to *convince* the council that saving a scared, dying boy was the right thing to do? Anyway, I could work this to our advantage still. I guess that's politics: convince everyone that your decisions are the right ones.

Then, there was what Darren said. I didn't even have a chance to think about it until now. There was a lot to unpack there. The crystals, could they be connected to time? Even if they were, why would they show Darren things about me? That didn't make any sense. It was true what he said about instincts, feeling like I've lived moments before, or at least like I just knew what to do somehow. I hadn't really thought about it until now. Though, he could have just twisted things like he always does. Maybe he knew just enough about the truth to make me believe a lie.

Then, there were "The Overseers". "Everything's just an experiment." How? What does that even mean, and why would Darren want to tell me? I guess his main objective is to survive. If somebody ever defeated The Ekklesia, he would certainly be on their hit list for his failure. He did seem genuinely afraid of them, but again, it could all be a mental trick - a mind game to either work toward his freedom, or just cripple me. He would probably like one just as much as the other.

I was sitting on the ground, leaning against the bunker when I heard the elevator arrive. I winced, expecting it to be a council member here to lecture me. The door opened. I was sitting around the corner, so I couldn't see who it was, but I immediately sensed a familiar presence. I relaxed.

Blake poked his head around the corner of the bunker and smiled when he saw me. He walked over and sat down next to me. He didn't say anything. It wasn't awkward though. I guess we'd both had a long day already. We just needed to sit, and having the other there made it better.

I closed my eyes and leaned my head against the bunker. We were shaded from the sun where we were sitting. The shade and the breeze made it the perfect temperature. I tried to relax my mind, but there were too many things knocking around in there, each one leading to thoughts about the other in a never ending cycle.

"So, do you think they're gonna kill me?" I asked Blake, referring to the council.

"Well, they need you too much to do that," Blake joked, but not really, "I'm sure they'll have a lot to complain about though."

We both looked out over the mountainous landscape. "You just need to make them eat their words," Blake said passionately, "Whatever they say, whatever they complain about, take it, and win."

I looked at Blake, who was already looking at me, "How do I do that?"

"They're going to complain about you saving Lucas because you lost a crystal," Blake explained, "Well, follow him and bring back him *and* his sister."

"That's easier said than done," I complained.

"But we can do it," Blake said, sentimentally.

I couldn't help but be encouraged. Any doubt I had in my plan was gone for the moment. Just in time too.

"Sorry to interrupt, but the High Council is calling for you," ALI informed us.

I sighed, but had gained a bit of confidence. Blake and I stood up and he put his hand on my shoulder.

"We just have to keep doing the right thing, whatever that is at the moment. If we do that, the rest will fall into place."

I smiled. He was right. He pulled me into a brief hug, and then we headed inside.

I marched down the corridor that led to the War Room, Blake keeping pace beside me. I could see Bailey ahead, waiting outside the door with General Raddick. They were talking about something.

"Where's Ana?" I asked, as I approached.

"She's following Lucas," Bailey informed me.

"On whose authority?" I asked, annoyed. That would be a dangerous job, a risk I would rather someone else take.

"Her own, apparently," General Raddick laughed, "She'll be fine. She's a great pilot."

I knew it was true. She would be fine. I just hoped she would be around when we took on Lucas, and hopefully his sister.

The four of us walked into the War Room. Everyone had been engaged in loud chatter until I walked in, and the room fell silent. Most everyone looked angry or at least confused. Word had definitely got around quickly. It would take a lot to explain myself, but I knew results would be the only thing that set things right.

Everyone took their seats, and I took my place as well, only I stood to talk.

"I know everything that happened a few minutes ago happened very quickly, but I want to inform you on everything that you may not know," The room was silent, waiting for me to explain my actions.

"We left this morning to go see Darren. He was little help, but we did learn that Lucas has a sister who is a crystal bearer. Their energies work together. Lucas can't survive without his sinister's energy to dampen its effects."

Still, no one said a word.

"Immediately after speaking to Darren, we were alerted that Lucas' damping device had stopped working. He was burning up. In order to save his life, I set him free, but he must return to his sister."

"You've been tricked!" Sparks yelled, "The old Parasite twisted your mind. The bearer probably doesn't even have a sister. He just needed you to set him free."

A chatter broke out among the other council members. I sensed their agreement with Sparks.

"We are tracking him!" I said with a raised voice, which hushed their conversations.

"We have a stealth ship following him back to wherever he's going. If it's not the capitol, it's likely been in communication with it. We can trace the communications back."

"That would involve a full scale assault of an Organization base," The Intelligence director said.

"Would it not be worth it?" I said.

"It depends on whether or not we can actually take it."

"There hasn't been a confrontation like that in months!"

"If we move cruisers to carry out this kind of mission, parts of our territory will be unprotected."

"We had a crystal in our possession! Why would we just let it go? What is the point of such a mission now?"

"We're trying to win a war, not just battles," Blake defended.

"Says the child," Sparks insulted.

"I'm more of a man than you," Blake snapped back.

Just as the group was devolving into chaos, a light began to blink on the Hologram projector in the center of the table. We were receiving a transmission. A hush fell over the council. Ana's voice began to play.

"Lucas just landed. We're in Siberia," she informed us. A howling wind threatened to overtake her voice. "I'm getting my initial scans of the base. It's small. Manageable. A skilled strike team could probably take it if Dylan and his team come."

"Are you sure we can take it?" I asked.

"No shields, minimal air defences. I don't think they were planning on fighting any battles here. It looks like a research facility."

I looked around at the council members. "You all can stay here and fight each other. My team and I are going to fight The Organization."

I walked away from the table and out of the room, closely followed by Bailey and Blake. As we entered the hallway, a voice called out to us. It was the intelligence director.

"Director, wait," I turned around to him, "Bases like what she described, they aren't built to fight. They're prisons. I'm not sure what you'll find, but may want to see who they are keeping there before you leave."

"Thank you," I said. Not only did we really need that advice, it felt good to know someone else was still on our side.

I saluted him. He did the same to me and said, "For the nations, Director."

"For the nations." I said

"For the nations," my friends repeated.

Then, we briskly walked down the corridor toward the elevator. "ALI, assemble my personal strike team."

"They're already waiting for you in hanger 5," ALI said.

He must have summoned them during the meeting. I don't know what I would do without his help.

"Perfect," I said.

"I also have a new suit for you there as well."

This made me laugh. I'd done that whole meeting in this scorched thing, full of holes. "Oops, that was real professional of me."

Everyone laughed, and I think, if ALI could, he would have laughed too.

We entered the hangar. It was crammed full of brand new transports and fighters, mostly Stingray models. All of the new stuff: integrated Ekklesia, Dorodin, and U.S. technology. They were really cool.

Because it was my personal strike team, everything was fitted with white Unitum armor. It was an expensive addition, but was tradition under my father, so it carried on to me as well. Though, I'm not sure the council would approve something like this anymore. These ships were the picture of both elegance and firepower. Every one of them had massive guns, missiles, and shield generators. Their systems were directly entangled with my crystal.

All of the troops wore their grey uniform with the flag and Ekklesia dove on their shoulder, but in addition to that, they wore a purple band around each wrist. I must admit, this was one of the best perks that came with my job.

I was met by Commander Cashner, the leader of my special division of troops. The best soldiers from every nation were represented here.

"Director," he saluted, "We're ready when you are."

"I'm ready," I said, "We can discuss strategy on the way there."

"Yes, sir," he said, then turned to the rest of the hanger. "Load up and move out!" he yelled.

All of the soldiers ran to their ships. The transports could carry twenty soldiers and there were ten transports. We had an escort of forty Stingrays, each having two pilots. We also had ten jet style fighters, which were mostly for carrying missiles.

I reported to the command center. It was a transport, but slightly bigger than the troop carriers. It was marked on the outside with a golden Ekklesia dove on either side of the ship. The emblem sat on top of the sliding doors and nearly took up the entire thing. They stood out beautifully against the white Unitum behind them.

Inside the ship, there was a table that ran lengthwise in the hold. It used the mist like what my suit was made out of to make 3D models of the battlefield. It used sensors outside the ship and on the other ships to scan the environment. We could see where every troop, craft, and structure was during a fight.

Along the walls, there were still a few seats. I sat in one. Blake took one on my left and Bailey on my right. Commander Cashner hopped on board and sat on the opposite side.

The hum of the engines grew as we took off out of the hangar. We couldn't see out, so I watched the display on the table. The black mist formed every single ship that was traveling with us. I inspected the image for details. It showed every rivet, dent, and gun crafted from the tiny black particles.

I'm not sure how long this entertained me, but between that and the small talk among our little group the flight went quickly. I informed the commander of what we were walking into and gave him the same advice that had been given to me earlier.

We decided that Ana, Bailey, and I would arrive first (We would meet up with Ana just before we arrived). Since we were bears, it would make sense for them to send out the other bearers to meet us. I would leave the fight at some point, leaving Bailey and Ana to fight the bearers while Blake and I infiltrated the base and hopefully found information leading us to the capitol.

It sounded perfect, but of course, nothing ever goes according to plan around here.

Chapter 7

As we flew, I noticed the natural light coming in through the front windshield beginning to fade. I knew we hadn't been flying long enough for it to be night time. Plus, we were flying west, so we should be chasing the daylight, not leaving it behind. I got curious enough to ask the pilot, and he said we were nearing the arctic circle. It stayed in a sort of eternal night time during the winter and was just beginning to receive daylight hours. Still, there wouldn't be much more than twilight when we arrived.

Finally, the announcement was given. We were five minutes out. Ana was using her jetpack to fly up to the command transport I was on. Then, she, Bailey, and I would all fly down to the base together.

We were getting very close to the base. Ana's people had advanced our cloaking technology by incredible bounds, but even it would be no match for the powerful short range scanners of an Organization base. Our cover would soon be blown, but we would still have the element of surprise.

Bailey had walked up to the pilots to look out through the windshield. Blake had elected to take a quick nap. Which was smart since we had learned once a battle started, sleep was hard to come by. Cashner was at one of the control panels observing the stats of the ships flying with us. I sat in one of the chairs that went with a different control panel, but I had pivoted around to look at the display over the table and admired our fleet.

I watched a little human shaped cluster of black particles appear at the bottom of the display. It was Ana. I watched her fly, maneuvering through the swarm of ships, to this command ship. When she reached it, I spun around in my chair and pressed the button that opened the door.

It slid open and a blast of the coldest air I had ever felt rushed into the cabin. The noise of rushing air and the cold jared Blake from his nap and Commander Cashner whipped around in his chair to see what was happening. Ana made her way into our view and glided in through the opening, landing gracefully inside our ship.

"Nice landing," I complimented.

"I've had practice," Ana replied, the closest to a thank you I would get.

Bailey poked her head in from the cockpit, "Does that mean it's time to go?"

"Anything to get this door closed," Blake complained, "It's freezing!"

I started to press the button to close the door, but the ship was rocked with a violent explosion. Green light lit up the twilight sky outside.

I stumbled and knocked into the table display, causing the mist to briefly scramble and reform. Ana nearly tumbled out of the ship, but Bailey grabbed her hand and pulled her back in. I looked at the display to see where the blast had come from. I could see turrets spaced out on the tundra below. Stingray fighters were breaking off to destroy them. At the very edge of the display, a structure was coming into view.

It wasn't much, probably no bigger than our high school back home. It was a series of barrack like structures, likely thick steel. They had rounded roofs and straight sides. They surrounded on three sides what looked like a courtyard, though I'm not sure why anyone would want to go out in this kind of weather. That would be our landing zone.

I pointed to the spot, "We'll land there. ALI, guide us in."

More explosions rocked the ship.

"On it, sir"

"Bailey, Ana, with me," I walked to the open door, then looked back at Blake, "I'll see you in a minute, don't do anything dangerous."

"Define dangerous?" Blake joked.

I smiled, turned, and then jumped out of the ship. The second I was in the open air I nodded my head for the helmet to form around my head. It was warm inside the suit.

I could see on my display a green trail to follow to the landing zone. I sensed Bailey and Ana following behind me. The three of us used our senses to maneuver through the blasts of green energy coming from the defences below.

We threaded the needle and reached the base. It was exactly as the display had depicted it. Though, now that I was outside the ship, it kind of felt like I was on a different planet.

The stars twinkled to my right, but to my left, the first notes of a sunrise were peeking over the horizon. In the middle of the two was a waning moon. The icy ground reflected the scene above.

I spotted the landing zone, shaded bright green by my heads up display, but I saw something that hadn't been on the display. Two people were standing alone in the courtyard. They were arrayed in the typical black Organization uniforms. It was strange that they were alone. I already knew what they were before I got close.

The two soldiers did nothing but stand there. I slowed down a bit as I prepared to land, but not too much. I allowed the energy from my crystal to spread over my body, concentrated it at my hands and released concussive blasts at the last second. This stopped me abruptly. I still landed hard enough that I had to bend my legs and put one hand down to break my fall. Though, I thought it made for a pretty good "superhero landing".

Ana had a similar sort of landing slightly behind me on my left side while Bailey gently floated down on my right. We were about thirty feet in front of the soldiers. I could have a good look at them now. The one standing closest to me was a woman, a bit shorter than me, and wore a blue crystal on her chest. However, it wasn't blue like mine used to be. It was a light, shimmering blue. To her right was a man, taller and decently fit. He wore a grey crystal on his chest. However, It was more like a rock of some sort. It didn't glow. Instead, a foggy grey haze flowed out from it in wisps that ran across his body. Our two little groups stared at each other for a moment as the shots rang out behind us.

I retracted my helmet first, "You must be Lucas' sister," I greeted, "I'm Dylan Vale, leader of the Ekklesia."

She retracted her helmet revealing her pale face. Very pale. In fact, her skin was so light that it was almost blue. Her hair fell down behind her. It was white as well, and she wore it in a braid.

"I know who you are," she said. She had a thick Russian accent.

"That should make things a lot easier then," I said, "I returned your brother safely to you, so now I feel that it's only fair you do something for me in return."

"You returned my brother to me nearly dead," she snapped, "You deserve the same fate."

"Your brother tried to kill me and would have died in our prison if I didn't let him go," I rebutted.

"You lie!" she scowled.

Bailey retracted her helmet now, "You don't believe that," she said. I knew she was reading her mind, "You're conflicted. You thought you knew what you were doing until something changed. You met someone."

The girl's eyes grew wide, and she cut her eyes to look at her friend. He still had his helmet on, but I could tell this was the signal for him to do something. I readied myself to fight, but let Bailey keep doing her thing. I sensed Ana tense up behind me. She must have noticed it too.

"And you," Bailey turned to the other soldier, "You foster a deep wound, but it's not one you can see. It weighs on your mind even now," He clenched his fists and his grey energy, or whatever it was, began to flow over his entire body. "We can help you," Bailey offered.

"If you want to help us, then leave," the Russian girl suggested.

"We can't do that without collecting what we came here for," I interjected.

"And what is that?" the girl asked.

"The location of your capital base," I said.

The girl looked like she was going to be sick, "You'll have to kill me for that. They say you don't do that sort of thing, though."

"I don't," I agreed.

"Well, I do," she snarled.

When she said that, her teal energy shot across her body and she lunged toward us. At the same time, the other bearer spread his grey tendrils of energy into the air.

Bailey shot a blast of her energy at him while Ana moved to counter the girl. I stood ready to intervene or break away, whichever was most appropriate.

Bailey's blast reached its target first, but he dodged out of its way. As he did, the grey wisps of energy brushed along the white bolt. When they touched it, they turned to the same white energy. This reaction traveled across each grey tendril until it made it back to the bearer. When it reached him, the energy across his body mimicked Bailey's exactly and his grey stone began to glow white.

He immediately sent a bolt of his now white energy to Ana, who was just reaching the girl. I conjured a beam of my purple energy that intercepted it before it reached her. This saved Ana, but immediately, the white energy turned purple in the same way it had transitioned the first time. My energy was the most powerful. I knew instantly that he was just trying to get me to use mine, and I had fallen into his trap.

I ran toward the bearer and reached to draw my staff, but I sensed a blast coming from my left. I ducked out of the way and drew my staff in the same motion. When I looked back, I saw Ana pinned by the girl. Her hands and feet were bound to the ground by chunks of ice.

I looked back at Bailey. The other bearer was attacking her, but we had sparred so many times that she was holding her own for the time being. I knew that he could still overpower her, but I had to help Ana first.

The girl had drawn her atom sword and was lifting it over her head for the kill. Ana squirmed on the ground as she tried to break free. I held out both hands in that direction, and just as the girl swung her blade, my energy smashed into her side and sent her hurtling through the air. She slammed into the side of one of the metal structures. When she hit it, the metal made a sound like a bell that radiated through the courtyard.

I ran over to Ana and used blasts of energy to break her hands free. Then, I offered her my hand to help her up.

"She's too powerful for me," Ana said. Her helmet was retracted now too.

"I'll take her," I said, "You help Bailey,"

"What about the plan?" Ana asked.

The other bearer had Bailey pinned down now. She was holding up a shield around herself while he poured out a flood of purple energy. He wasn't letting up and she couldn't counter. I knew she couldn't.

"Stick to it," I commanded, turning away from Ana and to the girl who had recovered from my attack.

Ana did as I said and went to help Bailey. I was hoping I could remove this girl from the battle somehow.

I drew my staff as the girl began to shoot icy blasts of energy at me. I realized how cold they were when intercepting them with my staff caused frost to form on it and my hands.

I blocked each one as she grew closer, but I knew I couldn't keep it up. The cold was starting to make it through my suit. I didn't want frostbite.

I made a break toward the girl, dodging a couple blasts and then ramming into her. This threw her backward and off balance. I sent a pulse of energy through my staff that leapt off the tip and erupted across her abdomen. She stumbled to the ground, but rolled onto her knees.

I shot a few more blasts that she flipped and ducked away from before she was back on her feet. When she had gained her footing, she formed a slender icicle that floated just above her hand. It came to a sharp point on both ends. She shot it at me. Then, another. And another.

I knocked a few out of the way with the staff, but one made it through and exploded against my chestplate. This broke my concentration enough that the next one escaped my senses entirely and grazed my neck.

I instinctively raised a shield and grabbed my neck. ALI had used the suit to patch it up before any blood came through, "How bad?" I asked.

"Just a scratch, sir,"

That was a relief, but now I was determined to end this fight. As I sat behind the shield, this girl had summoned a continuous stream of energy that bombarded my shield. She was trying to pin me down like her friend had done to Bailey (Who was now putting up a good fight with Ana's help).

Though I could tell her energy reacted strangely with mine, at least, it felt different than any other energy I had encountered, I could tell that I was stronger. Much stronger.

I held the shield up with my left hand and stretched the staff out in my right. I aimed the tip at the beam of bright blue energy that was slamming into the shield. Then, I summoned my own, bigger beam of energy just as I released the shield.

The purple beam sliced through the blue like it wasn't even there and met with the bearer on the other end of it. I had angled it so that it hit her in just the right way to launch her into the sky. She barely cleared the roof of the building behind her as she was thrown out of the battle. Her scream echoed through the tundra as she flew.

She'll be alright, I told myself. I looked back to check on the girls. They were holding their own. The new bearer's inexperience with my energy was helping them out a great deal.

I then began to look for Blake. I didn't have to look long though because he floated down right in front of me. He had apparently been hovering above the fight the whole time.

"You showed her," he laughed as he landed and his helmet retracted.

"I'm sure that won't last long," I worried, "Let's get inside."

Because of the cold, we both had our helmet reform around our heads. ALI had already scanned the building for an entrance and directed us out of the courtyard, to the end of one of the buildings. There was a steel door.

I could have just let ALI break into the system and unlock it, but to save time, I placed both hands on the door and summoned concussive blasts. The door was blown from its hinges and skidded down the concrete floor of the hallway.

I hadn't noticed how strong the wind was until we walked inside. The building was just one long hallway that made a horseshoe around the courtyard. It was lit with fluorescent lights that buzzed on the ceiling above.

"Where's the security?" Blake asked.

"I think those bearers are it," I said.

"Almost," ALI said, "There are a group of robots headed down the hall."

Sure enough, as he spoke, the marching of androids echoed through the hall. The tall, black humanoids rounded the corner. There were twenty of them walking two by two toward us. They had some impressive looking guns in their hands. Blake drew his Atom Sword.

I just stepped in front of him and held out my hands. My purple energy flowed in gentle streams toward the bots. It then surrounded them, coiling around their rigid bodies. I raised my hands a bit and they lifted off the ground. They were suspended in mid air. They tried to move, but I didn't let them. Smoke rose from some as their circuits overheated. Then, I clenched my open hands into fists. The energy retracted around them and crushed each one into a heap of metal. Some sparked or caught fire as I dropped the scraps to the floor.

"What am I even here for?" Blake complained light heartedly. He retracted his sword and clipped it back to his waist.

"Moral support," I smirked.

We made our way down the hall, stepping over the mess of robot pieces. ALI had analyzed the wiring in the building and found that most of the power was being used in the far section. That would be where the good stuff was.

I knew that it must have been good because when we turned the corner, there were ten real soldiers waiting for us. Most opened fire, but two ran at us with their swords drawn. Blake and I drew our staves. He sent his into the crowd that was firing at us. They had a small shield that separated us and them, but Blake was smart enough to aim his staff at the wall. The shockwave bounced off and knocked out a few of the soldiers.

I took the two coming at us and had them knocked out in just a few moves. I then turned toward the five or so cowering behind the shield. I summoned a blast powerful enough to overload the shield. Their small shield projector exploded.

The soldier closest to it was thrown backward and the others scattered into various rooms. Blake and I casually walked down the hall, stepping over the unconscious bodies. I wasn't worried about the ones that got away. They were scared enough that they wouldn't be any trouble.

We turned the final bend and began to make our way to the room at the end of the hall. ALI had it highlighted on our heads up display as the control room for the base. It would have the records we needed.

We walked toward it, but as we made it about half way down the hall, something stopped me. I sensed a familiar presence. I looked around and saw that I was standing next to a door. It was slightly different than the others though. It was thick like the door that we had entered through. Around its hinges, the cinder block wall was cracked. There was a lever in the center of the door.

I pulled the lever down, releasing the locks. The door squeaked as it opened. I peeked in. The room was totally different from the rest of this base. It was white, kind of like the rooms at the mountain base. The floor was divided into sections with seams that looked like they could raise and lower. One of those sections was up. It was a hospital bed, and on it was Lucas.

He wore only black boxer shorts. The rest of his body was covered in gruesome scars and new looking, pink flesh. He was hooked up to an I.V. in one arm and had a feeding tube that went up his nose. He didn't sit up, but he was awake. He turned his head to look at me.

I pushed the door open all the way and walked into the room. Blake followed in behind me, but I turned back to him, "Go get what we came for."

He nodded obediently and walked out of the room. I looked back to Lucas.

"Are you okay?" I asked.

"Do you really care?" he asked back.

I understood his distrust. We were the ones that had subjected him to torture. Whether The Organization had done that to him first, I didn't know, but we were certainly the most recent.

"Yes," I replied truthfully.

"Why are you here?" he asked. His accent wasn't as Russian as his sister's. I couldn't place it though.

"I'm looking for something," I said, "Why are you here?"

He didn't say anything. He didn't strike me as evil. I saw something in him. A spark, but not from his powers. A spark of good. I looked deeper.

He was scared. He was hiding. That's why he was here.

"You can't take what you came for," he said. His fear broke through to his expressions. .

"What do you mean?" I asked, intrigued.

"If you leave here with the location of the capitol, millions will die." His eyes simmered with terror, as though he were cornered by a terrible beast.

"You'll have to give me more than that," I said. He seemed genuine, but my senses could be fooled by someone who was well trained.

"You helped me once, so now I'm helping you," Lucas said, now stone faced, "On the other side of that wall, there's another crystal," Lucas pointed to a mirror wall across the room. "Down the hall, there's a kid who can wield it. He's our prisoner, so I'm sure he would love to be on your side. Take the crystal and him, and leave the information you came for."

I swung my hand toward the mirror and threw a ball of energy at it. The glass shattered revealing an observation room. There wasn't much in there, but against the far wall, there was a stand with a glass box on top. Inside the box there was a strange black force that flickered and pulsed, almost entirely snuffing out the glow of a light green crystal.

"How do I know this isn't a trick?" I asked.

"There's a new leader in Flyhe's place," Lucas warned, "Darren wanted a world left to rule. This man doesn't care if it all burns down. If you attack the capitol outright, it will. Take my offer."

I looked at the crystal in the next room, then looked back at Lucas. "Deal," I agreed..

I was sure we would find out soon if he would keep his word or not. I couldn't explain why, maybe it was me sensing his emotions or maybe I really had gone crazy, but I believed him. There were so many ways that this could be a trap, not even a clever one, but I believed him.

"Blake," I called over the coms, "You found the capital yet?"

"No, just a bunch of prisoner manifests and studies of these bearers' powers," he replied.

"Good, take what you have and leave," I said.

"What? But we're so close. It's here!"

"Leave it!" I repeated, "That's an order."

I hated doing that to him. I didn't think of Blake as a soldier I could order around, but I had to get the point across. I could explain later.

I walked through the broken glass and stepped over into the other room. I made my way to the glass box. The crystal was smaller than mine, about the size of Bailey's. It was a bright, leafy green color, but I could tell its light was made dim by whatever this black stuff was. It pulsated in vibrating waves that zipped around the crystal. I would call it energy, but it wasn't quite that. It was more like… anti-energy.

I took my staff, drew it back, and swung it at the box. I wanted to be ready in case the anti-energy was a trap and somehow attacked me. The glass shattered. Rather than attack me, the black void dissipated and the crystal fell to the floor.

I knelt down and picked up the crystal from among the shards of glass. When I stood up, I held it up in front of me, twisting it in my fingers to see it at every angle. It was beautiful. Its light was a bright green, but the crystal itself was a bit darker. The flat surfaces of the crystal refracted light in such a way that I think every possible shade of green may have been represented in this one crystal.

I walked back over the broken glass and looked at Lucas to say goodbye, but he was asleep, so I left him alone. I walked out into the hallway and found Blake walking toward me. I had the crystal enclosed in my fist now.

"What are you doing?" Blake asked.

"We just got a more important mission," I said, being intentionally vague. There was no time for details. Lucas' sister could be back at any moment.

I had Blake follow me down the hall to the only other vault door. It had to be the cell Lucas was talking about. I placed my hand on the lever and unlocked the door. Then, I swung it open. It was a heavy door and it moved slowly, creaking all the way. The room on the other side was dark, the only light came from the hallway, which cast mine and Blake's shadow ominously on the far wall of the room.

I heard a bit of shuffling coming from inside. Both Blake and I stepped into the room so that we could see around the door. If I hadn't sensed him, I would have overlooked him. In the far corner of the room, a young boy cowered.

He wore what looked like grey scrubs. He was thin, but not skinny. I couldn't tell much more about him. I could mostly just see the light reflecting off of his wide, scared eyes.

I sensed such overwhelming fear in him. Not just fear though, hurt - deep, deep hurt. I retracted my helmet revealing my face and Blake followed suit.

I smiled sympathetically and took a couple of steps toward the boy. He stood up, but kept himself pressed as far into the corner as possible. I stretched out my hand toward him and opened it, revealing the crystal.

It cast a bit of light into the dark corner and illuminated the child's face. He looked at the crystal for a long moment, then looked up at me. He wanted to trust me, but he was having a hard time doing so.

I spoke in the most gentle voice I had.

"I think this belongs to you."

Chapter 8

The boy looked up at me, and back at the crystal, then at Blake. He repeated this a few times, keeping his back pressed as tightly into the corner as he could.

"We're gonna get you out of here," I promised, "Trust me."

We looked into each other's eyes. I could tell he was trying to sense my intentions. He must have had some sort of training. That's not something you really just figure out.

Finally, he broke eye contact, looked at the crystal and held up his hand. He summoned the crystal to it and clenched his fist around it. The light green energy surrounded his fist. He nodded his head. I nodded back and turned to the door.

Blake gave me a confused, but compliant look as I walked past him. The boy trailed close behind me, and Blake followed behind him. We briskly walked down the hallway, back around the horseshoe to where we entered. We stumbled over the crumpled robots and finally reached the doorway.

I noticed the boy was already shivering. We would need to rush him back to the ship to get him warm.

I don't know what I was thinking. My mind was so distracted by Lucas and now this new bearer that I had let my guard down. I walked out into the cold and turned back to my companions. I was about to take hold of the boy to fly him back to the transport when I was hit with an icy blast.

I was blown across the tundra, sliding on the snow and ice beneath me. I felt something slice into my side before I finally came to a stop, just in time to roll out of the way of an icicle. It stabbed into the ground beside me. Another one followed it, but I used my energy to swipe it away.

I then put my hands at my side and blasted myself into the air. The ice bearer was standing right beside the door of the bunker. I blocked a few more icicles before landing right in front of her. I summoned my energy to my fists and prepared to fight, but just as I did, I noticed something had changed. The energy had faded from her body. She was just standing there with a blank expression on her face, staring into the bunker.

I stopped what I was doing and followed her gaze. She and the boy had locked eyes. The boy looked firmly into her eyes. He had looked so timid when we found him, but now he looked resolute. It was like he was testing her. I looked at him, then back at her. She looked at me. Her eyes were tired. She was stressed. I could see her gritting her teeth and sensed her fear and compassion. Strangely, the fear was brought on by her compassion.

The girl nodded her head and took a few steps back. She was letting us go. I didn't understand what was happening, but there was no time to figure that out. I turned back to the boy and held out my arm, "Come here," I said, keeping the ice bearer in my field of vision.

He obeyed and walked to my side. I put my arm around him and pulled him up next to me, "Hold on tight," I commanded, "ALI, fly us back."

We lifted off the ground. The boy's grip tightened. I nearly threw up as his fingers dug into my fresh wound. "Faster, please, ALI," I choked.

Even though the sky was clear, the strong wind blew the snow creating a haze near the ground. I noticed the girl just standing there, looking up at us as we flew off. I wondered what her relationship was with the boy, or if they even had one. Maybe he had some sort of mind powers. This was turning out to be a strange mission.

The sounds of the battle that had been loud earlier were quietening down. The fighters had likely destroyed most of the cannons by now. With the exception of the blistering cold, it was quite peaceful up here.

The faint sunlight we had seen when we arrived was brighter now, and as we climbed higher, it finally peeked over the horizon, casting a golden glow on the tundra. The ships ahead of us reflected the golden rays, their Unitum armor glistening as they flew. The boy, who had buried his face in my shoulder, was now staring at the sunlight. I sensed it melting something inside him. He was still shivering though. And he was still digging his fingers into my side.

I easily spotted the command ship, and ALI guided us into the open door. I landed a bit harshly and pushed the boy from my side. I couldn't help but inhale dramatically, now that my wound was free. I stumbled over to the table and leaned against it as I caught my breath.

Blake entered the ship right behind me. The boy we had brought along looked utterly confused, but this was mostly covered up by his violent shivering.

Blake guided him away from the door while I pressed a button on my vanguard. It was one, just above my wrist that only I and other commanding officers had. When activated, it gave the signal for all troops to withdraw from combat as quickly as possible.

The door to the cockpit opened and Commander Cashner rushed out. "So you got it?" He asked. He realized we had a new passenger while he was asking his question.

"We got something," I winced, forcing myself off the table to look more assertive.

Blake closed the door to the cabin and we both retracted our helmets.

Cashner looked at the boy, then at me. "Does he know where the capitol is?"

"I don't know," I answered, "We haven't gotten the chance to talk very much yet."

Cashner stared at me blankly. I looked back at him, trying to be sure of my decision, though, seeing his reaction was making me doubt it.

"Why did you recall the troops? This was going to be an easy extraction."

"I made a deal," I explained, "This boy is a bearer. He's holding a previously unknown crystal in his hand right now. I took him and the crystal in exchange for leaving behind the information we came for."

"We could have taken them both!" the commander raised his voice, "This was going to be seamless. You could have taken all three of the other bearers if you wanted. You could have taken all of their crystals. And we would have had the location of the capitol."

"Well, it would have been difficult to defeat all of the bearers and take them hostage," I defended. I admit, it wasn't a good defence. I didn't have a good defence. All I knew was that there was something deeper going on and I wasn't willing to risk becoming over ambitious.

"We can find the capitol at another base," I continued, "This was a one time deal. He needed our help."

"The world needs our help," Cashner said, "If you want to help everyone, you're going to have to leave some behind."

"Not today," I snapped, pointing my finger at him.

I could tell he was still upset, but the conversation was over. He walked back into the cockpit and closed the door behind him. It wasn't long before the door of the cabin opened again and Bailey flew inside.

"Where's Ana?" Blake asked.

"Headed back to her ship," Bailey replied, "Did we…" She stopped speaking when she saw the boy. "Who is this?"

"We haven't had time to introduce ourselves yet," I acknowledged, looking down to the boy. He was cowered down in the chair furthest away from the door. I walked over to him. "I'm Dylan," I held out my hand to him.

The boy spun around in the chair to face me and shook my hand. "I'm Hunter," he mumbled, cutting his eyes up to look at me.

Bailey walked over, "I'm Bailey," she smiled, kneeling down to shake his hand.

"Hunter," he mumbled again.

"I'm Blake," Blake said from across the hold.

"It's nice to meet you Hunter," Bailey said softly, "How old are you?"

"13"

Bailey and I exchanged disgusted looks. How despicable could one be to imprison a 13 year old boy in a place like this, all alone?

"How long have you been here," she asked thoughtfully.

He stared at her for a long time. His eyes were glossy as though he were reviewing a memory. Tears filled his eyes, but never escaped. "I want you to take me home," Hunter requested.

Bailey looked at me again. I knew taking him anywhere but the mountain base would seal my fate with the council, and it already wasn't looking good, but this was the right thing.

"Of course," I agreed, "Where are you from?"

Hunter's face scrunched up like a prune and turned red. His green energy lit up his eyes, but he kept it from flowing across his body. He composed himself just long enough to squeak out the word, "Boulder."

"Colorado?" Blake questioned, a bit insensitively. We all knew the fate of the town.

I thought hard about how to tell this kid that there was nothing left of his home. Colorado was one of the hardest hit states when The Organization bombed the west coast. The squadron of bombers that flew through that region were among the first to attack and went on the longest without being intercepted. They hit many major cities and the smaller ones surrounding them, reducing them to little more than ash and dust. Boulder was one of those cities.

"Kid, I umm," I stared. Hunter stared back at me, stone cold and composed now.

"I know," he said shakily, "Take me home."

I nodded. He must have been there when it happened. I couldn't imagine what he must have seen that day.

"Pilot," I called, turning to the cockpit.

The door opened and a voice called back, "Sir."

"Break off from the convoy, take an escort of three Stingrays, and set a course for Boulder, Colorado."

"Boulder?" The pilot questioned, "There's nothing le..."

"You have your orders," I cut him off. There was no need for Hunter to hear again what he'd already lived though.

"Yes, sir," he replied and the door closed.

Now that I was still and the adrenalin was wearing off, my side was beginning to throb. "Guah," I grunted, holding the wound.

"What's wrong?" Bailey asked.

"The Ice Queen hit him with an ice spear," Blake answered for me.

"It's not that bad," I said, not actually knowing if it was bad or not. I hadn't looked at it.

"Take your armor off so I can see," Bailey commanded.

"I'm fine," I countered, "I'll get it looked at by a medic when we get back."

My armor detached on its own and drifted over to rest on the wall, and the grey outer part of my suit turned to mist revealing the black fitted T-shirt and pants underneath. "ALI," I complained.

"This wound requires attention," ALI said.

I noticed Hunter perked up a bit, but I didn't have much time to think about it. Bailey was already hard at work, assessing my wound.

It was a deep gash, but it seemed to miss everything important. It was about five inches long and an inch deep. The suit's onboard med kit had stopped the bleeding, but it definitely needed stitches.

"Oww!' I complained, as Bailey prodded the wound.

"You need stitches," she concluded.

"No kidding," I jabbed.

She gave me a dirty look.

She was probably going to say something about how I needed to be quiet and let her fix it, but we both turned our attention to Hunter when he stood up.

"I think I can help," he said.

"It's okay," Bailey said, "He's just a baby. I'll get him stitched up real quick. You just focus on staying warm."

He didn't respond. He just walked over and wedged his way between Bailey and I. Bailey and I were both a bit taken aback. I didn't have a clue what he was doing.

"Umm, if you really want to help, why don't you just let Bailey show you what to do," I suggested.

He still didn't say anything. Instead, he raised his hand and stretched it out over the wound. When his hand was about an inch above my side, he allowed his green energy to flow down his arm.

It moved in geometric patterns, right angles and sharp corners, but it created a mesmerizing pattern and a shade of green that was even more so. As the energy reached his hand, it trickled down onto my skin.

A warm sensation filled the area around my wound and the pain ceased.

“That’s enough,” Bailey said sternly, placing a firm hand on Hunter’s shoulder. She likely read my shock as terror.

“No,” I said bewildered, “Let him.”

Bailey stood ready to rip him off of me, but I knew that wouldn’t be necessary. Blake was making his way around the table to see what was going on. I looked at him and smiled in disbelief.

The deep wound was slowly becoming more shallow and closing up from the ends. The red oozing flesh turned to a soft pink. What little bit of blood that was left dried up. The green energy was weaving the flesh back together again.

I looked down at Hunter. His eyes were closed as he concentrated on his work. He continued this way until the wound was nothing more than a scar. When he was done, the energy subsided and he removed his hand.

“Feel better now?” he asked.

“Like new,” I said, rubbing my hand across my new scar.

Bailey and Blake nearly pushed him over trying to get a good look. Both of them were touching it, testing to see if the miracle was real.

“Alright you two,” I smiled, pushing them away. I hopped down from the table and put my hand on Hunter’s shoulder. “Thank you.”

The corner of his mouth tilted up as he attempted to smile, “You’re welcome.”

“How did you do that?” Blake asked.

“That’s just how my powers work,” Hunter replied, sitting back down in his chair, “You should probably eat something,” he suggested to me.

"ALI," I said, "Do we have a spare puck on board?"

"Yes, sir," he said over the coms, "Under the display table. Third compartment to the right."

I turned around and reached for the cabinet.

"ALI?" Hunter exclaimed, "ALI, ALI! It's me!"

I grabbed the puck and stood up to join my friends in confused staring.

"ALI, do you know each other?" I asked. The table displayed his emblem over the center to make himself visible.

"Of course we do!" Hunter said, "He trained me."

ALI's bubble wavered as though he were confused as well, "I'm sorry, young man, but I have no memory of you. Would I know you by a different name? Maybe you were younger when we met?"

Hunter's spirits dropped. "You're the original," Hunter sulked.

"I wasn't aware there was anyone besides the original," ALI said.

My father had left behind countless books of secrets for me to rummage through, some of them ALI didn't even know, but if this was in there, I hadn't come across it yet.

"I met a man named Daniel Sons the night I got my powers," Hunter explained somberly, "He gave me a puck with a copy of ALI to help train me. I guess he removed your memory of it."

"Daniel would never have erased my memory!" ALI sounded offended at such a proposal.

"Well, he must have this once," Hunter said.

"Wait," I butted in, "You met Daniel Sons?"

"Yes," Hunter replied.

"That's my father!" I informed him enthusiastically.

"I know," Hunter said, "My ALI and I got your message."

"The Ekklesia call?" I asked.

"If that's what you call it."

"When did you meet Daniel?" Blake asked, just as curious as I was.

"In the summer before The Organization took over," Hunter said, "However long ago that was."

"Last year," I added, hoping to give him back his bearing of time, "Did he tell you anything?"

Hunter looked down. I could tell he was gritting his teeth, and I sensed overwhelming regret.

"Maybe that's enough questions for now," Bailey suggested.

I wanted to know everything Hunter knew. If he met my father and ALI didn't remember it, then he might have information that we didn't have. But Bailey was right. We were overwhelming him.

"How long until we get to Boulder?" Hunter asked. He sounded defeated.

"About three hours," I answered.

Hunter curled up in the chair and we all watched as he drifted off to sleep.

Chapter 8

'Is he asleep?" I asked Bailey. I didn't want to talk about Hunter if he could hear us.

"Out cold," Bailey replied.

"Ok. Good," I said.

"Right, so, what just happened?" Blake asked.

"His energy oscillates at the same frequency as ATP, the energy that supports all life," ALI informed, "He gave Dylan's body unlimited energy, which it used to heal his wound."

"Right," Blake said. He definitely didn't understand what ALI was saying, and also, he didn't care. He was more referring to my actions.

I explained what had happened with Lucas to both of them. They seemed to agree with my decision to take Hunter and leave the information. That answered most of their questions, so now it was time for mine.

"ALI, are you sure you don't remember Hunter?" I asked.

"I have gone through all of my memory banks. I can't find so much as a mention of his name," ALI replied.

"Are there any gaps in your memory?" I asked.

"None that stick out," ALI said, "I have to do a systems reset now and then. Those are the only gaps that I have."

"Is there a record of one of those happening last summer?" Bailey asked.

"Yes," ALI answered, "One about four weeks before the take over."

"That must be it!" I said, "Maybe we can ask him more when he wakes up."

"I don't think that would be wise," Bailey said, "I sense that he is…" she paused for a moment to find the words, "I've never sensed such brokenness and sorrow. He's lost everything. He's been isolated for almost a year. We should just let him be for now."

I knew she was right. That didn't keep me from wanting answers, but they would have to wait.

The three of us stood for a while, looking at Hunter as he slept. Which might seem a bit odd, but he was just such a mystery. His crystal was unknown. His powers were strange. And any record of him had been erased by my father.

Even stranger though, was the fact that I couldn't shake the feeling that I knew him, despite also knowing with certainty that I had never met him. It was like having a memory that was just out of reach.

He sat there, curled up in the chair. He was wearing one of the gray tactical suits now to keep him warm. He had placed the crystal in the puck on his chest without any instruction. He'd known exactly what to do when we handed him the puck. Now, it sat nestled in its proper position just as snuggly as Hunter was nestled into his chair.

Eventually, the three of us each found our own chairs as the flight drug on. We were all just thinking. I was mostly thinking about what I was going to say to the council. I couldn't come up with anything that would even sound remotely enticing to them, so I gave up and elected to just figure it out in the moment.

After this line of thought ended, I began to think about where we would go from here. I honestly had no idea what was going to happen when we got to Boulder. Then, I had no idea what would happen when we got back to the base. But after that, we would need a plan for finding the capitol.

I did still want to find it, but what did Lucas mean? Did he mean people would die if we went to the capitol at all, or just if we took it from that specific base? Maybe there was some sort of stipulation on the bearers for if they failed, similar to the Taken, but larger in scale.

I wished I could talk to him again. I was sure I would get the chance to. There was no way we had seen the last of them.

"Entering Boulder now," the pilot's voice played over the P.A. Hunter jumped, startled by the sudden noise.

Blake had fallen asleep himself but woke up when the announcement was made. Bailey had stayed awake though. She had been fiddling with one of the monitors. We all exchanged glances, and I stood up.

"We're here," I said to Hunter.

"I heard," he replied sharply. He was troubled. The sound of his aching heart was deafening to my senses. He was using all of his focus to hold back his tears. My heart ached for his.

"Do you have a place you'd like us to land?" I asked.

"Evergreen Avenue," Hunter replied, "On the West side of town."

I relayed the information to the pilot and watched through the windshield as we made our approach. Boulder must have been beautiful before the bombing. It was seated in a high elevation valley, with the towering peaks of the Rocky Mountains in the background. I imagined fittingly beautiful architecture, though there was no evidence of it.

Everything was leveled. A few lucky buildings stood sporadically, having blown out windows and crumbling walls. The raised overpasses were collapsed. Craters littered the landscape. If the vegetation hadn't started taking over, it would look more like the surface of the moon than a scene from earth.

It had only been a year and already nature had begun to reclaim the abandoned city. Grass and weeds grew out of control and young saplings were beginning to sprout in yards.

Our ship came to sit at the end of what had once been a road. Now, it was a grassy path with busted pavement and blast craters. The hum of the engines grew dim and the door to the cabin slid open. I turned from the cockpit and looked at Hunter, along with my friends. Hunter took a moment to look at each of us, finally fixing his gaze upon me.

"Thank you for saving me," he said somberly, "You can leave now."

He walked to the open door and hopped out of the ship. Bailey walked behind him to the doorway, "Hunter, wait," she implored, "You can't just stay here alone."

Hunter didn't say anything. He just kept his same steady pace, walking away. I could sense he was crying now, but he hid it well. I put my hand on Bailey's shoulder and spoke softly, "Let him have a second," I suggested, "We'll fly off, and I'll circle back to him."

She nodded. "He needs you," she said, her own tears welling up in her eyes.

Bailey had seen in so many people's heads that she was more accustomed to seeing hurt. Mental hurt, though she had much empathy, never seemed to get to her for this reason. For her to become emotional at what she saw in someone's head was a big deal. I knew how bold his emotions had been to my senses. I wondered what, and how much, Bailey saw.

I turned from her and told the pilot to take off and meet back up with the escort, "You should fly just outside the city," I said, "I'll call you when I'm ready to be picked up."

"Yes, sir," the pilot said.

Cashner was still sitting in the chair beside the pilot. I turned, and he gave me an impatient look, "Will this be a long adventure?"

"Nope," I said cheerfully, "We'll be back with enough time to go to church just before my lecture from the council."

He actually cracked a smile. Cashner had been around me long enough to know how I worked. He didn't always agree (and made it known when he didn't), but I always felt that he trusted me, or at the very least, respected me. Although, respect is a difficult thing to sense, and I never felt right asking Bailey to see if he did.

The ship took off, and I returned to the cabin. The sliding doors stayed open on both sides, letting the warm summer air blow through the ship. It was a much welcomed change from the Arctic air. I held onto one of the grab bars overhead and leaned out of the ship. Blake came up beside me and did the same.

"You gonna put on a jetpack before you jump or just freestyle it?" he yelled over the rushing air.

I had put my tactical suit back on when I gave Hunter his puck, but I left the armor and jetpack off. "I would freestyle, but I think the landing would be a bit jarring for our friend."

"Good call," he said, "You want me to go with you and hang back?"

"Nah, I think I'll handle this one," I replied, "There's nothing to worry about here. Just pray I can get him to come with us."

I wish I only wanted him to come with us for noble reasons, like giving him hope and watching out for him, and I did. But I also selfishly wanted him to appear before the council so they could see what I traded the mission for.

Blake gave me a salute and I answered with a nod, forming my helmet around my head. I leapt from the ship and a jetpack quickly shot out of the ship after me. As I fell, it fastened itself to my back and began guiding me back to where we had left Hunter.

He was easy to spot, the lone sign of life moving down the broken road. I noticed he had stopped at a crater in the road. He had climbed down into it and was on all fours. I landed at the top of the crater.

There was no pavement left here. It had all been stripped away by the blast. All that was under my boots was grass and soft dirt. I stood for a while, looking down the embankment. It was a gentle slope that was about three feet deep in the center where Hunter was. He was lamenting, weeping. He pounded the ground. His green energy raced over his body in waves and bolts. He groaned, but never had enough in him to make a full word. I knew how he felt.

Seeing him like this brought back memories I hadn't visited since they happened. I fought to keep from revisiting them now. Looking down at him, it was impossible not to. I wanted to tell him the hurt would fade and that things would get better. I wanted to tell him that there were people who cared for him, even if he didn't feel like it now. But there were times that I struggled to believe these things myself.

I thought back to when my father died, both times. There were two things that got me through that: my God and my best friend. It seems he didn't have a best friend anymore, but I could offer him God.

I waited until his sobbing had turned to sniffling. Then, I walked down into the crater. Hunter was sitting back on his knees now, staring ahead of him. I felt his senses turn on me. He knew I was there.

Just before I reached him, he spoke, "I should have listened to him."

I didn't know who he was talking about at first. I stood just behind him and let him finish.

"He said he could protect us," Hunter sniffled, "I…I was confused… I didn't believe him and now…" He stopped talking, unable to cry, but unable to keep going.

I realized the only person he could be talking about was my dad. That's the only reason he would be telling me this. I put my hand on Hunter's shoulder from behind, "There was no way you could have known," I consoled, "None of us knew the truth." I looked off into the same void Hunter was staring into as my own words affected me, "We still don't."

"And they died… they died because of it," The emotions finally overwhelmed him enough to push out the last tears he had.

I walked around to the front of him now and knelt with him. I put both hands on his shoulders and pulled him into a hug. "Too many have," I whispered, to both Hunter and myself.

His crying intensified, not because of anything I said, but because of the love in the embrace. I sensed he hadn't had this in a very long time. He wrapped his arms around me, pressed his head on my shoulder, and cried.

"It's okay now," I said, "You're safe."

I knew the real problem was that the ones he loved weren't safe, but I couldn't fix that. I could make him safe now. So I assured him of that.

I'm not sure how long this lasted exactly. A while. When he did finally cry his last tear, he refused to let go for yet a while longer. Then, when I thought the time was right, I pitched my offer.

"I won't force you to go with me," I said, "But at least let me offer you something." I knew he was listening. I pulled away from the embrace and stood up. Hunter remained on his knees. "There's someone I'd like you to meet back home. Come with me to meet him, then we'll go to my base."

"You sound just like him," Hunter said nostalgically. I couldn't tell if the memory was a good or bad one.

"Who?" I asked.

"You're dad."

I smiled and held out my hand, "Will you come with me?"

Hunter reached up and took hold of it. "Yes," he agreed. I pulled him onto his feet, keeping eye contact with his sad, red eyes.

"Good," I said, and we walked out of the crater together.

"ALI," I called.

"Yes sir," His voice played from a speaker in my puck so Hunter could hear.

"Call the pilot back," I commanded, "Tell him and the escort to set course for Tullahoma. We're going to make a pit stop there before heading back to the mountain base."

"Yes, sir," ALI replied.

"Where are we going?" Hunter asked.

"We're going to church," I smiled.

I put my arm around his shoulder and we walked down the broken road. Together.

At the end of the road sat our transport. I didn't really think Hunter would feel like making the trip back by jetpack. The side door was open and Blake was standing in the opening waiting for us. Without a word he offered us both a hand up into the ship.

Bailey sat at the workstation in the furthest corner of the ship and watched us as we walked in. She smiled when she saw that Hunter had come back with me. I noticed her white energy flickering through her irises and knew she was collecting the full story of what just happened. Her smile grew a bit bigger.

Commander Cashner sat in the copilot's chair of the open cockpit. "How was your little outing?" he asked.

"Productive," I answered, "Now, if you and the pilot could take us to Tullahoma, please."

"What are we going there for?" Cashner asked, not defiantly, but definitely impatiently.

"I told you," I smirked, "We're going to church."

Cashner rolled his eyes. I didn't sense frustration though. He was worried. He was very "by the book". It's what got him so high in rank. Funny how he ended up getting paired with me. He knew the council wouldn't take to my actions and worried. Despite him disagreeing with my methods, we made a good team. He didn't want a new boss.

"And Commander," I turned back to him before the cockpit door closed, "Contact the council. Tell them we will meet virtually in fifteen minutes."

"Yes director," he said gravely.

"It'll be okay, Commander."

He nodded and the door to the cockpit closed. I rejoined my friends.

Hunter was sitting next to Bailey now and Blake was standing behind me. "You're going to meet with them now?" Blake asked.

"Better I call the meeting now, than they have me at their mercy when I return," I explained, "Plus, it makes me look stronger if I call the meeting now. I'm confronting them, rather than hiding from my actions."

"Politics," Blake said.

"Politics," I agreed.

The transport took to the air as Blake and I leaned against the display table. "So what are we doing exactly?" Blake asked quietly. I only now realized that the only person who knew my plan was me.

"I'm taking Hunter to meet Pastor," I explained at the same low tone.

"What's he going to do?" Blake asked.

"It's not so much him that I'm counting on doing something," I hoped. I leaned in and whispered, "This kid is broken… He lost his entire family, his home, and then was tortured by The Organization. That's not a wound I can help fix on my own."

Blake looked up, now understanding my plan. "It won't happen in a day," he said, concerned.

"I know," I stared straight ahead, deep in thought, "...I remember."

The last bit of our fifteen minutes was spent in silence. I don't know what Blake was thinking about, but he was just as reminiscent as I was. Most of the memories were cold and closed now, and I did have a lot of new ones to bury the more painful ones under. The bad ones didn't hurt anymore. They just existed. I hoped that day could come soon for Hunter.

"Sir," ALI broke the silence, "You have one minute until the meeting. The council is already logging onto the secure server. I have your spot ready to go."

"Thank you ALI." I sat up off the table, as did Blake. The door opened and Cashner walked out of the cockpit. Bailey stood up and Hunter observed from his seat.

"Hunter, why don't you go sit in the cockpit for a few minutes," I suggested.

I sensed mistrust. Bailey must have sensed more, because she spoke up, "We're not keeping secrets. It's just..." She searched for the right words.

"Politics," I said, "I'm sure you'll be dealing with the council soon enough."

I left out the detail that, as a crystal bearer, he would be on it (per my dad's instruction). He could figure all that out once we actually got back to the mountain base.

Hunter nodded and walked to the cockpit. The door closed behind him.

"Good luck," Cashner said, taking a seat at one of the work stations.

"It's never luck," I recited.

Cashner cracked a half smile. That was my only answer to that particular statement now. It was to lighten the mood, but it was also true. It is never luck.

The display began to ripple as the members of the council began to form. They weren't life sized like the projections on the holotable back home. Because this was a smaller display, it just showed a simulated aerial view of the War Room. Above that, the face of the person speaking would be projected. All of this was formed from the black mist, so it didn't have color, only dimension.

"Good Morning everyone," I greeted.

"It's anything but that after the stunt you just pulled," Captain Sparks blurted out.

"Let him speak," General Raddick reprimanded.

"What I pulled, was no stunt," I defended, "I was calling to report a successful mission. Though the original objective was not accomplished, a greater one was achieved."

The room was silent, so I continued.

"As of this morning, the Ekklesia is in possession of another crystal, a friendly crystal bearer, and critical intelligence."

There was chatter that rumbled through the council. The intelligence director spoke up, "What intelligence?"

"The Organization is now under control of a new leader," I explained, "I had a brief conversation with the bearer, Lucas. This new leader is a radical even among their own."

"Is this Lucas an ally now?" General Raddick asked.

"Not fully, but I believe he may be conflicted about his loyalty," I speculated.

"And what of the new crystal and its bearer?" The science director asked.

"He's a 13 year old boy from Boulder, Colorado," I informed the council, "He was taken at the time of the Organization's bombings and has been captive ever since. His powers are unique to anything we have seen."

"This is all speculation!" Captain Sparks yelled, "Can you all not see it? None of this can be confirmed. We're going off the word of an enemy operative and a child that may or may not have his senses about him. Why would we believe the people who gained power through lies?"

Sparks' words were backed with "Yeah's" and "That's right" from some members of the council.

"I can sense deception and I detected none," I defended.

"A sense that can be fooled with the right training," the director of science pointed out pragmatically.

"I move that we assemble the fleet and go back for the information," Sparks announced.

"I made a promise that we would not move on the capital at this time," I said, "It would be unwise to act rashly. Let's at least gather intel first."

I noticed this meeting was moving in an unfavorable direction.

"He's right," General Raddick said, "We've come too far to become reckless."

"Let's at least give it some time," I suggested, "The information we were after has likely been moved or destroyed anyway."

"And yet it was within our grasp a few hours ago," Sparks wined.

"Sometimes chess requires you to sacrifice a pawn," I said.

"Indeed, it does," Sparks snarled.

He had flipped my words around quite effectively. I saw from the overhead that the council members were looking around and whispering to one another.

"We will meet again when I return to the base," I suggested, trying to take back control of the room. Sparks had won this round. "In the meantime, I will send each of you the mission report to review."

And with that, I pressed the button in front of me and logged off the meeting. "Well, that could have gone better," I sighed.

"Really?" Blake smiled, "I thought it went pretty good." He was joking of course, which did lighten the mood.

"It could have been worse," Cashner agreed as he walked back to the cockpit. The door opened. I could see through the windshield that we were flying above some storm clouds. The morning sun was ahead of us. Hunter was mesmerized.

"You never flown before, kid?" Cashner asked.

"No," Hunter answered, not taking his eyes off the view.

"It's beautiful isn't it?" I said, poking my head in the doorway.

"I've never seen anything like it."

For a second, he actually sounded a bit happy, but it didn't last long.

"You can have your seat back now," he said, solemnly.

"Why don't you keep it for now?" Cashner suggested.

"No, thank you," Hunter sulked. He then stood up, pushed his way between us, and sat back down in the dark corner of the ship. I guess when you've seen such horrible things, even beauty begins to hurt. Like eyes adjusting to light after being in the dark.

Chapter 9

The pilot announced that we had begun our descent over Tullahoma. We were to arrive around 10:45 am. It would just barely give us enough time to catch Pastor before service began.

I took my jetpack off and hung it on the wall with the rest of my armor. I felt the gentle bump as the landing gears touched down. I'd had to use this sort of transportation to get to church so often that we had installed a landing pad in the back parking lot. It came in handy for times like this.

The door of the transport slid open. The sunlight poured in and everyone squinted. "We're here," I said.

"Where's here?" Hunter asked, the only one still sitting. Cashner and the pilot had emerged from the cockpit.

"Tullahoma, Tennessee," I replied, "My home."

Hunter didn't reply and didn't stand up.

"ALI, how about you put us in something a bit more appropriate," I suggested.

"Certainly sir," he replied.

Everyone's tactical clothing became surrounded with a mist matching the color of the gear as it changed form. Blake and I ended up in a full suit, mine light grey and his a darker shade. Bailey's formed into a long white dress with ¾ length sleeves and ruffles around the bottom. Cashner and the pilot were now in grey polos and pants and Hunter was in all black: a button down shirt and dress pants.

"Much better," I congratulated, "You ready?" I looked at Hunter.

"For what?" He asked, still sitting in his chair.

"To meet the man I said I wanted to introduce you to," I reminded him.

"I guess."

"Good," I said.

"You'll have to hurry," ALI said, "You only have about ten minutes."

"Let's go then," Blake said as he hopped out of the transport.

Hunter finally stood up, but he waited for everyone else to exit. Bailey walked out in front of me, and I waited at the door before Hunter and I exited together.

We all started walking that way, but I noticed Cashner standing beside the ship, not following us. I stopped and looked back. Hunter stopped with me, sticking close by my side.

"Aren't you coming?" I asked.

"This isn't really my thing," Cashner denied politely.

"Sure it is," I said cheerfully, "You just don't know it yet."

Cashner smiled, "Maybe so, but I think I'll just keep the engines warm today."

I nodded, and we continued with the group.

We entered through the front doors along with the stragglers who had missed Sunday school. We were met by the greeters who shook our hands and told us good morning. I spoke to brother and sister Brinkley momentarily, but kept my eyes peeled, looking for Pastor. I wanted Hunter to at least meet him before service, even if they didn't get to talk very much until afterwards.

My friends spread out, speaking with their acquaintances. I saw that Blake had found our parents. I wanted to talk to them and introduce them to Hunter, but that would have to wait.

I finally spotted Pastor at the front of the sanctuary. He was speaking to a young couple that I had never seen before. "Ah, there he is," I told Hunter, gesturing toward the tall middle aged man, "Let's go say hi."

Hunter nodded and trailed closely behind me. We made our way down the center aisle. The young couple was just walking off as we reached him.

"Dylan!" Pastor's face lit up when he saw me. I loved this about him. It was like every time he saw you was the first time he'd seen you in years. There was always so much joy and love in his voice. He shook my hand, "It's so good to see you!"

He looked around me to Hunter, who was standing directly behind me, "And it's so good to meet you." Pastor held out his hand, and I stepped out of the way a bit, "My name's David."

Hunter shook his hand, but he never made eye contact with him, "I'm Hunter."

"Hunter," Pastor repeated (now he would never forget it), "It's nice to meet you."

"Mm, hm" Hunter nodded and pulled his hand back.

"We were on our way back to the mountain base and wanted to stop by for some church," I conversed, "You know I try not to miss a service and with the war picking back up again, it sounds like this might be my last chance for a little while."

"It's good to get it while you can," Pastor agreed.

The conversation sat for a moment, so I turned to Hunter, "Hunter, this my Pastor. He helped me when I lost my father and when I got hung up in this war. He's a very wise man."

Hunter looked up at Pastor.

"Well, it wasn't all me," Pastor admitted.

I mediated the conversation a bit more, "We just rescued Hunter from an organization base a few hours ago."

"Oh my," Pastor frowned, "I'm so sorry you had to endure something like that."

Hunter forced a sort-of smile, as if to say "Thanks", but the words really were empty to him. And I can see why. I was sure Pastor would try to connect on a deeper level when he had more time.

"Hunter, I would love to speak with you after church if you wouldn't mind," Pastor offered.

"Yea, sure," Hunter said solemnly.

Hunter definitely did mind, but I think he agreed out of either obligation or just a hint of trust that he had in me.

"Very good," Pastor said lovingly. Then, he walked up on stage to open service.

As he welcomed everyone and listed the various announcements and prayer requests, I walked Hunter over to my usual seat, on the far section of chairs, two rows from the back. Blake and Bailey were already sitting there with two seats in between them for Hunter and I.

Bailey sat on the end of the row and beside Blake sat Alex. As we entered the row, he stood up and shook my hand, "How'd it go?" He asked, not taking his eyes off Hunter.

"About like usual," I said.

"That bad, huh?" Alex joked, except, it wasn't really a joke.

"Not all bad," I said optimistically. I looked at Hunter.

On the row behind us sat the Vales and the Bridgers (Alex's parents). As well as Alex's little brother and Kinsley. I smiled and waved at all of them, and they did the same back.

Since I had moved into the row, Hunter was already sitting beside Bailey, so I took the open seat between him and Blake. Right about the time I sat down, Pastor asked everyone to stand and pray. I obeyed, as did Hunter and the rest of the congregation.

As we all prayed, the worship team began to play music and when Pastor had finished his prayer, they began to sing. They sang songs about joy, and love, and peace. They sang about the goodness of God. I sang along. So did my friends and much of the congregation, but Hunter just stood and watched. At times, I could see him clenching his jaw or biting his lip. The occasional tear would slip down his cheek, but he would quickly wipe it away.

Once the singing was over, Pastor returned to the platform and began his message.

"In Numbers 6:24-26, Moses gives a blessing to the people of Israel, He says, 'The Lord bless you and keep you; The Lord make His face shine upon you, And be gracious to you; The Lord lift up His countenance upon you, And give you peace." Pastor paused to let the words of the scripture sink in, "I will speak for only a few moments today. If I could title this thought, it would simply be, The Blessing."

From here, Pastor talked about the blessings that would be spoken over people in the Old Testament. He talked about specific Blessings that God gave to people. He spoke poetically about the scripture, but purposely did not relate anything to today or our own lives. He told a masterful story.

Then, he pivoted. "And I tell you all this today, simply to show you the record of our Lord. All of these people faced hardships and challenges both before and after the blessing," he paused "But they were still blessed."

Pastor looked around the room. I could tell even he was emotional. The congregation was silent with the exception of a few sniffles. "I came with a message for someone today, through all of life's storms, even in your lowest low," he almost whispered, "the Lord will keep you."

This was the crescendo of the message. It was so full of passion and conviction, it could have pricked even the most calloused of hearts. The air in the room was thick. I could sense a wave of emotion, not hurt or loss or fear, but resilience and peace. I sensed a room of people gracefully broken. I sensed it most strongly right beside me.

I could sense the walls Hunter had built up around himself beginning to crack. He was frantically trying to patch them, frantically trying to recede back into his shell, but he couldn't.

Pastor asked the congregation to stand and the worship team began to play music once again. Pastor promptly ended his message and left the stage. People flocked to the front of the church to pray.

Over the roar of breaking chains a piano and a woman's voice rose, singing a song that simply put the words of the scripture to music.

"The Lord bless you and keep you; The Lord make His face shine upon you, And be gracious to you"

I was initially focused on the song and message myself. It had touched me. I felt a peace about re-entering this war, assured that the Lord would keep me - assured that I was blessed.

Then, I sensed something. Not with my powers but with my spirit. I looked at Hunter.

He had stood strong for as long as he could. Now he was on the floor in a broken heap. Inwardly, his walls were falling revealing the shattered and broken landscape of his heart, more broken and desolate than his home, but at its center, there was something. Something glowing. Something beautiful and whole. It had long been dormant. It had almost died, but now it was awakening.

I heard his cries begin to rise over the sound of the music (though the music was loud enough that people couldn't have heard it more than a row in front or behind). I knelt down, put my hand on his shoulder, and began to pray for him.

Sometimes I had long prayers, occasionally even elaborate ones, but right now, I had nothing. Nothing but the scripture and the words of the song. I prayed in this manner for a while. I felt Blake's hand on my back and noticed that Bailey had put her hand on Hunter's other shoulder. We all prayed together.

Eventually, I heard a noise. It was a chair scooting across the floor. Pastor was pulling one chair out of the row to be able to reach

Hunter. Once he had cleared a path, he placed his hand on Hunter's head.

Hunter's crying grew louder as more hurt was brought to the surface, as more walls began to fall. He leaned forward and buried his face in the carpet. The hurting and broken parts of himself were being removed, purged by the light of the presence of God - by the blessing of the Lord.

I noticed that during all this, his powers never surged across his body. There wasn't so much as a flicker of green. Usually when a bearer is emotional, it's impossible to stop some sort of discharge. Though, I think, in this moment, he just needed to be human. So he was.

After a bit longer of this, Hunter finally sat up. His face was red and snotty. Tears stained his cheeks. His eyes were bloodshot. He looked rough on the outside, but on the inside, I sensed a more sightly change. I guess all that ugly that was on the inside, had made its way to the outside. It was a good thing too. What was once impossible to deal with, could now be fixed with some tissues.

"Do you feel better now, son?" Pastor asked Hunter.

The words he was about to say made him cry a bit more, "Yes," Hunter choked.

"I thought you would," Pastor grinned.

"What was that?" I heard Hunter sniffle.

"That was the Holy Ghost coming to clean up your broken heart," Pastor explained, softly and lovingly. He was beaming from ear to ear. "I think He did a pretty good job too."

"Yea," Hunter actually laughed. Which made him cry. Which made him laugh.

Pastor chuckled and looked up at me. I was so happy for Hunter. I couldn't hide my smile. I don't exactly know what I expected to happen when I came here today, but this was certainly more than I expected.

"Thank you," I told Pastor gratefully.

He stood up and cautiously maneuvered around Hunter. He gave me a hug and spoke softly in my ear. "This isn't the end," Pastor instructed, "Everything doesn't just get better now. I know you know that. He's going to need your help to get through what comes next."

"Yes, sir," I accepted.

"The Lord bless you and keep you," Pastor prayed.

"You too," I said.

We ended our embrace, and he walked away. There were still a couple other people praying. Everyone else had either sat down or moved to the foyer to socialize.

I reached down and took hold of Hunter's hand, pulling him up off the ground and into a hug. He began to cry again, but this time it was happy tears. "I'm so happy for you," I congratulated.

Somehow, I had only known this kid for a few hours, but it already felt like I had known him my whole life. I couldn't sense it, but something told me it was the same way for him.

This lasted for a while as well. I wasn't really sure how long we had been here, but my stomach told me it was far past time for lunch. When Hunter was finished hugging me, he hugged Bailey and then we all walked toward the exit. All of us: my friends, the Vales, and the Bridgers. I put my arm around Hunter as we walked.

When we made it to the foyer we started talking. I helped introduce everyone to Hunter. He was instantly just a part of our little makeshift family. I could tell that, like me, he already wouldn't trade the world for it.

Mrs. Cassy told us that she was making lunch for everyone and invited us all over. We all agreed that it would be great. The council never even once crossed my mind. They could wait. It was time to celebrate.

Everyone carried on in joyous conversation as we made our way into the parking lot. Hunter was mostly soaking it all in, but he was smiling and his eyes were bright.

We boarded our transport and quickly flew to my house. We parked the transport in my dad's driveway and walked down the sidewalk. We had beaten everyone else there, but by the time we walked down a few houses, the Vales and Bridgers were pulling into the driveway.

We all went inside and sat down, some sitting at the table, some in the living room, and others on the back porch. It was a full house. The sun was high, but today was cooler for a Tennessee summer. Still, my group chose to eat inside.

We all made our way around the kitchen island where there were four crockpots with roast and potatoes, green beans, mac and cheese, and pinto beans. Mrs. Cassy pulled a cheesecake out of the refrigerator and placed it on the counter. Everyone filled their plate to the brim.

The Vales sat with my friends and I at the dining room table. I was asked to say grace, so I blessed the food, blessed the people there, and thanked God for what he had done today. When I was finished, everyone said "Amen", and we dug in.

There wasn't much conversation for the first few minutes because everyone was so focused on eating the delicious food, but after our plates were cleaned, people began to conversate.

"So," Mrs, Cassey said, "Where are you from, Hunter?'

I almost choked on my food. Of all the questions she could have asked, why this one? I knew she didn't mean anything by it. It was just small talk, but she could not have picked a worse conversation starter. I tried to jump in and cut her off, but my mouth was to full of roast.

"Well," I tried to say.

"It's okay," Hunter stopped me, "I'm from Boulder."

He said it with resolve. There was pain in his voice, but it was like a bandaged wound. Manageable. Healing.

"Oh, I'm so sorry honey," Mrs. Cassey felt so bad, I thought *she* might be the one to cry, "I didn't know."

"It's fine, really," Hunter assured her. "Where were you during the attacks?"

"Right here, actually," Mrs. Cassey said, "They tried to take over Tullahoma, but Dylan and his father stopped them."

"What are we?" Blake said, gesturing to himself and the rest of my friends. He pretended to be offended.

"My bad," Mrs. Cassey admitted, "And Blake, Bailey, and Alex."

"That was a day before the bombings though," I informed him. "And we technically lost," I added, humbly.

"We're all here," Mr. James said, walking back from getting seconds, "Looks like you won to me."

"I guess we eventually won," I agreed.

"Battles aren't fought in a day," Mr. James added.

"Enough of this depressing stuff," Mrs. Cassey said, "Let's talk about something else.

And we did. We talked about church, our lives before the war, and all kinds of much more happy things. We dug out old board games and played a dancing game on an old gaming system. We found out that Hunter liked to fish, so as the sun began to set, I took Hunter down to the lake.

We walked side by side. All evening he had refused to leave my side, but I did notice that he was allowing a bit more distance between us now.

We reached the dock. On it sat two old, rusty fishing poles, just as they always did. I opened the metal can next to the dock and threw out some fish food. Then, I reached down to the bottom and pulled out our tackle. I baited the hooks, and we began to fish.

Every cast we reeled in Brim. I had worried that the underground base being active again would hurt the fishing, but it was just the same as it has always been. It was refreshing.

Eventually, we got tired of catching all the fish, and the fish got tired of being caught. They stopped biting, so Hunter and I sat on the side of the dock, rolled up our pant legs, and dangled our feet in the water.

The colors of the sunset illuminated the sky: orange, yellow, and purple. The scene reflected off the surface of the water, doubling the beauty.

We sat there, relaxing in the final notes of the sunshine. Until, Hunter yelled, "Oh!" and yanked his feet out of the water. He rolled head over heels and his green energy shot across him.

I sprang to my feet and summoned my purple energy across my body, raising my fists ready to fight. "What is it?" I questioned. Looking around and trying to sense a threat.

Hunter answered by bursting with laughter. He chuckled as he rolled onto his back, sprawling out on the deck.

"What?" I half laughed, still not understanding. I was perhaps more surprised by his laughter than the initial jolt. This was the first time I'd heard him laugh.

"A fish," Hunter wheezed, "It…" he chuckled some more, "It bit my toe."

I started laughing now, "Hunter, you scared me to death."

"It scared me to death!" he laughed.

We both laughed and joked about this for a while. Until The sun was below the horizon and the water was beginning to feel warmer than the air.

"It's good to hear you laugh," I smiled.

Hunter kept looking at the sunset, "It's good to be laughing." He sat for a moment. I could tell he was looking for words. "My best friend, Brady, we would go fishing like this all the time. My other friend Austin would go sometimes too, and my dad. My mom and my brother Trent never cared much for it, but they would tag along too." He reminisced, "that's how I found my crystal. We went camping. There was this big lake in the Rockies. We were gonna fish and hike. My friends and I found the crystal in a cave."

"It was just on the ground?" I asked.

"No," Hunter replied, getting invested in his story, "It was actually crazy. We went through this one chamber and it opened up into, like, a whole little jungle. There was a temple too. The crystal was in the temple."

"It was an underground ecosystem?" I questioned. I wanted to sound clueless, but I knew this sounded like the handiwork of Ana's people.

"Yea!" Hunter exclaimed, "And a pyramid. It looked like the Mayan ones we learned about in school. And there was this big light in the ceiling. But it blew up."

He was going to continue, but ALI interrupted us. "Sir, I'm sorry, but I must ask Hunter a question." We had changed clothes, but I still had my puck in my pocket. That's where his voice was coming from. I pulled out the puck and ALI's emblem formed between us.

"What is it, ALi?" I asked.

"Hunter, what did you say your best friend's name was?" ALI asked with urgency.

"Brady," Hunter said slowly, "Why?"

"What was his last name?" ALI ignored his question.

"Skott," Hunter said a bit agitated, "Brady Skott. Why!"

"Because he's alive, and I know where he is."

Chapter 10

"ALI, I think you need to explain," I urged. Hunter looked like he was about to explode. I sensed both hope and uncertainty swelling within him.

"During our last mission, I was combing through Organization files looking for their capital," ALI explained, "I didn't have time to find that, but I did go through some of their ship manifests. One was a slave ship headed for a ship-breaking ground in South Africa. It caught my attention because there was only one American on the list. Brady Skott."

"He's alive?" Hunter asked with urgency.

"The manifest is a few months old, but I would presume so," ALI answered.

Hunter looked at me. His eyes were wide and his breathing was heavy. "We have to go save him," he pleaded.

I agreed. I wanted to save him too. I knew I would be desperate to rescue Blake if we were in the same situation. "We will," I promised, "But we need to get a plan together first."

That short statement included a lot. I didn't know how well this place would be protected, but that wouldn't be our biggest problem. I would need resources allocated by the High council in order to run a successful mission. The problem would be getting them to greenlight something like that.

We were already stretching thin trying to patrol our borders. Moving cruisers now would mean leaving something unprotected.

"Do we know what we would be up against?" I asked ALI.

"We've actually scouted this base before," ALI said, "We would face three light cruisers, fully armed and stocked. The base has an airfield: mostly stingrays and bombers. The facility itself is protected by robots rather than soldiers."

It was doable. We would need at least three of our own cruisers and a strike team to infiltrate the facility and free the prisoners. South Africa was fringe Organization territory. If we worked quickly, we could be in and out before reinforcements arrived.

"We can do it right?" Hunter asked.

"We have the ability to, yes," I sighed, "It's convincing the council to give us what we need that will be the problem."

"I thought you ran the Ekklesia?" Hunter asked.

"Sort of," I stood up from the side of the dock, "My executive power is limited by a board of leaders. I have to get them to agree with me."

"This is the right thing," Hunter made his case, "Why wouldn't they agree?"

"I ask myself the same question all the time," I admitted, "But don't worry. I'll find a way to save your friend no matter what they say."

I extended my hand to Hunter and pulled him up. Then, we briskly walked up the hill, back to the house. I noticed Bailey was sitting on the back porch. She had been watching Hunter and I. She was sitting in a rocking chair, but when she noticed the urgency in our stride, she stood up and met us at the door.

"What is it?" she asked.

"Let's get Blake, then I'll explain," I suggested.

We slid the glass door open and walked in the house. "Blake!" I called. Mrs. Cassey and Mr. James were sitting on the couch. They both turned around.

"Is everything alright?" Mr. James asked.

"Yes," I replied, "We just got some new inforation."

Blake came down from upstairs followed by Alex. I guess the two of them were hanging out while I was with Hunter.

"What's up?" Blake asked.

"Come sit at the table," I subverted. I didn't want to have to repeat the story over again.

We all walked to the dining room table. Except for Alex. He walked toward the front door. "You can stay," I offered. I knew any intel would be safe with him.

"I think I'll leave the hero stuff to y'all," he smiled, "If it's life or death, then you can give me a call."

"Isn't it always?" Blake retorted.

"You know what I mean," Alex replied. Then, he walked out the front door.

When everyone was sitting. I explained to the group what ALI had just shared with me. For a moment there was silence, as my friends digested the information.

"So when do we leave?" Blake asked, already on board with the mission.

"We need to leave right now," Hunter replied, almost before Blake had finished the sentence.

"Unfortunately, it's not that easy," I said, "Despite the council, we still need a plan. A good one."

"You're usually the one with the plan," Blake said, "I know something's kicking around in that big brain of yours."

He was right. Something *was* kicking around, "Maybe just bits and pieces of a plan," I admitted, "Nothing definite yet."

"We'll stand with you no matter what the plan is," Bailey said. She sounded exhausted. "But I agree, we need to go soon."

Well, they were absolutely no help. Although, I did usually like to follow my own plan. I just kind of hoped they would have some ideas. I would need some time to think.

"Okay," I said, "Let's get some rest. I'll try to come up with something good by the morning. We'll leave first thing to meet with the council. Hopefully we can leave for South Africa shortly afterwards." I looked at Hunter. I knew he would prefer us to already be in the air. "I know that's not what you wanted to hear, but I'll send a scouting party to see what we're up against. That will take at least 24 hours anyway."

"What if he doesn't have that long," Hunter looked a bit angry, but mostly sounded worried and eager to see his friend.

"It will take us longer than that if we go in unprepared," I taught him, "It's just the waiting that's the hard part."

Hunter gave me a look of agreement. I looked around the table. Blake looked satisfied, but Bailey looked a bit rough. Her eyes had bags under them, and she was resting her head on her arm.

"I'll see everyone in the morning then," I announced, "We leave at 5:00."

We all stood up, Bailey a bit more sluggish than the rest. I walked to Blake and Hunter's side of the table. "You can sleep in my room," I offered, "I'll bunk with Blake."

"Are you sure?" Hunter asked, "I can sleep on the couch."

"I insist."

Hunter smiled a bit. I knew he wouldn't get much sleep, but he could at least enjoy some comfort after what he had been through. I told Blake to show him to his room. We would need to get some good rest since it would probably be hard to come by for a little while.

As I spoke to them, Bailey slouched by, headed for the stairs. I could tell something was wrong. I sent the boys on their way and walked to Bailey, putting my arm around her when I reached her. I guided her to the side as Blake and Hunter raced each other up the stairs.

"Is everything alright?" I asked, "You don't look so good."

"Yea," she groaned, rubbing her forehead, "I just have a migraine. It came on hard during Mario Kart."

"Do you get those often?" I asked. I didn't remember her having one before. I didn't even remember her mentioning anything about it.

"I used to get them before I got my powers," she explained. "I haven't had one since." She paused to rub her eyes. "I guess it was just luck."

"Do you need anything?" I asked as gently as I could.

"Ibuprofen, a dark room, and some sleep," she said groggily.

"And a hug?" I offered.

She smiled as best she could. "Just a gentle one."

I pulled her into my arms, and she pressed her head into my shoulder. I guided her like this into the guest bedroom (which was beside the stairs, opposite to the basement staircase). I didn't have a free hand, so I used my telepathy to open the door and turn off the light as we entered.

I let her go so that she could get into the bed, and when she was under the covers, I rolled onto the bed, beside her. I put my arm back around her and pulled her in close.

I'd never had a migraine, so I didn't really know what it was like. But I knew if it had her down like this, it must be pretty rough. As we lay there, she groaned a couple of times. I could sense her frustration at the pain.

"See if this helps," I offered.

I allowed my purple energy to flow across my body, casting a soft glow across the room. It flowed down my arm and around her. She answered by allowing her own energy to flow out of her. The two mingled until both our bodies, and the whole room, were covered in an elegant swirling pattern of purple and white.

The two energies cascaded off the edges of the bed, forming rivers of energy on the hardwood floor. They spun, and swirled, and flowed to every corner of the room where they then began to climb up the walls like unruly vines until they created a solid canvas. A gentle mist came from them, creating a fog that clung to the floor, illuminated by the energies below.

Bailey turned toward me and opened her eyes. I sensed this and opened my eyes. They met. Veins of white and purple flickered across her face. Her eyes shimmered with white energy that surrounded her irises, but unlike every other time, it was now mixed with my own purple energy. I knew mine looked the same.

"Better?" I asked, almost in a whisper.

"The pain, no," Bailey smiled, "But yes."

I smiled back. She still looked pretty sick, but she was just as beautiful as ever. I ran my hand through her silky blonde hair. Not breaking eye contact. She lifted her hand out from under the blankets and placed it on top of the one I had on her head. She closed her eyes.

"We better get some sleep," she whispered.

I sighed. I didn't want this moment to end, but it had to. I allowed my energy to fade, as did she. I gently rolled out of the bed, careful not to jar her. When I was on my feet, I leaned forward, kissed her softly on the head, and left the room.

I quietly closed the door behind me, and headed up the stairs. Just as my foot touched the first one, I heard a voice behind me.

"Sounds like you're about to be on the go again." It was Mr. James. I stepped back off the stairs and turned around.

"You know us," I raised my hands and then let them fall back to my sides.

"The boy can stay here if he needs to," he offered.

"I wish he could," I admitted, "He doesn't need to be caught up in all this." I shook my head, "He's been through enough."

"Then why not leave him?" Mr. James asked. He wasn't challenging me. He was just curious.

"He's going to have to testify before the council," I explained. "Possibly ours and the Mayan council. It sounds like he may have gotten the crystal from one of their forgotten cities."

"They have more than one?" he asked.

"I honestly don't know," I admitted, "Blake dates a Mayan and even he doesn't understand them... I actually don't think she does either." I paused for a second. My mind became distracted thinking about the Mayans. "Anyway, he also needs training. I think he has some, but I need to show him how to protect himself. I don't have any extra time, so that's going to have to happen on the battlefield."

"You'll do good taking care of him," Mr. James complimented, "You've always been good at taking care of Blake." He paused, "And other people too."

"Well, Blake takes care of me just as much as I do him," I admitted.

"Maybe so," Mr. James said, "But most everyone else doesn't do the same."

"Certainly not," I laughed. It was more of a spiteful laugh though. I became more sincere, "Some do though."

"Better keep *those* people close," Mr. James charged, finding space for a life lesson.

"I always do," I smiled.

"I know," Mr. James smiled back, "I just thought I'd remind you."

He started walking toward the couch and called “Goodnight” from over his shoulder. I said the same back and walked up the stairs. I turned and walked down the hall, all the way to the end where my room was. The door was cracked, and I looked inside. Hunter was in the bed, staring at the ceiling. He looked at me.

“Comfortable?” I asked.

“You have no idea,” Hunter said. I could tell by his voice that he had been crying. I remembered those nights. I knew it would happen more. It was part of healing.

“Good night,” I said.

“Good night.”

I left the door cracked and walked to Blake's room. I heard the shower going, so I just decided to lay down on the bed. I leaned back on the pillow and rested my eyes. I started to think about what I would say tomorrow to the council. How could I convince them to let me go on this mission with full resources? No doubt they would want me and my friends to be cutting our way through the heart of The Organization, not going to fringe territories like South Africa.

There was the fact that shipbreaking was a major source of materials for them. They harvested all of the useful parts from their decommissioned or severely damaged ships there. It was the only one that we knew of. The reason we hadn't already struck it was because we knew of the slave labor force.

Destroying it would cost the lives of the prisoners. Plus, even if we did destroy this one, it wouldn’t be hard for them to just make a new one. At least now we knew where it was and could keep an eye on it. At least, that was the case I had made in order to keep my colleagues from bombing it, prisoners and all. It would be difficult to go back on my word. Unless… Yes… That might work.

It would be a stretch, and a bit shady, but it was the only choice. Yes… That should… work…

***

I woke up to the horrific sound of my alarm. ALI must have set it to go off at 4:30. I did say I wanted to leave at 5:00.

Blake was rolling out of the bed as the alarm blared. "Alright ALI!" he exclaimed, "We get it!"

I took a deep breath and stretched. The alarm shut off, but gave a final loud beep just to spite Blake. He and ALI had an ongoing "frenemy" situation.

We quickly grabbed our pucks and started to get ready. I took a shower, put on my suit, armor, and gear, and then went into my room to wake up Hunter. He was already awake though. I assumed the alarm woke him up too. He looked like he had at least gotten a little bit of sleep, but he was eager to leave, already dressed and ready to go. His hair was a bit of a mess though.

"Go fix your hair," I told him.

"Why?" he questioned, "It's just gonna get messed up by a helmet or the wind while we're flying. It would just waste more time."

"You need to look put together for the council," I said, "Quick! I have a comb and some gel in my bathroom. First drawer on the left."

"Fine," Hunter agreed.

I walked down the hall and down the stairs to the guest room, but I saw that the door was already open. I looked around and saw that Bailey was already up too. She was standing at the back of the house, looking out through the glass doors at the lake.

I walked up behind her. "You ready?" I asked.

"Yes," she answered. She didn't turn around, but her voice sounded stronger.

"Are you feeling better?"

"Yea," she answered again, "The headache is gone. It just wrecked my body. I'll be fine once I get going."

"Good," I hugged her from behind, "We've gotta have you at full strength."

"I'll be back to one hundred percent soon," she said and she kissed me on the cheek.

I held on a bit longer, until I heard Blake and Hunter headed down the stairs. Bailey and I both turned around to them as they reached the bottom.

"Everyone grab a granola bar," I suggested, "It's gonna be a long day."

They all listened. We took a few snacks each and crammed them in various pockets and pouches on our uniforms. Then, We walked outside to meet Cashner and our pilot, who already had the transport engines running and ready for take off. We were off the ground and on our way almost before we could all get onboard. I had to yank Blake up into the cabin as we took off.

The flight was short. As we flew into the base, I sent Hunter to the front to look through the windshield. The pilot chatted with air traffic control as Hunter looked out in awe. I could only imagine what he was thinking. The sight of the mountains below, the shield, the cruisers in the sky, the fighters patrolling the area, the mountain base itself. It was a marvelous feat of human achievement. I never got over the flights going in. It truly was amazing what we had done. Even if we did get bogged down in politics from time to time, it was amazing that it even existed.

We landed in the hangar bay we had left from. All of the other ships had returned from the mission and were already cleaned and polished.

"This place is huge!" Hunter said, looking around as he exited the transport.

"It's pretty awesome," Blake agreed.

We made our way down the hall. It wouldn't be a long walk to the War Room. As we made our way down the corridor, a group of soldiers walked by, each wearing a shoulder patch with a different flag.

"What do the patches mean," Hunter asked. It was the only bit of individuality on the grey uniforms, so the small patched stood out.

"They represent what country the soldier is from," I answered patriotically, "When we called for help, people from every country came here to fight with us. The Dove pendant above the patch shows that they're all a part of this Ekklesia, but they wear the flag to represent what we are fighting for."

"What are we fighting for?" Hunter asked.

"Our homes," I replied.

"What about the ones that don't have a home anymore?" Hunter asked. He was subliminally referring to himself.

"They fight to avenge what they lost and make it possible for them, and others, to have one again," I explained.

"That's pretty noble," Hunter assessed.

"It's moral," I corrected, "It's just the right thing to do."

By the time our conversation reached this point, we had reached the War Room. The council would be waiting inside. Everyone, all 12 of the other members, would be in attendance today. Probably because of what I did.

I looked at Hunter, "You just tell them the truth," I instructed him, "Don't let them intimidate you."

"I'm sure I've seen worse," Hunter replied confidently.

"I'm sure you can handle it," I affirmed. I looked at Bailey and Blake who were standing behind us. "Follow my lead, but don't say much."

"Ounch," Blake punned.

"You know what I mean," I didn't smirk showing how serious I was. I wasn't sure of what I was about to do. I hadn't even decided fully on my plan until just now, and there was no time to explain it. I pushed the door open.

The council members had been talking to one another, but the room instantly fell silent when I stepped through the door. All eyes were on me at first, but they soon all turned to Hunter, who stepped behind me a bit.

"Good Morning gentleman," I greeted as though nothing out of the ordinary had happened.

Everyone silently took their seats, including my friends. Ana had beaten us there and was already sitting in her spot. I let Hunter sit in my chair since there wasn't one for him yet, and I stood behind him.

"I would like to start by introducing the newest member of our council, Hunter Hogan," I said cheerfully. I wasn't cheerful on the inside.

Everyone stared.

"And shall we add the three other bearers you encountered to this council as well?" Sparks insinuated snottily.

"Should they have a change of heart," I said, doing my best not to snap back at him. "But that's not our topic of discussion for today. I've been thinking, and I agree with Captain Sparks."

Everyone's eyes grew a bit wider, and I thought that Blake might fall out of his seat. Sparks looked like he had been betrayed. How could I do this to him? Agree?

Raddick was the only one who remained unchanged. He was trying to see what web I was spinning. It was a big one. I continued.

"I shouldn't have left behind the location of the capitol. I should have just completed my mission and taken it. It was a lapse in judgment, and I'm sorry," I tried to sound sincere. I definitely had everyone's attention. "Thankfully, I believe we've been given a second chance. ALI and Blake were able to obtain some records from the Siberian research facility, and I was able to obtain what they were researching."

"And what about that second chance?" The intelligence director asked.

"The records don't contain the exact location of the capitol, but they do contain an incomplete map of shipping lanes that we believe lead to the capitol. We just have to visit one more place on the map to find the rest, a shipbreaking facility in South Africa. ALI, could you explain please?"

His bubble appeared above the table and wavered for a concerning amount of time. I hadn't talked to him about this before now. I hoped he would come through.

"Yes," He said, but paused for an even more concerning amount of time, "Yes, sir. It's simple really. This is the map we recovered," The table projected a map showing the world on a flat surface, divided like an old school paper map. It had lines traveling from Russia, to Australia, over Antarctica, and up to South Africa.

"This is a showing the route of a single supply ship that would visit the Siberian base often. Its records indicate that it supplied many facilities along the way before reaching South Africa."

I breathed a sigh of relief. I knew ALI would come through for me.

"How do we know that South Africa wasn't the last stop on the route?" General Raddick asked. The council was intrigued.

"The manifest of the ship included one more batch of deliveries," ALI continued, "They don't carry exact coordinates, for security purposes I'm sure, but are simply marked 'Capitol Supplies'"

"So you believe that we could recover the final leg of the route from the ship breaking facility?" Blake asked, helping along the conversation.

"Exactly," I said pointing at him with enthusiasm. I was thankful ALI had fabricated such a convincing story.

"How do we know that you won't just botch this mission too?" Sparks insulted, trying to remain disagreeable. "The last was significantly less challenging than breaking into this facility will be."

"First, I didn't 'botch' the mission," I defended as politely as I could. I needed to save face. "I came back with something that I stand by as far more valuable. Second, am I not allowed one error? Does a decision that I made in the heat of the moment warrant such criticism if it was, at its heart, still a good decision. Maybe just not the best one?"

That was a mouth full, but I hoped I had elegantly stated my point.

Many of the council members exchanged agreeable looks. It was time to drive it home. The last thing I needed. "ALI determined from the log books that the ship is there as we speak. This was confirmed by an intelligence team that I sent there yesterday. If we act quickly, we can take the route straight from the ship."

Now a low chatter ran through the council members. "We should act immediately," one member blurted.

"We must review the intel from the reconnaissance team first," The Intelligence Director said.

"Their mission is scheduled to be completed within the hour," ALI informed them.

"I suggest we review all the information we have and then see what resources we will have to relocate for a mission of this magnitude," General Raddick added.

"Can the council at least agree that we must act today?" I asked, pushing for a determinate vote.

"This does sound like our best option," the ambassador for the Mayans agreed.

"Then we'll vote," I announced, "All in favor of sending me and an adequately sized division on a retrieval mission before the end of the day?"

A simultaneous "Aye" came from the council and my friends. I could feel Hunter's ambition soaring.

"All opposed," I asked as a formality. No one said anything. Sparks didn't say anything either time. I think I finally shut him up.

"Then it's settled," General Raddick said standing up, "We should all get to work on this immediately."

"What about the boy?" The Mayan ambassador asked, "We were supposed to question him.

"I believe this matter takes president," Radick attempted to defend him.

"Not to my people," The ambassador said coldly.

"You won't learn much from questioning because he doesn't know much," I said, "He's told me everything he knows."

"I would like to hear it from him," the ambassador prodded.

"This will waste valuable time," the intelligence director added. He was backed by the emotions of the rest in the room.

"If it's so important to you, why don't you just take him to your own council for them to interview while we prepare?" Sparks asked.

That wasn't going to fly with me.

"That is acceptable," the ambassador agreed.

"Not without me," I defended, "And he will accompany us on this mission."

"We can determine that," the ambassador said.

"He's not under your protection," I scowled, "He's under mine."

"Why don't we just fly down ahead of the mission," Ana spoke up, "The four of us can go immediately to El Dorado, and then the two of you can join the convoy on its way to the mission. Cruisers are slower than transports anyway."

This proposition seemed to satisfy everyone involved. I don't think Hunter was entirely pleased, but I knew he didn't fully understand what was happening. This was a good outcome. I wished that he didn't have to appear before the Mayan council. I did it once and it was tough, but I felt he could handle it. Plus, I would be there to help him.

"It's settled," I said, "Council adjourned."

Everyone stood up and immediately went to work. Some began discussions of strategy with others. Some began reviewing intel. Some made straight for the door, namely Sparks and the Mayan Ambassador.

It wasn't long before my friends and I were also headed for the door, closely followed by General Raddick. We entered the hallway outside the War Room, and I breathed a sigh of relief. I did it.

"That was some pretty good stuff," General Raddick congratulated.

"Thanks," I said.

"Why didn't you tell us any of that?" Blake asked.

I sensed that we were alone. "Because I made it all up."

"What?" Blake exclaimed. Bailey gave me a concerned and disappointed look. Ana didn't look so happy either. Hunter was just along for the ride and Raddick was grinning from ear to ear (which I had never seen him do).

"I lied," I admitted, "I had to convince them that we needed to go there, so that we could save Brady. We just have to hope that they actually have the coordinates to the capitol or else they'll have my head."

General Raddick laughed. I looked back at him confused. He slapped me on the back and squeezed my shoulder. "There you go," He congratulated.

"What?" I was confused.

"Now you're thinking like a politician."

Part 5: The Protectorate

"A state that governs itself internally but is under the protection of a greater power"

Chapter 11

Hunter, Blake, Ana, Bailey, and I all walked toward the main hangar bay together. Bailey walked beside me, and Hunter trailed closely behind. Blake and Ana walked together ahead of us.

“What if we don’t find any information about the capitol?” Bailey questioned. She didn’t even criticize me for lying. Which made me feel a bit more guilty. She was just focused on the result of it.

“I don’t know,” I admitted, “But at least we’ll have Hunter’s friend.”

“And you’ll be expelled from the council,” Bailey worried, “Even Raddick won’t stand by you if this doesn’t work.”

“Then they’ll finally be left to do things their way,” I replied. “And we’ll deal with that if we come to it. Right now, it hasn’t.”

There was too much happening in the present for me to become caught up in the “what if’s”. We needed to get this mission underway.

We walked into the hangar. The massive room was alive with mechanics performing maintenance and repairs of various models of ships. An instructor was teaching a group of about fifteen future pilots how to fly a Stingray in the back corner.

On the far end of the hangar was a Mayan transport. They were similar to Ekklesia transports in nearly every way on the inside, but their shape was a bit more ovular, while ours were more of a box. It had four feet that stuck out as landing gears and its door opened vertically, lifting up over the side of the ship, rather than sliding back.

“Blake,” I called ahead of me, “You two come here real quick.”

Blake and Ana turned and closed the gap that had formed between us. Hunter walked up from behind me, and we formed a small circle.

"Blake, Bailey," I addressed, "I need the two of you to stay here and ride in with the convoy. Help them get everything in order and ready to go."

"Why can't we go with you?" Blake asked. Bailey's expression backed up his question.

"My people don't allow outsiders except under very specific circumstances," Ana intervened, "The only reason they are letting anyone in is because your friend is a new bearer."

"I didn't get an interview when I was new," Bailey pointed out.

"That's because we knew about your crystal," Ana retorted. "I'm already shocked Dylan is getting in. The only thing he has going for him is that he's been before."

My friends seemed content with this answer. I knew they wanted to see the city. It really was amazing. Plus, I would rather not let either of them out of my sight. There was just no way around it this time.

"You know I'd let you come if I could," I told both of them.

"We know," Blake agreed.

Bailey nodded.

"I'll meet up with you two somewhere over Brazil," I promised.

Everyone was in agreement. Ana, Hunter, and I walked toward our transport, while Blake and Bailey watched. I sensed tension. Everyone was on edge.

Something was building up to a breaking point. It was below the surface now, but I could tell it was getting ready to blister. I couldn't tell if it was us, the Ekklesia, or the war itself. Maybe all three. It was just that feeling again. The one Darren had described. It was like I had lived this before, but couldn't remember what would happen next.

Each step that I made across the hangar made me want to turn back even more. My chest grew tight and my heartbeat quickened. My feet grew heavier with each step. I felt like I was walking toward a threshold from which there would be no turning back. I felt an overwhelming urge to stop - to throw in the towel and go home.

Just as we reached the shuttle, I noticed my crystal glowing. Its usual soft purple glow had intensified ever so slightly. Enough that only I would notice. I noticed something else.

Hunter's eagerness to leave had been replaced by an uncertain look. His eyebrows were scrunched, and he too was looking at his crystal.

"You sense it too?" I asked, making more of an observation than a question.

"Do you know what it is?" Hunter asked.

"No," I breathed. I turned around to look at Bailey and Blake.

Blake had walked off, but Bailey was still standing there, her hand gripping the crystal over her heart. We locked eyes. Her long blond hair, usually in a braid, was down and blowing in the breeze that came from the door of the hangar.

In that moment, it was like the world and time itself stopped. The busy sounds of the hangar were silenced. The weight of the war and the politics fell away. I took a step toward her, ready to leave it all behind.

Then, an overwhelming voice took over my thoughts with only one echoing word, "Go." It was Bailey.

I looked back at the transport as I entered back into time. The sounds of the hangar filled my ears once again as a group of Stingrays took off, leaving the hangar. Ana was standing up in the cabin looking at me.

"What is it?" she asked.

I realized she hadn't been a part of whatever Bailey, Hunter, and I had just experienced. I looked back at Bailey. She was standing there just as she had been. She nodded, confirming her command.

I looked back at Ana. "Nothing," I said, "Let's go."

I jumped up into the ship followed closely by Hunter. The door of the ship began to close. I looked out until the last bit of the hangar disappeared from view, and the door latched shut.

This transport had seats along both walls and little else. I walked over and took a seat. Hunter sat beside me and Ana sat across from us. The ship's engines grew louder, and I felt us lift off the ground.

It was strange. All of the emotion from what had just happened was gone, as though it had never happened. I actually questioned if it did. Everything was as it was before I walked across the hangar. I was determined to finish this mission.

I dug in my pocket and pulled out a small device we called a data key. It was a metal box with one button on the side. When you pressed it, a metal stub flipped out of the side carrying a unique engraving. This could be plugged into a computer and the information on it could be accessed. It was basically an old fashioned thumb drive, except it could hold terabits of information. It was also encrypted so that it couldn't be hacked, traced, or corrupted. I could put it in any computer and know that the information was safe.

At the back of the transport, there was a desk with a monitor. I waited for the transport to reach cruising altitude, then I told Hunter to follow me. We walked to the desk, and I sat down. Hunter looked over my shoulder. Then, I plugged the key into the appropriate port on the desk.

A holo screen projected up from the desk and a keyboard illuminated on the table. It was a hologram too, but it was projected on the surface of the table so that the user would have something for their fingers to type on.

"This is a data key containing all of my father's knowledge," I explained to Hunter, "I picked it up while we were home. It contains everything he learned about The Organization, life, and the crystals."

"What are you looking for?" Hunter asked.

"You," I replied, smiling at the screen in front of me.

I scrolled through the endless fines under the section dedicated to the crystals.

"Finding El Dorado"
"The other side of the entanglement"
"The effects of crystal energy on the metabolism"

"What's that one?" Hunter asked.

"What?" I asked back, scrolling back the other way.

"That one right there." He pointed at a file titled 'Aaron's breastplate'. "I remember hearing that name somewhere."

"You probably remember it from Sunday School," I said as I clicked on the file. When it opened, a lengthy text appeared, divided by a sketch of the artifact. It was a perfect square, with twelve sections, each one containing the Hebrew inscription of one of the tribes of Israel.

This was one of the first of my father's secrets I read when I received the key. I scrolled down the page as I gave a summary of the information.

"My father had a theory about the origin of the crystals. There's a story in the Old Testament about a man named Aaron, the cousin of Moses and the first High Priest. He was commanded to make a breastplate that he would wear in the Tabernacle. On it were twelve different types of precious stones."

"The Crystals?" Hunter observed.

"That's the theory," I continued, "He believed that the breastplate would allow the wielder to bear all twelve crystals at once. We can't confirm any of that though since the rest of the crystals and the breastplate are still lost."

I reached the bottom of the file. The last attachment was a map. I explained that too, "He was looking for it. Probably came close to finding it too. But then The Organization took over, and he had more pressing things to take care of."

I clicked off the file and resumed my search for information about Hunter.

"Do you think he was right?" Hunter asked.

"He was right about most things," I admitted, "He was probably right about this too."

I continued scrolling.

"Anti-matter Hypothesis"
"Tracing the crystals across history"
"The effects of radiation on those with lower gene purity"

"Ah, here we go," I said, clicking on a file, "List of all known bearers. Let's see if you're on here." Hunter leaned in and I read through the list aloud. Each bearer had their name listed, with a lengthy passage describing their personality, backstory, and powerset. I skipped over that part. "Darren Flyhe, A.K.A The Parasite. Bailey Boone. Daniel Sons. Dylan Sons. Ana Cantun…" The list ended. "No you."

I leaned back in my chair and looked at the screen with a puzzled expression. I stroked my chin.

"Well, I did meet him," Hunter insisted, "And he knew I had powers."

"I believe you," I said to reassure him, "It just looks like he went through great lengths to make sure no one knew that you met him."

"You can't find anything, Sir?" ALI asked from the coms in our suits.

"Nothing yet, ALI," I said.

"I don't understand why Danial would keep this from me," ALI actually sounded frustrated.

"He was probably trying to protect Hunter," I offered.

"What if he erased other important events from my memory," ALI worried.

"I'm sure he wouldn't take them to his grave," I knew my father, and I knew he would leave me everything he knew, "I have some journals at home that may contain what we are looking for. He put the most sensitive secrets in those journals."

"I'm more important to him than all these other things on this list?" Hunter questioned in disbelief.

"You must have been," I observed, "He definitely saw something in you."

"Or perhaps we should consider the fact that he never saw him at all," ALI said, only in my coms.

"That's absurd," I shot down his line of thought. I knew Hunter was telling the truth. I could tell ALI was upset. "I didn't know you could be affected by your emotions."

"What did he say?" Hunter asked.

"It doesn't matter," I defended, "He's not thinking straight."

"You are right sir. I'm sorry." ALI apologized.

"It's alright," I said, "You're made to be human-like. That means stuff can still get to you."

"Perhaps if you could just give me access to the files on this key, I could find some information that would ease my mind," ALI suggested.

"You know I can't do that, ALI," I said, "Dad left specific instructions in case you were ever compromised. Plus, it's encrypted. You couldn't access it even if I allowed you."

"I suppose you are correct," ALI said sadly, "I will leave you two to your research."

"Thank you, ALI," I said.

We looked through the files the entire flight. When I realized I wouldn't find anything about Hunter in these, I decided to show him some of the harmless, cool stuff.

The UFO recovery at Roswell. My father found reports in The Organizations Archive that said it was a time traveler, but he couldn't tell if that was a codename or a misdirect. Either way, they recovered new technologies from the site.

The real cause of WWI and WWII. The red crystal was in Europe at the time and everybody seemed to want it. The Organization funded the rise of the Nazies and tried to use them as a proxy to take over the world. That was their first real attempt, and it almost worked. They came so close that El Dorado almost intervened. That is, until Einstein defected. He was the top researcher on the red crystal at the time and he smuggled it to the Allies. With his help, they constructed a device that could harness its power. That device was only used twice, before being deemed too dangerous, and was dismantled.

How The Organization took over. Slowly, over time, they used parent companies to buy up most of the food supply and the banks. They use that money and power to loan to governments until they become dependent upon them. At the same time, they implanted themselves in every level of the world's military. They used their power, influence, and money to win elections. They used their troops to carry out strategic assassinations. They never let more than a select few know their intentions. The company owners thought they were running a company. The troops thought they were working for their own country's military. The politicians actually thought that they were making the world a better place. All the while Darren and his own council of leaders were pulling all the strings. I wouldn't be surprised if most people still didn't know what was actually happening.

It was a masterful plan, and they nearly succeeded. My father was the man who saved the world. I guess that left me to be the man to fix the world.

Hunter was amazed. "So basically every conspiracy theory ever is real?"

"Basically," I chuckled. It was funny in a disturbing kind of way. If we had listened to the conspiracy theorists and whistle blowers, though they only had crazy bits of the truth, we might have been able to put together the whole picture. Ironic.

"Coming into El Dorado now," the pilot announced over the intercom.

I quickly stood up from my chair and started toward the cockpit. "Come on, you're gonna want to see this," I urged Hunter. He followed.

We entered the cockpit and looked through the windshield. Below us was a vast expanse of jungle (the Amazon rainforest). We were flying over the heart of Colombia, across a towering mountain range. The sky was overcast, and a misty fog rose up from the forest.

"What am I looking for?" Hunter asked.

"Just wait," I said.

We flew, decreasing in speed and altitude until we were skimming just above the canopy of the trees. We were flying along a valley. Mountains towered on both sides. We dipped a bit lower. The pilot began to talk on his coms. I knew it was Air traffic control.

Just as it looked as though we were about to take off the tops of the trees, the pilot took a sharp left turn toward the mountain. Hunter gasped. He probably would have screamed too, but he didn't have time for that. We turned right into a rocky portion of the mountain where there was an opening just big enough for our ship to fit through. We traveled through the tunnel for only a couple seconds before our eyes were forced to adjust to bright daylight.

We had reached El Dorado.

Chapter 12

Our eyes adjusted to the light of the artificial sun in the expansive cavern. The hidden city had stayed hidden for so long because it was carved from the inside of a mountain.

The vast expanse of the cavern housed its own ecosystem that mingled with the architecture of the city. Massive pillars made from the bedrock stretched from the ground to the ceiling of the mile high cave. On these pillars were ledges that contained bits of forest, recreational areas, and landing pads for aircraft. One of the larger ledges housed a small forest. On the edge was a pond that spilled over the side, creating a waterfall. Within the pillars themselves were houses, offices, schools, and everything else needed for a city. These pillars not only served as skyscrapers, but as city centers.

On the ground was a forest, so perfectly curated that you could consider it a park. A winding river made its way through the center of the cavern, snaking from one end of the expanse to the other. Some sections of the forest were missing. In their place were sections of city. Some had boardwalks that traveled alongside the river. Others had what we would consider normal sized skyscrapers.

In the back corner of the cavern was a unique structure. It stretched from floor to ceiling and contained countless rows of rectangular cut outs. Each one was a hangar bay cut directly from the rock. I remembered this from the last time I was here, but it only now struck me as to how large their fleet was. It certainly wouldn't outnumber the Ekklesia's, now that we had converted all of the U.S. fighter jets to be effective in modern warfare, but it would still be able to give us a run for our money. They probably would have been able to take over the world themselves before the war. If they wanted to.

The most striking part of the city was the center pillar. It was where they ran their government and their military (which overlapped in nearly every way). It was the largest pillar, a bit more narrow at the top and bottom and wider in the middle. It had lots of ledges, but the pillar was so large that most didn't even stand out enough to notice them. Except for one. Around the middle of the pillar was a wide, flat ring. It housed a shallow body of water that spilled over the edge, perfectly cascading over every inch of the ring. It spilled down onto the forest below, creating a gentle rain. At the top of this pillar was the artificial sun, a blinding ball of white light seated where the pillar connected to the roof of the cavern, perfectly seated to reflect off the ring of water. It was bright enough that it lit every corner of the cavern with daylight.

Every pillar was alive with movement, transports and shuttles flying people from one spot to another. There were also distinct sky lanes - lines of aerial vehicles creating highways through the open air of the cavern. We joined one of those lanes headed for the central pillar.

Hunter's mouth hung open as he looked out through the windshield of the cockpit. We were both taking it all in. One visit wasn't enough to remove the awe of this place. In fact, Ana looked out in similar fashion. Though, she looked more proud than anything.

"It's pretty amazing isn't it?" Ana commented.

"It's more than amazing," I said, not taking my eyes off the sight.

"How did they do all this?" Hunter asked with awe.

"Hundreds of years of hard work," Ana said, "And a lot of help from the bearers of my crystal." She looked out nostalgically as she cited the story from her childhood, "The crystal was passed from one bearer to the next, each one charged with furthering our society. For the first few generations, that involved a lot of digging. Now, it's about protecting what they created."

Nothing else was said as we flew to our destination. There was no time to waste any more of our attention on words.

We flew down to the ring of water surrounding the center column. There was a landing pad off to one side. The pilot sat us down there. In front us was a long staircase leading to an iron door. This was their version of our War Room. The place where they deliberated the course of their nation.

On the stairs were guards: two standing across from one another every five stairs. They were dressed in tan uniforms, long pants and long sleeve shirts. A flowing white cape draped off of their backs, blowing in the underground breeze. Their white armor sat on top of their clothing like the uniform Ana had been wearing when we first met her. Instead of guns, they held a white Unitum staff in their right hand. Each guard faced forward, looking out over the cavern. They were definitely there out of ceremony and tradition, but even I would feel uneasy going up against these warriors. I was glad we were on the same side.

Ana, Hunter, and I left our places in the cockpit and exited through the open door in the cabin, onto the stone ground of the landing pad. The air here was fresher than anything above ground. It felt like it took less effort to breathe. The light of the artificial sun was bright, but soft. It had the same warmth as the sun at the beach, but didn't feel as though it would burn my skin.

A group of the same guards were marching out of the iron door and down the steps to meet us. They walked in two rows of three, with one lone soldier leading the group. We reached the bottom of the stairs at the same time as they did.

"Is this the boy here to stand before the council?" the soldier in the front of the group asked.

"Yes," Ana said. She stood in front of Hunter and I. Hunter clung close to my side.

"We'll take him," the soldier said, "The other bearer will have to wait here."

Hunter moved a step closer to me. "That" Ana cut me off.

"That won't be necessary," Ana defended, "He's with me."

"We have our orders," the soldier said, "and they were very specific."

Ana turned and looked at me. Her look asked for my permission. I looked at Hunter.

"You go with Ana," I said, "She'll watch after you."

He didn't look convinced.

"These people are our alleys," I assured him, "They just don't want me to taint your answers in any way." I smirked and playfully nudged his arm, "Plus, you're a crystal bearer. You can take care of them if you need to."

The lead soldier gave me a dirty look. I sensed his condemnation of what I had said. "It was a joke," I added, looking up at the soldier. I looked back at Hunter and winked, letting him know that it wasn't a joke.

This made him smile, but it was quickly replaced with his nervous expression. When the soldier asked Hunter to come with him, he returned to his solemn, glossy look he'd had when I found him. I wasn't sure this council was going to get many of the answers they were looking for.

As they started up the stairs, Ana followed, but looked back at me, "There's a training facility not far from here," she suggested, "You might be able to… reduce some stress." She smiled and resumed following the ground up the staircase.

At first I was completely closed off to the idea. I was going to wait right there until Hunter walked out of those doors. Then, I thought about what I said. These people were our allies. This place was safer than the mountain base. The Organization didn't even know where to find it. Plus, I could blow off some steam.

The iron door at the top of the stairs opened. The soldiers walked in first and flanked either side of what I could see of a long hallway, leaving Ana and Hunter standing together in the doorway. Hunter looked back at me one last time. I smiled and nodded encouragingly. Ana placed her hand on his back and guided him inside. The door closed behind them with a loud clang.

I looked up the stairs for a moment. I wish I could say I was praying for Hunter or something, but I was actually just standing there. Really I wasn't thinking about much. For a moment, the last moment for a long time, my mind was clear. And for no particular reason. It shouldn't have been, but it was.

I just looked at the intricate spiraling vines crafted into the iron of the door, this design contrasting the very bland staircase and surrounding rock, which was cut with sharp edges and corners and lacked decoration. It really summed up these people. What you see is what you get with them. They are functional, directed, and good at what they do. Then, there are these few little spots with such intricacy one could never hope to decode it all. And together, it makes a place as amazing as this.

When I was done with this, I walked back to the ship and climbed inside. I told the pilot to take me to the training center Ana was telling me about. He agreed and we flew up the same pillar a few hundred feet until we reached a landing platform.

This one was close to the pillar itself, but beside it, was a platform that stretched out from the pillar. It was connected by a thin walkway, and then opened up to a large circle, perhaps fifty yards in diameter.

"Is that it?" I asked.

"Yes," the pilot answered, "You walk out on it and the training session begins. You try and see how many rounds you can make it through."

It sounded simple enough. I followed his instructions. I exited the ship and walked to the training pad. As I stepped onto the walkway, a hologram projected in front of me, moving ahead of me as I walked. A woman's voice played.

"Your training session will begin when you step onto the arena. Scans indicate that you carry a staff and two atom swords. Your opponents will be equipped accordingly."

I continued walking. I determined that I wouldn't be using my powers for this. That would make it too easy.

I wasn't sure what kind of opponents I would be fighting. I assumed misty ones like the training program ALI used.

I stepped out onto the circle. "Round 1" the voice said. I drew my atom sword in my right hand and waited for my opponent to materialize. Instead, a door opened at the start of the walkway. A metal clanking came from inside.

I sensed two large objects coming my way. I saw something glowing in the darkness, just before the body stepped out of the doorway. It was a large robot, humanoid, and lanky. It had long, thin arms and legs, and a properly proportioned torso. Its head was round and had two glowing white sensors for eyes, purposely human-like. There were two of these walking in tandem.

They were likely made of steel painted black, but they had armored plating that looked like Unitum. I didn't see any weapons, but I was sure they had them.

They marched down the narrow path. I waited patiently. I stood in the very center of the pad, the fresh wind blowing by. I closed my eyes and took a deep breath, keeping my senses trained on the two opponents. They stepped onto the circle and drew their swords. The three swords hummed at the same unsettling frequency, growing a bit louder with the wind gusts. I opened my eyes. We looked at each other for a moment. Then, I charged.

They took a ready stance. I swung my blade at one, anticipating that it would be deflected. As soon as the blades clashed, I blocked the second robot's swing. The two blades hissed at one another and the white energy surrounding them lept from one to the other. I took my blade off of his to dodge a swing from the other robot. When his attack missed, I swung my blade back at his unguarded torso. It was a clean hit between the armor, but it didn't go deep enough to kill him.

The robot staggered backwards as his friend attempted to take up the slack. He swung the blade with enough power to knock a regular human off the platform, but my strength allowed me to hold my own. (I didn't count that as using the crystal since I couldn't really turn that power off.)

I deflected his swings, and when I saw my opening, I rolled to the side and swung at the robot's leg. I hit his armor. My blade screamed and bounced off the metal.

I rolled evasively to miss the robots counter. His sword wized by my side and bounced off the rock floor. His blade was on training mode, so it didn't slice through the rock. Mine on the other hand left a molten trail behind as I rolled.

I jumped to my feet and lifted my blade just in time to stop an attack from the wounded robot. I swung my sword from one robots blade to the other. They were on either side of me, trying to gain the upper hand. They didn't. Just as the one in good condition rared back for a powerful swing. I ducked, using my sword to block the wounded robot. When he swung, his sword sliced through the head of the wounded robot.

As he was forced to follow through, I lifted my blade and sliced off his arm. When it was severed, it retained its momentum and slammed into a shield that I only now realized protected the platform. I twirled my sword into a reverse grip. Then, with one defaced and one disarmed, I swung my sword and sliced them both in half. The fell to the ground.

"Round 1 complete," The voice said, "Commencing Round 2"

***

I flung my staff across the arena, hitting one of the white, misty figures in the chest. It dissipated. Since I couldn't call it back, I was forced to draw my sword from my hip. It extended just in time to catch the blade of a robot. I guided it out of the way, forcing the robot off balance. Then, I pulled my sword up, slicing through his midsection as far as the armor would allow me.

I pushed him out of the way and intercepted the blast of a gun with the sword. One of the white figures was firing at me from the edge of the arena. I sensed two more robots coming up behind me, so I advanced quickly. I moved the sword methodically, sensing where each blast would land before it was every shot. I reached the figure.

I'd had ALI add these from his training program to make it more challenging. They represented people. I couldn;t use lethal force on them.

I used the sword to slice through the fake white mist gun, then punched the figure in the face. He staggered back against the shield. Then, I grabbed him from behind and flung him onto the ground. He dissipated.

And not a moment too soon. The robots had reached me. One swung. I dodged and immediately sliced him in half. The sword screeched as it tore through the metal.

While my right hand was occupied with this, I drew my second shorter sword in my left. I held in in a reverse grip to better deflect the oncoming attack of the second robot. I did, and now my other hand was free.

I swung the sword in my right hand at the robot, simultaneously flipping the other sword back to a regular hold. I swung again and again, pushing the robot backward across the platform, until I finally was able to slice through his arm. I'll admit, I decided to have a bit of fun with this one. I sliced off each limb in a matter of seconds until the robot was only a torso lying on its back. Then, I sliced off its head with a screeching slash.

I had made it back to where my staff was, so I retracted the swords, clipped them back on my sides, and picked up the staff. I turned back to the arena, expecting to see more opponents, but all that was there was the carnage of my victims.

"Round 45 complete" The woman's voice played.

I waited for her to announce the next round, but she didn't. Instead the shield around the platform retracted and she announced, "Training session ended. New high score: 4,000"

I was proud to be the new champion of the arena, but a bit upset that my session had ended. Was this just as high as the levels went?

I looked down the walkway. The little cleaner robots that came out every five rounds were rolling out to clear the battlefield, but behind them was a man wearing a navy suit, buttoned at the waist, with a white shirt and a navy tie. His hair was black and slicked back. I recognised him, but at this distance, I couldn't place who he was. I knew he was important, though.

I retracted my staff and placed it on the back of my waist belt. Then, I walked to meet the man. We reached each other where the walkway turned into the arena.

I finally realized who he was. It was Ana's father, the previous bearer of her crystal and the chief of the Mayans. I had seen him a few times, once at Christmas last year, once when I appeared before the council, and when his people came to help us at the mountain base. He was just as set in their traditions as the rest of his people, but was a bit of a softer personality. He had surprised me a few times though. Once, when he agreed to spend a week at Christmas at the mountain base, and once when he agreed to let Ana stay behind. I imagined he probably received a bit of push back from his people for those things. It made me respect him.

"Chief Cantun," I shook his hand, "Is the meeting over?"

He laughed, "The meeting's been over for about an hour, son."

My eyes widened, and I cocked my head. How had I lost track of time that badly? And what had Hunter been doing for an hour?

"We didn't want to disturb you," he added, "You were putting on quite the show." He gestured to the arena. I cut my eyes in that direction and looked back at him.

"We broadcast the arena 24/7," he smiled knowingly, "I think you turned every head in the city."

"Where's Hunter?" I asked, not really concerned with his compliment. Although, I should have been more flattered. A compliment from a Mayan is rare. I learned that from hanging around Ana.

"He's on a tour of the city," the chief said, assuring me of his safety, "Having the time of his life I would say. Ana is with him too."

I felt relieved to know he was doing okay. The chief continued.

"I know you probably have a certain view of us and our council because of how harshly we interviewed you when you came here the last time."

"Harsh isn't the word I would use," I said, deflecting. Interrogation is probably the word I would have used.

"In any case," he continued, "We had to be that way to judge your character. And your intention." I sensed sincerity, "I hope you don't leave here with that sort of taste in your mouth this time."

"I hope not," I smiled. "So what brings you here?" I pointed out.

The chief grinned. "I thought you might be interested to know what we learned."

I leaned in. I was intrigued, but worried how Hunter might have taken to the questioning.

"The boy was more than willing to tell us what we needed to know, even eager once we got going," The Chief started.

"I'm surprised he wasn't more reserved," I reasoned, "He has a lot of hurt surrounding the information you were after."

"Well, of course, he stayed away from the topics surrounding the day of the take over, but it was what came before that that we found so interesting."

I waited for him to continue.

"He found his crystal in a much smaller version of what you sit in right now. An underground ecosystem, certainly a forgotten Mayan site…" He paused in thought, "Or more likely, a purposely hidden one. It seems it was created to house and protect a crystal. You no doubt know that your friend, Bailey, found a similar site, though her's was above ground, and we knew about that one."

"So you think your people created it to house a crystal and then wiped it from the record?" I questioned.

"Not exactly," He answered, "I am of the opinion that our founder created it without the knowledge of our people."

"Ah, the time traveler," I scoffed.

"Yes," The chief snarled, quickly regaining his professional composure. As did I. I didn't mean to make fun of such a revered part of their history.

Their legend stated that a time traveler came to their people some 2,000 years ago and gave them this technology before returning to his appropriate time. It sounded crazy to me. Then again, who was I to call anything crazy anymore.

"Anyway," The Chief continued, "I've sent a team to the coordinates Hunter provided." He paused and his facial expression changed as he shifted the conversation, "Now, what I find more interesting is what he said about the other bearers."

"Yes, I met the three of them a few days ago," I confirmed.

"Not three," The chief corrected, "He spoke of powers we can attribute to no known bearer."

"Another one?" I questioned, "He saw this?"

"No," The chief said, "He just described the moment he was captured. He was subdued with a black energy that countered his own."

"I've seen this before," I remembered, "They were using it to house his crystal at the facility. It did seem to dampen the power of the crystal."

My mind was cluttered with thoughts now. Was there really a bearer out there who could subdue our powers? Maybe this was just a new technology. That thought was even more concerning.

"He also had some interaction with the other bearers," The chief continued, "He insists that they aren't totally in it for The Organization."

"That would support my observations."

"He also said that *they* spoke of another bearer," The Chief added.

"Could that have been Darren?" I reasoned. Hoping there wasn't actually another.

"No," The chief said, crushing my hopes, "He met Darren. And, they mentioned this after his capture. They weren't referring to him."

I placed my hand on my chin and began to think about what I had been told. The Chief placed his hand on my shoulder, "These things will reveal themselves in time," he assured me, "I just wanted to make you aware in case you weren't already."

"Thank you," I said, truly grateful, "You seem to trust me more than my own council." I said this in a moment of vulnerability. I instantly regretted showing my weakness, but the chief didn't prey upon it.

"I'm removed from your politics here," he said, "I can see you for what you are rather than through the tainted view of a council." His eyes glazed over as though he were thinking of a memory. "I had my own council to deal with when I was a young bearer. Now, so does my daughter. I know what it's like."

I thought about it and realized we likely had a lot of shared experiences. He would have had a similar role to fill here when he was given his crystal. I noticed him looking at the one on my chest.

"Thank you for trusting me," I said, sentimentally.

"The mind reading ends up being something you learn how to do without the crystal," he said, "I can tell you're good. That's rare these days."

We smiled at one another and eventually ended up looking out over the city, the breeze blowing in our faces. "Speaking of that," he added, minutes after the conversation had seemingly ended, "I can sense the same thing in that boy."

"There's just something about him, isn't there?" I said, "I sense it too."

"You may not see it, but you both have it," the chief said, "I don't know what *it* is, but I know I've never seen it before." He paused again, admiring the view and gathering his thoughts. I waited, contemplating his words.

"Here, we have a tradition, one of many," he continued, "Each man, of fighting age, takes on an apprentice from the generation below him. The older one becomes 'Aj Kanul' to the younger. He trains him up until he has nothing left to teach him. And the cycle continues."

I scrunched my eyebrows, and I thought about what he was saying. "What does that word mean?" I asked.

"Aj Kanul?" he repeated, "It doesn't have a direct translation. It refers to a teacher, but it's more than that. It's a guardian. A protector. That's what he needs."

"That's what I'm trying to be," I admitted.

"Well, maybe you should make it official," he suggested. He pointed at a ship veering off of the skylane. It was the same model transport that had shuttled me here. It landed beside my transport and the door began to raise. Before it even opened all the way, Hunter was already outside and sprinting over to me.

"I'll leave you to it," the chief nodded, "Good luck."

"It's never luck," I corrected, as I always do.

"Hmm" the chief thought, "So it isn't. God go with you, then." He patted me on the arm and walked off down the walkway, back toward the transports. The two passed on the catwalk, but Hunter ignored him and ran up to me.

"How'd it go?' I asked.

"Great!" he said, not even breathing heavily, "They weren't near as scary as you said they'd be."

"I'm glad," I agreed, "They weren't near as scary as I remember them."

"So, can we go now?"

"Go where?" I teased.

Hunter's smile grew serious. He stared me in the eyes. Then a half smile returned. This time, a weight had resurfaced. He had remembered the weight of what he was begging to do.

"We'll check on the convoy," I said administratively, "I'm sure they're close."

"Good," Hunter said, "We're already behind."

"ALI," I said, "Can you…"

"Already on it, sir," he cut me off, "They are just flying off the coast of Brazil."

"Sounds like they're ready," I said. I was thinking about what the chief had said, "One more thing before we go."

Hunter gave me all of his attention.

"I want you to stick close to me. I'm going to let you help on this mission. I am going to teach you everything I know, so that you can protect yourself and the ones you love from now on. If you'll let me, I'd like to be your teacher," Hunter was about to respond, but I continued, "I'll protect you, but you have to listen to every word I say because it will be the difference between life and death, victory and defeat. Everyone from now on will either want to kill you or control you. It won't be easy."

Hunter's gaze glared determined. His breathing was controlled. He wasn't letting his emotions get the better of him. For the first time that I had seen, he was confident.

"When do we start?" He asked, a note of innocence still in his expression.

"Right now."

Chapter 13

We left El Dorado and headed for the convoy. We would meet it somewhere over the Atlantic Ocean. Ana decided to stay behind and spend some time in El Dorado. As we flew, ALI and I explained some of the secrets we (and my father) had learned about the crystals.

"So what if someone else ever became entangled with my crystal," Hunter asked.

"Only one person can wield a crystal at a time," ALI explained.

"Yea, but like, what if?" Hunter continued.

"Well, given that it is impossible, I suppose we'll never know," ALI said matter-of-factly.

"You're no fun," Hunter wined.

"I'm a computer program, what more do you want from me?" ALI complained.

"Come on, ALI," I said, "You're more than that."

"Definitionally,"

I cut him off, "Doesn't matter. You've become more than you were created to be. You're our friend."

"I struggle to see your point when I can't remember important details about the past, erased by my friend."

I thought that ALI had been a bit quiet lately. He must have been trying to recover his memory, or at the very least, he was thinking about it. Hunter looked at me around ALI's emblem, which floated between us in the cabin of the transport.

"That doesn't mean Daniel wasn't your friend," I consoled.

"It means that he used me like what I was created to be," ALI calculated, "A tool."

"You know that's not how he viewed you," I argued.

"I thought I did," ALI said, "But perhaps he just removed my memory of every time he treated me like a tool."

This was not a conversation I was not prepared for. I didn't realize ALI was in such a crisis. How do you even get through to someone who is programmed to see things logically?

"ALI, I can't speak for my father, but you are one of my best friends. Can't that be enough?"

ALI was silent. Likely calculating his answer.

"And your copy was always my friend too," Hunter said, "I never just thought of you as a program. I usually forget that you're not a real person."

I wasn't sure if bringing up the whole thing about the copy was a good idea. I nervously waited for ALI's reply.

"I suppose the past can be left where it is at," ALI said, "I thank both of you for being so kind."

"Of course ALI."
"Yea, anytime."

"It's striking how similar the two of you are," ALI observed, his misty emblem rippling, indicating deep thought.

"Us?" Hunter and I said at the same time, gesturing to one another.

This made us both laugh, and if ALI could laugh, I think he would have to.

Our conversation continued on a lighter note until the pilot announced that we were now joining the convoy and were preparing to land on the command ship. Hunter's demeanor turned serious.

I walked to the cockpit and looked out. It was dark now. All that could be seen were the stars above us, the lights of the ships flying with us, and the black void of the ocean below. It was almost like we were flying through deep space.

I recognized the silhouette of one of the cruisers. It was my lead cruiser (the one we had fought the parasite on during the Battle of Big Valley). It was difficult to make out in the moonless night, but I could see the light from the bridge reflecting off of the Unitum Ekklesia dove on the bow of the ship.

We flew up on it from behind and circled to land on the platform beside the bridge. As we circled, I could see the crew busily working at their stations through the large glass front of the command center. I couldn't make out who was in the captain's chair, but I prayed it wasn't Sparks.

We landed and the door of the transport raised open. I thanked the pilot and Hunter and I exited the ship. The cruiser was moving fast and the wind was strong.

The door to the bridge opened. Hunter and I shuffled our way there, doing our best not to blow away. We walked through the doorway as our transport took off behind us.

The first thing I noticed was that Blake and Bailey were not on the bridge. The second thing I noticed was that rather than turning to greet me (as was customary) the captain had kept his chair turned away from us, looking straight ahead through the front window.

I tracked his gaze, looking to see if there was some ominous threat up ahead. As I did, my senses detected a familiar stench, a mixture of pride, contempt, and ambition. My jaw clenched and my countenance shifted.

Slowly, the man in the captain's chair turned toward me. I stared directly at him.

"Good evening, Director," Captain Sparks snarled, "It feels good to be back captaining the flag ship."

"I'm sure," I remarked. I elected to keep our conversation as short and civil as possible. "What is our ETA?"

"About three hours," he said.

"Then we'll retire to our quarters for now," I said.

"As you should," Captain Sparks smiled, "This is an important mission for you."

I squinted, trying to read him. What did he mean? Did he figure out my lie and now knows that it's a personal mission, or was he just referring to finding the capital being important?

"Important for all of us," I said, not offering him anything else.

I walked out of the bridge. As soon as I was in the hall and the door closed behind me, I asked ALI, "Does he know?"

"Nothing besides the official story that I know of," ALI replied, "But I will see if he has accessed anything that might say otherwise."

"Good," I said, "Can you get Blake and Bailey on coms?"

"You are connected now," ALI said.

"Where are you guys?" I asked.

"We're in the barracks," Blake's voice said.

"Barracks?" I questioned, "You guys are supposed to get officers lodging."

"It's a long story," Bailey joined in, "Where are you?"

"Hunter and I just left the bridge," I said, "What is Sparks doing here?"

"Long story," Bailey repeated, "Meet us in the hangar bay."

"What's happening?" Hunter asked.

"Let's find out," I said.

We hurried down the halls and corridors of the ship until we reached its belly where the hangar bay was. It was largely empty with the exception of a few soldiers who were on patrol. We easily spotted our friends next to the large metal doors of the hangar. We walked over.

We greeted one another. I hugged Bailey and clasped hands with Blake, pulling into a "bro hug". Bailey and Blake both patted Hunter on the shoulder. Bailey gave him a side hug. You would have thought that we'd been apart for a week instead of a day, but really, a week's worth of stuff had seemed to happen to both parties. I admittedly held on to Bailey for a bit too long. Our interaction at the last hangar we were in had spooked me a bit. It was just good to see everyone.

"So what's going on?" I asked.

"Sparks hijacked the mission," Blake said, "He convinced the council to let him captain the ship. Then, he wouldn't let us on the bridge."

"And he brought all of his little minions along," Bailey said. I knew she was referring to the council members who supported Sparks. "He put them in the officers quarters and exiled us to the barracks."

"There's enough room for all of you in there," I argued.

"His words were 'you're soldiers, so act like it'" Blake imitated Sparks demeanor and voice. Pretty accurately, I must say.

"He's trying to unofficially demote you," ALI said.

Everyone's face contorted to the same confused look as we listened to ALI over the coms.

"He's trying to take away your power without an official action," ALI rephrased, "Keep you out of sight, boss you around, ignore your orders."

"How could he do that?" Hunter asked. The same question was on all our minds.

"The office of 'Crystal Bearer' is a very open ended position on the council. There's not a job description, so you could take that as meaning you have lots of power or very little," ALI explained, "He's trying to make everyone think the latter."

"And he can do it because there's nothing saying he can't," I observed.

"But there's nothing saying he can," Blake added, "Which means we can stand up to him,"

"Only if we have the support of the council," I corrected.

"Exactly," ALI said, "You have as much power as the council thinks you have."

"Well, I don't exactly see how we can spin this," Bailey said. We gave her our attention, "If we succeed, not just in freeing Brady, but finding the capitol, Sparks will take credit for it. But if we don't find the capitol, Sparks will blame it on us, and his people are here to back him up."

"He definitely played the politics," I said.

We all stood silently, trying to think of a way to spin this back in our favor. Even ALI couldn't think of a way to save this one.

"Well, we can at least save Brady," Hunter said. I knew he was about to explode, more so the closer we got to his friend.

"Of course," I said, "That's why we're here." I put my hand on his shoulder, "We'll just stick to our plan: save Brady, see what else we can find."

Hunter smiled, but it was forced. Forced, not because he wasn't happy we were saving his friend, but because of his fear. I sensed that he was terrified of what he would find. He knew how the Organization could break people, how they had broken him. It was reasonable to think "how could someone without powers survive what one with powers barely could?"

“Perhaps you should all get some sleep before the mission,” ALI suggested, “I’ll wake you up when we reach land.”

We listened to his advice and headed for the barracks. Bailey was forced to break off from the group to go to the female barracks, so I broke off and walked her there, sending Hunter with Blake.

When we reached the door to the barracks, I hugged her and kissed her on the cheek.

“Goodnight,” I said softly.

“Goodnight,” she returned.

Just as she was walking into the barracks, she turned back. She leaned on the door, half of her body hidden, the other half leaning into the open space.

“You’re not going to do anything crazy to Sparks, are you?” she asked.

She must have been reading all of my intrusive thoughts I was having about him on the walk over here.

“No, of course not,” I said, "Hopefully someone else will, but not me.”

“Dylan,” Bailey cut her eyes at me.

“I’m joking,” I held up my hands. I shrugged, “Sort of.”

She smiled and shook her head, “Goodnight,” she repeated.

“Goodnight”

I waited until she closed the door. Then, I walked back to the Men's barracks. The barracks consisted of a long hallway with sectioned off rooms. The front of the rooms were open, and faced the room in front of them. Each section had two small bunk beds. It reminded me of the dorms at my church camp when I was younger, except… metal.

I walked until I found Blake and Hunter. I was glad I had heightened senses because the corridor was dark. Everyone else was asleep, so I followed my senses to the only two people still awake and moving. They were at the very end of the hall, on the right side.

Blake was in a bottom bunk on the left side of the room. Hunter was in the top bunk on the right. Under him was a sleeping soldier. I climbed up to the bunk over Blake. I only realized that I still had my armor on when I laid down, but I was so tired, all I took off was my jetpack, which floated up, resting on the low ceiling.

The bunks were so close together, Hunter was only about three feet away from me. He was lying on his back, staring up at the ceiling. His breathing was quickened, and I could sense his emotions swelling. So much so that some energy was beginning to leak from his crystal, traveling across his chest in the area closest to his crystal.

"Hey," I whispered. Hunter looked over at me. I could see tears in his eyes, but he wouldn't let them out. "I know there's a lot of crazy happening, but we're gonna get Brady. Everything else, I'm not sure, but we're getting Brady."

Hunter shook his head and rolled over to face the wall. The first thing I thought was that I couldn't imagine what he was going through, but the truth was, I could. The last time The Organization had my best friend, I punched through a wall. I was sure Hunter was ready to punch through some walls too. He would get the opportunity soon enough.

***

"Stay close to me and watch what I do," I instructed Hunter as we walked to the bridge, "Training starts today."

"Maybe we should worry about that when we aren't in a real battle," Hunter suggested.

"I wish we could," I admitted, "But I don't think we'd ever get the chance."

We reached the door to the bridge, and I turned around to face my friends. Blake and Bailey had been training behind us. "Everyone knows what they're doing right?" I asked.

"If they don't, I will remind them," ALI said.

"Good enough," I replied.

Then, I opened the door to the Bridge. Hunter walked beside me while Bailey and Blake flanked us. I could see our fighters advancing on the shipping yard below us. With them were bombers. My stomach flew into my throat. This was not a part of the plan, which was now officially falling apart after about two seconds of being a real plan.

"Why are you sending in bombers?" I almost shouted at Sparks.

He answered without turning to face me, "We must weaken the base before we advance."

"There are civilians down there," I argued.

"Wars have casualties," Sparks said coldly.

"What if you destroy the coordinates we are looking for?" I argued, trying to find something he might care about.

"They would be far better protected than anything hit in a surface bombing," Sparks snarled.

I looked at Hunter. He stared straight ahead, clenching his jaw.

"Recall the bombers, Sparks," I commanded.

Some of the people working at their station in front of us turned to look at me. Sparks slowly stood up and turned to face me, taking a few steps toward us.

"And how would you suggest our people get on the ground if there is a base functioning at full capacity, not to mention the three cruisers we are about to engage?"

"I'll take care of it," I said. I stared directly into his eyes for a moment. He was having too much fun with this. Once I had looked at him long enough to hold my dignity, I turned to the door and walked outside, onto the landing platform. My friends walked out with me.

The wind wasn't as strong as it was last night. It was much easier to stand now. I nodded my head and my helmet formed around it. "You guys focus on getting to the ground," I said, "I'm going to take out some of the defences."

"I'll help," Bailey said.

"I've got it," I insisted.

"We've got it," She countered.

I knew I wasn't winning this one. "ALI, Teach Hunter how to use a jetpack."

"Yes sir," ALI said.

"Blake, keep Hunter alive, please" I requested.

"You kidding? He's gonna be keeping me alive," Blake slapped Hunter on the back.

"Let's go, then," I said. I ignited my jetpack and took off.

Bailey followed me at first, but she was faster since her powers allowed her to fly. She pulled ahead, weaving through the already tangled mess out our's and enemy fighters.

Orange blasts of energy flew past us, some exploding in the air, some crashing into fighters. Some reached the shields of our three cruisers.

The bombers were slow, but still coming behind us. I knew if we didn't clear these defenses before they got here, they would drop their payload.

Bailey reached a turret first. It was positioned in the open area out from the base. She blasted it with her energy. The white bolts leapt across its surface and the barrel of the cannon turned toward the ground. She had overloaded its circuits.

She continued this, allowing some of her bolts to sweep through multiple turrets, and in this manner she cleared all of the loan turrets before I was even within range.

Now, we lined up for our attack on the base. The base had a relatively thin shield. Our bombers could likely overload it. The shield protected a base similar in size to the surface of the Montana base. It had a few tall buildings and a few bunkers. Its defining characteristic was the landing zone for transport cruisers, the war equivalent of a barge. The shipbreaking yard was behind this. A sprawling, unprotected expanse of scrap. Downed cruisers, pieces of fighters, and decommissioned military equipment from the governments The Organization had overthrown. What wasn't covered in scrap was flat and grassy. In the distance there were some rocky cliffs. The scrapyard backed all the way up to these mountains.

All of the remaining turrets either surrounded the base of the shields or were housed underneath the shield (these would activate if the shield were to be destroyed or if something made it on the inside, like me).

"Bailey, make me an opening," I requested as she flew up beside me.

She nodded her head and flew ahead of me. She charged up until she was nothing more than a white streak cutting through the dim morning light. When she was finally close to the shield, she released a massive blast that sent white ripples through the entirety of the orange tinted shield. It was permeable now, but it wouldn't last long.

I conjured a concussive blast from each of my hands. This thrust me through the air. Another blast came from me as I broke the sound barrier. A white fog appeared around me.

I burst through the shield, turning my feet in front of me and conjuring another blast to slow me down. I reassessed.

Bailey was zippling around the outside of the shield, but she was now being pursued by a swarm of Organization fighters, which was being pursued by a swarm of Ekklesia fighters. This would slow her down a bit.

As I hovered, I sensed the turrets inside the shield turning in my direction. I began flying again, just as they opened fire. I bobbed and weaved, using my concussive blasts to throw myself this way and that. They could never get a lock on me.

As I did this, I would randomly fire a concentrated blast of my purple energy at the turrets. I knew they were unmanned, so I didn't hold back. The blast ripped through the turret, leaving no evidence that it ever existed.

Fly, dodge, shoot, dodge, dodge, fly, shoot, dive, fly, shoot.

I buzzed around the inside of the shield until all of the turrets were dead. Smoke rose from where they had once existed. I flew up and looked out onto the battlefield. Bailey was just wrapping up her job as well. I spied what I was looking for. The squadron of bombers was making its way toward the base.

"ALI, put me on the bridge coms," I requested.

"Yes, Sir."

"Sparks," I commanded, "Call off the bombers. It looks like we're going to be able to avoid a few of those casualties today."

There was no response from Sparks. I watched the bombers. It took them a second, but they changed their course and headed back toward our cruisers.

I smiled, having won this round, and took some time to assess the battlefield. The two sets of cruisers were holding their fire for fear of hitting their own fighters. Reasonable. But if The Organization, or probably Sparks too for that matter, started to lose, all bets would be off. So far, it was looking like The Organization was losing.

I looked below me. Troops were beginning to pour out of the various buildings. Except they weren't Human, they were robots. I smirked. This was a good teachable moment.

"Hunter, where are you?" I asked over the coms. I formed a shield around me like a bubble as the robots opened fire.

"Coming up outside the shield, right in front of you," Hunter replied.

"Look for the green flash," Blake said.

He must have sprung that on Hunter because it took him a second to do it, but sure enough, I spotted a green flash of energy not far from the base of the shield directly in front of me.

"Bailey," I started.

She knew exactly what we needed. She flew around the shield and hit it with a glancing blow. It wasn't as powerful as the first, but it was all she could do with the parade following her. It was just enough for Blake and Hunter to slip through.

I flew down to meet them, holding the shield as I went. Once I was on the ground, I expanded it to cover all of us, even though we were behind one of the buildings.

"Lesson one," I said, "Show me what you can do."

"Can't you just crush them and hurry up and find Brady?" Hunter begged.

I actually felt bad now. I knew this wasn't hindering anything, but I also knew how anxious Hunter was.

"You're right," I said, "Let's crush them together."

Hunter nodded thankfully and his green energy flew across his body. I responded by letting my purple energy flow across my body. Blake looked at us both and shrugged his shoulders, "I can't do that, but I'm ready to kick some tale!"

I chuckled, but Hunter didn't look like he heard him. He was focused on the mission. I let Hunter lead the charge, protecting him from blasts when I needed to and taking out as many robots as necessary to keep advancing.

Hunter ran at the robots, conjuring beams of energy that would slice through rows at a time. He was also good at shielding himself from their blasts. Though, his shields weren't like mine. Instead of being naturally rounded, they were rectangles. He kept up with the firepower pretty well.

After only a few minutes, I sensed Bailey enter the shield. As we fought, a white light surrounded us. Electrical zapping could be heard coming from every corner of the shielded base. White balls of energy zipped this way and that, faster than I could keep track of them.

In just a few seconds, all of the robots were laying on the ground, smoke rising from their fried circuits. Hunter looked around, confused about what had just happened, but I knew exactly what it was.

Bailey gently floated down between Hunter and I. "Sorry to take all of your fun boys," she said casually.

I retracted my helmet. Hunter and Blake retracted their helmets as well, while we enjoyed a bit of quiet. Relative quiet anyway. The battle still raged on outside of the shield.

"Alright, Hunter, you come with me, we'll start searching the East side of the base. Bailey, Blake, you two start searching the West side."

Blake saluted and Bailey nodded, and then we separated.

"Here's a real lesson," I said as we walked, "Be mindful of your senses. Sometimes they tell you things you weren't expecting them to."

"Like what?" Hunter asked.

"Like what door to enter, or what to do next," I said.

"How do they do that?" he asked.

"Honestly, I don't know," I admitted, "But it does. That's how I found you."

We searched a few different buildings. ALI conducted scans telling us which ones were likely holding the prisoners. After about fifteen minutes of searching (which is a lifetime in the middle of a battle) he directed us to a warehouse.

I blew open the door and prepared to fight a new wave of troops, but the building was empty. We walked in, and I received a call from Sparks.

"I guess you can put him through," I told ALI.

I was greeted by his warm, and sunny disposition, "What do you think you're doing?" Sparks yelled, "Get that shield generator down now!"

"The shield generator is still up because I don't want a rogue crashing ship to take out what we came all this way for," I retorted. Which was true, though I wasn't protecting what he thought I was.

"I want a strike team in there now!" he continued, "I want them turning over tables, and blowing the place to pieces until they find the capitol."

"Well, I guess we don't always get what we want, now do we?" I snarked. Then, I ended the call. "Something tells me that's not going to keep him out much longer," I told Hunter, "We better get a move on."

I was hoping that Bailey and Blake were having more luck than us because we had found nothing more than a few cowering soldiers in the buildings we had searched. A strike team would honestly be helpful to comb the place. The only problem is that they wouldn't be looking for the right thing.

The warehouse was dimly lit by fluorescent lights on the tall ceilings. I assumed this is where they cleaned up large pieces of salvaged equipment. There were abandoned tools and workstations scattered around the edges of the hangar, but the center was completely open. The only sound that penetrated in here was the humming of the lights and the occasional explosion on the surface of the shield.

When we had walked the full length of the warehouse, I suggested that we check the rooms and closets around the edges. Maybe there were people hiding in there.

"Sure," Hunter agreed," I'll start in the front and we…"

He stopped. His eyes grew wide and all of the blood rushed away from his face. His breathing grew labored. His lip quivered. I looked around frantically trying to see what had spooked him.

I didn't see anything. I was about to ask him what it was, but then I felt it. Cold.

A chill ran down my spine. The room wasn't cold though. It was as if life itself were being drained from the air around me. I narrowed my eyes and expanded my senses. What was this? Clearly Hunter had felt it before.

While I looked for the source, he snapped out of his petrification. He latched onto my arm and started dragging me toward the door. "We have to go," he warned, "We have to go!"

"What, Hunter," I pulled against him, "What is it?"

I was answered by a clanging noise and the ding of an elevator that I only now realized was in the warehouse. Hunter stopped pulling and looked toward the elevator, about fifty feet away from us, tucked in the corner of the warehouse.

The door creaked open. There was no light on inside of the elevator and I couldn't see inside from the angle I was at. Slowly, a figure emerged. The shadow that had enveloped him inside the elevator followed him out.

He was wearing a black uniform. On his chest was a solid black crystal, so black it was as though it sucked all of the surrounding light into it. Black waves of unstable energy flickered across his body. He wore a helmet concealing his identity. The light of my crystal flickered, as though it were already bowing to the superiority of this new player.

The figure slowly made his way to the center of the hangar, staring at Hunter and I. I made note of my senses. The door was about 200 feet behind us. In front of me was the figure. I knew this, but my senses told me there was nothing but an endless void.

"Who are you?" I asked the figure.

"We need to go," Hunter insisted. His voice was panicked as he hid behind me.

The figure said nothing. He only tilted his head a bit, as though he were actually thinking about what he wanted. Then, as though he had received the answer, he straightened up, held his arm out to the side, and flung a confusing ball of his black energy at us.

I pulled Hunter out of the way, throwing us both to the ground. As the blast erupted on the back wall of the warehouse, I sent my own black back at him. However, a few feet before it reached him, it dissolved into nothing.

He threw another ball of his energy. It wavered and pulsated as it flew silently through the air. All that could be heard was the wind as it flew by.

I dodged a couple times, throwing Hunter out of the way, but eventually I had to throw him out of my reach. When I did this, the figure turned his attention to Hunter.

I raised a shield to stop the blasts, but it crumbled after the first hit. The black energy ate at mine, ripping it apart. Hunter then raised his own shield to stop the second. The third struck him in the center of the chest and he was blown across the warehouse. He lay on his back, struggling to get up.

The figure took heavy steps in Hunter's direction. I broke out in a run toward the figure, drawing my staff in stride.

"Stay away from him!" I yelled.

I flung my staff at the figure. He dodged, but he was close enough to the wall that when the tip of the staff struck it, the blast knocked him off balance.

I called the staff back to my hand just in time to intercept one of his black orbs. This worked much better than the shield. I did this twice more, but the figure grew unammused, and blasted me across the hangar with the flick of his wrist.

Usually, I would break my fall with a shield or a concussive blast, but all of my powers were paralyzed. The black energy had enveloped my body.

I landed hard on the concrete floor. It knocked the breath from me. I gasped for air as I forced myself to stand up. I called my energy across my body, but it took a few seconds to fight off the infection of the black energy. The purple slowly spread out from my chest. I was restored.

The figure was reaching Hunter who was scrambling backwards on the ground. I called my staff up off the ground and to my hand. I caused my energy to concentrate around it and then I unleashed the most powerful beam of energy I could conjure at the figure.

Hunter saw what I was doing and blasted him at the same time I did. The two reached the figure at the same time, and to my surprise, they briefly mixed like mine and Baileys do.

This extra bit of power caught the figure off guard too. Hunter stood up, maintaining his beam of energy, and walked back toward where I was.

When he was at a better angle, the beams mixed more perfectly, creating a perfect mix of purple and green, evenly distributed through the beam after the two came together.

I thought we might have him pinned, but no sooner than the thought crossed my mind, I saw the black decay beginning to spread up the beams.

I scrambled to come up with a plan. Then, I heard Bailey over the coms, “We found the prisoners.”

“Good,” My breathing was heavy, “Retreat!”

"What?" I heard Blake say. There was no time to explain.

"Hunter, You too," I instructed.

"What about you?"

"I'm right behind you," I assured him, "Now go."

We stopped contributing to the beam at the same time and dove in opposite directions. I redirected my staff and blew a hole in the ceiling.

Hunter's jetpack ignited, and he lifted off the ground. The figure threw some of his black orbs at him, trying to stop his escape, but I sent my own blasts to intercept them. When he was gone, the figure looked at me.

I formed another beam, sweeping it across the entire half warehouse in front of me. It passed only a few feet over the figure's head, which cocked to the side as though to say "you missed".

I didn't.

I had severed every single one of the heavy steel beams holding up the other heavy steel beams directly over the figure's head. He raised his hand to begin another attack, but I conjured two concussive blasts, launching myself through the air, just as the building collapsed. I popped through the hole I had made for Hunter and ignited my jetpack. I saw the ripple of the weak spot Bailey must have just created in the shield and propelled myself through it.

I looked back to see a reverberating black energy covering the rubble of the warehouse. I assumed that meant our attacker wasn't dead.

I pressed the button on my vanguard to signal a retreat and then pressed the one beside it to open the coms line to Captain Sparks.

"Recall the troops, Sparks," I said over the coms.

"Did you find it?" he asked, actually sounding hopeful.

“I found something worse”

Chapter 14

I flew until I reached the command ship. I noticed Bailey and Hunter still standing on the landing platform outside the bridge. I came in hot, carrying enough momentum that I almost missed the platform.

As soon as I had my footing, I made for the bridge, ignoring my friends, who I realized were arguing. I burst onto the bridge, out of breath.

“Turn the ship around!” I commanded.

Sparks was standing up out of his Captains chair facing me.

“Did you get the location of the capitol?” he inquired sternly.

“It doesn’t do us any good if we’re all dead,” I answered, “There’s a new bearer in play, and I can’t protect us from him.”

Sparks actually looked like he didn’t know what to say. His mouth hung open as though he were about to speak, but the words never formed.

I shook my head and started walking toward the operators in front of him. “Get us out of here!” I commanded again.

Just then, Hunter came running in, followed closely by Bailey. “We have to go back!” Hunter yelled, grabbing my arm. His eyes were full of tears, “I wasn’t thinking. I should have stayed and fought. We have to go back.”

I knew he was referring to Brady. I didn’t know what to say, but I knew we couldn’t go back. I noticed Bailey had run in behind him.

“I think you should come with me,” Bailey told him.

“No!” Hunter insisted, “If you won’t go back, I will!”

Then, he ran for the open door to the platform.

"Hunter, stop!" I called after him. He didn't listen, and I knew I wouldn't have either.

"We have Brady," Bailey told me telepathically.

I didn't understand why she hadn't just told him that, but there was no time to think about it. I had to stop Hunter. Just as he ran through the door, I latched onto him with my powers. The purple energy flowed through the air and wrapped around his body.

His arms and legs were bound and I lifted him off the ground, preparing to yank him back inside. Except, just before I could do that, he used his powers to strike the door's control panel, causing it to close.

We were separated by the door which severed my connection to him, and he was free. He ignited his jetpack and flew off, but before he could make it very far, it turned off, and he rolled down the side of the ship. ALI must have killed its power.

There was a steep slope leading down from the bridge platform, but it evened off eventually. I could see where he landed through the windows on the bridge. He was directly out in front of us, running toward the nose of the ship. If he jumped, ALI would be forced to reignite the jetpack, and there was no way for him to safely override Hunter's controls and fly him back.

I turned back to Sparks, "I'm going to handle this, you turn this ship around."

A sly smile spread across his face. At this moment, he and I both knew that he had won. We had no information on the capitol. My reason for coming here was exposed. And I was unable to control my own team, a bearer at that. I could hear all of his arguments now.

"And wipe that stupid smile off your face," I growled, pointing my finger at him. My body was consumed by my purple energy. We locked eyes only for a second. Then, I sprinted to the door. I conjured a relatively small blast and blew the door off the ship, ripping a hole in the wall where it had been. I'll admit, it was mostly out of anger, but the door was broken and I needed to get out quickly.

I ran through the new opening, igniting my jetpack and flying down to where Hunter was.

"You have to come back!" I yelled over the roar of the wind. I didn't want to use the coms since Bailey was clearly being secretive for a reason.

Hunter didn't answer, but instead, shot two of his green energy beams. I easily blocked them with my own energy and landed in front of him. I could see that his face and eyes were red, even through the green energy that surrounded his body.

"Stop," I said, sternly. My face was cold. I held my arms at my side, ready to stop him by force if I had to. He knew I could, so he pleaded.

"You don't understand," he said, "I would rather die trying to get him back than live knowing I ran away." He was sobbing now.

"Bailey, I'm gonna tell him," I thought, knowing she was listening in.

"He doesn't need to see him this way." She replied, her voice echoing through my thoughts.

"That's not for us to decide," I said out loud. I put my focus back on Hunter. "We got him out," I told him.

"What?" Hunter whimpered. He didn't know what to believe, and I didn't blame him one bit.

"Bailey was trying to figure out how to tell you," I explained, walking close to him now, "He's in rough shape, but Blake has him in the medical bay."

"Wh...Well, we have to go there," Hunter stuttered. He sniffled. The wind swayed his weak knees.

"Let's just head inside," I suggested.

Hunter agreed. We flew back up to the landing pad and walked though the hole in the side of the ship. Hunter looked at the hole with wide eyes. Bailey was standing on the other side.

I had my arm around Hunter's shoulder when we walked in, but Bailey took him from me and wrapped him in her own arms, escorting him off of the bridge.

Sparks and I locked eyes one last time. I sensed his malice and greed. He was bubbling over on the inside. He had observed exactly what he came here to see and so much more.

"Will you be needing anything else from the bridge, Director?" He asked as professionally as I had ever heard him sound. He was mocking me.

"Just take us home," I said.

"As you wish," he smirked and then took his seat in the captain's chair.

I left the room and found Hunter and Bailey still standing in the hall. "My mother is a nurse," Bailey was telling Hunter, "I've been around this type of thing, and I think you should let our doctors do their job for now. You don't want to see him this way."

"If it's that bad, then that means I have to see him now," Hunter said. He was holding his composure, but tears were still coming up in his eyes.

"I just think-"

"I might be able to save him!" Hunter cut Bailey off.

"It's okay," I interjected, walking up to them, "Maybe he can help." I remembered Hunter's healing powers, "Let's just go see him."

ALI instructed us on how to get to the med-bay and, we walked there mostly in silence, our pace ever increasing as Hunter led the way.

We finally came to a part of the ship with a grey sliding door, contrasting the white hallways. The door had a sign above it that read

MED-BAY, and on the door itself was a notice that read "please keep all surfaces sanitary and remove any contaminated clothing".

I assumed that we weren't contaminated, so I pressed the button of the wall panel for the door to open. It did, revealing a short corridor with five doors on each side of a short hallway. This was the area where emergency surgeries were performed and critical patients were kept. One might expect this area to be bigger, but anyone not in these categories would be expected to wait until we arrived at a base or would be shipped back on a medical transport.

We walked in and were promptly greeted by a nurse who came out of one of the rooms closest to us. She was wearing a white uniform, loosely fitted, with a skirt that reached about midway past her knee. On her sleeve was a red cross below her Ekklesia Dove pendant. I saw Blake standing outside the room at the end of the hallway on the left.

"What is your business here?" the nurse asked.

Hunter completely ignored her. She held out her arm to stop him, but he plowed through and made for Blake.

"We're here to see a patient," I said, then I pushed past her as well. She wore an upheaved expression, and I sensed her frustration. Bailey stayed behind to explain the situation while I followed Hunter.

He reached Blake who positioned himself in front of the door.

"Let me in," Hunter commanded.

"I'm not going to stop you," Blake assured him, "I just want you to be prepared."

"Why are people acting like this?" Hunter threw his arms up in frustration, "He's alive. I don't care how bad he looks, so long as he's alive."

Blake bit his lower lip and stepped away from the door. He looked at me and gently shook his head. I sensed that Blake had been shaken. He was hiding it well, but what he'd seen had enraged him against The Organization. Blake had seen a lot. It took quite a bit to shake him anymore. Now I was curious what condition this boy was in.

Hunter pressed the button on the wall and the door slid open. He took a few bold steps into the bright sterile room, then stopped. He turned back and looked at Blake, "You got the wrong person." Hunter's voice quivered with fear and anger.

"This is Brady Allen Skott of Boulder, Colorado," Blake assured him, "He was tagged with a microchip."

"This isn't Brady," Hunter insisted, looking back into the room. I heard him start to breathe a bit heavily, "This isn't..."

I walked toward the room, positioning myself so that I could see in. There was nothing in the room besides a hospital bed (riveted to the floor) and some medical equipment (also connected to the wall and floor). The sheets and pillow on the bed were a very light blue. A monitor beeped periodically in the background.

In the bed was the near skeleton of a boy. His face was sunken in and sharp. I could tell his skin usually held a deeper tan color, but it was washed and yellow now. His lips were white. His dark hair was shaven close to his scalp which was colorless and peeling. The rest of his tiny body was concealed by the blue sheets which barely moved with the boy's shallow breathing.

Hunter took a few steps closer to the bed. He was crying again as he realized that this was, in fact, his friend. He reached the foot of the bed and then lost his composure. He released a combination of screaming and crying. His green energy uncontrollably swept across his body. There was a metal rod at the foot of the bed that he had latched onto which crumpled like cardboard under his grip.

He was beginning to lose his grounding. He leaned forward then staggered backwards where he fell into my open arms. I managed to remove my breastplate just before Hunter buried his face in my chest. He squeezed me as tightly as he could, occasionally taking my breath, but I was strong enough to let him.

From the outside, it would have looked like he was crying over the state of his friend, and he was. However, it was more than that. This was an end of sorts for Hunter. He'd found a piece of his past. He'd taken back a bit of what the enemy had stolen from him. They weren't just tears of sadness, they were tears of joy and of a weight being lifted.

I allowed my energy to flow over my body and mingle with Hunter's as I had discovered could be done earlier. I did this partially because I knew it was comforting, it was the bearer equivalent to a hug, that could be felt in the darkest corners of our being. It also allowed me to control and tame the bits of his energy that wanted to slip out into the room around us (which now radiated with a mixture of our purple and green energy).

I looked over my shoulder at Blake and smiled. I only then noticed the tears in my own eyes. I didn't expect them to be there. I guess I just couldn't help but empathise with Hunter. I sensed his emotions and recognized them.

I noticed Bailey had shed a few tears herself. She was standing beside Blake, and I knew she was looking into Hunter's mind. It must have been full circle for her, seeing him when we found him, to seeing him now, only a few days later, well on his way to healing.

I held out my arm for her to join in and she walked over, allowing her energy to radiate across her body as well. Before she even reached us, the room was already filled with her energy in the mix of ours. She reached us, and put an arm around me and an arm around Hunter. When she did, I felt the energy explode with growth. I sensed Blake stagger backwards as it flowed around him and down the hallway. I knew that it had encompassed the whole ship (what a sight that must have been), but I didn't care. I only cared about this moment.

Slowly, Hunter's sobbing softened to a sniffle. The room grew quiet, the only noise being the residual hum of the engines that filled even the furthest corners of the ship and the beeping of the heart monitor.

Hunter still squeezed me, holding on for dear life, terrified to let go. Each thought that crossed his mind, both good and bad, threatened to send him spiraling once again.

Then, in the silence, there was a voice.

"Hunter?" it choked. It was dry and weak.

Hunter's head jolted up. He let go of Bailey and I, and spun around. It was Brady.

To all of our amazement, his color had returned. Although he still looked rough, he looked better. The healing energy from Hunter must have made some difference.

"Brady!" Hunter breathed excitedly. He rushed to the side of the bed and put his hand on Brady's tiny arm.

"I didn't think you were alive," Brady said in a raspy voice. It was hardly a whisper.

"Yea, same," Hunter cry-laughed.

Brady smiled a bit. "What happened to you?" he asked.

"To me?" Hunter asked, "What happened to you?"

"That story will have to wait," the nurse said, walking into the room, "Brady needs to rest."

"It's okay," Brady said, "Hunter can heal people."

The nurse cocked her head and looked at Hunter, "I can speed up bodily processes," Hunter corrected, "I think I could help though…If you give me what I need."

"If you really can do that, I think you should do it in a more equipped facility," the nurse suggested.

"I agree," I said, other things prompting my agreement, "I'll call Ana and have the two of you transported to El Dorado. You can do your thing there.

Hunter looked at Brady who was already dozing off. "What about you?" he asked.

"I have to go back to the mountain base," I said. I tried to sound strong, but my uneasiness seeped through in my tone. "You stay here with Brady," I suggested to Hunter, "Bailey, Blake and I have some things to take care of." I turned to them and urged them to follow me out of the room. I looked back at Hunter before walking out, "You good here?"

"Yea," Hunter nodded, still standing at Brady's side.

We walked out of the med-bay and down the hallway. I didn't want to talk until we were in the hangar. There was enough noise there that people wouldn't overhear our conversation. Once we arrived, we found a spot near some fighters being repaired. The clanging and welding would cover our words.

"So how'd you find him?" I asked, kicking off our conversation.

Blake's eyebrows narrowed. He clinched his jaw and stared at the ground. I sensed anger and remorse. Bailey looked at Bake. "Blake found him," she said.

"Them," Blake corrected, "At least forty."

"Slaves?" I asked.

"I don't...I don't know," Blake's voice cracked, "They were just sitting in an open room, most of them young. They were all starving, emaciated. Brady just happened to be in the front. ALI scanned the chip."

"They appeared to be workers," ALI said, "However, I don't understand why they would have been kept in the condition that they were in. These people likely lost the ability to work weeks ago."

"It's egregious," Blake scowled. His lip quivered "I've never seen anything like that. They were just laying on top of each other. Starving, and...I couldn't..." He stopped talking, unable to continue recalling the memory.

I knew he was distressed that he had to leave the others behind. It was a miracle that we even got Brady out, but I knew, after witnessing something like that, it must not have felt that way.

"I didn't make it to Blake before you told us to retreat," Bailey said.

"Why *did* we retreat?" Blake asked. He cut his eyes up from the spot on the floor on which he was focusing his attention, attempting not to become lost in his thoughts.

"There's a new bearer," I said, "The most powerful one I've seen." I looked up at the ceiling, trying to find the words to describe it. "It's like he can corrupt our powers."

"Corrupt?" Bailey questioned.

"It eats away at the energy, makes it unusable for a time. I have to use my energy to overtake it." I explained.

"I don't understand," Bailey said, which made sense, it was hard to explain.

"It leaves a residual field that eats away at my energy," I explained further trying to demonstrate with my hands, "When it's disconnected from the bearer, I can overpower it by sending more of my own energy to the affected spot."

"So it's like anti-energy," Blake said, still somber, but trying to focus on other things.

"Yes," I agreed, "Exactly like what was inhibiting Hunter's crystal when we found it."

"And it worked on you and Hunter?" Bailey confirmed.

"Yes."

"So if you can just send more energy to overpower it, why couldn't you overpower him?" Blake asked.

"I could only overpower the anti-energy when it was detached from him," I explained, "When it was connected to his crystal, it was just too powerful. Even Hunter and I together couldn't make a dent."

"So, okay, that's bad and all, but why is he just showing up now?" Blake asked, "If he's that powerful, why wasn't he just the first one they rolled out?"

“Maybe he’s new?” Bailey suggested.

“Or they’ve been saving him for when all the bearers were in play,” ALI suggested, entering our conversation through our coms.

“What do you mean?” I asked.

“Well, if you want to control the world, then you don’t want any group of people out there more powerful than you,” ALI brainstormed, “So you wait until all of them are fighting each other, then toward the end of the war, you roll out the one that can defeat them all.”

“If the Organization bearers knew about him, that would explain why they let us go,” I added. It was starting to make sense to me. "They may want insurance."

“We haven’t really asked Hunter what he knows about them,” Bailey said, “Maybe that’s a good place to start.”

“Let’s wait until after we see the results of this mission,” I said solemnly.

“It could have gone better,” Blake sulked.

“And we didn’t find the capitol,” I reminded them.

“Right, but we didn’t get a chance to look for it because of the new bearer, so you have an excuse,” Bailey proposed.

“That would work if Sparks and his people weren’t here to see how it all went down,” I said, “He has everything he needs.”

“To do what?” Bailey asked.

“To turn the council against me and take over the Ekklesia”

After our conversation, we spent a decent amount of time in silence. Everything was beginning to pile up, and what victories we had came at a price; a price to which I was deeply in debt.

When the silence had set long enough, I made a call to Ana and explained everything that had happened. I told her that Hunter and Brady needed to come to El Dorrado so that Brady could be treated. She said that she would send a transport immediately to get them.

I knew she was bending some rules to get Brady in there. Hunter had earned their trust, which was helpful. I felt that I had also gained the favor of Chief Cantun. I didn't fully understand how their council worked, but I felt that this would at least be good for something.

The three of us walked back to the med-bay. Hunter was sitting in a chair next to Brady's bed. Brady was asleep (or sedated, I wasn't sure which one). The nurse walked in behind us.

"There's a transport on its way to take you and Brady to El Dorado," I told Hunter. I turned to the nurse, "If you can take Brady to the hangar, the transport will meet you there."

She nodded and I walked closer to Hunter. "Stay with Ana," I instructed.

"Is something wrong?" Hunter asked.

"I wouldn't say it's right," I responded, "Just be vigilant and wait for me to contact you."

Hunter agreed, and I turned back to my other two friends. I extended my senses down the hallway behind them to make sure the nurse had left. "The two of you escort Brady to the transport," I said.

"What are you going to do?" Bailey asked.

"I'm going to the barracks to get some sleep."

Chapter 15

"We've reached the mountain base," ALI informed me, jarring me from my sleep.

The barracks were dark, purposely kept that way so soldiers could sleep at any time of the day. In this case, it was early morning. I noticed the empty bunk across from me and my armor floating up against the wall. I hopped down from my bunk and saw that Blake was asleep in the bunk under mine. He wasn't there when I fell asleep, and I was surprised I didn't sense him when he entered. I must have been in a deep sleep - a rare occurrence for me anymore.

I put my armor on and the shifting fabric made of the puck's mist formed over them. I wanted to take a long, hot shower, but those weren't an option here. Instead, I ran a cycle on my suit that would rid my body of any bacteria. Then, careful not to wake Blake, I walked toward the bridge.

Typically, when I was on a cruiser, I would spend nearly all of my time on the bridge, helping command, interacting with the crew, and admiring the view. With Sparks there, that was the last thing I wanted to do, but I thought my absence would give him too much pleasure. I wanted him to see that I was still strong.

As I walked, I thought. It had always felt like Sparks' vendetta against me was personal. He seemed to hate my guts. Some kid comes in, inexperienced and instantly successful, thriving in a position handed to him by his father. To a long standing member of the Ekklesia, I could see how that would be frustrating. However, the more I thought about it, the more I began to realize that it was more shallow than that; he just wanted power. He didn't care about me. I was simply an obstacle in the way of his end goal. The rest was a political performance.

I reached the door of the bridge. It slid open, revealing the crew. Sparks stood in front of the captain's chair, looking down on the crew in front of him. I took note of my posture, straightened my shoulders, turned my chin up, and walked toward Sparks.

I reached him and stood at his left side, placing one hand inside the other behind my back. He cut his eyes to look at me, then returned to his forward gaze. I matched it.

A section of the yellow shield was just opening in the distance to let us inside. The cruisers would each park next to a hangar to refill on resources. The crew would be exchanged and the leaders on board would head to an emergency council meeting.

The base was just as alive as it always was. Fighters were buzzing around the mountain. Squadrines ran practice maneuvers through the mountains and valleys.

In front of the captain's chair was a small ledge with three steps that led down to the rest of the bridge crew. I overheard one crew member giving air traffic control our clearance codes. I overheard another advising all of our support craft to report to an airfield rather than the main hangars in the base. The other eight members of the bridge crew worked busily at their stations.

“Enjoy it,” Sparks stated, not breaking his gaze.

I did the same when I responded, keeping a cheerful tone, “Enjoy what?”

“The view,” Sparks replied, “You won’t be seeing it like this anymore.”

My anger flared, but I told myself he wasn’t worth it. I bit my tongue, kept my posture, and held my peace. This lasted only as long and Sparks' ego could let it.

“A bit… drafty in here isn’t it?” he shifted on his feet and shook his head as though he were confused. We both kept looking straight ahead.

“Forcing your way though doors tends to mean you can’t close them back,” I alluded.

“Poetic,” Sparks smiled. I could sense his pride at what he’d accomplished.

"Is this really a door you want to force open?" I asked, turning now to look at him. He met my glance, cutting his eyes ever so slightly down, since I was shorter than him.

"I assure you, I've never been more sure." His face was cold and emotionless, but his heart was full of contempt and greed.

"Then don't be surprised when something uninvited walks in behind you," I warned.

We held each other's gaze for a time, then, as though we'd received the same signal, we straightened up, and assumed our forward facing positions.

The cruiser entered the shield of the mountain base and docked at the main hangar bay. The ship and hanger both erupted with movement. Sparks, his loyal council members, and I boarded a floating platform and were shuttled to the hangar.

I stepped off the platform first, leading the group of elites through the hangar. All around us, soldiers were working on damaged fighters and transports. Some were carrying crates of supplies. But all of them, no matter how busy they were, stopped what they were doing, straightened their backs, and saluted us as we walked by.

"Look at them sir," ALI said over my coms privately.

"What about them?" I asked, talking under my breath, "They always salute us."

"They aren't saluting us, sir," ALI observed, "They are saluting *you.*"

When ALI said this, I re-examined the soldiers. He was right. Their gaze never fixed upon Sparks or any of the other council members. They all looked at me, and only resumed their tasks after I had passed, often before all of the other members were passed by.

I realized then that the Ekklesia never ordered them to salute any superiors, including me. It was a gesture of respect that they had set aside for me - the kid who had defied the organization and brought them together.

ALI continued, "No matter what happens in this meeting,"

I cut him off. "Let's deal with that after the meeting, ALI," I mumbled.

"No, sir. It can't wait," ALI retorted, "Before you walk into this meeting, you must understand. You may not always feel like you have done a great job, but you have. You have become a symbol of hope to the people of the world. You, not your father, *YOU* single handedly united the nations of the world against The Organization. *YOU* became a strategist superior to even your elder counterparts, to the point that they all became jealous of you. *YOU* earned the respect of these soldiers. You earned the legacy of your father and have already crafted one of your own."

We were in the hallway now. The hangar was far behind us, but I hadn't even noticed the transition. I had tried so hard to stay out of my emotions, and ALI was sucking me into them. He knew he was. I wished he wasn't.

"ALI, I can't even keep a handle on the council," I grumbled, "I've failed upward. I've never actually planned anything great, I've just reacted and gotten lucky. It was bound to catch up with me sometime."

"And here I thought luck had nothing to do with it," ALI used my own words against me.

It made me stop and think. I really did believe that. Luck had nothing to do with it. Even the very notion was a lie. I was down on myself. No matter what happened, I knew it wasn't chance, and I could deal with it when it happened, no matter what happened.

"Thanks ALI," I said a bit louder than I had been talking. Enough that I knew Sparks heard me.

"Anytime, sir," ALI replied, "For the nations."

This actually made me smile. It wasn't happiness. It wasn't smug. It was joy. Sparks couldn't touch that.

We had reached the door to the War Room. I heard voices on the other side. I sensed the eagerness of those behind me. I closed my eyes, took a deep breath, and exhaled a short prayer. Then, I placed my hand on the panel and opened the door.

All of the other members were already in the room. There were four people entering with me including Sparks. The other six council members were standing in their usual groups. Typically they would be talking about what they were over and our advancements on the battlefield or in science, but today, everyone was talking about me.

Slowly, they began to realize that I had arrived. They didn't end their conversations. Rather they continued, taking turns cutting their eyes or half turning to look at me.

The meeting started in five minutes. I hoped my friends were on their way. I was beginning to wish I had made sure they got off the cruiser with me. I spotted my only source of safety, Raddick, and headed toward him. He had just ended a conversation with the director of resources.

"How far out are my friends?" I asked ALI, as I made my way across the room.

"They're coming down the hallway now," ALI replied.

I figured I could make our conversation last at least that long. I walked up with a smile and extended my hand for a handshake. Raddick looked a bit startled, as though he couldn't believe I had the audacity to walk up to him. I let my hand hang in the air for a moment, but retraced it when he refused to take it. My smile quickly turned into a look of confusion.

"What's the matter General?" I asked, my offence coming through in my tone.

"It would seem we have a traitor in our midst," he scowled at me.

"Excuse me?" I asked, genuinely confused. In the moment, I truly thought he had unmasked someone in our ranks working for The

Organization. Instantly, my mind suggested Sparks, but I quickly realized he was talking about me.

"So they finally got to you too, then?" I shook my head, "I didn't think you were easily influenced.

"By rumors," Raddick corrected, "However, it is hard to deny facts."

"And those are?" I jabbed. I was becoming emotional. I took a breath and tamed myself.

"Save it for the meeting," Raddick detested. Then, as I stared at him in disbelief, he walked away.

As he walked past me, he bumped into my shoulder. It unsteadied him more than me, but he put his arm on my back as though to catch me. When he did he whispered, "Politics."

I turned to look at him, hoping to catch his gaze, but he had already turned around, headed toward another group of men.

I had no idea what to think. How was I supposed to interpret that? He, loud enough for the entire room to hear, reprimanded and practically disowned me. Then, he says that it was just politics. Was that meant to say it was all a show or was it supposed to be another sideways jab?

As I stared at him in disbelief, I noticed Blake and Bailey walk in. I felt a bit of the tension lift with every inch closer they came.

"How bad is it," Bailey asked softly.

"I think they turned Raddick against us," I said, solemnly. There was more shock than sadness at the moment.

"What?" Blake said a bit too loudly. He noticed and corrected his tone, "There's no way."

"I guess there is," I replied, "He just…"

I noticed a hush fall over the room. I stopped talking so that they wouldn't hear me, but then I became curious about what had caused it.

At first, I thought it was just an awkward lul in conversation. However, I quickly noticed a man in the tan and silver Mayan uniform standing at the door of the war room. It wasn't the Mayan representative though. It was Chief Cantun himself.

The only time he had ever been seen by the council was during the days leading up to the Battle of Big Valley. He had made quite the name for himself during that time: bold, honest, and incredibly skilled in the art of war and politics. They respected him, or at least, they feared him.

I held a bit of fear toward him in the beginning as well. He was also skeptical of me. But he gave me a chance, and we had actually grown to like one another. Still, I wasn't expecting him here.

He never paid the room a bit of attention. He looked directly at me and spoke in a demonstrative voice, "Dylan, it's good to see you."

"Good to see you too, Chief," I smiled. I really was glad to see him. I knew I had an alley in him.

"Ana sends her best," he smirked and then took his seat at the round table. This was his way of saying that Ana had told him everything and demanded that he come and help smooth things over. I was certain his presence would tame the conversation a bit, but I didn't think it would do much more than that.

The men in the room followed his example and took their seats. I walked and stood at the head of the table. Blake and Bailey on either side of me.

The room was silent. Every eye was fixed upon me. I looked at each member of the council individually, making sure to hold eye contact for a moment, starting with Blake and following all the way around the table, ending with Bailey.

"I can officially report that the mission to South Africa was a success," I said. Every eye in the room simultaneously squinted. "You are all now aware that this was a personal mission. Hunter, the young bearer that stood before you a few days ago had lost his best friend to the war. That is, until ALI located him in a ship breaking facility in South Africa. Knowing that even the most sympathetic among you would never approve that mission, I lied, and took the needed forces to save Brady Skott."

I looked at Sparks. He hadn't lost that smug smile he had worn since we left that battle.

I looked back at the group, "We found him, emaciated and dying next to a room full of other starving slaves. In the meantime, Hunter and I stumbled across a new threat. A bearer more powerful than any we have encountered. We narrowly escaped, carrying out only the primary function of this mission. I am happy to report that Brady Skott is now recovering at El Dorrado, thanks to the generosity of Chief Cantun." I looked at the chief and smiled sincerely, "I truly thank you."

The chief nodded. The council members kept looking at me. I think they must have expected me to defend myself or call out Sparks, but I didn't. Now that I was finished, I took my seat, and waited for someone else to speak.

The focus of the room had shifted from me to Sparks. I quite enjoyed seeing him scramble to find words. Unfortunately, he eventually found them.

"We can agree that it was a noble cause, but I must also assert that it was a risky and childish endeavor," he smeared, "I detected our director's deception and assembled my own team to investigate this. We flew on this mission and I regret to inform you that it was a disaster from start to finish. What I witnessed was a child out of his depth and in over his head."

He pointed his finger at me. I said nothing.

"Do you have an accusation?" General Raddick asked.

"Well, if I must be blount," Sparks acted, "After what I have witnessed over these past few days, I have been forced to accuse Director Dylan Sons of treason."

"How dare you!" Blake blurted out, standing up, "He has shown nothing but loyalty to this Ekklesia!"

"He has shown nothing but loyalty to you, and your friends," Sparks corrected, "Such loyalty that he has none left for this Ekklesia. He serves you, not the greater good."

"He has burned his life in loyalty to this Ekklesia!" Blake retorted.

"All to protect you," Sparks said, "And when those two interests collide, he'll choose you. His loyalty is not here. It's with you."

I placed my hand across Blak's chest, and he eased back down into his seat. He was burning on the inside, but we needed to let this play out. I already knew there was nothing we could say or do to stop it.

"I can attest that it seemed the director could not control even his own team," the Intelligence Director accused.

"The door of our best cruiser can attest to that," the resource director remarked.

"We simply can't afford to have a director that isn't willing to make tough decisions when it comes down to it," Sparks said.

"There's no doubt, this child, no matter how sad the story is, should have never been the subject of a search and rescue mission, especially of the caliper," another added.

"And with the emergence of this new bearer, we could have lost all of our cruisers, our men could have died, thinking they were saving the world, but in reality they were saving one boney child."

"Perhaps if Daniel had time to teach him how to lead we wouldn't be in this situation now."

"Unfortunately, a child simply cannot lead a war effort."

Their conversation continued. I stayed silent. Eventually my weary eyes locked with Chief Cantun's resolute gaze. He was seated directly across from me. He looked back at me, sort of chuckled and nodded his head. I sensed a sort of nostalgia. He didn't care what these people were saying. I sensed that he still believed in me.

"What course is there for dismissing a supreme director?"

"Our bylaws clearly state that he has total power, even over the final unanimous verdict of the council."

"There is a provision under treason that states any council member suspected of treason would be under the scrutiny of the whole council."

"Does this include the supreme director?"

"He is not excluded in the wordage, therefore he is definitionally included."

I looked at Bailey. She didn't even notice. Her fists were clenched. Her face and eyes were red. Her irises flickered with her white energy. I knew she was reading the council members' every thought. I placed my hand on her leg. She looked at me, her face twisted with anger. I just smiled back. This forced her face to loosen. Now she just looked like she was in pain as she shook her head.

"They don't understand what you've sacrificed for them," she said telepathically.

"I can't force them to understand," I thought.

"We could force them to listen," she said back. Her white energy flashed across her body.

I just shook my head 'no'. I knew what she wanted. I admit, there were times that I wanted it to. I had the power to rule with an iron fist, but if I did that, then what was the point of all this? If I were going to be the all powerful dictator, then why not just let The Organization take over?

"Do you have anything to say for yourself?" Sparks asked me. The room had become silent. They were ready to vote.

"There's nothing I could say that would change your minds," I replied, showing both of my hands in a surrendering gesture.

"Under the allegation of treason, all in favor of dismissing Dylan Sons as our leading director, please say aye," Sparks said, faking a heavy conscience.

One by one, around the table, aye, aye, aye, and on they went, even Raddick voting aye. The first "no" came from Chief Cantun. Then, aye, aye, all the way to Bailey and Blake who both gave a much more emotional, "no", disgust and near hatred in their voices.

"The council is decided," Sparks announced, "Dylan, you are dismissed effective immediately. Your clearances have been revoked. Your rank has been stripped. You are a citizen effective immediately." It must have been torture for him to contain his smile.

I stood up, "You all will never know the extent to which you have erred in your judgement," I warned. Then, I began walking away from the table. Bailey and Blake stood up and began walking behind me. The council watched. When I reached the door, I turned around.

I thought about when I had given my first speech to this council: my plea to the world to join me here. It looked a bit different then. I couldn't help but smile realizing that it had worked. I guess I already knew that. Yes, I felt betrayed and hurt and angry, but above that I felt proud. At least I had given the world a chance.

As I prepared to leave, I took a breath and smiled. I looked at the place where I had stood that day, the door to my father's office adjacent to it. That office was empty now. It made me realize this place, the Ekklesia, wasn't my father's legacy. It was empty now. I was his legacy.

I nodded in solace and then spoke to the room. "For the nations," I said. Then, I turned and walked out.

Chapter 16

My friends and I walked silently down the hall. I was headed for the hangar. My friends were just following me. I don't think they knew what to do or say. For once, Blake couldn't read me, and even though Bailey could, the increasingly wide range of emotions I was experiencing probably threw her off too.

I was hurt to my core by the betrayal of the council, even though I wasn't all that surprised. My father gave his life for those people. I sacrificed my innocence. We all gave our loyalty. Still, we were betrayed, those sacrifices cast away like they didn't even matter.

On the other hand, I felt that if they thought they could do so much better, then let them. I was tired. I never got to sleep, and when I did, I woke up already tired. It wasn't even that my body was all that tired, since the crystal largely powered that. It was my mind that was exhausted. I had felt like I was in over my head from day one. So, if they wanted to take that upon themselves, maybe I could finally rest.

Then, there was the side of me that feared what would happen in my absence. I was, at many times, the only moral compass the council had. It caused most of my strife with them. I feared what they would become without me there to guide them. I feared they could become as heartless as The Organization. The Ekklesia's soldiers certainly wouldn't mind torturing, killing, or doing even worse things to The Organization's soldiers. They hated them. Such contempt can lead even the purest of causes to evil actions.

Above all, I was disappointed in myself. I looked back and saw so many things I could have done differently to prevent this. The first was going home. That was when I truly lost the council. I just wasn't here. It didn't even work out the way I wanted. I spent most of my time running missions, and the council never saw the value of what I was doing.

I didn't know what to think or which side to give into. That would come in time. Right now, I just wanted to go home and figure out what my life was going to look like.

I knew there was only one hangar that would be open for departure (since the rest were blocked by our cruisers still). I made for the hanger with my private strike team. Former private strike team, I guess.

As we walked, Blake caught up to me and matched my stride. For a minute, he didn't say anything. I mostly ignored him. I was attempting to avoid the storm of emotion raging in my mind. I had devoted the entirety of my focus to finding a transport to take us to Tullahoma. I walked fast and stared straight ahead.

Finally, he spoke, "Dylan I,"

"Let's save it for the ride home," I cut him off.

I noticed him grit his teeth, then focus his attention straight ahead, as I was.

I could feel my emotions rising: anger welling up within me, disgust curling my lip. I fought it. I wouldn't give in, at least not until I was out of the base. I didn't even allow the slightest bit of energy to escape my body.

Finally, the light of day overpowered the fluorescent lights of the hallway. I marched into the hangar. My fleet was just as beautiful as ever, the Unitum plating glistened in the morning sun. An ambient golden glow filled the hangar, turning the white walls the same hue as the sun. Any other day, I might have admired the beauty and power of this fleet, but today I purposely ignored it.

I spotted a transport near the middle of the hangar. It was in the front of a line of about ten others, arrayed five wide. There were Stingray fighters in front of them, but they sat low to the ground, making for an easy take off.

I briskly walked toward it. The hangar had little activity if any. In fact, I didn't even see anyone until Commander Cashner stepped out from behind the row of transports. At first, he stood beside the transport's open door as though he were going to give me the customary greeting, perhaps asking what the mission I had planned was. I tried to think of a way to get the transport without having to go through the story of what had just transpired in the War Room. However, as I drew closer, I realized that wouldn't be needed.

Cashner moved himself from beside the door, to in front of the door, blocking my path.

"State your business," Cashner demanded. I knew for certain then that he knew since there wasn't a formal "Sir" or "Director" attached to his inquiry. He sounded angry. I was sure the only information given to him was that I was removed for treason, neglecting to add any other details.

"I'm taking this transport home, Cashner," I said tiredly. I was at my wits end. I just wanted him to move, so that I could go home.

"Your access to Tullahoma has been restricted," he informed me.

"What?" I barked, "Where do they expect me to go?" My anger was showing through now.

"Somewhere without a base," he replied. "There will be an escort to take you somewhere soon."

They could do a lot of things, but they would not be stopping me from returning home. "No. Cashner, move" I dismissed.

Fed up, I stepped forward and raised my arm to push him aside. When I did, I noticed him place his hand on his atom sword, preparing to draw it.

"Cashner?" I questioned. I was appalled. Similar gasps came from my friends, watching all of this from behind me. We had been through so much together. I thought he had been loyal to more than a chain of command. For him to react this way hurt me. "What are you doing?"

"I'm not letting on that transport," he affirmed.

My eyebrows narrowed, "You can't stop me." I called a bit of energy to my palms as a warning. The glow of the crystal on my chest intensified.

"Maybe, but you'll have to move me," Cashner stood his ground.

"Have it your way," I shrugged. I'd had all I could take.

Cashner drew his blade, but before the blade had even fully extended, I flicked my wrist. With that motion, my purple energy surrounded his body and yanked him out of my way. He was tossed across the hangar, landed on his back, and slid to a stop a few yards away.

I didn't even look at him as I boarded the transport. Bailey hopped in behind me, but Blake was stunned. He stood where he was staring at Cashner. The wind had been knocked out of him, but he was quickly recovering.

"Come on!" I hurried. Blake was called out of his shock, but it was too late. Cashner was already running up on him, sword drawn. Blake ran up into the transport as I jumped back out, landing where Blake had been standing.

My energy swept across my body as I yelled, "Stop!". He didn't listen. He raised his blade and prepared to swing. Why was he doing this? He knew there was no way he could win.

Just before he reached me, I lifted my hand and caused my energy to bind his body. He was frozen. Slowly, I lifted him up off the ground. I forced the blade out of his hand, and it fell to the ground. The Atom blade screamed as it cut into the metal floor before retracting into its sheath. I pulled Cashner's arms to his side and bound his legs. He screamed as he fought it.

I debated whether I should question him or just knock him unconscious and leave. I deeply wanted to know what they had told him, though it was of no consequence. They would spin whatever story they wanted to. More than that though, I just wanted to go home. I prepared to toss him aside, but the second I made the decision, the rest of the soldiers in my special unit poured out of the hallways leading to the hangar.

They ran, guns and swords drawn, across the hangar and took positions to fight. Some with swords came close to me. Others hung back and secured spots behind cover, such as crates and other ships.

I dropped cashner to the ground. He fell to his knees gasping for air (I didn't realize I was squeezing him). "This is ridiculous!" I yelled. My voice echoed through the hangar, "When did I become your enemy?"

Bailey and Blake were now standing on either side of me. Blake had drawn his staff and Bailey's energy surrounded her body. The hangar was silent. My own emotions were so high, I couldn't sense those of the others in the room, but I could see the nervousness in their faces. Their brows glistened with sweat. They didn't want to do this. If for nothing else, out of fear. They waited for one of us to make a move or for Cashner to give an order.

Cashner stood up, but before he made an order, Chief Cantun ran into the hangar. "Stop!" he yelled.

Everyone looked. He had clearly ran here from the War Room. He was winded. "Stop," he re-emphasized.

No one took their eyes off the chief as he walked over, catching his breath now that he could afford to walk. As he neared us, he began to propose a solution. "This is nonsense," he began. He looked at Cashner, "Whatever you've been told to cause this, wasn't the truth."

"I heard from Director Sparks himself," Cashner countered.

The title "Director" instead of "Captain" made me cringe.

"Then there's been a misunderstanding," Chief Cantun replied, "Dylan is not our enemy."

I allowed my energy to fade, as did Bailey. The soldiers began lowering their weapons. Blake retracted his staff, but still held it in his hand. The tension in the room lowered. The chief continued.

"Dylan isn't going to Tullahoma. He's coming to El Dorado," The Chief gave me a look that said not to argue. I didn't.

"He needs to be under Ekklesia supervision," Cashner argued.

"He will be under *MY* supervision," Chief Cantun offered, "And if the Ekklesia has a problem with that, then I will withdraw Mayan forces and let you fight The Organization on your own."

Cashner stopped pressing then. Even I wasn't sure the chief would follow up on that threat. The two forces couldn't defeat The Organization alone. Still, the threat was enough as a threat.

Cashner called off his forces. They slowly backed away from the transport as Chief Cantun, Bailey, Blake and I boarded the transport. Blake went to the cockpit, and he and ALI piloted the ship.

The engines turned on, and we quietly levitated above the other craft in the hanger. Bailey and the chief retreated inside the cabin once we were flying, but I stayed in the opening. I held onto the bar above my head and stared at the men I once led. They were so confused that they might never know the truth. It was sad.

We pulled out of the hangar and the door of the transport closed. One section of the shield had been opened for a cruiser to exit through, so we filed out with it. I'm sure air traffic control was practically screaming at us over the radio, but I don't think we ever even turned it on. I took a seat in one of the spots along the wall in front of Bailey. The chief was standing in the cockpit with Blake.

I plopped down in the seat and let my head fall back onto the headrest behind me. It wasn't padded well, so it made a banging noise when my head hit it. It didn't hurt though.

I let out a sigh and rubbed my hands across my face, eventually interlocking my fingers behind my head, holding my arms up behind me. I pulled my elbows forward, covering my ears and then leaned down until my elbows rested on my knees and my face pointed down at the floor.

I didn't really know what we were doing, but I was glad we were leaving.

I don't know how long it was before Chief Cantun came and placed his hand on my back. I raised up. As I did, his hand slid to my shoulder.

"I'm sorry, friend," he consoled.

I didn't say anything.

"I know what it's like to report to a council like that," he continued, "I'm lucky that I never had to deal with the corruption you've been faced with."

"Well, I don't report to them anymore," I found a bright side.

"But you may still have to answer to them if you choose to involve yourself from here on," the chief warned.

He was right, but I wasn't looking that far ahead right now.

"I can offer you some protection from that," the chief offered.

"How?" I asked.

"My people are prepared to house you and your friends in El Dorado," the Chief explained, "I wasn't able to talk The Council of Elders into letting your whole family come, but everyone on this ship, and everyone there can stay."

"I won't go without my family," I rejected. I knew they were already being generous, but I couldn't protect them in Tullahoma anymore.

Chief Cantun must have seen why I didn't want to go, "I can station my own troops at Tullahoma with the express purpose of looking after your family. The Ekklesia will never know, and you will be able to check in on them at any time."

The arrangement was sounding good. The chief must have put a lot of effort into this, which meant he really wanted me to say yes.

"And another thing," he continued, "I'll let you come and go as you please. You'll have no oversight as it pertains to anything outside El Dorado."

"So if I do leave and go home for a few days?" I inquired.

"No questions asked," Cantun answered.

"And if I want to run a personal mission?"

"No questions asked," Cantun replied, "But we won't protect you from outside forces. You would be on your own… Unless you're helping us of course."

I felt like that was his true motive, or at least the motive of his council (for I felt he did offer this out of genuine kindness). Having this many crystal bearers in El Dorado would give them a lot of power. Power that, in my opinion, they deserved.

I looked around the chief at Bailey. She had been listening silently, waiting for my decision. "What do you think?" I asked her.

"I think it would finally give you some rest," Bailey smiled, but it wasn't happy. It was in hope that she would be smiling for happiness soon.

I looked up at the chief. "Thank you," I wasn't sure if this was appropriate in their culture, but I wasn't thinking about it at the time. I stood up and wrapped my arms around him. It wasn't a long hug, but it was a sincere one. "Thank you for sticking up for me."

"You have the heart of a Mayan," The chief complimented, "You and all of your friends." He smiled and placed his hand back on my shoulder, "Being Mayan is more than blood. And we protect our own."

We flew silently for a while. Bailey had her head resting on the seat. Her eyes were closed. She wasn't sleeping. I didn't sense her in my mind. I wondered if she and Blake were communicating. I didn't really care, but the thought made me decide to go sit with Blake in the cockpit.

I stood up and walked over to the door, which slid open when I pressed the button on the wall panel. Blake was flying the ship manually. The Chief was sitting in the copilot's chair.

"You're showing Blake how to get to El Dorrado?" I questioned, knowing how secretive they were about its location.

"I thought you might need someone who could get you back and forth," the chief answered, "Plus, it gave Blake and I some time to chat."

I briefly wondered what they had been talking about, but didn't have the emotional energy to ask. I caught myself staring blankly through the windshield. We were above the clouds. Below us was a thick white blanket. I caught my daydreaming when the chief stood up.

"You can take my seat," he offered and patted me on the shoulder as he exited the cockpit. The door closed as he left the cockpit. I stood for just a second before building up the energy to move. I sulked around the side of the seat and plopped down. I took a deep breath and exhaled.

I realized that I wasn't even sure what had motivated me to come in here. I didn't really want to talk about anything that had happened. I didn't want to talk at all. I know Blake knew that, but he asked anyway.

"So how are you doing?"

I knew what he meant, but my heart wouldn't tell him right off. "Tired," I answered.

"You know what I mean," he pushed, "We haven't talked about... everything, for a little while. I just want to make sure you're okay."

"I'll be fine," I said plainly.

Blake took his focus off of his piloting and turned his body sideways in his seat toward me. "No, Dylan, you won't be if you keep doing this," he said, troubled.

I turned my head toward him, but not my body. "What are you talking about?" I asked wearily. He sounded a bit upset, which upset me. If he had a problem, why bring it to me now? After all this?

"You've got to stop shutting us out," he said emotionally, "You keep trying to do everything on your own."

"That's not true," I defended.

"Dlyan," Blake protested, "You've hardly talked to me for six months. When we were in Tullahoma, I hardly ever saw you. All of us hardly ever saw you."

"I was trying to run the Ekklesia," I raised my voice, the memory stirring up my anger, not with Blake, but with the Council.

"By yourself," Blake retorted.

"I was trying to give you guys a normal life!" I turned my body toward Blake now. Behind us, our ship was beginning its descent. The white blanket turned into a thick fog.

"We didn't want a normal life, we wanted you!" Blake returned my emotion. Then, his voice softened, "We wanted to be with eachother." He leaned back in his seat and looked out the windshield.

I clenched my jaw and took a deep breath. Tears welled up in my eyes. My stomach churned. "I guess I'm a failure at everything, then."

I stood up from my chair and turned to exit the cockpit. I heard Blake say my name but I ignored him. I was struggling to contain my power. It was leaking across my body, and I couldn't afford an accidental discharge on such a small space. I walked out, but the door didn't close behind me. Bailey and the chief pretended not to overhear. They glanced at me.

Blake walked out behind me, "Dylan, I didn't mean it like that," he apologised.

I spun around at him, "You..." I raised my hand, but I noticed the energy concentrating around it. I clenched my fist and forced it down at my side. I ground my teeth. I tried to calm myself. I closed my eyes and turned my head toward where I knew Chief Cantun sat, "Chief, how long until we land?" I said in a low voice.

"About five minutes," he answered softly. He stood up and walked toward the cockpit. I took a few steps, and I slowly lowered myself into his seat.

"Dylan," Blake sulked.

"Why don't you help me guide the ship in," the chief offered. Then, he guided Blake back into the cockpit, closing the door behind them.

I buried my face in my hands and squeezed my eyes shut as tightly as I could. I bit my lip. My breathing was heavy. I tried to focus on something, anything but the bad, but there was nothing good, not that I could remember. I had failed as a leader, a friend, a son, an heir, and on the list went.

I sensed Bailey walk over. She was about to place her hand on my head, but I raised my hand, without looking up, to stop her. "No"

"Dylan," she whispered. She sounded as though she were about to cry.

My hand was trembling.

I heard the sound of the air passing around the ship change. I knew we had entered the tunnel leading to El Dorado. I stood up and briskly walked past Bailey, making sure not to look at her. I slammed my hand down on the button that opened the side door of the transport. It slid open just as we entered the light of El Dorado.

Without hesitation, I jumped from the ship. I fell for only a second before releasing the build-up of energy within me in the form of two concussive blasts, one from each hand. I was launched through the air. My energy erupted across my body, so that you likely couldn't have seen any part of me through the field. A long purple streak trailed behind me.

There was a clear cut area that left a gap between the wall of the cavern and the jungle. I landed there, but the blasts that broke my fall destroyed the vegetation a few layers deep into the forest. The solid rock under my feet turned to gravel. Tiny bits of it launched into the jungle like bullets.

I let out a low growly scream of frustration. I conjured a ball of energy and thrust it at the rock wall in front of me. It exploded against the slate, but the rock was mostly unphased.

Then, I just stood there. As I heard the trees crash to the ground, and I finally had room to breathe, the edge of my emotions began to dull.

And I realized… I finally had room to breathe.

Chapter 17

I didn't stay in the jungle long. I needed to think, and I did my best thinking when I had a good view. Luckily, ALI had sent my jetpack out behind me. I put it on my back, and began to fly around the Mayan city.

The city was alive - like a hive of bees. Transports swarmed the rocky city-pillars. Lines of ships crowded the busy sky lanes (straight lines of ships traversing from place to place around the cavern). These lanes formed a web that connected the whole city.

I stayed clear of the lanes of air traffic and began flying around one of the columns. I looked closely at its design. Glass elevators traveled through tubes up and down the rocky towers. Windows and terraces dotted the structures allowing natural light and fresh air into the rooms and tunnels within.The rock shell was rigid, as though it were not carved, but formed. I knew that wasn't true from Ana's stories, so it must have just been caused by the method they used to carve out the cavern. Across every inch of extra space there were trees, vines, flowers, and bushes planted directly into the rock (likely kept alive by some advanced form of hydroponics.) It was like the forest floor extended right up to the top of the cavern.

The artificial sun shone brightly above the central column, a few miles away. It cast long shadows of the pillars. The shadows defined the unique shape of each notch and crevice.

I flew up to the very top of the pillar and found a terrace that overlooked the rest of the cavern. The terrace was a half circle protruding from the rock. There were bushes and flowering plants in planters that were built into the rock. These plants formed a border around the edge of the platform. The terrace was only a few feet from the ceiling of the cave. There probably wasn't even enough room to land a transport. The pillar itself was close to the wall of the cave, and the terrace faced outward, allowing me to see the entire capitol city.

I landed on the edge of the terrace. There was a bit of space between two bushes, so I sat there and hung my feet off the edge. I leaned back and propped myself up on my arms, looking out over the scenery. It was unlike anything I had ever seen before. I knew I would never get used to it.

I looked down at the towers next to the base of my pillar. They were mostly glass. The light of the sun reflected off of them, casting a yellow glow on part of the forest. At the edge of the city, the buildings abruptly transitioned to jungle.

The river also ran nearby my column. It came out of the cavern wall and flowed from one end of the cave to the other. I could track its gentle flow all the way to the end, where it entered back in the wall. It was wide, cutting a winding path through the heart of the jungle. Its water was a light blue-green, contrasting the deep green of the forest.

As I followed the path of the river, my eyes fell on the central pillar where I had spent my time during my last visit. It was just as busy as any other pillar, but I knew there was much more going on inside, specifically in their council chambers. I knew they must be discussing everything that had happened in the Ekklesia today. I didn't know if it was just because so much had happened, but I was emotionally numb to the thought. Mostly, I was just glad that I didn't have to be there. I wondered if that was where Blake was.

I began to think about the past year. How everything had started. I had trouble seeing how that had led me here. Physically, I knew how I got here. I understood how the decisions I had made led me to this place, but I didn't understand how I had arrived where I was at in my mind.

When I found the crystal, the one now glowing on my chest, I was curious and innocent. I was a child (though you couldn't have convinced me of that at the time). In innocence and out of necessity I used my powers to save Blake and then my family. I never chose to fight battles then, they just happened. Until my dad was killed.

I realized that I had never chosen a battle to fight until after my dad was killed. That's when I made this war my own. For the longest time, I just thought that I inherited it, but after he died, in a way, I wanted to fight. I chose to.

I also realized that when I started choosing to fight was when I started pushing people away. Blake was right about that. I didn't choose to do that though. It just happened. I know I justified leaving them out to protect them, but now, I don't think that's really what it was. I don't know what it was. I think there was a part of myself drifting away. Each time I chose a battle, that part of me became bound a little bit more. Each time I appeared before the council, it was buried a little bit deeper. It felt free now.

That felt selfish. I was still the most powerful person on Earth (maybe besides the bearer I met the other day), even if I didn't have my political power anymore. Why did it matter how I felt? The Organization had to lose. There was no other option. But why did I have to be the one with the power to do it? It wasn't fair.

I wished I could just give this stone on my chest to someone else and let them worry about saving the world. I didn't know how to do that, and my father hadn't left me the answer. Who would I give it to anyways?

I noticed the artificial sun beginning to dim. The intensity of its white glow lessened until it cast a golden hue across the cavern. It was golden hour. I was disappointed that it didn't come with a sunset. As the sun captured my attention, I noticed something else. Someone was flying on a jetpack, coming from the center pillar. I knew who it was even before he was close enough to be more than a dot.

I watched Blake fly. He flew low, not far above the forest canopy until he reached the pillar that I was on. Then, he turned up and flew toward me. He was flying so close to the pillar that I lost sight of him until he popped up in front of me. He flew behind me and landed softly. After this, he walked and silently sat down next to me.

He hadn't even sat all the way down before he started, "Dylan, I'm-"

"Don't," I said. I turned my head toward him and gestured with my hand, "Don't apologize. I'm the one who should be sorry. You were right."

"Still," Blake answered, "It was the wrong time."

"Yea, maybe," I admitted. Then, I looked back out over the landscape.

We sat for a few more minutes. Then, I found more words to say, "I didn't mean to push you away," I explained, "I guess I was just trying to keep you safe."

"You were trying to do it on your own," Blake corrected, "He kept looking forward. "I should have said something sooner, but I didn't know how… It just all built up, and I couldn't keep it in anymore today."

"Blake, we've never been like this," I pointed out, frustrated at both of us, "We've always told each other everything." I huffed, "What happened?"

He sat silently. When I was younger, even last year, I would have told you that there was nothing that could ever come between the two of us. Even now, as we were obviously farther apart, I couldn't tell you what had separated us.

"I wasn't stronger than you anymore," Blake finally said.

"What?" I asked.

"Do you remember the day we became friends?" Blake asked.

I knew exactly what he meant. We had known each other our whole lives, but there was one event that we both knew was the day our friendship began. "Kindergen, recess. I was walking by the swing," I started the story.

"And I was playing on the slide." Blake added.

"I was minding my own business when a second grader tackled me," I continued. "I scrambled away, but he tackled me again. And then his friend joined in." We found out later that they wanted to play tag (that was their story anyway). I was never informed of this at the time, and I was not enjoying the game. "You saw me, rushed down the slide, and started beating up the second graders so that I could get away."

"And until last year, that was my job," Blake said, nostalgically.

Job? What did he mean? I asked him.

"I was strong, you were smart. I protected you, you helped me in every other way. Jock and nerd. Those were our roles," Blake smiled, but he had tears welling up in his eyes. "Then, all of the sudden, you were stronger than me. Faster. Braver. You didn't need me anymore."

My face melted. My heart sank in my chest, "Blake, of course I need you," I demanded.

"I wish you did," Blake choked, trying his best to keep his composure. "Bailey took my place. You tell her things that you don't tell me."

"Blake,"

"No, it's fine. You need her," he sniffled. "But then, you saved Hunter. And I'm glad you did. Now he protects you - better than I could, and he needs you. But there's just not anything left for me." A tear slid down his cheek. "And this is selfish," he scolded himself, "It's stupid! You've got too much to worry about without me getting emotional. I…" He turned away from me and started to stand up.

My heart broke. Everything else that had been on my mind went away. I put my hand on his shoulder and pulled him back down.

"Blake," I looked directly into his red eyes, "I'm sorry. I've been losing a part of myself. I didn't realize until now, that part of me was you." I could see him grinding his teeth. I sensed his shame. "I love Bailey. I need her. She's my rock. I'll marry her when this is all over. I love her like my spouse. I love Hunter too - like a son."

I took a deep breath. I narrowed my eyes, nearly staring into Blake's soul, "But you, Blake, you are my brother. I love you like a brother. You protect me from the things I can't see. You are my voice of reason. I can beat up my own second graders now, but I need you to beat up the demons that I can't fight."

Blake was crying now. I pulled him into a tight hug, and he hugged back. I knew then that I would never care what any council ever said again. I would protect this at all costs. I wouldn't choose battles. I would only fight the ones that chose me.

A new body was forming. Not one ruled by politics or war. One ruled by love and the bond of found family. A new power.

Golden hour ended, and the light of the artificial sun went out. However, Blake was shining brighter than ever. I could sense his inner light being reignited. His shame was gone. His focus was redirected on a new purpose. So was mine.

We let go of one another and looked across the Mayan city once again. It was hard to tell that it was a cavern anymore. The darkness made it look like it went on forever. There were no stars or moon, but there was light.

The pillars were illuminated with specs of light coming from their windows. The elevator shafts were lit with white light; the tubes climbed up the pillars like bio-luminescent worms. The sky lanes were still busy, the engines of the ships flickering like lightning bugs. The cities that dotted the floor of the cave were lit with spotlights that shown up on the buildings and down on their streets.

All of this reflected off of the winding river. Its ripples distorted it, creating a dancing light show on the surface of the water.

As we looked over all of this, I felt the anxiety of the past months lifting off of my shoulders. The tension that had been strung so tightly was beginning to loosen. It almost felt strange not to have that weight.

Then, in its absence, a light hearted thought came to mind. "Did you call me a nerd?" I asked Blake.

He smiled and looked at me. "Yea," he said, as though it were obvious, "because you are one."

"And who says that?" I asked, defending myself.

"Everyone," Blake quipped, "There's nothing wrong with it though."

"Yea," I agreed, "Except I'm not a nerd,"

"Dylan," Blake leaned in, "You modified both of our weapons – in the woods."

"ALI told me how to do that," I pointed out, inadvertently knocking on my own intellect.

"And you could do it," Blake pointed out, "I didn't have a clue what he was trying to tell you."

"Well…" I had to think of a defence, "Following instructions doesn't make me a nerd."

"You read all the time, you can engineer your way out of any situation, you remember stuff the first time you hear it," Blake readied the pinnacle of his argument, "You even walk like a nerd."

I took a gasp of air and placed my hand over my chest, purposely being over dramatic, "I do not!"

"You walk like a robot." Blake moved his arms stiffly up and down. "But that's okay," he consoled. He held his gaze for a moment. Then, with rigid movements, he raised his arm and placed it on my shoulder.

We held eye contact. I tried to look irritated, and he tried to look serious, but we both failed. Our stale faces disipeared as we burst into laughter.

I couldn't remember the last time we really just laughed. It felt good.

The laughter faded though, and we found ourselves looking at the landscape once again. We smiled. Though I couldn't name very much that was going right at the moment, everything felt right again. I felt safe.

It was hard to tell how much time was passing without the moon or a constellation to look up at - to track its movement across the sky. The view of the cavern was mesmerizing, and the presence of my friend was comforting. I didn't want to move.

I was growing tired, but those two things made me want to stave off sleep. Despite my best efforts, I found myself leaning on the small tree beside me. I told myself that I was only going to lean on it.

Questions began to clutter my mind. Where were my friends? Where would we be staying? Where would we go from here?

But those questions would have to wait until morning.

Chapter 18

A warm light shown on my face. A gentle breeze freshened the stale air. I took a deep breath and opened my eyes. With my head still resting on the flimsy tree trunk I had fallen asleep on, I looked out over the cavern.

It was just as alive as it ever was, but now it was daytime again. The walls were visible and the lights had faded, absorbed by the brightness of the artificial sun.

A low rumble came from the sky lane that passed under the terrace I was perched on. Usually they were mostly quiet, but a larger transport was towing a floating platform loaded heavily with crates. The added strain on the engines made their hum audible.

I watched the transport crawl through the skyline as a traffic jam formed behind it. It made its way through the cavern and finally ducked out of the lane when it made it to the grand, central pillar. It flew down and finally dipped out of sight when it circled behind the pillar.

Having lost my entertainment, I cut my eyes to look for Blake. He lay on the ground next to me. His head rested on nothing more than the cold hard rock that the terrace was made from. He must have been exhausted.

His jetpack sat a few feet away. He probably took it off to lay down. Past it, I noticed a door. It was glass and seemed to lead into someone's living room. I didn't realize until now that we were sitting on someone's balcony.

As I looked through the glass, a small child walked up. He couldn't have been more than three. He wore a red onesie. He put a hand on the glass, and then pressed his forehead to it, peering through his own reflection. We made eye contact. I smiled. He smiled. Then, he walked away, leaving behind a handprint and a smudge where his forehead had rested.

"I wish I was that age again," I thought out loud.

"The world would be waiting for you all the same," ALI commented from my coms. He startled me a bit, "Innocence can't last forever."

I started to dwell on what he said, but I decided to cast it from my thoughts. I didn't feel like getting that deep right now.

"You've been quiet lately," I pointed out.

"It never felt appropriate for me to jump in," ALI replied, "The two of you had it under control."

"Did you realize I was drifting?" I asked.

"I knew you had more on you than you could handle," ALI answered, "I just didn't see a solution." He paused, as if to think, "I believe the one that presented itself will lead to a favorable outcome."

"I hope so," I agreed. "So, have you found anything on the copy of yourself?"

"No, sir."

"What about the overseers?" I asked, "Was there anything in Dad's notes?"

"Not that I have access to."

"What about the new bearer?"

"Nothing, sir."

"Well then, it looks like we have work to do," I said, rather chipper.

"I thought you were done with all of this?" ALI questioned.

"I'm done fighting other people's battles," I corrected, "I still want answers. I'm not just going to disappear." I looked out toward the central pillar, "I owe it at least to the Mayans to try and find some answers...and my dad"

"So we're still going on missions?" ALI asked.

"I hope not," I admitted, "But there are other ways to find answers. I have a library's worth of notebooks from my dad that I can look through. There might be something in there."

"I'm also vital to the Ekklesia," ALI added, "They can't run their bases without me, so I'll be able to keep you informed if they find anything."

"Thank you, ALI," I said. Then, I looked at Blake.

I moved my leg, nudging Blake's head slightly. He didn't jump, but his eyes opened suddenly. They darted around and stopped when they locked with my own.

"You wanna go find the others?" I asked.

"Good morning to you too," Blake greeted. He took a deep breath of air and exhaled as he sat up. His jetpack levitated and attached itself to his back.

"Good morning, Blake," ALI greeted back.

"ALI, do you know where everybody's at?" I asked, hoping to skip having to search for them.

"I can track their coms," ALI confirmed. We waited for his response. "It looks like everyone is split up," ALI informed us, "Ana is in the courtyard outside the Mayan council chambers. Hunter is in the city below us, in what I would assume is the hospital housing his friend. Bailey is…" ALI stopped talking.

I leaned in, waiting for him to finish, but then, I sensed her. She was close. She was…

SWOOSH!

Bailey shot up from underneath Blake and I, popping up just out from the edge of the terrace. Blake jumped back and let out a startled "Oh!". Sensing her had dulled the surprise.

"Goodmorning, boys," Bailey chuckled, "Blake, did I scare you?"

"No," Blake shook his head and put his hands on his hips. "Not at all."

I caught myself staring at her. The white energy that surrounded her was calming. Her blue eyes sown through even the white glow that came from them. Her hair was down which allowed it to flow out behind her. The energy mingled through it like glowing white ribbons. It made her hair as weightless as the rest of her. It drifted out behind her like a golden cape. She was beautiful.

She caught my gaze and locked eyes with me. "What is it?" she asked.

"Nothing," I smirked, "Just you."

She smiled back, and I could have sworn time stopped in its tracks.

"You're clearly feeling better," Bailey pointed out.

"I think we all are," I agreed.

She floated over and landed on the terrace with us. Blake and I stood up. "I was going to ask if you wanted to go see Hunter this morning," Bailey proposed, revealing the reason for her visit. "I went to see him last night, and he was worried about you."

I smiled, "Of course!"

"How is Brady doing?" Blake asked, rather grimly. This caused me to remember how devastated Blake had been after seeing the captives in South Africa. It was clearly still bothering him.

"Much better," Bailey confirmed, "Hunter has been able to work with the doctors to develop a new treatment using his energy." She looked at me, "You'd find it interesting."

"Well, let's go see," I prompted eagerly.

And so we did. We flew across the cavern, toward the central pillar. When we were close, we dove through the traffic of the skyline and headed for the city at the base of the pillar.

The false sun was already reflecting brightly off the surface of the ring of water surrounding the column. The water that spilled over the side caused a rainbow to form over the city.

We flew through the water. The only part of my body that was exposed was my face. The water was cold, and actually felt nice. It would have felt better if we weren't moving so fast.

Once we were through the water, we flew toward the hospital building. ALI had pointed it out to us on the flight over. All of the other buildings were made from a blu-ish glass and steel, but the hospital was white and made from concrete. It stuck out from the rest.

We landed on the street in front of the hospital. It was strange. There were no cars there or lines painted on the street. These streets were made for walking. All of the movement from one to the next was done though the lanes of traffic above, by foot, or on a floating platform (a few of which we passed while we were landing).

Being on the street was almost like being on the streets of Nashville, just without the cars. Down here, it was easy to forget that we were in a cave.

We walked though the front doors and were led by a receptionist to an elevator. This took us up 33 floors to the top of the building. The hospital was long, skinny, and slightly convex. It was simple to navigate: just one long hallway with rooms on either side. The elevator came up in the middle of this hall. We turned left, per the instructions we were given at the front desk, and soon we came to room 3324. I could sense Hunter from outside the door.

I knocked, twisted the handle, and walked in, followed by Bailey and Blake. I immediately noticed Hunter. He was sitting in a well cushioned chair beside the hospital bed; a white blanket was draped across him. It seemed like he had been asleep until I opened the door, but as soon as he saw me, his face beamed with excitement. He cast off the blanket and hopped out of his chair.

I hardly recognized the boy in the bed next to him. His skin was dark. His hair was clean. His face was full. I could actually see the outline of his body under the cover of the sheets. Even though there were I.V.'s in his arms and a feeding tube in his nose, he looked peaceful. Even as he slept, the corners of his mouth turned slightly upward.

Hunter and I walked toward each other and hugged in the center of the room. "Good to see you, kid," I said as we let go.

"I heard what happened," Hunter frowned as he consoled me. He paused and looked at me. "You don't seem that upset."

"The opposite, actually," I smiled, "I'll tell you all about it later." I turned my attention to Brady. His eyes were open now. He was observing what was going on, "I'm more concerned with meeting your friend."

Hunter turned around and smiled at Brady. "Brady, this is Dylan," he introduced.

Brady scooted up in his bed until he was in a sitting position. Then, he pulled his right hand out from under the sheets. An I.V. was taped to his arm and white ring was on his pointer finger (likely tracking his oxygen). His arm was thin and trembled slightly as he held his hand out toward me.

"I"ve heard a lot about you," Brady greeted.

I stepped forward and gently shook his hand, "It's nice to meet you, Brady." I smiled and looked into the boy's soft, brown eyes. He was smiling back at me. I sensed his pain. Emotional. Physical. But under that, I sensed a strength. It didn't come from him; it came from somewhere else. It was a spring, a well of joy inside his heart. It was nearly contagious.

I let go of his hand. It fell onto the bed. I sensed something behind me. An emotion. Relief and sadness. I turned and saw tears in Blake's eyes. In the face of guilt in leaving the others behind, I knew it must feel good to know he saved one from the base. I waved him over to us.

"This is Blake," I introduced, "He's the one who rescued you."

Brady's face lit up. "You're Blake?" he asked excitedly. He pulled his other arm out of the sheets, and instead of holding out a single hand, he held out both arms.

Blake looked confused, but then he realized, and leaned over the edge of the bed, softly hugging Brady. "Thank you for saving me," Brady sniffled.

Blake pulled away and quickly wiped his face, "Yea, kid, you're welcome."

I sensed something within Blake healed during that hug. I'm sure Bailey had a better picture of it. I could only see the hole being filled. What was being buried, I couldn't see. I just knew that it looked like we were all getting better, and for that, I was thankful.

"So how are you feeling?" I asked Brady.

He sort of laughed. "I'm… better," he settled. "Hunter's patching me up pretty good."

"Yea," I agreed, "That's a pretty cool trick he's got."

"I just wish it worked faster," Hunter added.

"I'm just glad it works," Brady corrected.

As we talked, a young nurse wearing a solid white gown walked in. She carried a cup of water in one hand and a cup of pills in the other. Her skin and hair were dark like Brady's. As a matter of fact, she could have passed as his older sister. "Time for your medicine," she spoke in a stern, yet loving, voice.

"I guess I'm not getting enough through his thing," Brady raised his right arm slightly.

"Not quite," the nurse smirked.

While she helped Brady, I looked at Hunter beside me. "You wanna go for a walk?" I asked softly, nudging his arm.

"Oh, I… Um." Hunter looked conflicted.

"I'll be fine," Brady called out just as he gulped down a pill, "You need some fresh air."

Hunter looked at Brady, then back at me. He still wasn't sure.

"I'll stay here with Brady," Blake offered, "Since he's a part of the team now, we need to get to know each other."

"Well…" Hunter thought, "I guess I could leave for a few minutes. But he has another treatment in an hour!"

"We won't be long," I promised, "We can just walk down to the river. Surely the boardwalk will have some sort of ice cream or something." I wanted to treat Hunter and get his mind off of all of this. Maybe I could even explain everything that had happened.

We took a few steps toward the door. Bailey had been standing in the doorway, silently observing what was going on. When he reached her, she smiled and gave Hunter a quick hug.

"Bring me something!" Brady called after us.

"And me!" Blake added playfully.

"We'll see what we can do," I teased.

"Do Mayans even eat sweets?" Hunter asked me.

I held my hands up. "I have no idea," I laughed.

We walked out of the room, into the hallway, boarded the elevator, and walked out through the lobby. All the way, no one said a word. Once we had exited through the sliding glass door and stepped onto the street, Hunter broke the silence.

"You said you'd tell me later?" Hunter asked.

I knew what he was asking me; I explained the past few days as best I could. Bailey helped fill in gaps where I left out details. As I told the story I began to realize how long and convoluted it was (so long, that we were able to find the only ice cream shop on the entire boardwalk). I had to pull up details from long before I met Hunter to even make it all make sense. At times, I felt like Bailey understood it all better than I did. And in reality, she probably did. She carried the knowledge of her thoughts, my thoughts, and the thoughts of those she'd shared rooms with. It was amazing how much she remembered, how many dots she was able to connect that I couldn't. Still, in the end, the story was exactly as I had lived it.

All the while, as we talked, Hunter walked between Bailey and I, listening intently. I knew he hadn't been here for most of the story. It was strange that he had become such a big part of it so quickly, but I wouldn't trade it for anything.

"So Raddick?" Hunter asked, "I still can't tell if he was playing a game or if he actually believed Sparks."

"We can't either," I huffed.

"Why do greedy people always get to be in charge of the important stuff?" Hunter asked. It was a deep question. I had to think about it, but Bailey didn't. It was as if she had been pondering the same question.

"Greedy people are the only ones who seek the power," She said, "The selfless ones don't seek power, so their voices are drowned out by the selfish."

It made sense to me. That's what happened. Sparks wasn't right. He was just louder.

"But why don't people listen to the good ones?" Hunter asked, still struggling to understand.

"Because they can't hear the good ones," Bailey said.

That felt like it was a pretty good place to end the conversation. Plus, our ice cream cones were melting.

The boardwalk ran the entire length of the city, (about five miles). The river's water came right up to the street. There wasn't even a rail. The raised wooden walkway transitioned seamlessly to the river. There was only about a six inch gap from the bottom of the walkway and the top of the water.

All along the edge were benches that looked out over the river. We found a spot and sat down to finish our treats. The false sun cast its light in front of us. It lit the walls of the cavern, but it was easy to imagine them as overcast clouds. We were away from the noise of the city. All that could be heard here was the trickle of running water, the chatter of songbirds, and the low rumble of conversing Mayans who were also enjoying the boardwalk.

I put my arm across the back of the seat, around Hunter, and rested my hand on Bailey's shoulder. She reached her arm around, resting it back across on mine.

Hunter realized what was going on, and when his cone was gone, he spread out both his arms and put one around each of us. His sticky fingers coming to rest on our shoulders.

"I love you guys," he smiled.

"We love you too," Bailey and I said just slightly out of time with one another.

Hunter kept his arms around us but leaned his head on Bailey's shoulder, which really meant he rested on my hand. "Can we stay here?"

"Well, that's the plan, buddy," I said sentimentally.

"No, I mean forever," Hunter almost whispered, "There's no war down here. Can we stay in El Dorado?"

I knew that if this war ever ended, I would want to move back to Tullahoma, but I knew what he meant. It was peaceful down here, almost like the war hadn't touched it. He just wanted to stay somewhere he didn't have to worry about loss ever again.

"We're gonna do our best," I promised, answering his true question, "But we've got to prepare like we can't"

"Why?" Hunter asked, "It's safe here."

"Because we're still at war," Bailey answered for me, "It didn't stop just because we moved underground."

"Anything can happen," I added, "So we have to be ready for anything." The good Sumaritian spoke up within me, "Plus, there may be other people who need our help. You never know."

"But we protect each other first," Bailey clarified.

"And from now on, we stick together," I said, "No matter what."

"I like that plan," Hunter agreed, shaking his head.

Bailey looked at me. We locked eyes, "I like that plan too."

Chapter 19

Over the weeks that followed, we settled in to El Dorrado. We were given suits at the top of one of the residential pillars, near the wall of the cave. Blake, Hunter and I shared the penthouse, which had a terrace like the one Blake and I had sat on the night we arrived here. Bailey lived one floor below us in her own apartment. The council was supposed to be deciding whether or not our families got to come with us. I assumed that their answer would be yes, but they needed a good excuse.

Hunter wouldn't leave Brady the night we got our homes. The next day though, Brady was showing major improvement, even walking around the halls. The doctors told us that he could come live with us by the end of the week. Between that and I'm sure, some major convincing from Bardy, Hunter finally decided to start taking some breaks. He came and stayed in our penthouse, and the next day, after Brady's healing session, I convinced Hunter to do some training with me.

It was around noon when Hunter and I walked into the training circle. I had trained on one of the more public ones when I was here last, a small ring extending from one of the pillars. However, this one was in the forest. It was bigger too. The center was clear - a dirt floor, but trees surrounded the edges. The opposents would enter from the trees. All together, this circle was about two acres, one acher clear, one acher wooded.

We stood in the center of the arena. Both of us were fully suited up. We still wore our Ekklesia armor. I had spent these past few days here modifying mine.

It was still grey, but I now allowed the armor to sit on top of the material like the Mayans did. The metal was white and accented it well. I liked how it would catch the sunlight, not the best in tactical situations, but I liked it. Plus, when was I going to be doing anything stealthily?

I had removed all of my accolades. There were no bands or insignia. All that identified me was the purple crystal on my chest. Now, rather than over my heart, I wore it in the center. It made it look more even.

I didn't carry any gear other than my staff. It hung from its end on the right side of my waste.

Hunter still wore his darker grey suit. The Mayans had given him armor to wear. The suit accepted it, but other than the green crystal, he just looked like an Ekklesia soldier. He even still had the dove pendant on his shoulder. He didn't carry any weapons. I would have to make working on his suit my next project.

"The figures made of mist represent soldiers, the robots represent…robots," I explained, "We go nonlethal on the figures, but you can have all the fun you want with the robots."

"Cool," Hunter said. A flash of his green energy fluttered across his body.

I could hear the arena powering up. Beneath our feet, gears clanked and shifted as the robots that would attack us were put into place. A magenta pulse of light ran through the arena and a shield projected up from the edges (the source blocked by the trees).

"Round 1" a woman's voice played.

There was a louder clank. I sensed a passageway opening in the woods - four of them actually, evenly spread around the arena at the edge of the shield. One robot was coming from each.

"Do you sense them?" I asked Hunter.

"I sense movement," Hunter guessed, "Something beyond the trees.

"Close your eyes and focus," I prompted, "See it in your mind."

He listened. He closed his eyes and turned toward one of the quickly approaching enemies.

"It's tall," Hunter sensed, "Taller than me. It has long arms and… a small head."

"Good," I congratulated, "Now, let's see how good you fight against it."

Hunter opened his eyes. The four robots exited the treeline simultaneously. We were surrounded.

Hunter's energy ignited across his body. I waited to engage mine. I stood with my hands behind my back, while Hunter assumed a fighting position. The robots stopped to analyze us.

"You better do something before they have too much time to think," I suggested calmly.

"Aren't you going to help?" Hunter asked.

"Not yet," I said.

Hunter stood there, taking them all in. I knew they wouldn't move until he did. Hunter took a slight step forward, then he and the robots began their attack.

All four started by firing plasma bullets from guns that were fixed to their lanky arms. Hunter raised a rectangular shield behind him while he dodged the blast from the robot in front of him. He countered with his own blast of green energy that completely dismantled the robot.

He spun around and lowered his shield, immediately sending a beam where it had been. The robot anticipated this and was able to dodge. The blast erupted on a tree a little ways into the woods. The tips of the tree's branches grew a few inches and the leaves radiated with the green glow of his energy for a few seconds.

The remaining three robots were in front of Hunter. Two laid down cover fire from the tree line while one charged at Hunter. I casually leaned back as I dodged a stray bullet.

The advancing robot drew an atom sword which hissed as it cut through the air. It reached Hunter and swung the blade. He dove to the ground.

"They use real swords?" Hunter yelled, as he conjured a blast at the robot. It hit it in the shoulder, knocking the robot on its back.

"They won't cut you," I told him, "I think."

I actually hadn't ever tested it, but surely they weren't actually dangerous. The more I thought about it, the more I actually started to realize that they may actually be on a lethal setting. I had seen these blades cut through things before. I would just have to keep a closer eye on the battle.

Hunter rolled on the ground, trying to get away from the blasts of the other two robots. "This is ridiculous!" He yelled as he raised a square shield on either side of himself. "I've survived how many battles in this war? Why can't I kill four robots?"

He condensed the energy of his shields into two balls and flung them at the two robots that were shooting at him. They tried to dodge, but Hunter had purposely aimed them at the ground so that when they exploded, the robots were sent flying into the jungle.

The injured robot was reaching him now. It used the sword in its injured arm to advance at Hunter. Hunter dodged the swings and countered with blasts of his own, but the robot blocked them with the blade. The robot wasn't giving Hunter enough time to charge up a big enough blast to overtake the blade.

I could see him getting frustrated.

"You…Stupid…Robot!" Hunter got out between dodges. When he got out his last word, he raised his hand in front of the blade. He used his energy to catch it. The blade hissed as the green energy surrounding it impeded its trajectory. The blade hovered inches away from Hunter's right hand.

In the second or two that it took the robot to figure out how to get away, Hunter had already used his free hand to conjure a larger blast. This one hit the robot in the tiny, sensor filled head. The head flew across the arena, hitting the shield, then falling into the woods.

The robot tipped backward and collapsed onto the ground. Hunter took a deep sigh. Coming though the trees were the other two robots. They had their swords drawn.

I saw Hunter look above them. His gaze was fixed on one tree that stood taller than the rest in the arena. His eyebrows scrunched as though he had an idea.

The robots reached the edge of the woods and started to sprint. Hunter held his hand out in front of him, his palm facing the sky. Then, he jerked it upward.

I saw bits of his energy manifest in the air; then, from beneath both of the robots, massive roots burst out of the ground endowed with the green energy.

They bound their feet first, causing it to fall to the ground. Then, they quickly spread across its entire body. They coiled and grew thicker as they did. I could see their robot fingers clawing at the ground, but they were completely overpowered.

"Woa!" Hunter laughed, "I did not think that was going to work."

He looked back at me smiling, waiting for my approval. I smiled back. "Finish them off."

Hunter turned back to his opponents, lifted both hands, and conjured a blast for each of them. The blast erupted on the ground and destroyed both the roots and the robots.

"Round one complete," the automated woman's voice said.

Hunter walked back to me. "That was harder than I thought it was gonna be."

"Well, I did turn the difficulty up to 'expert'," I admitted.

"Why did you do that?" Hunter asked, almost offended.

"You're a bearer," I explained, "That gives you an advantage."

Hunter thought for a moment and then seemed to agree.

"I'm not sure I can handle much more than that," he admitted.

"Round two," The woman's voice mocked him.

"I guess we'll find out," I chuckled.

Hunter readied himself again. "Just don't let them cut me in half," Hunter requested. He was only sort of joking.

The clanking began again, and I sensed the new attackers entering at the outskirts of the arena.

"There are those mist things this time," Hunter sensed.

"Make sure you don't hit them too hard," I coached.

"I guess that depends on how hard they hit me," Hunter balled his fists and called his energy back to him.

A blast came from the trees. It was a ball of the black mist used to create the figures. They didn't use real weapons. What they used still hurt though.

The shot whizzed past Hunter and hit the dirt behind him, kicking up a cloud of dust. Three more followed it. Hunter raised his shield to intercept them.

All of the enemies were coming from one direction this time. I sensed seven of the figures. No robots yet.

Hunter looked back at me. "I think I'm going to go into the trees for cover," he proposed.

"Go for it," I said nonchalantly. I hadn't moved from my first position: feet apart, hands behind my back, back straight. I watched intently, and he lowered his shield and ran into the jungle. He quickly disappeared into the foliage.

I knew he was safe in the arena (at least when the robots weren't in here), so I forced my senses to be restrained. I only used my natural senses.

For a while, there was nothing. Just the gentle hum of the shield and the occasional chirping of a bird that had become trapped inside. There was the sound of blasts coming from the figures. I knew it was them because it was a low frequency thump. Following this, there was a couple of seconds of silence, followed by more blasts.

Then, there was a more energetic blast. I saw green energy travel up a tree. There was another larger blast, then a thud and an "Oof".

A branch began to break and trees shook. All of the sudden, I saw Hunter break through the treeline, flying backward through the air. He landed on his back in front of me, a bit of his green energy going before him to cushion his fall (an instinct common among every known bearer). He flipped over himself and slid to a stop just in front of me.

"Ugh," he groaned. He struggled for his breath.

"Looks like they knocked the wind out of you," I said, cutting my eyes down at him, but not looking down fully.

"...Yea" he choked.

I sensed three remaining opponents. They were nearing the edge of the treeline. Two were coming in with melee weapons. One was taking a position behind a tree, ready to lay down cover for the other two.

Hunter slowly pushed himself to his feet, and stumbled into a fighting position. "I didn't think they were going to be that strong," Hunter protested.

"I think ALI cranked up the difficulty to ten for these too," I answered.

"I did, indeed," ALI commented.

"You wanna help me like you help Dylan?" Hunter requested.

"I believe you can handle these on your own, sir," ALI declined.

"I wish I had my ALI back," Hunter grumbled.

The two attackers emerged from the trees. Hunter nodded his head, causing the grey metal helmet to form from the ring around his collar. He charged at his opponents.

"We ever hear anything else on that copy?" I asked ALI while Hunter fought.

"Perhaps," ALI alluded, "I was able to find the break in my code from which the copy was created. I've been working on a way to track it. I could still be out there."

I nodded, taking in the information, "I hope you are. Or, it is." I wasn't sure how to refer to the copy, "It would be good for Hunter to have a friend like you."

"Perhaps he, the copy, and Brady could be like our original little team," ALI suggested.

I smiled nostalgically, "I think that would be nice."

I wasn't really paying attention to Hunter until he came tumbling back at my feet. He secured himself quickly and raised a shield in front of him. It blocked both a blast and a swing from the fake sword of the mist figure. Hunter pushed the shield forward and the attacker back.

"They'll need a lot of training first," I observed.

"Well, sir, they weren't rigorously trained by their father from the time they were born," ALI pointed out.

"This is true," I agreed, "Maybe he just needs some way to connect something he loved when he was young, with battle." I was thinking out loud. I had quickly been able to transfer over my martial arts training to the gadgets and weapons of this war because they were so similar. Maybe Hunter just needed a little extra help making the connection.

"Hey, Hunter!" I called.

He dodged the swing of one of the attackers, then blasted it backwards. The attacker didn't dissolve, so the hit must not have been hard enough.

"I'm a little busy," Hunter said between heavy breathing.

"Did you ever play any sports or anything when you were younger?" I asked anyway.

"Umm, yea," He dodged a blast from the treeline and sent his own blast as a response, "Baseball." He continued fighting the other attacker and finally got the upper hand. He called his energy to his fist and punched the figure in the face. The green energy erupted from the punch and the figure faded. The other one was just reaching him.

"Were you any good?" I asked.

"Little," dodge, "League," punch, "State," dodge, "Champs" BLAST! A beam of energy sliced through the figure and it dissolved.

"Ooo," I scrunched up my face as I imagined what would have happened to a real soldier, "Um, You're supposed to try not to kill them."

Hunter turned around, sucking air through his teeth, "Sorry, I got a little carried away."

I was going to use this as a teaching moment, but the other figure was coming out of the trees, so Hunter had to focus on him. He used the same trick he had used on the robots to bind the figure, only this time the roots were aided by low hanging tree branches that bound the arms, while the roots bound the feet. Once he was secure, the figure faded.

"He only killed one of them," ALI read the stats, "The rest had a 98% chance of survival."

"Not bad," I brought my arms to the front of my body and crossed them.

"I was better at baseball," Hunter said out of breath.

I was going to continue our conversation about baseball, but I sensed something. I looked up and saw a magenta speck flying through the sky. It was Ana, and she wasn't slowing down.

Hunter tracked my gaze. We both decided at about the same moment that we needed to move. We scrambled backwards just as Ana burst, feet first, though the small shield protecting the dome.

She landed in the center hardly needing to slow herself. The shield and her jetpack had done most of that for her. She slammed into the ground and the energy that cushioned here pushed dust out in every direction. I turned my face as the particles flew by. Her energy quickly faded, as did the dust cloud, revealing her smile.

"Training interrupted," the woman's voice played.

"How was your date?" I asked, knowing that was Blake's plan for the day.

"It was good," Ana replied, "I came to see how the lesson was going?"

"Good," I said.

"Terrable," Hunter disagreed.

Ana laughed, "Is your Aj Kanul giving you trouble?"

"Well, he's just making it too hard," Hunter complained.

"I'm making you tougher," I countered.

Ana's smile turned into a smirk. "Maybe I should give the teacher a lesson," she suggested.

I head out my arms in an open gesture, "There's nothing left for you to teach me, old lady," I winked. This was an inside joke since she was a few years older than the rest of us.

"You're never too smart to learn." Ana called her magenta energy back across her body.

I smiled and called for mine. "Just like old times," I reminisced as we squared up. We walked in a circle around the arena.

"It's been a while," Ana agreed, "I hope you're not rusty."

"Rusty? Ha!" I taunted, "I'll take it easy on you."

Ana smiled. I sensed she was thinking of something distant, a memory. I wondered what it was, but wasn't given the chance to think about it.

Pillars of her energy began to shoot up from the ground around me. I flipped and dodged out of their way before using my own energy to sweep the ground around me. The purple energy ran along the ground, cutting off the stalks. The energy dissipated.

I had learned over our past sparring sessions that her energy was heavy in a way. It could form solid structure, but they had to be connected to Ana, and often, they had to be connected to the ground.

"You'll have to try harder than that," I teased. Then, I sent two blasts of energy toward her. She dodged both. After this, I spotted two large rocks near the treeline. I lifted them with my energy and threw them at her, one at a time.

A column of her energy rose from the ground in front of her and smashed through the first rock, turning it to gravel. Then, she conjured a beam of energy to do the same to the second.

She turned at me and cast that same beam, but I blocked it with a shield. We stood for a second, waiting for the other to think of some new move to try. We locked eyes, holding a smoldering glare. Her eyes squinted, then she turned and ran away into the forest.

I assumed she was going there for cover, but I still sprinted after her. I thought I lost her for a moment when we entered the trees, but I locked onto her magenta glow. She was running a few yards ahead of me.

Once we were out of the arena, the woods grew thick, but never too thick to run through. She was fast, faster than I remembered, but I kept up, keeping her glow just in view.

Finally, I saw her glow enter a clearing. I anticipated an ambush, but ran after her anyway. I broke through the trees, but I instantly skidded to a stop. It wasn't a clearing at all. It was the river, and I almost fell in. I still saw that magenta glow that I had been following. It was all the way across the river.

"How did she get over there so fast?" I thought. I knew she had a jetpack, but I wasn't that far behind. I thought about blasting myself across, but I didn't want to land in the water.

"Hey! No fair!" I called across the river, "I don't have my jetpack on!"

As I squinted across the wide open water, I noticed the glow fade. *What?*

Suddenly, I sensed something behind me, but it was too late. I couldn't even turn around before I was hammered in the back with pink energy. I was knocked off the bank and splashed into the river. The second I fell in, I felt my energy disburse into the water.

I popped up powerless, staring at the gleaming face of the winner of this sparring session.

"Got you," she taunted.

"Yea, yea," I waded out of the water and climbed up onto the bank, "When's the last time you won one of these?"

"When's the last time we had one of these?" Ana countered, "Maybe you're the one who's rusty."

"Well, I guess I've gotta let you win one every once in a while," I tried to make an excuse, "Plus, you live here. I didn't know we were so close to the river."

"I'm just hearing excuses," Ana flipped her perfectly dry hair.

"Yes," I admitted, "You are," then I shook my head of wet curly hair. The drops flew over onto Ana.

"Eww! Dylan," She complained.

I laughed.

We walked back though the jungle we had just ran through. Ana wasn't much of a talker, but about half way through, she spoke up.

"Can I give you some advice, Aj Kanul?" she asked.

I sensed that she was being sincere and not offering another playful jab, so I returned her sincerity. "Sure."

"Start slow with the kid," Ana suggested, "Let him have some wins in the beginning."

"I'm not trying to be too hard on him," I admitted, "I just don't want him to get hurt in a battle. He's got to know, and fast."

"I understand," Ana agreed. She trailed off a bit as she prepared her next statement. "My brother was supposed to be the bearer of this crystal. He was trained from the time he was born. I wasn't."

I had never heard this part of her story. I knew how private she was, even with Blake. I knew what she was revealing was a privilege to hear, so I listened all the more.

"He was killed on one of his first field missions," she said. She sounded sad, but resolved.

"I didn't know that," I said solemnly.

"It was supposed to be easy, but they ran into trouble," Ana explained.

Her description was vague, but I could only think of one thing that would give a highly trained bearer trouble. "The Parasite?" I inferred.

"Yes," Ana confirmed, "That's part of the reason why we joined your Ekklesia, but that's not the point." She redirected the conversation, "After that, my father trained me day and night. He wasn't, and still isn't in good enough health to wield the crystal anymore. He needed a successor. He pushed me hard. Too hard. It drove a wedge between us, and I almost gave up."

I thought about what she was saying. I hadn't even considered that I would be pushing Hunter too hard. I really hadn't even started his training yet, but when I reviewed my plans, I saw how I could do that.

"I just wanted to talk to you about that before you got started too far," Ana said, "You're a good teacher. Really, you're a father to him. I don't want you to get carried away."

"Thank you," I said genuinely, "I need all the advice I can get. I have no clue what I'm doing."

"You'll figure it out," she patted my shoulder, "The two of you can learn together."

We walked out of the treeline together. Hunter was sitting crisscross in the center of the arena until he saw us. When he did, she sprang up. "Who won?" he asked enthusiastically. Then, tilted his head, "Why are you wet?"

"Because she won," I rolled my eyes and grinned.

"I had to knock him down a notch," Ana teased.

"Mission accomplished," I sulked.

"So, I meant to tell you," Ana started, "I didn't just come here to kick Dylan's butt."

"Hey!" I interjected.

"I actually came here because Blake and I went to see Brady and they're releasing him from the hospital."

"Really!" Hunter almost screamed.

Ana and I both smiled at his contagious excitement.

"Yes," Ana grinned, "They're taking him to your penthouse now. Blake's with him."

Hunter looked at me with near 'puppy dog eyes', "Can we go meet them there?"

"How could I say no?" I responded, "Of course!"

"ALI, can you get our jetpacks?" Hunter requested.

"They're already on their way," ALI said.

As soon as he did, I sensed them coming over the treeline. The light of the false sun reflecting off of them made them visible from a good distance. The second they reached us and were secured to our backs, we flew off.

Hunter led the way.

Chapter 20

We landed on the terrace of our penthouse. The air at this height was a few degrees warmer than the forest we had just come from. It was still comfortable though.

The glass door to the living room was open. Inside was a couch to the right and a recliner. The Mayans didn't have T.V. Instead, their living rooms were centered around the window with the best view.

Past this was a kitchen with a bar that separated it from the dining area. Everything here was made of rock and wood. The floor was cut straight from the rock of the pillar and polished. The bar was a part of this same rock and topped with a dark, glossy wood. The barstools and dining set matched this wood. The living room had a coffee table that rose from the rock as well.

Past the dining set was a rock staircase that led to the bedrooms. They were directly to the right of the door leading to the hallway outside our apartment.

Hunter, Ana, and I walked inside. The house was empty.

"I thought you said they were here?" Hunter questioned.

"Well, they were on their way," Ana tucked her black hair behind her ear.

As if to add to their conversation, there was a knock at the door. I sensed Blake. I lifted my hand and used my powers to twist the knob. Then, I pulled the door open.

Blake stood on the other side. He was hunched over a bit and held a key where the lock had been before I opened the door. He straightened up and smiled at us.

"I picked up a homeless guy," Blake joked, "I hope you don't mind." He stepped into the doorway and held his hand just out of view into the hallway.

I heard a faint, "I've got it," and Blake retracted his hand.

Finally, Brady came into view. He was taking cautious steps. His balance still wasn't the best, but he was walking without any assistance now. He walked through the doorway, placing his hand on Blake's shoulder to steady himself.

"Hey, everybody," Brady greeted. He looked weak, but his voice was strong.

Hunter responded by bounding over the sofa and putting his arm around Brady. This functioned as both a hug and a help. They walked together into the living room. Blake followed behind them.

"How does it feel to be a free man?" I asked.

"Almost as good as it felt being freed the first time," Brady said. Everything he said came out with a grateful tone. I could hardly imagine how good he must feel, maybe not physically, but emotionally. Just knowing that he didn't have to worry. Knowing that he had people again. Still, I was amazed at his resolve.

Hunter and Brady sat down on the couch together. Ana leaned against one of the windows. Blake pulled up a stool from the bar. I sat down in the recliner.

"The doctors told us that this was the fastest they had ever seen an emaciated victim recover," Blake informed us.

"That's all thanks to Hunter," Brady thanked. He looked at Hunter, "You're still supposed to do whatever it is you do twice a day."

"I'll give you as much energy as you want," Hunter offered.

"Well, they said not too much," Brady corrected.

"ALI can help with the dosage," I told them. A white mist came from my puck and ALI's emblem appeared beside me.

"I can, indeed," ALI agreed. "Did the doctors take any kinds of readings on your energy?"

"All kinds," Hunter answered, "I'm sure you can get them if you ask."

"I will add it to the list," ALI replied.

"You're getting a pretty comprehensive list of our powers," I pointed out, "We need to look at getting your hardware transferred from the mountain base to here."

"That would be difficult," ALI admitted, "My data core is powered by the crystal there."

"Those stationary electron entanglers are obsolete," Ana said, "My crystal powers everything here, and I still wear it on my chest. I'll check into upgrading the mountain base so that you can have a mobile power source."

"That could work," ALI agreed.

"I think it sounds like a great idea," Brady added. We all looked at him seriously, but he started to laugh. "Yea, I have no idea what you guys are talking about."

Everyone laughed. Ana smiled.

"So, Hunter says he used to play baseball," I inquired, changing the subject for Brady's sake, "Did you play with him?"

"Oh, yea," Brady said, "That's basically all we ever did."

"That and camping," Hunter added. His eyes glossed over as he recalled his good memories.

"We were pretty good too," Brady added, "At both."

"We might have to get out and play a game or two one day," I suggested.

"There's something we could beat him at," Blake jabbed.

"I haven't played since I got my powers," I pointed out.

"Well, that's not fair," Blake complained, "You would have to turn those off or something."

"I'm sure we could figure something out," I agreed. I looked at Ana, "Where's a good spot to play baseball around here?"

"That depends," Ana folded her arms, "What's baseball?"

"You people don't have baseball?" Brady questioned. The entire room held the same shock

"I didn't realize you all were that crazy," Hunter tacked on.

"We have Pitz ball," Ana countered.

"Huh?" Hunter commented.

"She took me to see one of these one time," Blake spoke up, "They have two teams and they have to use their hips to bounce the ball through a stone hoop."

"That sounds…fun…I guess," Hunter replied.

"It's really hard to master," Ana admitted, "And usually only the men play."

"Well, only men play baseball too," Hunter explained, "But we have a girl version called softball. That's the kind guys and girls play together."

"And why do the girls need the softer ball?" Ana sounded a bit offended.

"Oh, trust me," I interjected, "There's nothing soft about that ball."

"Then they should give it a new name," Ana observed.

"I've always thought the same thing," ALI agreed.

Just then, there was another knock at the door. Everyone turned to look.

"Come in," I offered.

The door opened. It was Chief Cantun.

"Hey, Dad," Ana greeted, surprised.

"Chief!" I welcomed, "What brings you by?"

"I just wanted to see how everyone was settling in," he smiled. I sensed deception, but I didn't call him out on it.

"Good!"

"Oh, it's great."

"You couldn't have given us a better view!"

"How about Bailey?" the chief asked, "Where is she?"

"She wasn't feeling well today," I explained, "She gets migraines every once in a while."

"Oh, well, I hope she gets to feeling better soon," Chief Cantun consoled, "You know, we have had some very promising research regarding migraines. She should give one of our neuro-doctors a visit."

"I was telling her about that yesterday," Ana told him, "I think she has an appointment tomorrow."

Bailey had told me about her appointment this morning before I left to get Hunter. I had hoped she would go with us training today, but these things really put her under. Today's was a pretty bad one, according to her. Which, if she was saying it was bad, then it was pretty bad. I was supposed to go see her after this.

"Well, I hope they can do some good for her," the chief wished.

There were a few seconds of awkward silence. Then, the chief spoke again, "I wish I didn't come with business, but I did."

"What's the problem?" I asked. I held off my anxiety. Since the chief seemed to be in a good mood, I hoped that it wasn't anything tragic.

"Well, I wouldn't call it a problem," the chief alluded.

"Can I join?" a tired voice cut in.

Everyone turned around again. This time, it was Bailey at the door.

"Of course!" the chief said, "We were just talking about you."

"All good things, I hope," Bailey commented as she walked over. Her hair was a bit frizzy and she held her head down. I could tell the migraine wasn't gone. She must have gotten word that Brady was coming here and forced herself out of bed.

I stood up and offered her my chair. As she prepared to sit down, I spoke softly, "Any better?"

"I'll be fine," she brushed off. She sat down, and I sat on the cushioned arm of the seat.

I hated these things for her. I had prayed they would go away, but I guess that wasn't in the cards for us right now.

"So," the chief continued in his proper military countenance, "The Council of Elders has sent me with a request."

"I'm not sure we're up for any more councils right now," I declined, a bit rudely in hindsight.

"Well, I think you'll want to hear what they have to say," the chief urged. My comment was a bit harsh. I guess I had a bit of reluctance on this topic.

I nodded in acceptance and apology. He continued.

"They acknowledge that the people in this room are among the most powerful on Earth. They also acknowledge that you have sacrificed much to protect Earth."

Everyone listened intently and nodded in agreement.

"You work well as a team, and you can do a lot of good," He paused and looked directly at me, "When you're unrestricted and left to your own devices."

I tilted my head a bit as I tried to figure out what he was saying.

"They would like to offer you all a position as a proxy of El Dorado," he proposed, " You would be a Protectorate, not under our control, but under our express protection. We would handle the military and politics - and any necessary interactions with the Ekklesia. You would work as a team to handle... the things you want to handle."

We all began looking at each other. Ana was just as shocked as the rest of us. Although, I think more than anything, we were all just confused.

"So you're proposing that we do whatever we want?" I asked.

"Well, within reason," The chief answered, "As long as you don't go out attacking any of our own forces or something crazy."

"You know we wouldn't do that," Blake defended.

"Exactly," the chief pointed, "That's why we can give you full, unsupervised discretion."

"And you'll be able to stay in with the Ekklesia if we do something they don't like, because you can claim that you didn't know," Ana reasoned.

"Exactly."

"What's in it for El Dorrado?" I asked.

"Leaverage," The Chief explained, "We want you to stay. As long as you're here, we can keep Sparks from doing anything rash. He needs our support while the Organization is here. We don't want another war when the Organization falls."

"Why would we run any missions when we could just stay safe by staying here," Hunter proposed.

"Well, of course, you could do that, but with the full resources of El Dorado in your hands, I think you'll find some worth your time," the chief persuaded.

"Like what?" I asked.

"Like taking supplies to places under Organization control that need them," The chief looked at Blake now, "Like South Africa."

Blake's eyes widened and his mouth nearly hung open.

"Yes, son, there are survivors," the chief gestured to Hunter, "And thanks to him, we can treat any you can pull out."

I knew that from this point on, Blake was sold. Hunter would be sold too with some convincing from Brady.

"I still don't understand why," I pointed out.

The chief took a deep breath, "There are a few reasons. Well, besides the ones I named off. One of those is that we need both The Organization and The Ekklesia to see that you are all still active. Another reason is…" The chief caught himself as though he had to decide whether or not to say what he was going to say. He decided to say it, "Another reason is that we've found the capital of The Organization."

All of us, except for Brady, scooted to the edge of our seat in shock. We knew that this would mean the end of the war. There was both an excitement and an unease at that thought. The room was totally silent. If he didn't have our attention before, he had it now.

"How?" Bailey breathed.

"Well, as you all know, all of the satellites went down at the onset of the war. That's why we couldn't scan for it," the chief explained, "Except, we could. We started sending out stealth fighters across the globe to map it. The Organization couldn't detect them. It took a while, but we just located it about a week ago."

I felt my heart begin to flutter. So many thoughts were coming to my mind. This would certainly mean death. I wanted no part of that. But it would also mean the end of this war. If we failed to take the capital, it was safe to say this war was over, for now anyway. If we took it, it was safe to say the war was over. Only one end was favorable, and it would come with sacrifice.

"I actually wasn't at your base to see you removed," The chief continued, "I was there to present what I had found. Your political issues changed that."

"This war would be over if it wasn't for Sparks," Blake growled.

"Nevertheless, we do have the coordinates. It's a walled city on a Mediterranean island in Greece. They're calling it Jericho," The captain explained.

"Hopefully it ends like the last Jericho," I quipped.

"To ensure that, we need El Dorrado to have the final say in how that battle goes down," The Chief continued, "Even if you don't fight in that battle, and we are not asking you to, having your displayed loyalty will give us the advantage."

The Chief had finished his pitch and everyone in the room looked at me. I looked back at everyone. Then, I looked at the chief, "Let us talk about it," I offered.

"You can come find me when you have an answer," the chief agreed, "Take all the time you need." He tilted his head from side to side, "Not too much time though. I'd like to end this war."

"We do too," I assured him.

Then, he nodded, raised his hand, and headed for the door. He turned back and grabbed the door to close it. As he did he said, "For the nations," and he closed it behind him.

Everyone's attention turned back to me. I looked at the ground. I had to gather my words. I felt like the decision would be unanimous, but I didn't want there to be any reluctance.

I looked up, "What to y'all think?"

"I think we have to at least run the aid to the people who need it," Blake said immediately.

"I know I'm new, but I like that idea," Brady added, "Not sure if I get a vote though."

"Of course you get a vote," I told him, "You're a part of the family now."

"I'm with my dad on this one," Ana said, "For more than just the aid. I'll run missions for my people regardless."

"Might as well take us along for the ride," Blake said.

"What about you ALI?" I looked to the orb of white mist that still floated to my right. "I could use your critical thinking on this one."

"Everything appears to be well thought out," ALI observed, "The risk variables are high, as always, but I believe this is the most logical decision on every measurable front."

"Bailey?" I asked. I looked down at her, "What do you think?"

She had her arm propped up on the chair and was rubbing her forehead. "It's kind of hard to think right now," Bailey tried to joke, "But I'm in. It sounds like a good deal, and they need us."

"And it sounds like we could stop whenever we want to," Blake added, "Everything would finally be up to us."

"If it ever wasn't up to us, that would be the deal breaker," I tacked on. "What about you Hunter? You're the last one."

"I think I would be out voted if I said no," He sulked.

"That's not how this works," I retorted, "Either we're all in, or we're all out."

Hunter took a long look and Brady. He looked back with hopeful eyes, but whispered, “It's up to you.” Hunter closed his eyes and turned his head down. I could sense his conflict - his fear. Finally, he looked up.

“Okay,” he agreed. He paused. Then, he allowed his smile to return, “But we're gonna need a name.”

This lighted the mood (as Hunter always seemed to be able to do). Everyone smiled, our fear faded to resolve. We would give it a chance.

“Like a band?” Brady laughed.

“No,” Hunter corrected, “Like a team. Like baseball.”

“The Flying five!” Blake threw out.

“We can't all fly,” Hunter pointed out.

“And there are six of us,” Ana chuckled.

“Oh…right,” Blake looked down.

“The Sleepy Six, is probably closer to the truth most days,” Bailey joked, leaning back in her chair.

Everyone giggled. Then, Brady spoke, “What about what that guy called us?” he suggested. “The pro…Protectors?”

“Protectorate,” Ana corrected.

“Protectorate!” Brady confirmed, “That's it.”

The group began to nod and they mulled the name over in their heads. Protectorate…Protectorate…

“I think it has a nice ring to it,” Blake complimented.

“I like it,” Bailey agreed.

“I think it is a charming name,” ALI added.

“Anyone opposed?” I asked, “Any other ideas?”

The room was silent. It seemed like everyone had settled on the name.

“In that case, welcome to the Protectorate!”

Part 6: Victory and Defeat

"I see, in your victory, a grave defeat"
-Darren Flyhe

Chapter 21

The light hum of the engines filled the cabin of the Mayan stealth ship, but our happy conversations drowned it out.

"We would have won if Dylan wasn't cheating," Hunter wined.

"Cheating? Me?" I placed my hand over my heart, " I would never."

"I watched the ball curve right into your glove," Blake called me out, "And I was on your team." He said it as if that claim made his statement more credible.

I moved my hand to the back of my neck, "It was…the wind."

We all started laughing. I think if he had learned one thing today, it was that we were all equally competitive. Which worked quite well. That is, when we were on the same team. When we split up to play baseball, well, that's another story.

"This one has quite the arm though, doesn't he," I put my arm around Brady, changing the subject from me and my…special tactics.

Brady was wearing a uniform I had modified just for him. It was tan, the color of the Mayan uniform, and had the armor on the outside. Really, it looked just like theirs. What I had changed was the helmet. I wanted his to match the rest of ours, which were Ekklesia issued.

Brady smiled and put his arm around me.

"Don't let his flattery fool you," Hunter warned, lightheartedly.

I took my arm back to myself and held them out in surrender. "Okay, okay, I cheated. Now, don't we have a mission to worry about."

On cue, ALI came over our coms, "Preparing to descend over our target. Welcome to Spain!"

"Saved by the bell," Bailey commented.

"I've never been to Spain," Hunter changed the subject.

"I don't think any of us have," Blake added.

"I've always heard it was really pretty," Brady said, "My mom, umm," he stumbled over his words, "My mom went there when she was younger."

I guess we all still carried scars – some still fresher than others.

"Well, we're low enough to find out for ourselves," Hunter slapped Brady on the back to distract him. Then, he walked behind him and pressed a button on the wall panel. The door of the ship slid open.

Wind rushed into the cabin. It was a pleasant temperature and dry. We were only a few hundred feet off the ground now. The six of us crowded around the opening to take in the view.

We were flying over rural farm land: vineyards planted into rolling hills. Houses that looked like castles (and what might have really been old castles) towered over fields and tiny towns. It was nothing like the desert landscapes or fire charred remains of cities we were used to visiting in the month that we had been running supplies. However, these people weren't struggling with food like those places. Here, the war had polluted their water supply. Perhaps grape juice and wine could have sustained them, but the contaminants polluted the irrigation. Using it on the vineyard would have made the grapes toxic. We were bringing them purifiers.

Our target was a small town called Haro, where we had an informant. He and his small crew would distribute the technology across all of Spain as well as word of who was delivering it in hopes of gaining underground support.

Haro came into view as ALI, our pilot, circled us around to the landing zone. The city itself was on a hilltop. All of the buildings were stone and smushed so close together you could easily jump from rooftop to rooftop if you wanted to.

In the center was a massive building with a bit more space around it. It looked like an old cathedral. There was a road that led to the city, visible across the green planes. However, the streets of the city were so close together, I'm not sure where the cars would go when they got there. I don't think there was even enough room for one on the narrow pathways. Thankfully though, there was just enough room to park our ship. The two following us would have to park in one of the fields adjacent to the city.

As we neared the landing zone, I couldn't tell if it had once been a lush garden or a parking lot, but whatever it was, was destroyed and overgrown with weeds.

ALI sat the ship down, and we all immediately got out. Walking to meet us was a man. He was the only person in sight. He wore a blue checkered button up shirt and brown jeans. His sleeves were long, but rolled to just below his elbows. His hair was salt and pepper and combed straight back. He looked to be in his fifties.

"Any luck with the corn this year?" I asked the code phrase, making sure this was our allie.

"Oh, it's been fine," the man put one hand on his hip, "But in my experience, it's never luck."

I smiled, and he smiled back. I walked briskly to meet him and extended my hand. "I'm Dylan Vale"

"Manuel Perez," he introduced. I kept my senses keen. I didn't sense any deception. I felt that we were safe. "I'm sure glad to see you." His accent was thick, but he was easy to understand.

Ana stepped up from behind me, "My father sends his best, Manuel."

"Ana?" Manuel's face lit up, "Is that you?" He walked over, took her by the hands, and kissed her on the cheek. "Oh, you're so grown up." He tilted his head and spied the crystal on her chest, "And wearing the crystal well. Your brother would be proud."

"Do you two know each other?" I asked, interrupting the sentimental moment. This was a detail I was not privy to.

"Ana wouldn't remember me," Manuel explained, "She was about this big [He moved his arms into a cradling position] the last time I saw her. But I knew her brother and her father."

"I've only heard the stories," Ana added, a bit nostalgically.

"Those days live only in my memory now," Manuel sighed. He frowned. A defeated look took over his countenance, "We hoped this day wouldn't come in our lifetimes... Selfish, isn't it?"

His words sat in the air for a moment. No one was sure how to respond. That is, until Brady spoke up.

"I don't think so," Brady consoled, "We didn't want it either."

"But we got it," I hurried, "And if we stay too long, we'll be detected by a patrol unit."

"Of course," Manuel shook himself back to the present, "I'll send my people to load up the purifiers."

"We'll help," I offered, "We've only got half an hour."

"You can send your friends, but I was hoping to talk with you for a moment," Manuel offered, "I have some information to send back with you, and I need it personally delivered."

I turned back to my friends. "I'll catch up," I said.

The group agreed and headed to their job. All except for Hunter. "We don't go places alone," he reminded me. This was a rule we had established for running missions. I nodded, and he joined. I liked having him at my side anyway..

Manuel looked uneasy. "I would rather us be alone."

"He's my student," I told him. I knew if he had any connection to the Mayans, he would understand this significance.

"Oh, my apologies, Aj Kanul," He gave a slight bow and extended his hand toward Hunter, "Join us."

We followed Manuel up a set of stairs that led to the cathedral. It had massive wooden doors and walls made of handcut stone, each one stacked and mortared in a way that made them look like they naturally fit together. It was as if each stone had been formed by God himself to fit in its spot.

The doors were open and led to a gaping, round room with a domed ceiling, the paintings of which could rival those of the cysteine chapel (they were better than the pictures I saw in school anyway). Though they had faded from centuries of existence, the intricacies of the paintings were still visible.

They depicted different biblical accounts. The one on the ceiling above us depicted one of the prophets seeing into Heaven. I wasn't sure which one though. There were angels and other beings with strange lion faces, wings, and clawed feet. All of it was surrounded by clouds. On the left was the prophet with a book in his hand recording what he saw. Where the throne should have been, there was a skylight. The weather that entered through it had ruined the surrounding paint, but it was still beautiful.

There were other paintings on the plastered walls around us. The doorway that we entered through and the door way in front of us separated the two scenes.

One side was the battle of Jericho. A pile of rubble sat before a horde of soldiers rushing into the defenseless city. Off to one side was a brigade of trumpet players. Among them was a man that was clearly Joshuah. He held a trumpet in one hand and a sword in the other.

The other side was a depiction of the parting of the Red Sea. A massive wall of water towered from the floor to the ceiling, getting narrower to show perspective. In the center of the wall was a path of dry land. This must have depicted the moment the water parted, because the only person in the picture was Moses. He had his back turned to the observer. He wore a red robe that flowed in the breeze. His black shoulder cut hair almost seemed to flutter in that same breeze. One hand was stretched up toward heaven, while the other held his wooden rod out in front of him.

Hunter and I both spun as we took in the room. We looked in every direction. The curvature of the room made it feel as though we were a part of these stories in the moment they took place.

I took an affinity to Moses and walked over. I placed my hand on the wall of water and looked at the straight path ahead of him. I said a quick prayer that our path to victory would be as such.

"It's impressive, isn't it?" Manuel boasted, "Some say Da Vinci himself experimented on these walls." He shook his head, "Of course, they wouldn't give little Haro any of the fame."

"It's incredible," Hunter awed.

We walked further, begrudgingly leaving the chapel. I slid my hand along the smooth plastered wall all the way to the wood-framed door way ahead of us. The disappointment of leaving the first room quickly vanished as we walked into the second - a long rectangular chapel. Again, each of the side walls were painted. Except, this time, the sides and front wall all depicted one scene.

"Woa. Where are we now?" Hunter asked. I was pretty sure I knew the answer, but I let Manuel respond.

"This is the camp of the Israelites in the wilderness," he explained, "I believe this is supposed to be the day they finished the Tabernacle, but that's just a local rumor. It could be any day during the forty years."

I sensed both Hunter's Awe and confusion. He wasn't keen on his bible history like I was. He wasn't really raised in church. I wanted to explain it all to him, but I realized that the painting could speak for itself.

On the sides were the tents of the Israelites. It showed them doing their daily tasks. On the left, one tent displayed a blacksmith hammering away on a sword. Another showed a woman with two children. The mother seemed to be pushing them out of the tent to go play. This conclusion was supported by the three other young children who appeared to be waiting on them.

On the right, there was a man eating a handful of wafers: manna. To his right, there was a fire going with logs surrounding it, turned on their end to sit on. Some men sat with harps, drums, and other instruments that I didn't recognize. I tried to imagine their melody. It made me miss my guitar. I hadn't played since the war started.

In the front of the room was the pinnacle of the scene. Purple cloth sheets were hung to conceal a large tent that poked up just above them. Smoke rose from both that tent and the court in front of it. Above this structure was a cloud, thick and grey. It engulfed the horizon and shaded the front portion of the depiction. This was the Tabernacle and the glory cloud.

Near the corner of the room was a man who was dressed differently than the rest. He had white hair and a well kept white beard. On his head was something akin to a turban - a round and poofy white hat. His robe was thick and blue. He was walking toward the Tabernacle. What stood out though was what was on his chest. It was a golden square. On this were three rows of four gemstones. Twelve all together. It was held to him by a golden chain that went around his neck.

"Who is that?" Hunter pointed to this man.

"The High Priest, Aaron," Manuel explained.

"What's on his chest?" Hunter asked. I could tell he had a direction he was going with his questions. He was remembering our conversation we'd had about a month ago.

"That is the Breastplate of Judgement," Manuel answered, "One stone for each tribe would go before God, and the Priest would sacrifice to atone for the sins of the people." We all stared for a moment, then Manuel continued, "You know, some people think those stones you wear were a part of those twelve."

"That's what my father thought," I confirmed. I didn't know why, but I felt comfortable sharing that with this man.

Manuel winked at me, "I think he was a smart man."

We looked for a minute longer. Until, I realized we had a schedule to keep. "So what did you need to tell me?" I asked.

Manuel Manuel walked over to the part of the wall under Aaron. There, he pried up a loose board. He reached his hand up behind the wall and pulled out a small data key. "This." he grunted as he stood up. He walked over and handed it to me, closing my hand around it with his own. I looked back with a look that insisted more information. "I used to work for The Organization. The Mayan Chief helped me defect a long time ago. I used what I knew to send a team to get this. They gave their lives for this information."

"What information?" I asked.

Manuel looked around and leaned in. I didn't know how what he was about to tell me would be any more secretive than what he had just shared. "A full schematic of Jericho."

My eyes bugged. As if having the location wasn't enough, this would almost guarantee a successful attack. Well, it would at least give us the ability to plan a good one anyway.

I gripped the key in my hand as though the fate of the word depended on it, because of course, it did. Then, I extended my free hand to shake Manuel's. I looked him in the eyes, "Thank you."

"Don't thank me," Manuel replied, "Win."

Just then, a violent explosion shook the Cathedral.

"¡Qué barbaridad!" Manuel growled.

Hunter and I sprinted to the exit. All that I could think was the worst. That was too close. We ran out through the wooden doors and rounded the corner of the church. I looked wildly, trying to find the source of the explosion.

I quickly saw that both the ship on the courtyard and the ships in the field were fine. So what was it?

Up on the hill, one of those castles we had seen on the way in was pouring smoke. A section of it had collapsed.

I turned to see Manuel catching up to us. "What was that?" I asked.

"Those imbeciles blew up another one of our grain storages," he huffed, "That was the last one in the region. If they finish the job, we'll starve come winter."

I ground my teeth and looked at my vanguard. On it was a timer that tracked how long we had until we couldn't fly off without being detected by the next patrol. We had fifteen minutes. I lowered my wrist and looked at Hunter, "Wanna get in on some action?"

"Not really," he said, "But I wanna kick these guy's butts."

I nodded, both confirming our new mission and calling for my helmet. The metal rose from my collar and formed around my head. Hunter did the same, and then we both flew off.

"Where are you going?" Blake asked over the coms, "We don't have enough time."

"They actually have enough with a three second margin of error," ALI corrected.

"Just finish the mission and keep the engines running," I requested.

"We're here if you need backup," Bailey added.

Hunter and I flew up high enough to see everything surrounding this castle. It was on a hill taller than the one the little town was on. Once we were above it, I realized it was more of a fort than a castle. It was just a square with spires at each corner. The rock walls had a pathway that went all the way around the top. Inside these walls were bins of grain. Half here destroyed. The grain was burning on the ground. The other half had survived with little damage. I noticed men in grey uniforms quickly running for cover. Men in black uniforms pursued them. Orange and yellow blasts were exchanged from their guns.

"What is the Ekklesia doing here?" I thought out loud.

"Not just the Ekklesia," ALI added, "This is your former strike team. Cashner is here."

None of this made sense. Even if they had caught onto The Organization blowing up these grain storages, why would Cashner be sent here to stop it? And why would The Organization blow up their own grain? "Let's get a closer look." I suggested.

Hunter and I flew down to the section of wall that was still standing. We crouched down and peered over the side. It looked like the battle was winding up.

The Ekklesia troops were placing handcuffs on the Organization troops and they were lining them up against another section of the brown rock wall.

"Ten minutes till we've gotta pull out," one of the Ekklesia soldiers said. I recognized his voice, but it wasn't Cashner.

"Scout says Dorrado has ships in the valley," another soldier said.

These two flanked one with decorations on his arm. This was Cashner. "What are they doing here," he grunted. Then, he shook his head. "It doesn't matter. We've got a mission to complete. Set the new charges and remind me to fire the bomb tech."

"What? They were blowing up the food supply? The Ekklesia? Anger surged through me. How could Sparks pervert such a well intended institution. Resorting to starving the Organization made them no better. This wouldn't even affect many troops, only citizens.

"What do we do with them?" A soldier gestured to the defeated Organization troops (about ten of them).

"Execute them," Cashner commanded.

Absolutely not, I thought. *Not on my watch*. "Stay here," I growled at Hunter.

The Ekklesia soldiers lined up behind the unarmed Organization soldiers. They faced the wall on their knees, hands restrained behind their unprotected backs.

I launched myself off of the wall and landed between the two groups. "Stop!" I yelled. My energy consumed me. My helmet muffled my voice.

The troops lowered their guns a bit. I think this was done more in shock than anything. Cashner had been walking away until now. He turned around, ready to fight. When he recognized me, his helmet retracted.

"So you work for them now?" Cashner huffed, "I could have guessed."

I kept my helmet on, "Of course not," I growled, "But I could have pegged you for Organization. Blowing up food storages. Executing unarmed prisoners."

"Huh, it's almost like we're in a war," Casher raised his voice and stepped toward me, "It's almost like I'm a soldier trying to end it!"

"At what cost?" I retracted my helmet now and yelled back at him.

"Any," Cashner barked.

I remembered the Data key that was now in my pocket. Zipped up and tucked safely away. Cashner didn't know how close we were to the end.

"Leave," I commanded Cashner, extending him mercy.

"Not until I'm done," he refused.

"I said, leave," I narrowed my eyebrows and concentrated my energy at my hands, "We don't want this playing out like last time, do we?"

Cashner returned my scowl. Then, he smiled, "You're too late anyway. Light it up!"

We both expected an explosion. Instead, there was a green flash, and a soldier came flying over one of the grain bins. Then, he smashed into the rock wall about half way up. He bounced off and fell to the ground on his face.

Hunter peeked out from behind one of the bins. Then, he walked toward us, "I know you said to stay, but…"

I smirked, "Good job, Hunter."

Cashner started to scowl again. "How do you think this war will ever end, if you keep doing stuff like this?" He threw his hands up, "Pick a side!"

"I have, Cashner."

He only shook his head and walked away. There was nothing more he could do. He was outmatched and on the same time frame we were. His soldiers scooped up their friend Hunter had incapacitated, and they left.

Five minutes.

I turned to the soldiers I had just saved and began ripping off their binders. Hunter rushed over to help. I was strong enough to break the metal, but I had to be careful not to hurt them in the process. They were all very thankful as I sent them free. I really didn't expect this since we were on opposing sides. Then, I was even more shocked when their leader spoke.

"You're Dylan?" he asked.

"Yes," I replied, "You've heard of me?"

"Heard of you?" He almost looked offended. Then, he seemed to decide that I was joking. "Of course. I can't believe we're actually getting to meet you, Director."

I nearly laughed out loud, "Director?"

The soldier looked back at me blankly.

"You lead the Ekklesia," he informed me, "So, yea."

My brain began to churn now. I knew these were not Ekklesia troops. They wore Organization armor. They wore the Organization insignia. I didn't even lead the Ekklesia anymore. I certainly wasn't their leader.

Maybe they had gotten the armor on a mission and had to wear it to stay undercover, "Where did you get your armor?" I asked.

"From the Ekklesia." The soldier was clearly confused and irritated. The rest had formed an equally confused and irritated semi-circle around us.

"No, that's Organization armor," I informed them. "Who do you take orders from?"

"You!" he insisted.

"No, you don't" I insisted further, "You just fought the Ekklesia, and I don't even give them orders anymore."

"What?" the soldier took a step back. Then, he narrowed his glance, "Who are you?"

"I'm Dylan Vale!" I confirmed, "Who else can do this?" I waved my purple energy in between us. "Plus, you've seen my face in the message I sent out, right?"

The soldier thought for a moment. I felt him go through confusion. Then, anger. Then, cold terror.

"If I don't work for the Ekklesia, then…" his voice trailed off. He stumbled backward until one of his soldiers caught him. "No… no…" he whispered.

I returned his concern. "All of you," I gestured to the other soldiers. "You all thought that you worked for the Ekklesia?"

They nodded.

"One minute," ALI reminded me.

"I'm so sorry," I stepped back and grabbed Hunter's shoulder, "We've got to go." I tried to think of something that I could do for them. Something I could say. Something I could promise. There was enough room to take them with us, but the Mayans would never allow it. What if this was an elaborate ruse?

I knew Bailey would be able to tell, but she wasn't here and wouldn't have the time. I sensed the ship flying to retrieve us. I looked in its direction, then back at the soldiers. I sensed true fear and confusion. I ground my teeth.

"Bailey, I need you down here," I requested.

"Already on it," she replied over the coms, but I heard her voice beside me. She must have landed behind me and walked up.

"Thirty seconds," ALI reminded urgently.

"Truth or lie?" I asked.

She understood the assignment. Her eyes turned white. Our black ship appeared overhead.

"Truth."

"That's what I thought."

"Ten seconds"

"Open the door!" I commanded.

The door of the smooth ship opened. Without warning them, my energy surrounded the soldiers. I launched them into the air and shoved them through the opening.

"5"

Bailey, Hunter and I flew up.

"4"

"3"

We entered the cabin with the heap of soldiers in the middle. The door began to close.

“2”

“Punch it!” I yelled.

“1”

Chapter 22

There was a unanimous groan that rose from the pile of young soldiers beside me. I myself had dove into the cabin beside them. They were one big pile of arms, legs and heads turned every which way. I lay on the cold floor of the ship for a moment. I wasn't hurt. I could have gotten up. I just needed a second to process.

We had a ship full of soldiers that may or may not be loyal to the Organization. They were seeing - riding in - technology that they weren't even supposed to know existed, owned by a people who would explode if they knew they were in here. All of the Mayans who came before them were probably rolling over in their graves.

"Ana," I slowly stood up. Ana was staring down at me. "Call your father and see what we need to do."

"Who are these people?" she asked. I wasn't sure she even heard me. She was too busy worrying what trouble she would be in when she got home.

"That's what I'd like to find out," I alluded.

"They're Organization," Bailey explained from beside me, "But they think they work for the Ekklesia."

"That sounds like a trap," Blake said from the doorway of the cockpit. The soldiers were starting to stand up. Blake had his hand on his staff. He looked at the soldiers, "Why don't y'all just stay sittin' for a minute." He pointed at them when he spoke.

My senses told me they weren't planning anything suspicious, but Blake was right to not trust them. Some Organization troops have been trained to resist mind reading.

The leader of the group continued to stand, "I don't-"

"Sit down!" Blake scolded, "While we decide whether or not to throw you overboard."

The soldier tucked his tail and sat. Even Hunter looked as though he wanted to sit down.

I looked back at Ana, "Tell the chief that I need to see him in person, alone, right away," I explained, trying not to give off any information to the soldiers. "We also need a spot to drop these soldiers off. The Council of Elders will want to send a team to question them immediately."

Ana nodded and walked to the cockpit, grumbling something about how I'm "always getting her into trouble". Blake side-stepped to let her through, positioning himself just in front of the doorway. When she was inside, the door shut, and Blake leaned against it, arms folded across his chest.

The soldiers were silent. A couple looked around, but most just looked down at the floor. They looked like prisoners, and I guess they were for now.

Bailey and I shared an uncertain glance. I invited her to look into my mind and revealed what Manuel had given me. She was as surprised as I was.

"This is it, then," she communicated telepathically, "This will end the war."

"One way or the other," I thought.

I knew we were entering a situation similar to what we had faced at the mountain base last year, except the roles were reversed. If we won at the Organization's capital, then we would have won the war. That would be the end of The Organization in its present form. If we lost, the scales would once again tip in favor of The Organization.

"This will at least give us an advantage," Bailey replied.

"A huge one," I agreed.

While we were talking, something caught my attention. Hunter had gone over to the group of soldiers and knelt down next to one of them. The young man was holding his right arm and crouching forward a little. I realized that he was in pain.

"Can I see it?" Hunter asked softly. Bailey was paying attention now too.

The soldier reluctantly stretched his arm out as far as he could. He winced as he surpassed his limit and pulled it back a bit. Hunter took hold of the bottom of the arm to support it. Then, with his free hand he tore back the already tattered sleeve. This revealed a long deep cut. I could tell that it was from an Atom sword because the wound was cauterized. That was one plusses of being cut with one of those blades. It hurt like everything, but they didn't bleed much.

Hunter prodded the wound a bit. The soldier inhaled though his teeth as he ground them. Once Hunter had assessed it, he hovered his hand over the wound and allowed his green energy to flow down his arm and over his hand.

The energy flowed in geometric patterns. Light and dark shades of green came together as it trickled down onto the wound. At first, the soldier receiving the treatment looked terrified. However, I could see the moment that the pain started to subside. I could also see the moment the other soldiers realized what was going on. Each one's eyes slowly began to grow wider as the wound grew shallower.

Hunter moved his hand from under the arm to start pushing the sides of the wound together as it healed. It wasn't more than a few minutes before there was a fresh patch of pink skin in its place.

"How did you do that?" the soldier asked.

"Practice," Hunter smiled.

I saw that we had gained a bit of trust, and I hoped that the bizarness of what they had just seen would throw them off guard. I decided to ask a question.

"So, how did y'all join what you thought was the Ekklesia," I addressed my question to their leader who sat in the middle of them.

"We got your message," he explained, "Some of us were civilians, most of us were former military." I only now took time to note that he had the same accent as Manuel. "We heard that you had sent ships to retrieve us so we went-"

"Heard from who?" I cut him off

"A man that went from town to town," he redirected, "He wore a uniform like this one and told us that we need to come with him to a rendezvous with an Ekklesia transport."

"And you believed him?" Blake prodded, "No questions asked?"

"Of course we asked questions," the soldier snapped. He looked around the room, making eye contact with all of us. Then, he narrowed his eyes and glared at me. "We had just seen spaceships fly over our towns. Our technology didn't work. Our capital city had been destroyed...He gave us hope." He made sure to make eye contact with Bailey, Hunter and Blake once more before he finished, "What would you have done?"

I was less concerned with his moral dilemma than I was with what this meant. When I called the Ekklesia, people from all over the world came. Except, they came from the places my father had connections. The only way that they got to the Mountain Base was if they had a connection with someone who knew my father. Even the various militaries that had come were brought here by people my father knew, unless they were in our hemisphere. Most of our people came from the combined forces of the Mayans and the American military.

This meant that there would have been countless others who wanted to enlist that weren't in North and South America, that couldn't find a way here. It seemed as though The Organization had snagged up those people to reinforce their troops.

It was genius really. If The Organization had taken over purely by force, the world would have rejected them like a virus. In reality, they grew like a cancer, turning the body's own cells against it. They didn't even have to ensure their total loyalty. Just send them to do the little jobs, like protecting the grain storages, in order to keep them away from the real Ekklesia. Meanwhile, you use your truly loyal troops to fight the real battles.

But…Maybe you do send your deceived troops to fight battles too. You just make sure no one stops fighting long enough to ask questions.

This thought terrified me. When did we ever stop to think that the people we were fighting against might think we were The Organization? We could be solely fighting the people who thought they joined the Ekklesia while The Organization just sat back and laughed.

I bit my fingernails and walked to the back of the ship. I sat in the seat closest to the back wall. Brady had been sitting back there this whole time. He was in the seat across from me.

I put my elbow on my knee and rested my chin on my fist. I let out a long sigh. My mind drifted to the topics at hand until everything around me was dark and silent. I was in only the world of my mind.

I began to become surrounded by the glimpses of faces I had seen in battle. How many of those who died in Washington and at the Battle of Big Valley might have thought they were on our side. If they had really known who they were fighting for, would there have even been any battle at all?

"That bad, huh?" Brady spoke up.

"Hm?" I cut my eyes to look at Brady. I heard what he said, but my brain didn't process it.

"Are we in danger?" he clarified.

"Oh, no," I replied, "Well, I don't think so… I actually have really good news."

"It doesn't look like it's good news," Brady frowned.

"It's just heavy," I decided, "It's all very heavy."

Brady looked like he was trying to think of something encouraging to say. He never got the chance.

Ana opened the door of the cockpit. This took away the backing Blake was leaning on, which caused him to tumble backward into the cockpit. Ana caught him in her arms. Blake turned his head toward hers.

"Thank's, babe," he quipped.

Ana smirked and shook her head. She "We'll drop them off in Elsalvidor. The chief will meet you on the surface to talk."

"Sounds like a plan!" Blake answered for me. Then, he pressed the button that closed the cockpit door.

I guess they wanted some alone time. I didn't blame them. We were all really enjoying picking our missions lately. In fact, we liked it so much that we started doing it all the time. This made alone time scarce.

We were always in such a good mood since we moved to El Dorado - especially since we started running these missions. We were saving the world, helping people, and having fun doing it. We got to be together.

Bailey and Hunter walked back to join Brady and I. Hunter sat beside Brady, and Bailey sat beside me.

"Liven up," Bailey nudged my arm.

"What's wrong?" Hunter asked me.

I had to think about that. I wasn't really sure. Hunter actually figured it out before I did.

"Is it because of Cashner?" he asked.

"Yes… well, I guess," I reasoned, "That's part of it at least."

"Did you tell them what you told me?" Bailey asked, insinuating that we would talk about that later. She knew I could get in my own head. She stopped my spiraling.

"Hunter knows," I told her.

"Knows what?" Brady asked.

I managed a smile, but I stopped myself before I told him. I cut my eyes toward our prisoners. They were a few feet away, and the hum of the engines likely covered our discrete conversation. Still, I didn't want to risk it.

"Tell him, Bailey," I suggested.

I saw her crystal's glow brighten a bit. Then, I saw Brady's deminer change. At first, he looked excited. Then, I watched the weight of what he had learned hit him.

"So this could be the end?" He questioned.

"There's a good possibility," I nodded, "But I want to see the schematics myself. Plus, the Mayans. I trust them more than me on this one."

"And ALI," Hunter added.

Of course! ALI. I had almost forgotten about him. He could look at the schematics right now. That would certainly lighten the mood.

"Well, we can ask him right now," I suggested.

I removed the data key from my front pocket and walked toward the cockpit. I pressed the button on the wall and opened the door. To my surprise, Ana was sitting in Blake's lap. Which is normal for any other couple, but I couldn't remember the last time I had seen Ana show affection - for anyone. Not in any traditional way anyways. She looked embarrassed.

All I could think about was what a perfect couple they made. Blake, just a bit taller, Ana just a bit bolder. Her hair straight, his hair curly. Their personalities perfectly complemented one another: rigid meets emotional, logical meets impulsive.

I handed her the data key as she stood up. "Knock next time," she cowered.

I smiled and ignored her. "Plug this into the secure computer."

"What is it," Blake asked, agitated that I had ruined the moment.

"Worth it," I joked. I felt my mood growing lighter already. Though, I felt a nervousness in the pit of my stomach - a fear that the fortress would be impenetrable.

Still, I forced myself to be optimistic and closed the door behind me. I stepped over the prisoners until I made it back to my seat.

"ALI, what do you see?" I asked. Brady, Hunter and Bailey leaned in as ALI spoke over the coms.

"The base sits on an island. The initial exterior sweep shows a circular, walled structure that is 750 feet high. Each section of the wall has three pivoting cannons embedded in it and one on top."

"How many sections?" I asked.

"52" ALI replied.

That was a lot of guns, but nothing we couldn't handle.

"What really stands out is what the walls sorround" ALI said, "The walls don't protect the base. They protect some sort of ray cannon. It's the largest one I've ever seen."

"How big?" I Hunter asked.

"Well, the mouth of the cannon is about 300 feet across. Its neck extends into the earth's crust further than our data goes. If it were aimed down at the earth, it would destroy the planet. A large portion of it anyway."

"Why would they need a gun that big?" Bailey asked.

"I couldn't say," ALI answered.

"As long as it's pointed up and not down," Hunter added.

I stroked my chin. Why point a gun that large straight up? Why have a gun that large at all? What purpose could it serve?

Bailey interrupted my thought with more questions. "Where are the last two crystals?"

"They are housed in relay stations on either side of the cannon.," ALI answered.

"On the surface?" I asked.

"There is no underground component other than the cannon," ALI replied, "All of the base's activity happens in its walls. The walls are the base."

"You guys getting that up there?" I asked over the coms, "You're awfully quiet."

"Loud and clear," Blake replied, "Just thinking it over."

"Are you sure this is the right base?" Ana questioned, "Our reports didn't say anything about this huge cannon. They said it was a dome surrounded by walls."

ALI corrected himself, "A retractable dome covers the canon."

"That's important information," Blake nagged.

"It would be easier for you to understand if you had a visual," ALI defended.

"We're almost to El Salvador," I pointed out, "We can look at it after we drop the prisoners off."

"Agreed," ALI said.

As we flew, my friends chattered, but I was mostly zoned out. I couldn't stop thinking about the information we had just heard. Even though I knew I would see the real thing in just a few minutes, I couldn't stop trying to visualize it in my mind: the massive walls, the gigantic gun, the defencive cannons, the island.

Finally, after an eternity (A.K.A thirty minutes), we landed in El Salvador. The transition was largely uneventful. The prisoners filed out into the possession of the Mayan forces stationed there. I thought we would talk to the prisoners or at least the troops before we left, but they just followed their orders and rushed us along. Something about "protocol" in sensitive cases. In other words, they didn't want us to get attached to them. As much as I wanted to know about them, I wanted to know about this base more.

My friends and I gathered back in the cabin of the ship as it took off once again. From the ceiling, ALI projected the layout of the base through a blue tinted hologram, aided by his white mist for texture and realism. The light and particles worked together to create the picture.

It was probably the most sophisticated structure we had ever seen. If the island was natural, all of those parts were covered. What was visible was a perfectly circular structure, towering walls rising out of the sea. Directly inside the walls were structures that appeared to be offices, armories, and other things you would need in a capitol. The walls themselves had the huge guns ALI had mentioned, along with hangar bays, filled to the teeth with fighters.

From this, there was an inner ring, the dome that protected the cannon. It was made from solid steel, coated with Unitum. How they fashioned it was beyond me. The hologram imitated the dome opening to reveal the hole beneath.

The base was very clearly divided into two halves. One side was trademarked with dark green lines. Its cannons shot dark green energy blasts. The other side was Orange. The divide could be traced to two structures, one on either side of the dome. These were the last two crystals we knew of.

We all circled the hologram, taking it all in. New angles, however, didn't offer new insights. It was the same from every side.

“So why don't we just take all of our cruisers, fly in, and blow it up,” Hunter asked, “It doesn't have a shield, right?”

"It doesn't need one," Blake said, “Even if we could cloak our cruisers as good as the ship we're on right now, we'd never get close without being detected. Especially in the Mediterranean."

Blake was right, but I was more concerned about that cannon. It had to have a purpose, and I wouldn't want to get us close to it without knowing what it was.

"You know, there's probably a Mayan who could figure it out," Bailey suggested.

I looked up from my inspection, "Where's the fun in that?" I quipped. "ALI, can you calculate the approximate power of the beam from that cannon and run a simulation."

"Of course," ALI replied.

It wasn't long before the core of the gun began to glow. The hologram zoomed out a bit, and a beam of light appeared, shooting up from the hologram cannon, to the ceiling of the ship.

"Is that to scale?" I asked. Everyone had backed away to let me do my thing.

"Yes, sir" ALI affirmed.

I placed my finger on the beam as high up as I could reach. The white mist helping create it tickled my finger as it moved up with the beam. "What's the energy decay right here?"

"0.03%" ALI replied.

"Really?" I gasped, "At that rate, it could escape the atmosphere."

"It could escape the solar system," ALI corrected.

"Zoom out," I requested.

ALI zoomed out until the earth was about the size of an orange in front of me and the moon was near the door. The beam still shown out across the empty space as far as the hologram would project. "Track the moon's orbit. Does it ever intersect?"

The moon flew around the cabin, and the earth rotated on its axis, but never crossed over the beam. I huffed.

"The planets don't intersect either," ALI added, "No time of day, no time of year."

I stepped back until I could lean against the door of the cockpit. My friends looked between the hologram and me. "What's the point then?" I asked myself out loud.

Ana spoke up, "There's a man back at El Dorado who oversees our advanced research division. I think he may be able to help."

My heart jumped and sank at the same time. The idea finally clicked. It all came together. It came together in a way that made the answer undeniable.

"Overseers," I whispered.

"What?" Hunter asked.

Bailey sensed what I was thinking. Everyone else was lost.

"The Overseers," I said again, louder this time. "It's not a cannon. It's a beacon."

Chapter 23

Our ship landed in front of the steps to the council chambers in El Dorado. The door opened. On the other side was the Mayan chief. He was waiting to receive the data key.

I hopped out, extending my hand toward him as I did. "You'll want to see this."

"I've been pins and needles," he confirmed. He took the data key from my hand. My friends and I followed him up the white limestone stairs. Each stair we climbed we passed a guard. Their Unitum spears and armor glistened in the light of the artificial sun. Their tan capes spread out behind them, flapping in the gentle breeze.

I was walking between the chief and Hunter. I leaned over to my apprentice. "I wish I had a cape," I commented.

This made Hunter smile.

We continued walking up the stairs, and finally we made it to the huge wooden doors. They had intricate carvings on them, but I didn't get the chance to observe them. I could only make out vines and flowers before they swung open.

They revealed a room shaped like a cylinder. The walls were smooth stone. The ceiling extended up a ways before giving way to natural stalactite formations. This must have been a natural cave before the Mayans carved out the massive cavern.

In the center of the room was a marble circle seated in the floor. This was where those approaching the council were to stand. It was raised up just slightly from the limestone around it. In front of this were the elders.

They sat on three thrones. Despite the grandeur of everything else, their thrones were rather plain. They were carved directly from the stone, but they lacked added carvings or frills of any kind. They were just smooth and plain. Their bases were wide and the backs extended a few feet above the elders' heads. The elders wore long white robes and capes that folded around them. Their hair was white and their skin was as folded and creased as their robes.

The chief walked forward and stood on the circle while the rest of us stood near the wall behind him. The chief knelt in front of them. "I've brought you the data key," he informed them.

"Bring it to me," the elder in the middle commanded eagerly. His voice carried through the room unnaturally. The shape of the room amplified his voice to a thunder that rumbled in my chest.

Chief Cantun rose and walked to the elder. He handed him the data key, which the elder then placed into a slot on the side of his chair. The already dark room darkened even further. A projection shown down from the high ceiling. The hologram filled the entire room.

The chief returned to my side. The elders observed the schematic. After a few minutes of tense silence, the one on the left spoke.

"You," his voice boomed. He pointed in my direction.

I looked to either side to make sure he wasn't pointing at anyone else.

"Yes, you," he thundered, "You've already seen it."

How did he know that? He wasn't connected to a crystal. Was he still able to read my mind?

"He understands it," the elder on the right echoed.

"Tell us what you see," the middle elder requested.

I gave a brief bow, unsure of what exactly was customary, and then I walked into the projection. The structures around me flickered as I walked through the projected walls (which were taller than I was). Then, I began to explain everything we had discovered.

When I finished, the elders turned to one another and began to mumble. Their voices didn't thunder through the room when they were turned away. In fact, it was impossible to hear them. The longer they talked, the more I worried that I had said something wrong. I looked back at the chief, but he gave me a reassuring look as though this was normal. This made me feel better.

Finally, the elder in the middle spoke toward me, "Explain to us who these 'Overseers' are."

"I wish I could," I conceded. "All I know is what Darren Flyhe told me. Just that he seemed to report to them, and -he claimed- that there was no way to stop them."

"There is always a way," the elder on the left interjected. "Is there any way that we could question this man?"

"He's in Ekklesia custody," I informed him, "Even if you could get them to send him here, I doubt he would talk to you."

"You just leave that to us," the elder in the middle boomed.

I felt bad for Darren now. I was sure their methods of interrogation would be… unpleasant.

"Thank you for bringing this to our attention," the elder on the left thanked.

"Do you think we can take the base?" I asked timidly.

The elders looked at one another. Their stoic countenance briefly cracked as they smiled. "I wouldn't become overconfident," the middle elder boasted, "But if we can focus our resources, we should be able to end this war."

My heart fluttered. I could hardly believe my ears. One more fight, and it was all over. We could go home. Everyone could go home.

I turned back to my friends who were all beaming. Brady was clenching Hunter's shoulder as though it were the only thing holding him to the ground.

I bowed, "thank you," I said to the elders.

I took long strides toward my friends. Two guards pulled the doors open and we all filed out of the chambers.

"So this is it," Hunter said with nervous excitement, "It's almost over."

"The large-scale war is almost over," the chief corrected from behind us, "There will be many more battles to fight once we begin to reconstruct."

"As long as you keep handling the politics, we'll be just fine," I said.

"I wish we could fight this battle tomorrow and get it over with," Ana sighed, knowing it would take the wheels of process time to turn.

"Why don't you all take some time off until then," the chief suggested, "I know you don't like fighting battles anymore, but we'll need you for this one. And we'll need you rested up."

"I think that sounds like a great idea," I agreed. We all knew we would have to fight this fight. I think everyone was happy to if it meant the war would end.

"Why don't we go to Tullahoma and visit?" Blake suggested.

"I didn't think we were welcome there?" Ana reminded us.

"I could probably smuggle you in," the chief offered, "Let me see what I can do."

"Really?" I asked in excited disbelief. I missed my family. We had only been able to talk to them through holograms since my falling out with the Ekklesia. The chief did his best, but the elders would not let them live here with us.

"Anything for our star players," the chief said, "But I won't make any promises yet.

Bailey was walking beside me. When we reached the last step, I put my arm around her. "You're awfully quiet," I said softly.

"I think I'm getting another migraine," she sulked.

"That's the second one this week," I pointed out worriedly. "What's that doctor saying?"

I immediately sensed something was off before she ever responded. "Oh, he's still running tests."

I narrowed my eyes at her. She wasn't lying, but I knew she was leaving out details. I sensed unease. "Let's take a walk." I suggested.

Our friends were already filing around us to get on the transport. "Are you coming?" Blake asked from the doorway.

"I think we're going to go for a walk on the surface," I countered. I turned to Bailey and lowered my voice, "You think you're up for it?"

"It's better than laying in bed," she agreed.

"Oooooo," Blake and Hunter teased.

I smiled and winked at them.

The transport took off. Then, Bailey and I flew to one of the small doors on the ceiling that led to the surface. I think they served as some sort of ventilation shaft. I just knew that we could open them and fly up through the bedrock to the surface. That's exactly what we did.

We had done this a few times over the past month. Bailey, well all of us, liked to sit in the real sun from time to time. The shaft wasn't very long and we quickly popped out of a pile of rock surrounded by bushes.

We were underneath the thick rainforest canopy. Not much sunlight made it here. It was still beautiful though. Rays would break through the trees and dance on the ground. The burst of light would occasionally highlight an Iris or hibiscus flower. The white sunlight would bounce off the petals in vibrant reds and purples. I found one such flower by the opening and picked it.

"For you, my lady," I handed it to Bailey and bowed in jest.

She smiled. "It's beautiful." She sniffed it and tucked it behind her ear. It seemed like the migraine might have been a false alarm. I sensed her tension fading. I hoped it was going away.

We walked down a trail through the jungle. There was a tiny clearing not far from here. This time of day, the sun would peek through a gap in the canopy where a tree had fallen. It just so happened that the tree was on the side of a clif, so it also opened up a view into the valley.

We walked hand in hand.

"Is your headache any better?" I followed up on my hypothesis.

"I think it might be going away," she hoped.

We walked a bit, then I asked, "So what all is the doctor saying?"

"He's trying to figure out what kind of medicine will work best," Bailey answered. I could tell she was still holding back. "I think they're analyzing some bloodwork. I think the fact that my blood glows might make it hard to analyze." she chuckled.

I chuckled back. I wanted to press, but I knew she hadn't felt good. I could just ask the doctor in person. I promised myself that I would go with her next time she went.

We finally reached our destination and sat down. The view was beautiful. It reminded me of the mountains back home. These were just a bit more jagged, but other than that they looked the same.

The sky was clear and blue, pierced by the green peaks of the mountains. A soft breeze blew. It was humid, but a bit cooler today than usual. Here, that still meant it was pretty warm though.

We sat on the wet ground, not worried about the mud that would be clinging to us when we stood up. Our suits kept us dry. Bailey leaned over onto my shoulder. I put my arm around her and placed my head on top of hers.

"It's almost over," I whispered in disbelief.

I felt a hot tear soak into my sleeve. "I'm so ready," Bailey breathed. She wasn't crying out of sadness. She wasn't really crying at all. I sensed a release - a weight close to being lifted.

"Do you ever feel like you don't belong here?" I asked, "Like it should have been someone else?"

"Of course not," she sniffed, "We're right where God put us."

"Well, I know that but..." I trailed off, looking for the words to express what I was feeling.

"We have an assignment from God," Bailey continued. She sat up and looked at me now. "He's just been putting us where we need to be to complete it."

"What happens when we complete it?" I asked.

She leaned back onto my shoulder. Her answer didn't come for a moment. She was deep in thought. Finally, she whispered, "He'll finally call us home."

She didn't mean home to Tullahoma. She meant home. Home with God. I realized I had failed to take peace in that. It was a hard thing to do. I had spent a lot of time fighting to keep everyone I loved alive, but at the end of the day, when the dust settles and the smoke drifts away, no matter what, I know that we'll be together again. I guess that's why I tried so hard to make sure we fought the right way. Like Pastor said, what good is winning a war if you lose yourself?

As we sat, my mide drifted here and there as it often does. I thought about what the Overseers could be. I had nothing to go on, so my mind quickly came to how we would fight the battle of Jericho. I assumed we wouldn't be marching around the walls, though I was almost certain whatever happened would be just as crazy. It always was.

I couldn't decide if I wanted the other bearers to be there or not. On one hand, if we captured them there, we wouldn't have to worry about them anymore. On the other, I wasn't sure if I could defeat the Onyx bearer - especially in the middle of a battle on that scale.

When I couldn't make my mind up on this fact, I drifted to thinking of what would come after. What would the Ekklesia become? Would their alliance with the Mayans hold? The horrid thought of a second war between the two made me feel sick, so I forced myself to look at the best case.

I would be back with my family. I would be with my friends. I realized that I wasn't sure what we would actually do with all of that free time. I assumed we would still be running aid. If not, we could help rebuild. There was so much destruction.

I would be with Bailey too. We could raise a family in a peaceful world. We could have kids. I knew I wanted at least three. Bailey probably wanted more. I imagined us in my house on the lake. Taking a canoe out on the water, watching the sunset, one day teaching my kids how to fish. I would teach them to swim. I would teach them to appreciate the things I always took for granted: peace, friendship, the sunset.

We would go on vacations to the mountains. One day I would revisit all the battles I fought, teaching my children about the war. Would they have my powers? I didn't have my dad's as soon as I was born. I don't think I did. But, I wasn't sure if he had his powers before or after I was born. Plus, my mom didn't have powers.

"Let's get married"

As I was thinking, I became so excited that the words just escaped.

"Huh?" Bailey raised up. I think she was almost asleep.

"The war's almost over. We've got a little bit of time before the last battle. Let's get married," I proposed.

I spun around onto one knee and took Bailey by the hand.

"Dylan, my answer is yes, but I thought we would wait until after the war?" Bailey questioned.

I guess this was rather spontaneous. We would need to talk through it, “Well, I just thought there was no harm in doing it now,” I offered, “That way we can have a jump start on everything after the war.”

“What about our families?” Bailey asked.

“We’re going to see them, remember?” I reminded her, “We’ll do it when we go to Tullahoma.”

Bailey thought for a moment as she still tried to wake up. I could see as she weighed the options. I can’t read exact thoughts, but I was almost sure I heard a “Why not?” just before a huge smile spread across her face.

“Yes” she bubbled.

“Yes?” I affirmed

“Yes!” She shrieked. I had never heard her do that.

She sat up on her knees to hug and kiss me. I think her knee hit a rock or something because she lost her balance and fell toward me. We both fell backwards, giggling all the way. (I could have stopped it, but I didn’t)

After a moment, she rolled off of me, and we both lay on our backs and looked at the sky. “I have so much planning to do,” Bailey realized.

“I can call Pastor and see if he’ll come to my house,” I suggested, “We can get married on the dock.”

“At sunset!” Bailey added, “The pictures will be beautiful.”

“I hope you weren’t hoping for something more extravagant,” I apologized.

“I thought you would know the one you proposed to better than that;” Bailey joked.

I smiled. We really were perfect for each other.

"Do you think we-" I was cut off by a sense of dread. I knew Bailey felt it too. Her face changed in an instant. We sprang to our feet, ready for action. I sensed something behind us. I used my energy to pull apart the trees until I could see the sky beyond them. In the distance, there was a small fleet of cruisers.

"Are those ours?" I asked Bailey.

"Doesn't feel like it," she said.

"ALI,"

"Putting you through to the chief now," he said before I could finish my request.

"Chief," I called, "Are these cruisers out here ours?"

There was a long second of silence. Then he said, "I'm watching them now. They're Ekklesia."

"What are they doing here?" I asked. I couldn't shake the sense I was having.

"They told us that they were moving some of their cruisers south, but they veered off their projected trajectory this morning," he explained, "I'm trying to get through to them, but they won't respond."

"I thought they didn't know where El Dorado was?" Bailey pointed out.

"They aren't supposed to," the chief said, "It could be an honest mistake because of that. We think we are just going to let them fly over."

That sounded reasonable. I let the trees go and they flung back together, "Just checking, thanks chief," I said.

"Thank you for reporting them," he added. Then, the comms channel closed.

I did my best to bury the sense of doom I was feeling. I tried to tell myself that I was on edge and they just startled me. The problem was, I hadn't been on edge at all, and they didn't startle me.

"They ruined our moment," I joked, but not really.

Bailey tried to smile, but I knew she was feeling it too. It was that feeling Darren had described, and we had felt. It was like we had lived this before and we knew it didn't end good.

All of the sudden, I saw Bailey's crystal begin to glow brightly, she grabbed her head and let out a sharp wail of pain. I took a step forward to help her, but my crystal did the same.

The world around me began to close off. A shrill ringing appeared in my ears. Then, over it, there were loud explosions and crumbling rock. I heard screams. I recognized them. The first was Ana. Then Hunter. Then Blake. Then, Bailey. Bailey's lasted the longest and faded into slow heavy breathing.

I fell to my knees, unable to move, unable to fight what was happening. Voices filled my mind, echoing and overlapping.

Ana - "I'll die with my people"

My own - "Blake!"

My father's "What happens now is up to you, son"

Darren - "I see, in your victory, a grave defeat."

Then, there was fire falling from the sky. I saw the pillars of El Dorado collapsing. I saw the Onyx Bearer standing in front of the council chambers.

Again, voices filled my mind, this time, too many to distinguish "Wake up" "I need your help" "You absorb 100% of your crystal's energy." "You failed" "He was commanded to make a breastplate" "Bailey's is 68%" "none of it matters"

The voices continued to echo as they were replaced with screams. Then, the screams merged together to create the ringing in my ears. Suddenly, my eyes shot open.

When I came to, I was screaming and holding my ears. I quickly got to my feet. I saw Bailey had passed out, but she was moving, so I moved to the next most important thing. "ALI!"

"Sir, are you okay, your vitals-"

"Get Cantun back on the coms,"

"He's back," ALi replied immediately.

"Chief, You need to unleash everything you have on those cruisers!" I yelled.

"What?" the chief snapped back, "That will reveal our location."

"They already know it!" I pleaded, "They're going to try and destroy El Dorado!"

There was silence over the coms. "Chief!"

He had to listen. I didn't fully understand what had just happened, but I understood that.

I sensed something else above us. I looked up and could just make out a fiery dot. "What is that ALI?" I asked.

"Inital scans indicate its metal and about 40 meters long."

As I focused in, I noticed more behind it. Then, the ground began to shake. I heard rock breaking. It sounded like a massive landslide, but I couldn't find it. Then, there was an explosion on the mountain across from us. Bits of rock were sent flying into the air. The entire side of the mountain gave way.

From the site of the explosion rose the biggest gun I've ever seen. It was black and had two sections. In the middle was an open trench that reverberated with magenta energy. The energy gathered at the ridge until it was blinding to look at. Then, it shot off in a beam toward the incoming ships. Its boom echoed through the jungle. I heard three other shots ring out after it.

After this, my attention was turned back to the metal poll crashing through the atmosphere. It was an orbital attack clearly trying to crack into El Dorado.

I allowed my energy to consume me. I lifted my hands and forced my energy up toward the poll. I began to push back on it with all my might.

The ground beneath me cracked. Energy leapt off of me in every direction. Tiny rocks began to float around me as they were lifted by the excess energy.

Thick ribbons of energy traveled up a central beam. They wrapped around the poll, but hardly seemed to slow it down. It was getting closer.

Finally, it was only a few hundred feet away. I screamed as I used all my power. It screeched to a stop just above my head. With what little bit I had left in me, I pushed it over to the side and off the cliff. It banged and clanged down the mountain side.

I looked back up and, to my horror, there were ten more to take its place, and ten more behind them. I ran over to Bailey and held under her arm. “We’ve got to go,” I pleaded.

She groaned, but couldn't pull herself up. I wasn’t sure if she was still having a vision or not. It didn’t matter. We had to go. I scooped her up in my arms. Just before I turned to run, I heard the roar of one of the beams approaching. I instinctively raised a shield around us, but it didn’t land close by. Instead, it plunged into the gun that had just risen from the mountain at the very second a shot was being fired.

The energy from the metal rod ripped the gun to shreds. When it hit the rock underneath, it exploded with the force of a bomb. The entire cap of the mountain was removed. House sized pieces of rock flew through the air, but before those arrived, the shockwave came. It slammed into my shield. I wasn’t expecting it to be that powerful, so it broke through and set Bailey and I both flying through the air.

Before we hit the ground, I caught Bailey with my energy, but this meant that I couldn't catch myself. I hit the ground with full force. My head hit a rock and my brain became foggy.

I felt the blood running down my face. My body didn't want to move, but I forced myself up. I staggered for a few steps, then I was back to a sprint. I made it to Bailey, and I picked her back up. Blood dripped down my face. Then, the rocks reached us.

They crashed through the trees around us, some landing only a few feet away. I kept my senses keen and was able to keep them pushed away from us. I sensed another poll coming down right above us. Thankfully, the access hatch was just a few feet away. I saw the pile of rocks that concealed it and lunged for it. I heard the explosion of the other poll landing behind us. We slipped through the hatch just as a wave of fire moved overhead. The hatch sealed behind us.

Chapter 24

We fell through the dark shaft before abruptly entering the light of El Dorado. Above us, explosions rumbled. Below us, sirens blared. I allowed us to free fall for a ways. Then, I ignited my jetpack. I gently slowed our fall and headed for the Hall of the Elders. I located the central pillar and its water filled ring. As I flew, I began to feel Bailey stirring as she returned to consciousness.

I landed at the foot of the long staircase. The usually stoic guards were holding their Unitum spears in attack position. They relaxed a bit when they saw it was me, but they still stood at the ready. I laid Bailey on the first step and knelt down beside her. She turned uncomfortably and moaned. Her eyebrows were scrunched together and her face was wrinkled up. I squeezed her hand.

"Bailey!" I called, "Come on."

I knew the vision might have been a lot for her - if that's what happened - but I was starting to get worried. She should be recovering by now.

The rumbling grew more tangible. Little rocks around me began to bounce and jump. The sirens clogged my ears. I saw Bailey's lips move, but I couldn't understand her with all of the commotion.

"What?" I asked, moving my ear next to her lips.

"Hunter," she whispered with all her might, "Find...Hunter."

"He'll be fine," I promised, "I'll send Blake to get him."

"Go!" Bailey commanded. She had actually managed more than a whisper. I had no choice but to obey.

I looked up at the nearest guard. "Watch her," I commanded, "I'll be back in a minute."

It wasn't his job. He was supposed to protect the elders at all costs. Still, he nodded, and I trusted him.

I ran toward the writhing water that surrounded the pillar. I leapt out toward the middle of it and ignited my jetpack. I flew out into the cavern. The usually organized sky lanes had devolved into an angry swarm of ships transporting troops to their stations. I was sure that they were boiling out the sides of the mountain.

Their computers kept them on course without crashing, but I was forced to dive and weave through the web of ships.

"ALI!" I called, "Where's Hunter?"

I skidded along the belly of a troop transport.

"He's in the penthouse," ALI informed me, "But he's not wearing his coms, so I can't pinpoint or contact him."

"Leave that to me," I commanded, "You get everyone else to the Hall. Locate the chief and see if I can get an audience with him and the Elders."

"They are already calling for you," ALI said.

I used two concussive blasts to boost me up and around a group of tic-tac shaped fighters.

"In that case, tell them I'll be a minute," I replied.

I finally reached our pillar on the far end of the city. I landed on the terrace and barged through the sliding glass door. The apartment seemed deserted, but I had an idea of where to look.

I jumped over the sova, dashed up the stairs, and slung open the door to his and Brady's room. I immediately saw Hunter. He was curled up in a ball between their two beds. He wasn't just crying; he was balling uncontrollably. Brady had knelt down next to him, trying to console him, but it wasn't working.

The poor kid looked horrified. Tears were running down his face. I hurried over and placed my hand on Brady's shoulder, comforting him and pulling him back a bit so I could intervene.

"What's happening?" Brady asked. His voice was trembling.

I was forced to ignore him. He would find out soon enough.

"Hunter," I consoled. He didn't acknowledge me. He must have seen something other than what I saw. I wished I had Bailey's mind-healing energy, but I didn't. I would have to do this one on my own.

I grabbed his hands and pulled them off of his legs. Then, I placed them around me as I picked him up off the floor. He squeezed me and buried his face in my chest. His sobs grew louder before they dimmed. I wrapped him in my arms, placing my right hand on the back of his head. He squeezed me tighter.

"It's okay," I promised, "I've got you."

"We need to stop," he cried, "We need to hide."

"It'll be over soon," I promised again.

"I can't lose you too."

I squeezed him tighter now. He sobbed, and I felt my own tears welling up. I wouldn't admit it, but I was scared too. I finally pulled him off of me, keeping my arms on his shoulders. "Look at me," I commanded gently but firmly, "I'm here. Whatever you saw, it wasn't real. I'm real. And I'm not going anywhere. Okay?"

His sobbing had finally turned into sniffling. He nodded his head and coughed. His face was blood red, soaked with tears and snot. "Come here," I pulled him into my embrace once again. Once he was secure, I pulled in Brady too.

We held onto each other for a while, but another violent rumbling brought us back to the reality of our situation. We looked around without letting go. I heard dishes falling from the kitchen cabinets downstairs.

"Get suited up, and come with me," I instructed. We let go and the boys hustled to get out of their normal clothes and into their underclothes for their suit. While they got dressed, I filled them in on what I knew (which wasn't much). Once their tight, black T-shirt and shorts were on, they each pressed their own pucks to their chest. The black mist flowed from them and a white wave of energy passed over their bodies leaving behind a grey and tan suit. Armor floated out of their closet and attached itself to their bodies. The only thing that distinguished the two was the green crystal in the center of Hunter's chest.

When they were done, I clapped my hands together, "Alright, let's go."

We ran back down the stairs, past the dining room table, through the living room, out the glass door, and leapt off the balcony. ALI helped us back to the central pillar by mapping a course through the cloud of ships and fighters.

We arrived back at the base of the stairs to find Blake and Ana standing with Bailey. She was sitting up on that first step now, rubbing her head. They all gave me a funny look as we walked to them.

"Are you okay?" Blake asked.

"Yea," I answered nonchalantly.

Blake gestured to his face. I was confused, until I remembered smashing my head on that rock. My adrenaline had numbed the pain. I pressed my hand to my forehead and then pulled it away to look. It was covered in blood. I felt around some more until I realized that it had run down the entire side of my face. No wonder Brady had looked so horrified when I walked in on them earlier.

I wasn't hurt badly, so I brushed all that aside, "How's Bailey?"

"She's-" Ana started to talk, but Bailey cut her off.

"I'm fine," Bailey said as she forced herself to her feet.

"The Elders are requesting all of you inside the chambers," ALI said over our coms.

I walked to Bailey and put my arm around her. "Are you sure?" I confirmed.

"Yes."

We all hastened up the stairs and through the huge wooden doors. Immediately, I noticed that the marble circle in the middle of the room had raised up to form a round table. The elders stood at one side. The chief stood opposite of them. Between them were people who I assumed were something like generals. There were eight people in total, and all of their attention turned to us when we walked in.

The chief left the table to greet us. I extended my hand and shook his. "Thank goodness you called me when you did," the chief congratulated, "How did you know they were hostile?"

We talked as we walked toward the round table. "I honestly couldn't explain it," I conceded.

"I understand," the chief said, surprisingly calm for the gravity of the situation, "It's that way with the crystals sometimes."

"How did this happen?" I asked. The entire table gave the chief their attention.

"We've been betrayed," he frowned.

"By who?" I asked.

"The Ekklesia," the chief explained.

A stunned silence fell on my friends and I. Sure we had been at odds lately, but I never for a second thought that we were on opposing sides.

The chief continued, "They were supposed to be moving forces to the South. They submitted a route and clearance codes that we approved. They veered off this morning and started toward us." The chief trailed off.

"Since they aren't supposed to know where the city is, we thought it was a mistake on their part," one of the generals continued the story in a gruff voice, "They would have sealed us in and been right on top of us without your warning."

"So the Ekklesia sent their own ships to attack us?" I pressed. This didn't sound right to me.

"No," the chief said, "The ships are Organization, but they were given Ekklesia codes and the location of our base. We don't think it's an Ekklesia wide betrayal. There's only one man that could do it."

"Raddick," I rationed.

Everyone at the round table shook their heads. I was shocked. I never thought that Raddick would work for The Organization. I didn't like him, but I thought he was just self-serving, not a traitor.

"We played the politics by bringing you here," the chief said, "Raddick felt threatened because we had all of the bearers. He's trying to eliminate a threat to his power."

I stepped up to the round table and took a spot beside the chief and my friends spread out behind me. "How can we help?" I asked.

"The Orbital strikes have taken out two of our four guns and sealed off two of our three main exits." one of the elders said.

"We can keep the cruisers at a distance so long as those two guns remain operational, but we need those exits open to counter attack." another elder explained.

"Are there any of you strong enough to move the rocks?" the final elder asked.

It was strange to hear their normal voices, rather than the booming, echoes I'd heard earlier.

"I can," Ana volunteered behind me.

"Yes, I can too," I offered.

"Then you each go clear an exit," the elder suggested.

"What about the rest of us?" Bailey asked.

"I'm sure we'll need you," said the chief, "Just stay here for now."

I nodded and turned from the table. I walked past my friends and Ana fell in behind me. Hunter was standing in the back. He grabbed my arm when I walked by.

"We need to leave," he ground his teeth.

I felt something. I didn't know what it was. I actually wanted to listen to him, but I knew we had to protect this place. As we stared at each other, Bailey walked up behind him. She took hold of the hand that was holding my arm. "Go," she whispered sentimentally, pulling him off of me.

I nodded my head and told Hunter, "We'll be fine." Then, I ran out, igniting my jetpack once again, and flew out through the giant doors. For as long as I could, I sensed what was going on behind me. Bailey wrapped Hunter in her arms. She told him something, but I couldn't make it out. I sensed comfort, so I felt okay leaving them. Not that I really had a choice.

I knew that I wanted to talk to both of them about what they had seen as soon as this was over. Our crystals were clearly linked, and we clearly all saw different things. I hoped that when we put everything together, we would be able to understand what it all meant.

Ana and I wove our way through the ever growing swarm of ships. The traffic jams at the exits were causing them to stack up inside the cavern. At some point, Ana broke off and headed to her exit on the opposite end of the city. I spotted a wad of fighters hovering in front of where they were supposed to exit. If we didn't act fast we would be risking a crash.

I flew out in front of them and made my way down the wall of the cave. The exit was a tube that traveled through the side of the mountain. It was positioned about halfway up the walls of the cavern, so I estimated that it would come out somewhere near ground level.

I cut in front of the ships and squeezed my way around the traffic jam in the narrow corridor. The closer I got to the exit, the louder the explosions of the bombardment became. I could see the walls shaking violently. I began to wonder how long I would be able to keep this exit open. I couldn't hold up the whole mountain.

I finally reached the end. I landed and walked up to the pile of rocks. It was dark. Light from the entrance found it difficult to make its way around all of the eager to leave fighters. I relied more on my senses than my sight.

I walked up to the pile of boulders and placed my hand on one of the larger ones. I sent a pulse of energy through them to see how much of the tunnel I needed to clear. It turned out that there was only a thin layer blocking the exit.

I allowed my energy to spread across my body. The dark tunnel illuminated with a purple glow. I held both hands out in front of me and sent my energy across all of the rocks. It slowly wrapped itself around each one.

The ground beneath me shook with the impact of another titanium rod.

I began to lift up and push the rocks out of the clogged passageway. I was careful to hold onto all of the rocks above the entrance as well. I didn't want to cause a larger rock slide.

Once the rocks were out of the tunnel, I dropped them and allowed them to roll the rest of the way down the mountain (only about 100 yards).

Finally, daylight filtered by thick smoke and dust began to overpower my own purple glow. I choked as it filled my longues.

I let go of the cleared rocks, only holding onto the loose ones above me. I stepped out of the way and the fighters poured out. The most common model was the tic-tac black fighters. The Mayans called them Whisps. They were the fastest, most maneuverable ships to ever make their way onto the battlefield. Their shields were fitted to their exact shape and strong for their size. They could out-manover a jet any day.

The rest were Stingrays. They were my favorite to see in action. They had a rapid fire rate and, unlike the Whisps, they carried a good stock of missiles. They could quickly disarm a cruiser of its anit-aircraft cannons to clear the way for bombers.

I admired our fleet, but my heart sank to see the landscape. What had just been a beautiful rainforest minutes earlier was a dreary wasteland. Not a single tree was left standing. Most of them had been disintegrated by the force of the orbital strike.

There was only one thing left standing here. On the top of the next ridge was another one of the Mayan super-canons. It was firing every minute or two. The Organization's shields would probably be able to stave off the blasts if they stayed at a distance. I hoped that we had taken a few ships down before they could raise their shields.

I began trying to move the rocks above to a more stable position. The constant rumbling made that difficult. Although, the rumblings were coming further apart, so I hoped that the Orbital strike was almost over. I couldn't really see the sky where they were coming from or where they were hitting. This side of the mountain appeared to be blocking them.

While I was keeping an eye on the steady stream of fighters heading around the mountain, I noticed a fiery streak fighting the traffic. It was Lucas, and his attention wasn't on the fighters, it was on the cannon.

"Dylan!" the chief called over the coms.

"I see him," I acknowledged. "On my way to intercept."

"No," Bailey's voice spoke up, "You keep that tunnel open. I've got him."

"It took both of us before," I reminded her.

"It won't this time," she snarled. I could feel her anger through the coms. She was now a mother bear protecting her den. I wouldn't want to be the one in her way.

It wasn't long before Bailey came zipping out of the tunnel I was protecting. She was flying faster than I had ever seen her move before. I sent a blast of my own energy after her. It hit her and she used its power to conjure a powerful beam of purple and white energy. It plowed into Lucas just before he reached the cannon.

I saw him flip through the air and disappear behind the mountain. Bailey was soon over the peak and out of sight.

"We've got another one going after the north cannon," the chief informed, "Looks like the ice one."

"I'm on it," Hunter volunteered.

"No," I overruled, "You come hold this. I'll take her."

"No," Hunter insisted, "Trust me. I need to go for her. We know each other."

I didn't like it. He was good. Really good, but I had only been training him a month. She may have trained her whole life.

"If we're gonna stay and fight, you have to trust me on this one," Hunter pleaded, "In my vision, I saw her fighting with us. I think she'll turn."

I took a deep breath, "Okay," I agreed, "But the second you see anything going sideways, you get out and let one of us take over."

"Yes, sir," he agreed.

I decided that I couldn't be stuck here. I needed to secure these rocks. One by one, I began to move the most precarious ones away from the entrance.

As I worked, I heard a loud explosion come from the other side of the mountain. "What was that?" I asked over the coms.

"We just took down a cruiser," ALI informed me.

"So we're pushing them back?" I asked.

"Hard to tell," he informed, "We are taking heavy casualties. The Organization came prepared."

This is ridiculous. I raged. *One rock at a time?* I focused my frustration into my energy and pushed it through the entire mountain side. I dug its tendrils into the ground and clawed away every bit of loose material. Every rock,every tree, every speck of dirt. I scraped the side of the mountain totally bare and let everything tumble down on either side of the tunnel.

"There," I congratulated myself.

"Why didn't you do that sooner?" ALI asked.

"I guess I forgot I could," I admitted. I had only pushed my powers to their limits a couple of times. Really, since I had united the two halves of my crystals, I hadn't seen what it could truly do. We might find out today.

I ignited my jetpack and flew up to the top of the mountain. Fighters were swarming the ten or so remaining cruisers. I could see that many of them had been equipped with tiny, anit-aircraft missiles. They were eating through our forces almost as quickly as we could supply them.

"Bailey," I called over the coms.

"Yea," she replied. I could tell she was in the middle of a fight still.

"We need you at the cruisers. Swap out with me," I suggested.

"I've...just about got him," there was an explosion in the background as she talked.

"For his sake," I joked (half-joked). "Plus, you're the only electrical one here. I need you to stop some missiles."

"Fine," she huffed.

I flew over the valley and past the super-canon. Crossing over the mountain was like flying onto another planet. The forest was still lush and green (with the exception of a few smoldering patches).

I instantly spotted Bailey and Lucas exchanging blasts. I drew my staff and focused a beam of energy in his direction. He dodged, but it was more to signal to Bailey that it was time to tag me in.

We made brief eye contact, and then she flew off over the mountain. Lucas turned his attention to me, instantly throwing as many fireballs as he could in my direction. I threw my own balls of purple energy to intercept them. Some would have missed me, but I didn't want to take the chance of them hitting the cannon.

We flew toward one another until we collided. We deflected off of one another.

"I thought we were friends," I quipped.

"I told you we were even now," he barked in his thick accent.

I threw my staff at him and charged at the same time. He dodged the staff. When I reached him, I took hold of both his arms, all the while directing the staff at his back. He tried to pull away, but it was too late. The blue wave of energy spread across his flame engulfed body. I let go of him and he tumbled through the air until he crashed into the mountain behind us.

He quickly recovered and launched himself out of the jungle. When he reached me, we engaged in a mid-air fist fight, each blow extrapolated by our powers.

It didn't take long before I landed a good blow on his jaw which once again sent him flying backwards. He didn't crash this time. Instead, he used the momentum to fly toward the cannon.

"Oh no you don't," I said out loud. I charged toward him. My jetpack was slower than he was, so I propelled myself with concussive blasts.

I called my staff back to my hand as I flew. I would have to be more delicate as we fought around the cannon. I caught up and tackled him just as he prepared to destroy the cannon. The ball of fire shot off into the sky, and we crashed beside the gigantic machine.

I was on top of him now, holding him to the ground by his neck.

He coughed as I tightened my grip. I wasn't trying to kill him, but I knew if I let up he'd get away. He began to panic and his energy began to consume us. My own energy protected me from the heat. When I thought the time was right, I pulled him up, flipped around behind him, and put him in a sleeper hold. It wasn't long before the flames subsided, leaving behind scorched earth and a scorched suit.

"Is he out?" I asked ALI.

"He seems to be unconscious," ALI confirmed.

I let go and stood up. I pushed his motionless body to the side. I hoped that all this was almost over.

"Bailey, Hunter, how's it coming," I asked.

"Amelia is not interested in swapping sides at the moment," Hunter informed, out of breath.

"It's chaos, but I'm managing here," Bailey said, "Go help Hunter."

"On it," I said.

"Dylan, what are you doing back in the cavern?" Blake asked.

That seemed out of pocket. "What do you mean?" I asked.

"If you need something, I'll grab it for you," he continued.

I began to question if he was talking to me. "Blake, what are you talking about? I'm standing beside the cannon." I was sure he could hear the blasts coming from it over the coms.

"What?" Blake responded, "I literally see you right there. You're the purple one." He almost laughed.

"Blake, that's not me!" I nearly shouted.

Suddenly, there was a loud explosion over the coms. Then, only static.

Chapter 25

"Bailey, help Hunter," I commanded frantically, "I'm going inside."

There was no response. I wasn't sure if she could hear me. I could only pray that she did.

I prayed the most desperate prayer of my life as I flew across the valley toward the opening I had cleared earlier. These bearers had executed a perfect plan. Draw all of El Dorrado's bearers out, get me to use my power, sneak in unquestioned. Now there was no one to protect the inside. We had played right along.

I quickly spotted the entrance because of the bare ground above it. I soared through, whizzing by the few straggling fighters exiting the tube. I popped out on the other side to horror.

Purple energy exploded around the base of one of the pillars. The rock was blown out from underneath and the top broke away from the ceiling. The entire structure crumbled as it fell and smashed into the jungle and one of the city blocks below. A huge cloud of brown dust swirled up around it. Another had already fallen before I got there.

A swarm of Whisps attacked the bearer, but he disposed of them with only a few blasts of energy. I flew toward him as fast as I could. It was a long way across the cavern to where he was at. I could only watch as he destroyed another pillar. He had destroyed three of the nine that surrounded the central pillar. When he saw me coming, he turned his attention to the central pillar.

We both raced to reach it first. He directed a beam of stolen purple energy at its base, but I conjured my own to intercept it. They clashed at the base of the pillar. I was sure it took damage, but I had saved it for now.

Before he could take another shot, I slammed into him. My hands gripped his neck as I pushed him backwards through the air. He clawed at them, his eyes wild with hate, mine narrowed with determination.

I forced two concussive blasts from my feet just as we reached the cracking ceiling of the cavern. It must have been a thin spot (likely caused by the orbital attacks) because we exploded through the rock and tumbled across the side of the barren mountain.

As we rolled through the ash and dirt, I lost my grip on him. Even with all of my adrenaline kicking, I laid stunned for a moment, facedown in the ash. The smells of the scorched Earth filled my nostrils. The white sun glared down, heating the black, sooty ground. The sounds of nearby explosions barely broke through the ringing in my ears.

I pushed myself off the ground. Once my feet were under me, I saw the thief doing his best to stand just a few feet away. Before rushing into another fight, I thought to sense his emotions. He was angry - filled to the brim with hate. It wasn't directed toward me though. I wished Bailey was here to understand what it meant.

"Why are you doing this?" I yelled, "You don't believe in it."

"I don't believe in anything anymore," he snarled. Purple energy ignited across his body. He raised his hands and focused a beam on energy in my direction.

I raised a shield to intercept it. Our fight ensued.

Our powers were evenly matched, but he didn't have as much experience with the energy as I did. He fought with his hatred. I knew it made him weaker.

"I could help you," I offered as I dodged a ball of energy. It hadn't yet set in just how many people he had killed by destroying those pillars. I wouldn't have offered it otherwise.

"I've heard that before," the bearer scoffed. He conjured another blast.

"Suit yourself," I conceded. If I was holding back before, I stopped then. I called my energy to my fists and began throwing punches. Once I had landed a few, I drew my staff. I swept his legs out from under him and tried to jab at his chest. He grabbed the staff with his hand and pulled it to the side. The tip of the staff marred up in the dirt.

The bearer rolled out of the way, kicking me in the chest as he did. I was knocked backward, leaving my staff stuck in the dirt. I never lost my footing though.

Before he could stand up, I had already balanced myself and called the staff back to my hand. I prepared to fight again, but as he stood up, a bolt of white lightning fell from the sky. It took both of us by surprise. The bearer fell over, unconscious.

I looked up and saw Bailey and Hunter flying down to me. "Nice shot," I congratulated her. The two of them landed just in front of me.

"Thanks," Bailey said quickly, "Is everything okay inside?"

As if to answer her question, the ground beneath us began to shake. This was even more violent than what he had felt with the orbital beams crashing. All of our eyes were equally wide as we exchanged worried looks. Then, with one mind, we ran for the opening I had just created on the side of the mountain.

We jumped through and flew toward the central pillar. Dust and small rocks were falling from the ceiling as cracks spread. Coming toward us were strange vehicles. They were almost rectangular, but they had hoses connected to robotic arms on the outside. They were clearly from El Dorado, so we didn't engage them. I did look behind me to see what they were doing.

They each went to different places along the ceiling. From their hoses came some sort of clear liquid that crystallized when it made contact with the rock. They were repairing the cracks.

The cavern was still swarming, but no longer with fighters. Now it was filled to the brim with medical ships, all of them headed for the collapsed pillars. As I examined the debris, I saw a magenta glow spreading through the rubble. Ana was helping the recovery teams.

"ALI" I called.

"Sir,"

"Are our coms back up?" I asked.

"Yes, sir," ALI confirmed, "That bearer took out El Dorado's communications, but I'm running ours through a short range system."

"Blake, Brady, you there?" I asked, hoping he could hear me now.

"Yea, we're still here," Blake answered for both of them.

"Alright, we're gonna go help Ana," I informed him, "You keep us updated on what's going on outside."

I turned toward the fallen pillars. Hunter and Bailey followed. The dust from their fall was beginning to spread through the cavern like a thick clay fog. As few flew into the cloud, we had to rely more on our senses than our sight.

As we grew closer, I could sense the overwhelming pain. I hated being in catastrophes like this one. Each survivor's cries of pain, fear, and sadness filled my heightened senses. I knew it must be even worse for Bailey, but she handled it well.

We landed near Ana who was lifting a large boulder off of a survivor. Her pink energy cradled the bottom of the rock with arms of energy that extended up from the ground. One of the first responders swooped in and drug the poor woman out. Her lower body had been crushed. I doubted she would ever be able to use her legs again. If she survived.

I took a step forward. I was going to ask Ana where she needed us, but a hand grabbed onto my arm, stopping me. It was Hunter. I turned around to him. Bailey was standing behind him. I could tell she was reading him.

"We have to go," Hunter demanded, tears welled up in his eyes, "Everyone needs to leave right now."

He was desperate for me to listen to him. His hand squeezed my arm. His face wrinkled as he tried not to sob. I put my hand on his shoulder.

"Hunter," I started, looking at Bailey for help. She didn't offer any. Maybe this vision had affected him more than I thought. "Maybe you and Bailey should…"

A cold shiver traveled down my spine. Hunter's expression changed. His tears died up, and he let go of my arm. I saw that Bailey felt it too. A sinking feeling in the pit of my stomach. The light of my crystal flickered. I knew exactly what this was.

"Chief, Chief!" I called over the coms.

"He can hear you," Blake answered, "Is everything alright?"

"Evacuate the city," I commanded.

"What?" I heard the chief's voice in the background, "We've almost won."

"No we haven't," I said. I felt the sensation growing stronger. Ana had stopped what she was doing, and walked over to us.

"What is that?" she asked. She felt it too.

"Not what," Hunter said softly. His mind wandered off to the past, "Who."

We all looked up. Through the dust, I could see the flaming silhouette of Lucas. It started a fuzzy glow, but sharpened as he drew closer. As he came closer, the glow of two other figures broke through, one light blue, Amelia, and one white, Ryder using Bailey's energy instead of mine now.

They all stopped a good distance away from us. Anticipation of the ensuing fight rose in my chest. As I watched them, another figure slowly emerged, descending in front of them. This silhouette was black. Not just a shadow, but a shadow that absorbed all of the surrounding light. Vibrating waves of black pulsated out from him as he descended.

Ana, Bailey, Hunter, and I all called our energy to ourselves. It lit the particles of dust around us with our respective colors.

"Hunter, get to the central pillar," I commanded, "Get all of the leadership out. Bailey, Ana, protect the central pillar."

"What are you going to do?" Bailey asked.

"Buy us some time."

No one moved. I looked back at them, "Go! I'lll be fine. We've got to keep this place standing for as long as possible."

Finally, they turned and flew off toward the central pillar.

"That was a mistake," a low voice boomed. It was the Onyx bearer.

I closed my eyes, clenched my fists, and took a deep breath. "The power of a star," I reminded myself of ALI's first lesson. I looked at the four bearers, through the veil of dust suspended between us.

I looked past them with my senses and locked onto the crumbling wall above them. I sent my energy past them and pushed its tendrils into the cracks of the rock. Then, I pulled back on it, simultaneously sending a beam of energy from each of my hands as a distraction.

Ryder raised a shield around them all to intercept the purple beams. When the energy hit his white shield, it turned purple. As all this happened, the ceiling above them crashed down.

I saw Amelia fly out to one side; she disappeared in the falling debris. Ryder acted quickly, lowering his shield and attempting to stop the rocks with his telekinesis. A few began to float as they fell, but more fell on top, breaking through his defences. It wasn't long before they had all completely disappeared into the flying debris.

I knew they would survive, but I hoped that it would split them up. It worked. Sort of.

Amelia was the first to recover. She came flying in on my left. I dodged a few icy blasts, then stopped a spray of ice cycles with my shield.

I focused my own energy back at her. Jetpacks aren't very nimble, so she wasn't able to dodge out of the way. The blast made contact with a loud SMACK. She was sent flying backwards. Just in time too, because Lucas came flying from my right.

I stopped two fireballs with my own balls of purple energy. They exploded violently on one another, the sound echoing through the hollow mountain.

"One tale whooping wasn't enough for today?" I taunted.

Lucas responded by focusing a contentious stream of fire at me. I raised a shield to stop it. The smell of burnt air swirled in the hot wind blowing off the fiery energy.

As I tried to come up with a way to end our little fight quickly, I remembered how I had withstood his energy quite well back at the mountain base. I had an idea it would either work, or it would hurt. Maybe both.

I nodded my head to form my helmet. Then, I readied myself, feet braced, fists pointed toward Lucas. Then, with one motion, I lowered my shield, ignited my jetpack, and launched myself forward with a concussive blast from my feet. I propelled myself forward, through the pillar of fire. I felt the intense heat building up around me, but just as it grew uncomfortable, I reached Lucas.

I grabbed him around his waist, pushing him through the air. His fists jabbed into my unprotected sides, but I ignored the pain. I felt around on his belt until I found what I was looking for: his power dampener. It was smaller, and better attached than before, but I was sure this was it. I placed my palm on top of it and focused a small blast of energy there. I destroyed it.

I could feel Lucas' body change when he realized what I had done. I pulled myself up to his shoulders. He was flying in a frantic weaving pattern, trying to throw me off. I lowered my helmet. "I'm sorry," I said, then I let go.

I hated to do it, but I didn't feel bad. This would keep him and his sister busy. I hoped.

I heard his screams as he flew off. I gritted my teeth and tried to regain my bearings. I never got the chance, because a blast of my own energy knocked me out of the air. I tumbled head over heels until I crashed into a section of the jungle that was still intact.

A shield formed around me to cushion my fall, but it didn't feel like it helped very much. I landed on my back.

I heaved, trying to catch my breath. Over my own wheezing, I heard someone approaching behind me. I sensed the chilling presence of the Onyx bearer. I forced myself to roll over and attempted to push myself up onto my feet. It wasn't going very well. From the ground, I looked up at the shadowy figure approaching. He walked until he was standing directly over me.

"Such a waste of talent," he detested. His voice was made gravely by the modifier in his helmet.

I tried to think of something to quip back, but I couldn't breath, let alone talk. I heard the explosions of bearers fighting. I tried to look, but I couldn't see over the trees.

Then, the Onyx bearer grabbed me by the back of the neck and lifted me up. The black energy on his hand spread out, making it nearly impossible to even sense my own crystal. I grabbed at his hand, but I couldn't reach it.

He pointed me toward the central pillar. Blasts of green and white and magenta lit up the sky as they tried to take down the purple speck buzzing around the pillar.

I saw Bailey slam into him. She and Hunter combined their powers and focused a beam at Ryder. He dodged, but it clipped his foot, which pushed him away from the pillar. Two pink tentacles of energy stretched up from the floor of the cavern and wrapped themselves around Ryder. They jerked him down, but he freed himself with a purple blast that went in every direction.

As I was forced to watch the battle, the Onyx bearer raised his free hand and summoned his black anti-energy. It quivered and glitched as it consumed his left arm. I felt my body growing lethargic as the energy spread across me as well. My limbs grew limp and my eyes grew tired.

"This is the end of your insurrection," the bearer growled, "Now the Earth will bow to me. And you, and your rebellion, and your friends, will bow."

"I'll never bow to you," I choked.

"Then you will die."

The Onyx bearer thrust his left hand forward. The anti-energy pulsated out from his arm in a line that glitched to this side and that. It rumbled as it split the air. In less than a second it had reached its mark: the artificial sun seated above the central pillar. For a split second, there was an eerie silence, as if the explosion that was building were absorbing all the sound in the cavern.

All at once that sound was released in a white disk that erupted from the sun. That disk traveled outward just below the ceiling, crashing through every remaining pillar. It passed overhead and then, all at once, slammed into the edge of the cavern. The cavern shook, everything went dark, and the same silence filled the air once again. Then, as I fell to the ground, so did the cavern. Our oasis had been destroyed.

Chapter 26

I expected darkness. I expected death. I expected the weight of the mountain to come crushing down on me. I didn't get any of those. Instead, my strength slowly returned as my purple energy was able to spread across my body again. I dug my fingers into the dirt, forced my eyes to open, and pushed myself off the ground.

The first thing that I noticed was the pink glow. It was bright, lighting the forest around me. There was a low rumble, a straining and cracking noise as the cavern threatened to cave it. It didn't, and I quickly spotted the reason why.

In place of the central pillar was a new pillar made of Ana's magenta energy. It reached up and spread across the top of the cavern holding everything in pace. All around me, more of those same pillars of energy were rising. I didn't know where the Onyx bearer, or any of the others had gone, but I knew they would be trying to take Ana down.

I ignited my jetpack and launched myself off the forest floor. I had to find my friends.

"ALI! ALI!" I called frantically.

"Everyone's alive," he answered before I could ask.

A weight instantly lifted off my mind. I could think more clearly now.

"We need to get everyone and get out of here," I commanded, as I dodged a massive boulder falling from the ceiling.

I sped to the new central pillar. Its light was nearly as bright as the artificial sun. I quickly spotted Blake and Brady at the base. Blake was yelling into the beam.

I landed between them, "Where's everybody else?" I asked Brady.

"Bailey scooped us up and put us here," he replied.

"Ana!" Blake yelled. Brady and I interrupted our talk to look at him. "We've got to go. You can't save it."

I could hear her screaming over the roar of the energy beam itself. Her crystal wasn't made to push this much energy.

"I think she went to find Hunter," Brady continued.

"Did the chief and the elders make it out?" I asked.

"They got on a ship just before the explosion," Brady answered.

"Okay," I refocused my mind, "Stay here, don't let him do anything stupid. I'll find Bailey and Hunter."

As I turned to search for Bailey, I saw the black anti-energy crawling up one of the furthest out energy pillars. They had fooled me once, they wouldn't fool me twice.

"Don't leave Ana's main beam," I commanded over the coms, "They're trying to draw us out." I watched the attacked beam flicker, then its light faded completely. Its section of the cave collapsed. There was so much mountain on top of it that the rubble filled in completely without allowing sunlight through.

"ALI, get us a transport," I commanded.

"On it," he confirmed.

"Bailey, Hunter, where are you?" I called.

"On your left," Bailey's voice said.

I looked, but the only thing to my left was Ana's energy pillar. They must have been on the other side. I ran across the rubble and jumped up on top of a giant piece of steel. I only now realized that everything under my feet used to be a city. I hoped people had time to get out.

I peered around the side of the beam and saw flashes of white and green energy, tainted by the pink glow in the cavern. It was dark, so

I couldn't see what they were fighting. I leapt off the steel and used my jetpack to fly toward them. It wasn't long before a purple blast shot up from the ground near them. Their fight must have never stopped.

"Keep him distracted," I said. I tried to position myself so that he wouldn't see me. If they could keep his attention, I hoped he wouldn't sense me.

It worked. I flew up behind Ryder and tackled him. I pinned him against a large rock. He struggled, but he couldn't get away.

"You should have taken my offer," I scorned through gritted teeth, "You'll pay for all the people you killed today."

Ryder grabbed both my hands, but he couldn't move them. "How? You'll kill me?" he mocked.

"No," I admitted. I was going to smart off until I noticed a pink aura forming around us. It grew thicker until the ground was completely covered in the energy. "But she might," I worried.

I let go of Ryder and jumped to the side just as a beam of energy formed where we were sitting. Ryder couldn't move in time. He was carried upward until he reached the ceiling. The pillar crashed into the roof of the cave and kept going. I assumed, if he survived, he had been spit out on top of the mountain again.

I ran to meet Bailey and Hunter. We reached each other all at once and engaged in a group hug. "I told you we needed to leave," Hunter said, "I saw this in my vision."

"I should have listened," I admitted.

"We can say 'I told you so' later," Bailey suggested, splitting up our hug, "Ana won't be able to hold this much longer."

"I can't believe she can hold it at all," I added. "ALI, where's that transport?"

"On its way now,"

As Bailey, Hunter and I flew back to Ana and the rest, I saw another pillar go dark in the distance. Its section of the cave collapsed. This time, it left an opening in the ceiling of the cave. A ray of sunlight shone in like a spotlight. A few seconds later, I noticed tiny black dots ascending up the spotlight. At first, I thought it was ash, but I didn't see a fire. I realized that it was survivors. Some on jetpacks, some in transports. They were escaping the doomed city.

When we landed, Blake was still yelling into the beam of energy to no avail. Brady gave me a concerned look. I quickly walked up to the pink pillar.

"Ana-" I put my hand on Blake's shoulder and pulled him back a bit.

"Ana, it's time to go," I called into the beam.

"Then, go!" she yelled back. It was hard to hear her over the rumble of her energy beam. I could tell she was exhausted and in pain. She had pushed herself far beyond her limits.

Another pillar went dark. The deafening sound of another section collapsing filled the cave. The dust began to choke me.

"Ana, you've done everything you can do," I urged.

"Then…I'll die with my people," she demanded.

"Ana! No!" Blake cried. He pounded his fist off the energy beam, but he was thrust backward. He landed on his back.

I heard a ship coming. It was the transport ALI had ordered.

I knelt down next to Blake. "I have a plan, but you have to trust me," I told him, "Come on." I took him by the hand and lifted him up. "Get on the transport and get everyone out of here," I commanded.

He pulled away from me. "You're trying to get rid of us," he accused, "I thought we weren't splitting up any more."

"We're not," I promised as another beam died. "I just need to know all of you are out of here."

"So you can what? Sacrifice yourself? And Ana?"

"I hope it doesn't come to that," I said.

Blake shook his head, "No way, not both of you. Not one of you! There's a better way."

I put my hand on his shoulder, "Find a spot to lay low a few miles away and keep the engines running," I told him.

"If you die, I'm gonna kill you," Blake's voice quivered as he attempted to joke.

"You have my permission," I granted, "Wait for my signal."

"What signal?" Blake asked.

"I don't know," I admitted, "But you'll know it when you see it."

I looked at the rest of the group. I called my energy across my body. "Get in the transport," I commanded.

"What about you?" Hunter questioned.

I didn't answer. I needed Blake to take care of that. I turned back to Ana's beam and walked toward it. When I was close, I pressed my purple hand against it. I pushed hard, and my hand slipped through. That was what I needed to see.

I turned back. Bailey was forcing Hunter onto the transport. Everyone else was on board. Once he was inside, the door closed and the transport took off.

I closed my eyes and took a deep breath. "Ana, I'll buy you some time," I promised. I stepped away from the shield to see another bean give way to the black anti-energy. I prayed my friends would be able to navigate through the falling debris. There were three beams left standing behind me. All of the ones on the other side of the cavern had been destroyed. I figured that he would ignore the ones still standing and go straight for Ana herself. I was right.

A ball of the black energy soared above my head. It crashed into Ana's beam, biting a chunk out of its side. Its vibrating waves ate away at the pillar.

I couldn't sense the Onyx bearer's exact location, so I just fired off a purple blast in his general direction. I wanted his attention on me. I need to buy my friends and the surviving Mayans time to escape.

My purple beam exploded against a section of destroyed skyscraper. I still didn't see the Onyx bearer, but I did sense another ball of his anti-energy headed our way. I hit it with my own ball of energy which was quickly eaten away by his. It saved the pillar though.

Finally, the bearer showed himself. He emerged from the shadows just a few feet away from me. I jumped back, startled. He had hidden himself in the darkness.

"Bow," he grumbled.

"No," I scowled. I took hold of my crystal and removed it from its place on my chest.

"Then die," The bearer lifted his arms and directed a powerful blast of his dark energy.

I focused as hard as I could and pushed all the energy I could conjure through the crystal. For a moment, they met in the middle. The anti-energy consumed the purple energy as fast as I could supply it. Then, he started trying.

The black pulsating waves of anti-energy crawled up my purple beam. The crystal shrieked as though it were about to break. Finally, the time was right. I yanked my crystal toward me and jumped out of the way.

His torrent of black energy slammed into Ana's pillar, bringing it down all at once. Ana collapsed on the ground.

Luckily, the bearer was standing precisely where I wanted him. He didn't know it, but we were standing over the underground river. The rock and debris had just covered it up.

I focused my energy again, this time boring a hole through the ground. I focused it as much as I could, crushing and melting the rock below us. Instantly, the ground gave way and began to slide.

The bearer lost his balance and his attention turned back to me. Before he could comprehend what was happening, the ground dropped out from beneath him. I heard him splash into the water below. Now he was powerless. I hoped.

I ran as fast as I could toward Ana. Giant boulders rained down around us, the force of their impact tossing me from side to side. I could hardly keep my balance as I ran.

One boulder threatened to fall on Ana, but I pushed it back with my powers. It narrowly missed crushing her.

I couldn't see anything now. I was running using only my super senses. Just as the collapsing roof reached us, I dove on top of Ana and raised a shield around us. A crushing weight built up on top. I could hardly hold it.

There was a deafening sound of crashing rocks. It felt as though the earth beneath us might give way, if my shield didn't give way first. I reached my breaking point. I couldn't hold it.

I screamed. At first, it was just a scream of desperation, then, it formed a word, "JESUS!" It was the most eloquent prayer I could form.

Still the weight grew more. The rumbling grew louder. Then, suddenly, it all stopped, and there was nothing but silence and darkness.

Chapter 27

"Ana" "Ana, wake up"

It was no use. She was out cold. Her breathing was shallow. She had pushed herself too far. She would be lucky to survive, let alone help get us out of this mess.

I was laying on top of her where I had fallen. My arms were on either side of her. My elbows were pressed into the sharp gravely dust that was beneath us. I was using all of my might to hold together a shield above us. It had been pressed down by the rock above until it was pushing down on my back. It provided a little light, but not really enough to see. Not that there was much to see.

"When we get out of here, let's agree not to tell Blake about this part," I attempted to joke. It didn't lighten the mood.

Dust particles burned my lungs. Occasionally, I heard a rock shift. Each time I thought it might be the one that would crush us.

"What was I thinking," I asked myself, "Bury the creepy bearer. Save your best friend's girlfriend. Everyone will be so happy." I coughed.

"I must be running out of oxygen," I thought.

I bowed my head and rested it on the tiny bit of ground beside Ana's. My head throbbed. My muscles ached. Every second that passed made letting all of this fall on top of us seem like the better option. Was there another option?

"God, it's times like this that make you realize you don't pray often enough," I pointed out, "I'm sorry for that. I guess I could make plenty of excuses, but I don't think that would help," I coughed again, trying not to do so in Ana's face. "Anyway, I'm sorry for that, but if you don't help me out, I think I'm gonna be seeing you real soon."

"Not that I don't look forward to that," I admitted, "I just think I have a little bit more work to do here first. Plus, who's gonna watch out for my family? And who's gonna make sure this war ends? And make sure it doesn't happen again?"

Then, something strange happened. My busy mind instantly quieted. Following the quiet was a voice, not audible, but so loud I couldn't mistake it, "You will."

A fire of sheer willpower and determination willed my eyes. I gritted my teeth and pulled energy from my crystal. I thought I had already been pulling as much as I could, but I found more.

My energy began to weave its way through the debris above me. A second wave of strength filled my muscles. The shield once pressed to my back began to push upward. The purple glow around me intensified until it was blinding, illuminating our air pocket like the sun itself had arrived.

I made my way onto my hands and knees. I looked down at Ana. I noticed Ana's eyes flutter, but they didn't open yet. I looked back at the rocks above me, their grey tone made purple by the light coming off of me.

I pulled one foot under me so that I was kneeling. I raised my hands over my head and pushed the rocks further. My energy spread through the collapsed mountain side. Like roots seeking water, they broke through rock and dirt.

Streams of purple energy swirled out from the crystal on my chest, rushed across my arms and leapt off my hands. A contentious river of energy rushed off of my hands and up into the rocky prison.

I finally pushed the rocks far enough to stand. Ana lay at my feet. I noticed her start to stir. I nudged her with my foot.

"Wake up," I grunted under the strain of the weight above me.

"Ugh," she replied, rolling her head back and forth.

I focused back on the rocks. Slowly, I started forcing them to the side. There was no way I was going to lift up the whole mountain, but I could move it enough to make a tunnel to the surface. Little by little, the way out became clear.

"Time to go," I urged.

Ana rolled over and did her best to get on her feet. The best she could do was all fours. I held the mountain above us with my right hand. With my left, I leaned down and placed it around her waist. I scooped her up, and she put her arms around my neck.

"Hold on," I requested gently as I ignited my jetpack.

Slow and steady, we began to rise toward the surface. As we moved up, I allowed the rocks below us to collapse, focusing my energy on the path ahead. We moved up in a little bubble of safety. The further we pressed, the easier it became.

Then, finally, we burst through the surface. I expected the sun to be shining, but it was night. The moon hid itself. The stars were the only light - that and my own purple glow. Waiting just above where we surfaced was a transport filled with worried faces. I rose up and landed in the open side door.

"You're alive!"
"Thank God"
"Don't ever do that again"
"Are you alright?"
"Ana!"

I passed Ana off into Blake's arms. "She'll be alright," I assured him, "Hunter, she could use your help."

Before he would attend to her, he ran to me and buried his face in my chest. We nearly tumbled out through the open door. I wrapped him in my arms "I told you I wasn't goin' anywhere, kid," I smiled.

He cried.

Bailey came up behind him and sandwiched him between us. We kissed and she put her forehead on my shoulder. I felt her own hot tears begin to soak into my tattered uniform.

We lost. I think it was only begging to set in just how badly we had lost. Everything was turned on its head. The city that had once offered us sanctuary was now a graveyard beneath our feet.

I guess I could have cried with them, but I didn't see much point in it. We could cry for the dead later. Right now, we needed to focus on who was still alive.

I looked at my other friends. Brady was doing his best to help Blake and Ana. I could tell he was just as distraught.

"Brady," I called. I took one arm off of Bailey and Hunter and extended it toward him. He looked for a moment. Then started walking our way. It was only a few steps, but he grew heavier with each one. By the time he had reached us, all he could do was fall forward into the little space left between Bailey and I. We each offered him an arm and he pressed his head into his friend's shoulder.

Ana was sitting up now, holding her head. Blake looked from her to me for a moment and I gestured with my head for them to come over. Blake slowly helped Ana to her feet and he half carried her over to the rest of us.

Ana propped herself up on Bailey, but soon, the emotion broke through to her as well. She and Blake leaned in, Her front leaning on Bailey, and Blake holding her from the back.

And then we stood there. The big blubbering mess that we were. Ana had failed her mission to protect her people. Millions were dead. Bailey heard the cries of every trapped, crushed, and broken Mayan that was killed, and no doubt the ones that were still buried.

Hunter and Brady had watched the only place they had been able to call home since the takeover crumble around them. They were refugees once again.

Blake had watched his future fall apart. His plans of marrying Ana meant he would help rule their people one day. He had a heart for the Mayans. He loved them, and he was just begging to be accepted by them.

I had watched the full betrayal of a system my father had built for my future. Everything I thought I knew and many things I trusted had destroyed peaceful people, murdered in cold blood. The war that was set to end in our favor now appeared to be extended indefinitely and swayed by greed in our opponents benifit.

I didn't know what to do. I didn't even know where to go. Where would we be safe now? Surely the entire Ekklesia wasn't against us. The chief had said we were betrayed by Sparks. He held the blame for all of this. He expected us to die. We held the evidence to dethrone him.

"ALI, take us home," I requested. Still not letting go of my friends.

"Sir, they'll be looking for us in Tullahoma," he advised.

"Take the long way," I suggested, "Activate the stealth shield and bring us down near the old Arnold Base. I can have Alex come get us once we land."

"Yes sir," ALI agreed.

"ALI," I called back.

"Sir"

"You're in this hug too, even if we can't see you," I consoled, "I know it's hard for you too."

"Thank you sir," ALI's inflection turned down. He was sad.

I'm not sure how long we stayed like that, but eventually, we agreed to let go. Bailey and Blake helped Ana to a seat. Brady walked to the cockpit. Hunter let go, but he stayed behind.

"Does everything we see in the visions come true?" he asked, his voice shaking.

"I don't know," I admitted, "I guess it's up to us whether it does or not."

I saw fear in his eyes and sensed pain in his heart.

"What did you see?" I asked.

Hunter's eyes glossed over and he looked at the ground. "I... I saw... I saw us split up. We couldn't be together anymore. We lost."

I put both hands on his shoulders, "Then we'll just have to make sure we don't let that happen."

"How?" he asked. His breathing was heavy as though he might start crying again.

"Our choices are ours to make," I explained, "The future isn't set for us. We choose what we make it."

This seemed to suffice him for now.

"Why don't you go help Ana," I suggested.

Hunter agreed and walked over to them. He summoned his green energy and began waving his hand across her body. The energy seeped into her skin and I almost instantly saw the color return to her face (even in the dimly lit transport). Once Bailey saw that Ana was going to be fine, she walked away from the group and joined me next to the door of the cockpit.

She put her hand on the side of my head. "Are you okay?" she asked, pressing her finger on the wound I'd forgoten about.

"Oww!" I pulled away. "I was." I took her hand and placed it on my neck instead of my forehead.

We must have been a sight to behold. Everyone in the group was covered from head to toe in a thick layer of brown and grey dust. Our hair was madded and tainted the same shade. Our uniforms were filthy and ripped. Bailey and I hadn't been wearing armor when the attack started, so our uniforms were even more torn. You could see our skin in some places. For those wearing armor, the armor was scratched and filthy.

I had dried blood caked up all down the side of my face. I could feel sore spots on my back and ribs...and arms...and legs beginning to fight through the adrenaline. I was definitely bruised, and possibly broken in a few spots.

I placed my dirty hand on Bailey's cheek and pushed it back through her dirt caked hair. A small dust cloud formed. "Are you okay?" I asked.

He placed her hand on top of mine, "The worst wounds aren't the ones on the outside," she whispered. She bowed her head and bit her lip, "All those people…The children… Not enough escaped."

I started to pull her in for another hug but she pulled away, "No," she insisted, "We have to be strong right now. I'll cry when the war's over."

"You don't have to keep it all inside," I offered.

"Neither do you," she retorted, lovingly.

"Fair," I admitted, "When we get a second to breathe, we can let it out to each other."

"Deal," Bailey agreed.

We stood, leaning on the door and each other for a while. A long while. It was hard to move. It was hard to think about anything very long without a more pressing thought taking its place.

Once Hunter had finished treating Ana, he secluded to the back corner of the transport. Blake and Ana sat next to one another in the seats that lined the side of the ship. She laid her head on his shoulder, staring out into nothingness. I'm not sure she blinked once. Over the hour that we flew, I watched her eyes slowly shift from crushing sorrow, to flaming hatred. Blake looked more stunned than anything. I sensed a sort of helplessness. I knew he felt useless in battles like that because he didn't have powers like the rest of us. I knew he wished he could have done something more.

"Sir," ALI called, jarring me from my thoughts. I immediately noticed that he was only speaking in my coms. "What is it?" I asked softly. Bailey lifted her head and listened in.

"I don't mean to alarm you, but a Mayan transport, much like the one we are in, has appeared on the radar. It also had a stealth shield. I just happened to run a decloaking scan. It's about two miles behind us."

"Survivors?" I asked.

"I'm sure they are, but I found it strange that-"

I stopped listening. A familiar cold chill ran down my spine. Again? Already?

"ALI, take evasive manovers!" I commanded.

Nothing happened.

"ALI!" I called.

Nothing.

I burst through the door of the cockpit, startling Brady in the pilot's seat. "Look out," I said, and I pulled him out of the chair.

I sat down and took hold of the controls. A crowd had already amassed at the door.

"Blake, co-pilot," I commanded.

He pushed through the crowd and sat down. I swerved the ship just as a fiery energy blast illuminated the horizon. He missed.

"What's happening?" Brady asked.

"They're trying to finish the job," I answered, jerking the ship to dodge another fireball.

"I thought they were dead," Blake nearly yelled and he took control of the rear cannon.

"Obviously not!" I responded, turning the nose of the ship up.

A white glow filled the cockpit. "I'll take them down," Bailey offered, turning for the door.

"No!" I yelled, "No, we need you here. Give us a shield."

Her shield would be stronger than the one that came with the ship. Unfortunately, before he could raise her own, the ship was jarred forward.

Sensors across the dashboard lit up like a christmas tree and alarms blared.

We were hit. And we were going down.

"ALI, where are we?" I called.

No response.

"ALI!"

"Looks like we're on our own," Blake said.

"Everyone strap in," I instructed, "Open up the side doors to slow us down."

A white glow spread across the windshield. "Better late than never," Blake quipped.

It was nearly impossible to see the ground for the darkness. There wasn't a city light in sight, only endless rolling mountains. Except, I knew these mountains! And that Lake. And… I realized we were in the Great Smoky Mountains. I used to come here all the time when I was a kid.

We were flying low now. In the distance, one mountain stuck up higher than the rest. A spiraling structure stood on top. I knew this mountain. It was a tourist attraction, the highest point in the Smokies.

On the side opposite to us, I knew there was a parking lot. It would be the only place to set the ship down.

Another blast erupted on the ship. I shook us, but Bailey's shield prevented any damage.

I pulled up, trying to slow us down. Our landing zone wouldn't be very big. It sat just down from the peak and had large drop offs on every side.

"I could really use ALI to tell me if this was possible," I wished.

Blake fired the reverse thrusters. Above us and to the right, I saw the other ship flying alongside us. Its side door was open and Lucas was standing there, his orange fire consuming his body. He fired at us again.

Suddenly, a white bolt of energy appeared between our ships. It struck their engine which turned into a brighter inferno than Lucas. The ship veered to the side and began its own crash landing.

"Nice shot!" Blake yelled.

"I'm sure they'll be back," Bailey said, "They just keep coming back."

The parking lot was in view now. In fact, it was coming into view way too fast.

"Hold on!"

Chapter 28

"Is everyone okay?" I asked when the ship finally screeched to a halt.

"Yea"
"All good"

I unclipped myself from my seat and looked over at Blake. He hadn't responded, but he seemed alright.

"Thanks for not putting a tree through my leg this time," He joked.

He was fine.

"Seems like I recall you were flying that ship just as much as I was," I defended.

Bailey leaned into the cockpit from the door behind us, "Seems like we crash every time the two of you fly one of these things."

We all had to chuckle. What had been terrifying and stressful to live through, we looked back on fondly now. I doubted this would age in the same way.

"What happened to ALI this time?" Blake asked.

"We lost our comms link with him," I said, observing the screen on my vanguard. "It's on his end, not ours."

"Guess we'll have to fix this thing without him," Blake sighed.

"Or we'll be doing another cross country jetpacking," I suggested. We were close enough to home now that, even though it would be long and uncomfortable, we could get there on our jetpacks.

I stood up and walked into the cabin. Bailey stepped out of the doorway to let me pass. Blake followed behind me. Everything looked intact. I could see through the open door that we were on the very edge of the parking lot just before a sheer drop off. The ship was seated in a deep scar it had cut though the ground and pavement when we landed. I congratulated myself on a job well done. The parking lot was probably smaller than a football field and quite uneven. It was a miracle we had been able to stop.

Hunter and Brady were standing next to one another. Hunter was healing a cut Brady had received on his forearm during the crash.

"Everything good?" I asked the boys.

"Yea," Hunter answered, "It's not very deep."

I looked around the cabin. Something was off. Something…someone was missing.

"Where's Ana?" Blake asked. I could hear the worry in his flickering voice.

Brady and Hunter looked at one another. Then, Brady used his free hand to point out the door. "She walked out as soon as we landed."

We all followed his finger out the side door and across the parking lot. Beyond our path of destruction, there was a path leading up to the peak of the mountain. Ana was walking briskly up it.

"What is she doing?" Blake wondered out loud.

"One way to find out," I suggested.

We all walked out of the ship together. Blake led the way. The scar in the landscape divided the parking lot into two halves and led almost directly to the entrance of the trail. Abandoned cars from the Organization's initial wave of attacks littered the landscape. They would have been exactly where they were parked over a year ago if our ship hadn't plowed through a few of them.

The power for quantum batteries went out across the entire world on that first day. I guess the people vacationing here never came back, even after the power turned back on.

I noticed Bailey was in the back, trailing further as we walked across the dark parking lot (what used to be a parking lot). I tagged back with her, sensing something familiar and unwelcome.

"I know that look," I worried, "Even in the dark."

"I'll be fine," Bailey assured me.

"The other bearers won't be held up long," I pointed out, "Are you going to be able to fight with a migraine?"

"I guess I'll have to," Bailey sighed, "Maybe it'll hold off a little bit longer."

"Don't push yourself too hard." I didn't want her getting sick.

"I don't think we get to choose that," Bailey started walking faster. I sped up with her.

"Seriously," I continued, "Hold back and let the rest of us fill in for you."

"We couldn't beat them when we should have had the advantage," Bailey raised her voice. Not because she was angry with me. She was angry we lost, and angry at herself over this headache. "We don't get to hold back. Don't treat me like I'm sick either. Let me fight."

"Okay," I agreed. "But this time, we don't split up. We take all of them all at once."

"Deal."

The rest of our walk was brisk and silent. The trail was paved but extremely steep. Looking ahead, I could tell Brady was getting tired. He didn't have the stamina of a bearer. The only reason Blake could keep up was because he had been doing it for a while. He was just always strong. He could keep up. Brady was new to this. We had all been up since probably this time the day before. Even the adrenaline and energy from our crystals wouldn't be enough to keep us going much longer. I worried we would become wreckless.

Finally, we reached the top of the trail. It flattened out and a bend in the trail promised an end to our trek. Brady and Hunter had fallen back to Bailey and I. Blake had pushed ahead and turned the corner before us. A section of Pine trees blocked our view. As we neared, I realized Blake's silhouette was still standing in the opening that led to the overlook at the peak. We all walked up behind him.

I looked over his shoulder. In the darkness, I could see Ana standing in the middle of a round paved area. Large, flat limestone slate pieces were set in the pavement. A short stone wall surrounded the circle on two sides, our path entering through one opening and exiting on the opposite end. Where the path continued, a narrow spiraling ramp rose from the ground. It gently climbed into the air until it met with an observer tower. The tower was supported by a concrete cylinder and had a round platform on top. It was about three stories tall, offering a view above the evergreen trees.

In front of this tower, there were no trees. Only rocky ground that dropped straight off. It offered a view of the mountains and valleys without having to climb up to the tower. Ana was looking out from her place into the valley below. Her arms were together behind her back, one hand resting inside the other. Her back was straight. Shreds of her tan Mayan skirt blew in the gusty mountain breeze.

I put my hand on Blake's shoulder. He didn't move. He just stared at Ana.

"We don't know if her dad made it out," Blake said. His voice was cold. He trailed off. "The Elders didn't."

I didn't know how he knew this. The only explanation was that he knew because he witnessed it. He would have likely been in the council chambers when the pillar collapsed. Brady too.

"I'm sure he made it," I assured him.

"I'm not," he stated. The emotion had left his voice. We were reaching the end of our emotions. The situation demanded we pay more, but we were out of payment. Everything was begging to callous in our tired, dreary fog. Or we were just stunned.

I moved my hand across Blake's back to give him a reassuring side hug. Then, I pulled him forward. We all walked to meet Ana. She was colder than he was. Her demeanor was anyway. On the inside, she was burning with hatred.

"They're coming," Ana said coldly as we walked up. She didn't take her eyes off of the dark landscape before us. A thick fog was settling in the valley below. It made the rolling mountains look like islands in the sea.

There wasn't a single light from a city, which was strange since I knew of a few we should be able to see. There was however, the light of a fire in the valley just beneath us. It cast a flickering orange glow through the ominous haze. No doubt, this was the remnants of the hayjacked transport.

"We'll be ready for them," I promised. I focused my conversation on the group. "We don't split up this time."

"About time," Hunter jabbed.

I nodded, agreeing that I was wrong to split us up the last time. "We watch each other's backs. We take out the three colorful ones. Then, we can focus on the black one."

Everyone nodded. Then, everyone's eyes simultaneously narrowed as a familiar cold chill returned. I think even Blake and Brady could feel it.

"Brady, you need to hide," I commanded, "Blake, you protect him."

"I want to help," Brady offered.

"I know you do, but there's not much you can do this time," I consoled, "Let the bearers take this one."

He begrudgingly agreed, and then he disappeared into the nearby forest. I took inventory of his exact location with my senses. The rest of us lined up facing the direction of the evil energy. I stood in the middle. Hunter and Bailey stood at my sides. Ana stood beside Bailey and Blake stood beside Hunter, keeping his eye on where Brady had entered the woods.

The crisp wind blew through my damaged suit. It wasn't nearly as hot here as El Dorado. I wasn't used to these temperatures anymore. The evil aura of the Onyx bearer hung in the air, chilling it further. It gripped my heart and made it difficult to breathe. It was different than it had been before. It was thicker, more volatile. I think he was angry.

The realization made me even more angry. What right did he have to be angry at us? He just destroyed our home. He was upset because, what? He didn't destroy it enough? We got away?

I heard an atom sword ignite. I looked. It was Ana. Her pink energy burned in her eyes. Her mouth turned down into a scowl. "I won't be playing by your rules tonight, Dylan," she seethed.

I didn't say anything. My own anger was begging to rise. I could have given her some speech about how they were tricked or fooled, that it wasn't really them who did it, but The Organization. I didn't. I only drew my staff and planted it into the ground. A blue ring spread out underneath us.

Bailey and Hunter drew their staff. Blake, flanking the opposite side from Ana, drew his sword as well.

The only sound was the wind and the hiss of the two blades. Their white glow lit the area a bit, as did the ever intensifying glow of our crystals. As our emotions rose, their light brightened. It began to leak out and spread across our chests and arms.

I felt Bailey gritting her teeth. The Migraine was setting in, but she was stronger than the pain it caused her. I prayed we all would make it out of this fight alive. It was a miracle we had all made it this far.

The evil grew nearer until finally, an orange glow could be seen just over the trees. Lucas flew up the side of the mountain and landed in front of us. Fire appeared on the opposite side of us and again flew to our front. It was Ryder mimicking his powers. Next, Amelia flew in, her body consumed with her cold, teal energy. Her jetpack set her gently between the two boys. A patch of frost formed under her. Finally, the

Onyx Bearer emerged from the trees, following the same path we had. Amelia moved over allowing him to take the center position.

For a moment, we just looked at one another. Usually, there would be some sort of discussion before a battle like this. Darren certainly liked to talk when I fought him. This team was different. They didn't talk much. I wasn't sure my group had much to say this time either. Everyone waited for someone to make the first move.

Ryder turned white. Lucas drew his atom sword which flamed with his energy. Amelia and Hunter locked eyes. His energy intensified. She drew her sword. Bailey set her sights on Lucas. Ana glared at the Onyx Bearer, but he ignored her. He was focused on me.

Of course, I was angry at all of them, but I really just wished this fight didn't have to happen. I couldn't see one way that this ended good for any of us. A death would be required before the first thought of stopping occurred. I feared that would only intensify it.

As everyone prepared to move, I had an idea. A good one. I worried we wouldn't have enough time before the pressure cracked, so I sent a bit of my energy to combine with Bailey's and a bit to combine with Hunter's. I needed them to pick up on what I was asking without setting off the bomb.

Bailey nodded in agreement. She remained looking forward. However, Hunter looked up at me. They both knew what I wanted, but he accidentally set everything off.

Amelia saw her chance to act. She lunged forward. Ana blocked her with a wall of pink energy. Ryder flew forward at Ana. She barely blocked his swing with her own sword. Lucas blasted a fireball at Blake. Thankfully, I had made a new gadget for him: a Unitum shield that retracted into his vanguard. It deployed just in time, but Blake was sent tumbling backward.

Bailey and Hunter both hurriedly supplied me with their energy. The white flowed up my left arm; the green traveled up my right. I placed both hands on my staff where the three were able to combine and directed a beam at the Onyx bearer.

He conjured his own beam to try and block it, but the three energies working together began to overpower it. The mountaintop illuminated with a rainbow of colorful blasts.

Bailey and Hunter used their free hands to form a shield around the three of us. Amelia tried to thrust her sword into the side, but she was blown backward. Lucas focused a pillar of fire on us, but it couldn't break through. The Onyx bearer began to slide backward. Our beam was held off only inches from his own hands. If we didn't overpower him right now, I knew he would falter to one side or the other and our opportunity would be lost.

He pushed back with all his might. The black anti-energy began to eat away at our beam, gaining back a few inches of what he had lost.

"On my signal, lower the shield and give him everything you've got!" I commanded my friends. They looked at me and waited for my command.

"NOW!"

The shield around us dissipated. I dropped my staff. Bailey, Hunter, and I each focused the most powerful beam we could muster at the evil bearer. They combined midway between us. There was an electrical ZAP. Then, the combined beam exploded out into the horizon as far as we could see. I sensed the Onyx bearer was gone.

We stopped contributing our energy to the beam, but still green, white, and purple embers lingered in the path of the surge. We had narrowed our fight down to the weaker bearers.

"Did we get him?" Hunter asked as he shielded an attack from Lucas.

"Probably not," I assumed. If a mountain couldn't crush him, I doubt that disintegrated him. "Let's focus on putting these guys down."

Amelia summoned a torrent of tiny ice cycles in our direction. I learned my lesson from the last time and used my telekinesis to take hold of each individual one as it flew through the air. They stopped just in front of me. I turned the sharp ends back toward their sender and returned them with the same speed.

Amelia flipped and dodged, but when she finished, I saw her grab her cheek. A drop of blood ran down. She tilted her head to the side as a sort of respect. But now she was angry.

I called my staff to my hand and ran at her. I figured now was a good time for a conversation. I swung the Unitum rod at her and she blocked it with her sword. The blade screamed in anger, as it was unable to slice through the indestructible metal.

"It doesn't have to be this way," I offered, driving her backwards with my advances.

"You have no idea what you're talking about," she growled. She fought in anger.

As she advanced at me now, she suddenly stopped, almost falling over. She pulled at her feet, but they would budge. They were bound by glowing, green roots.

"He's right," Hunter said from behind me. "You're not like them. You're not evil!"

Amelia's blue energy began to flow around the roots. Hunter's energy grew dim and its flowing movements slowed. Amelia ripped her feet up from the ground.

"Good and evil live on both sides," she lectured, "Yours is no better." She put her sword to her side and focused a beam of her own energy at me. I blocked it with a shield.

"You're right," I admitted, "But there's more good in the common people than your organization wants you to believe."

"Thats not the problem," she doubled down on her blast. I felt my hand growing cold and numb. I felt my shield losing strength. "The problem is that the common people always lose because they give power to evil. That's why evil rules on every side."

Ryder erupted out of the woods and began to fight with Hunter. Ana pursued him, riding a wave of her own magenta energy. I didn't know she could do that.

"Then let's cleanse the evil," I begged, "We can make something new."

"You're naive," she scolded, "They'll never let us."

My shield lost its integrity and I was forced to roll out of the way. I stood up quickly, but didn't attack her back. "They can't stop all of us," I pointed out.

Amelia stared at me. Her energy still ran across her body, but she didn't attack. I continued, "They only win if we keep fighting each other." She looked like she might consider what I had to say. "I fell into it too. They try to make it look like two sides. Ekklesia against Organization. That was never true. That was never even the point of the Ekklesia. It's not right against left, it's us against them."

I felt a fire in my soul as I spoke it. I knew it was true, but I had never verbalized it. We had allowed the Ekklesia to grow centralized. I don't think that my father ever meant for that. It was supposed to be a place for the little guys to come together so that maybe, just maybe, we could take down the rulers of darkness.

Amelia and I stared at one another. I could tell the words sparked something in her too. I sensed there was something, one thing, holding her back. A thin wall between she and I.

Our moment was disrupted by a fireball coming from behind me. I told my energy to make a shield, but it had been made lethargic by Amelia's cold energy. The shield didn't form in time and I was hit in the chest with a fire ball.

I wasn't hurt. My body could absorb the energy. In fact, it warmed me back up to normal. It did knock me on my back and my superheated chestplate fell off. I chose to use my momentum to flip head over heels and land back on my feet. I landed directly beside Amelia.

"Come on!" I yelled at Lucas, "How many times have I beat you? You really want me to do it again?"

Amelia glared at me. I flenched, expecting her to attack me, but she didn't. "Don't hit his dampener again," she warned. Her Russian accent was especially thick when she said it.

"You'll think about it then?" I asked.

She answered by giving me an icy punch to the chest. I stumbled backward. My entire body felt frozen. It only lasted a second though. When I could think clearly again, she was gone, and Lucas was barreling down on me once again.

As he began his attack I heard a scream. "Dylan!"

It was Blake. I used a concussive blast to knock Lucas back, then I whipped around in the direction of the sound.

He was beside the pillar holding up the observation towar. Brady was running away and Blake was squared up with a void figure emerging from the woods. The Onyx bearer was back. His energy covered him so thick that he was only a silhouette in the dim light.

Blake blocked a black blast with his sword, but it shut off immediately and retracted into the hilt. Blake dropped it and stumbled backward.

"Hey!" I screeched. I threw down my staff. Lucas was coming in for another attack. I locked onto him with my energy and yanked him out of the sky. With one fluid motion I stole his atom sword and locked my arm around his neck. I used my free hand to hold the blade to his neck.

"Stop this!" I commanded.

The entire battlefield fell silent. The intense flashes of color dwindled to the individual glows of the bearers. Lucas didn't struggle and did his best to press his body into mine, away from the sword. I felt his fear, but it wasn't greater than mine.

Blake backed up a few steps, about three feet away from the base of the pillar. The Onyx bearer stood about five feet away from him. Brady was cowering at the base of a tree nearby.

Amelia watched on from the top of the observer deck. Her hand was clasped over her mouth. Ana was on the spiraling ramp. She had been attempting to sneak up on Amelia. Bailey and Hunter were behind me. They had Ryder pinned down. Now, everyone stood and watched.

"You give me my guy, I give you yours," I suggested.

I couldn't see the Onyx bearer through the shroud of his anti-energy. I could tell that he moved, but I couldn't tell what he did. I could see him look at Blake.

Without a word, he raised his hand and thrust a ball of his black energy into Blake's chest. Blake was slammed against the concrete pillar and fell to the ground.

I couldn't even react to this before a loud bang rang out from the same direction. Instantly, pain filled my chest. I stumbled backward. What kind of power was this?

I dropped the atom sword. I heard Lucas gasp. As I stumbled backward, he fell forward. He fell face first on the ground. Blood began to leach out of a hole in his back shoulder. His fiery energy faded.

He was dead.

I heard Amelia scream. She leapt from her perch and began to fight with the Onyx bearer. I tried to run forward, but I tripped over my own feet. I stumbled and fell. When I landed on the ground, an even sharper pain filled my chest. I rolled over on my back.

I saw Ryder fly over me, engulfed in purple.

I placed my hand on my chest. I felt a divot. It wasn't my scar though. There was a hole in my uniform. It was wet.

As the world became fuzzy, I saw Bailey standing over me. Then, Hunter.

"What's happening?" I questioned. I wasn't sure if I actually made a sound or if it was just in my head.

"Hunter, heal him," Bailey commanded. Then, she flew off.

I thought I heard crying.

I saw green.

Then, I saw nothing at all.

Chapter 29

"Run!"
"Go!"
"I don't think I can do it."
"Pick 'im up"
"He doesn't have his jetpack."
"Get in the car. Now!"
"Step on it!
"Move!"
"Give us a shield!"
"Get off me."
"I think we lost him."
"We've gotta get the bullet out first."
"Let him rest. We'll let him tell us himself when he wakes up."

I heard running water. A creek. It bubbled and sloshed. I could smell the fresh water as the wind blew across it. I heard birds singing their morning songs, chattering as they woke up the forest. I felt the sun on my cheek. I felt its warmth on my hand. I heard leaves rustling as they brushed against one another. I could taste metal. I didn't feel any pain.

I opened my eyes. I was looking up at the sky through a canopy of trees. It looked like home. A rock was pressed sharply into my shoulder blade. I tried to sit up.

"Woah there," I heard a tired voice say. It was Bailey. She leaned over me and helped me up.

"What happened?" I asked. I saw that her eyes were red.

"You got shot," she smiled a painful smile.

"Blake?" I asked, remembering a bit of what happened.

"He's alive," She answered.

I heard a commotion behind me. Crying. "Everything's shutting down. It's the black energy. He can't fight it."

I forced myself further up. “Blake?” I saw a tear slip down Bailey’s cheek. I leaned forward and did my best to stand up.

“Don’t hurt yourself,” Bailey commanded, her voice shaking.

“Help me up,” I commanded.

She did. When I was up, I realized we were next to a road. We were in a valley. It looked like we had ridden in an SUV and pulled off the road here.

Blake was laying on the ground a few feet up the creek. Brady and Hunter were standing over him. Hunter tried to straighten himself up when he saw me coming.

“What is it?” I asked. Bailey kept her arm around me even though I was certain I could stand on my own.

“We’re bearers,” Hunter sniffled, “We can fight the dark energy. He just can’t. Even with my help.”

I looked down at Blake. His face was pale. His breathing was shallow. He didn’t move. He looked as though death had already begun to take over.

“Your energy can’t cancel it out?” I asked. I knew when it got on me, my own energy could undo it. I assumed any energy could work.

“It's not like when it gets on us,” Hunter explained. He was more composed now. “Our own energy can fight it because it's our energy. He doesn't have energy.”

I looked back down at Blake. I took my right hand and placed it over the crystal on the center of my chest. I ran my fingers across its smooth surface, changing their tilt with its different faces. Slowly, I summoned it out of its spot.

I pulled away from Bailey and stood on my own. I pushed all the energy in my body toward the crystal. The purple bands flowed out of me, running up my legs, across my chest, and out into the crystal. It swirled down my arms and leapt off of my hands.

"What are you doing?" Hunter asked.

Bailey stepped back. She knew.

"Blake was always stronger," I smiled, "I'm just putting things back to the way they're supposed to be." I'm pretty sure Hunter thought I had gone crazy. I had been reading my fathers journals on crystal power transfer a few weeks ago. This was the only thing that could save him.

Bailey smiled, but it looked painful. I couldn't tell if it was because I was giving up my powers, or because she was actually in a lot of pain. Probably both.

I placed one hand on either side of the crystal, about five inches from touching it. The energy concentrated there. The crystal began to spin.

As it spun, a low hum filled the air, followed by an electrical crispness. Bailey's hair began to rise in the static. She brushed it down with her hands. The crystal spun faster.

A bubble of energy began to materialize around the crystal. It took on the same vibrant purple color of the crystal. It condensed until it formed a smooth purple sphere around the crystal. The crystal spun faster, and the humming grew louder.

Blueish-purple dots projected themselves from the crystal, They began to orbit it in complex patterns - coming close, but never colliding. These blueish-purple dots began to orbit so fast that they formed solid lines of the same color, contrasting the deep purple glow of the nucleus. They organized until there were three rings around the crystal, each one oriented in a different direction, and each one intersecting at the poles of the crystal. The hum grew to a roar.

"God, save my friend," I prayed.

I leaned over my friend and focused my attention on him. I aimed the crystal at his heart. Then, I willed that my connection with the crystal be passed on.

The roar ceased. For a tiny fraction of a second, everything froze. Then, everything turned purple. Bright purple.

There was a loud crack followed by a deep BOOM. I was blast backwards. I bounced off the side of the bank and rolled into the creek.

There's a chance I would have lost consciousness if not for the frigid water. My chest squeezed in on me and I gasped for air. I flung myself out of the water and ran onto the bank. Only one thought was on my mind. "Did it work?"

I ran over to Blake. Bailey was a few feet away. She had raised a shield to cover her and Brady just in time. Hunter, on the other hand, was laying a few yards away in the middle of the road. I was sure he was fine.

Blake still lay on the ground. A bit of smoke rose from the hole burned in his brown tactical suit just above his heart. I knelt down and placed my hand on the side of his head.

"Blake!" I called.

I expected him to jump right up, but nothing happened.

"Blake!" I called again. I realized his face was still pale. "No," I breathed.

I placed a finger on his neck. I couldn't feel a pulse. "No, no, no," I whispered, "Blake!"

I slammed my head down onto his chest. No breathing. No heartbeat. "No!" I screamed.

I took hold of the hole in his shirt and ripped it open. A raised pattern had been burned into his chest. It was red and angry looking.

I placed one hand on top of the other, intertwined my fingers, and began pressing down on his chest. "Blake!" I called. Tears formed in my eyes. He was dead, and I had killed him.

Ana ran up behind me, "What did you do," she cried. "What did you do!"

"Hunter!" I called, "Help!"

Hunter ran over and began to focus a slow flow of energy on Blake as I continued compressions. I paused to listen to his heart. Still nothing.

I pinched his nose, held his mouth open, and pressed my mouth onto his. I blew into his lungs. Still nothing. I continued pumping his chest.

"God, please," a tear slipped down my cheek, "Please."

I heard Ana begin to cry as her mask shattered. She couldn't be strong any longer. I was losing the ability myself.

Hunter continued the flow of energy, but he began to cry too. "This is what I saw," I heard him say.

I couldn't let this come true. I tried harder.

Still nothing.

"Blake!" I called again, hoping the message would finally reach wherever he was.

I leaned over to resume mouth-to-mouth. But Bailey stopped me by pulling back on my shoulder. I tried to pull away, but when I did, she gripped harder and yanked me off of Blake.

As her body replaced mine over Blake I heard her say, "I saw this too, but I saw how it ended."

She raised her hand, white electricity arced from one finger to the next. With one motion, she thrust her hand down onto Blake's chest. His body tensed up. White nodes of energy jumped across his body, spreading out from his chest. Then, nothing happened.

I sat on the ground to Blake's right where Bailey had left me. Bailey fell to the other. He was breathing heavily and holding her head. We all watched with hope, but with every painful second that passed, that hope faded.

Ana fell to her knees and laid herself over Blake's body. Her tattered skirt covered their legs. Her hands grasped each side of his head. Her head lay on his chest. She sobbed.

My head felt light. The world began to spin. I felt nauseous. "What have I done?" I pulled my hand down my face. Tears followed it.

My other hand clawed into the ground. I ripped up a handful of creek pebbles and slammed them back down. I stood up, ready to storm away. I took one step. Then, I heard a deep gasp, followed by coughing and heaving.

"Oh!" Ana exclaimed. The line of her crying changed.

I flung my body back toward them.

Blake was upright and in Ana's tight embrace. He was facing toward me and looked very confused. He was still coughing. I saw a washed look come across his face. He shoved himself out of Ana's arms and turned away just in time to vomit into the creek.

Ana was having a hard time composing herself. Bailey on the other hand was leaned back against a rock. Her eyes were closed. Her face was pointed toward the sky, and she was smiling.

I let out a heavy breath in disbelief. "Oh, God," I exhaled, "Thank you!"

My misconstrued face melted into a joyful grin. I had to force myself to stay back while Ana tended to him (and herself). Hunter looked like he didn't know whether to cry or laugh. He and Brady consoled each other.

I had just decided to walk over to them when a voice behind me spoke. "Glad *your* friend got a happy ending," a thick Urban accent complemented.

I looked over my shoulder. I couldn't place the voice, but I recognized the face. It was Ryder.

I lifted my fists to fight. I felt my energy surge inside me. It consumed my hands and arms. My energy?

My eyes cut down to my purple arms. I thought I had given that away. I didn't understand why it was here, but I was glad it came. "Hey, we've got company!" I alerted the group.

No one really reacted. Including Ryder. He just looked at me with a smug smile. He looked sad. He didn't look like he was trying to attack.

"Stand down, soldier," Ryder held up his hands, "Seems I'm on your side now."

I loosened my stance. I heard Hunter's snotty nose coming up behind me.

"He, uh," Hunter sniffed, "Him and Amelia helped us get away from the Onyx bearer."

My first instinct was to question their sincerity. Then, I remembered the lifeless body of Lucas falling out of my arms. The thought caused me to rub my hand across my chest. There was a bandage under my shirt. (It was only now that I realized I was in my tighter fitting shirt and shorts that went under my tactical suit.)

"Where is Amelia?" I asked. I knew how close we had just come to being in the same situation just now. Unfortunately, there wouldn't be a second chance for her brother.

"She's burying her brother," Ryder ground his jaw.

"Alone?" I questioned.

"She is now," Ryder wrinkled his nose. Then, his face loosened. He was blank now, and he turned and walked off.

"Where's Amelia?" I asked Hunter.

"What about Blake?" Hunter asked.

I looked at Blake. Ana was going on about how he was dead and came back, refusing to let go of his hand or take her eyes off him. I smiled, "He's busy right now."

Hunter smiled too. "She went off in the woods that way," Hunter pointed across the creek. "She's really angry. I don't know if I'd go looking for her right now."

"Noted," I said. I look concerned, as though I might listen.

"You're gonna go anyway," Hunter realized.

I grinned, "Yep. Hold down the fort. Yell if anybody else tries to die."

"Will do," Hunter saluted.

I turned and trudged across the creek. I also realized I wasn't wearing shoes. My shorts clung to my thighs. The wind had little success blowing them. The water that sloshed up on them made them stick tighter. All this, made me decide I might need some gear.

"Hey, Hunt!" I called, "Where's my gear?"

I looked at me, then looked back at the SUV parked on the road. He held out his hand and a puck, endowed with green energy, floated out through the window. He pulled it to his hand and then tossed it to me.

"Here ya go!"

I caught it. "Thanks!"

I waded to the opposite side of the creek and then pressed it on my chest. The grey mist poured out and secured itself as the white energy wave moved across my body. It didn't leave behind anything other than the tactical suit and an empty spot over my chest where my crystal was supposed to go.

I remembered calling my powers when Ryder had startled me. I decided to summon my crystal with my dry hand. It popped out of the creek and flew to me. I examined it.

I looked just as it had before except… I couldn't put my finger on it. Something was different. I shrugged it off, having more important things to worry about and pressed it into its spot.

It didn't fit right and fell back into my hand. I looked at it again.

The crystal was smaller than it had been. It was the shape that was different. It looked like it had before it had combined with Darren's crystal. Or, actually, this looked more like Darren's crystal. Mine was a bit more pointed. I realized the crystal had split back into two.

The thought of a stray crystal running around worried me. I lifted my hand again, and tried summoning my crystal. Nothing. I had my crystal.

Just as I began to search the bank for the fragment, I saw something in Blake's hand. A soft purple glow. A shiny surface reflecting the sunlight that made it through the trees. He had the other piece. I smiled, realizing it was his now. We both had a crystal. At least something good had come out of today.

We would have much to discuss, but I wanted to make sure Amelia was okay. I wanted to secure a new ally, but more than that, I knew she needed a friend.

I walked through the forest in the direction Hunter had pointed me. I felt much more at home in these woods than I did in the jungles of El Dorado: the soft fern leaves, the crunchy leaf litter, the creeping ivy, the mountain laurels. It was familiar and soothing to me.

The air was warm and humid as it often was in the summers here. However, as I continued my journey into the words, the warm air turned cold. The yellow sunlight turned white - almost blue. The air was sharp and the soft crunchy leaves turned solid.

The colorful greens faded into a frost bitten brown. A white layer of frost coated everything. A dusty white powder rested on the coarse tree bark. At its center was a young woman hunched over a fresh, unmarked grave.

She wore a frayed, black, Organization issue tactical suit. Her armor was cast off into a pile a few yards away. Her mid length white hair had fallen out of a tight bun and hung messily around her head. The knot still held together at the end. A hard to see teal energy leaked out onto the ground around her.

I stood back at first. I wasn't sure if she sensed me or not. The woods were eerily quiet, and I assumed she would have at least heard me crunching through the forest floor. I saw her tilt her head to the side a bit. The fresh scratch on her cheek I had given her faced me.

"Did he just trade this Hell for another one?" she asked softly.

"What?" I asked. I stood behind her.

"You're the righteous one," Amelia growled. Her accent poked through more than usual, "Did he stop burning in this world just to burn in the next?"

I felt my face turn as pale as her cold skin. I opened my mouth, but no words came out. How do you answer that?

She forced herself off the ground and turned toward me slowly.

"Answer me, Soldier Who Wouldn't Kill," she demanded.

I certainly wasn't an expert on the subject. I knew he didn't live the greatest life, but that wasn't up to me.

"Answer me!" she yelled. She began to sob.

She broke down now. She stumbled forward. I caught her.

Her tears froze as soon as they touched the air. They bounced off her cheeks and stuck to my clothes. I gave her the awkward hug that she needed. I was glad that I couldn't imagine what she was going through.

"Answer me," she whispered again, her hands grabbed into my clothes.

I had hoped I would get out of answering her, but it didn't seem like that was going to happen. I just told her the truth. "I don't know. It's not up to me."

Amelia dug fingers into my back. Her sobs became further apart. She pulled away and faced the grave. She fell back to her knees.

"When you make a deal with the Devil, don't be surprised when he comes for your soul," she thrust her fist into the ground. A teal tidal wave of icy energy spread out from it. Amelia picked her hand back up and clenched her heart. "Our mother used to tell us that."

As I stood over her, I couldn't help but hate how long we had fought each other. These were just people. Just kids. Just like me. They just happened to find themselves on the other side when all of this started. Lucas would still be alive if we had just sat down and talked it out instead of throwing so many punches. Instead of letting the forces behind us drive us to war.

"It's true." I agreed, "But the best thing about the Devil is that he's a loser."

Amelia listened but she didn't look.

"He never wins," I explained, "Not even once. Even this, even right now, if you give it time, he'll lose. You know why?"

She turned her head to look at me. I think she was beginning to regret asking her question.

"Because those with us are greater than those with him," I smiled a true smile, "Because we're stronger than he is. All we have to do is decide that we want to fight him."

"How?" Amelia hung her head again, "How do we fight him?"

I extended my hand toward her. She turned, thought for a moment, then took hold of it. I pulled her up to her feet.

"Together."

Chapter 30

We walked out of the frosted section of the forest. I led the way out and Amelia trailed behind. She wasn't done grieving. That would take more time than we had. Now that everyone was back to, well, at least functioning, we needed to leave.

We walked out of the woods. Across the creek I could see all of my friends standing around talking. Everyone but Bailey. She still leaned against her smooth rock, resting her eyes. This migraine must have been a bad one. The first person to notice our return was Ana.

She first caught a glance of us, cutting her eyes in our direction. When she realized who it was, her nose turned down and she looked back at the group. Her hand gripped Blake's a bit tighter. This caused him to look.

"Dylan, behind you!" he called. He pointed and readied himself for a fight. I didn't look behind me.

"She's with us now," I informed him. Ana refused to turn around. Bailey forced herself to stand. She needed to mediate.

"She and Ryder saved our lives," Bailey informed Blake and I.

"And that makes up for the millions they killed," Ana butted in aggressively. She wasn't questioning her. She was challenging her.

"I think we could use all the help we can get," Bailey defended.

I hated what had happened to El Dorado. I don't think I had really processed that it had even happened though. I don't think any of us had. I knew I didn't blame these people for it. I blamed the Onyx bearer. I blamed The Organization. Above all, I blamed Sparks.

"They didn't give the order to destroy the city," I added.

"They followed it," Ana detested. "They deserve to pay for that." She took another step toward me, "You know, I don't know what all of you are doing," she gestured to all of us, "We outnumber them. We out power them! They should be on their knees begging for our mercy."

"Ana, I-"

I was cut off by an icy crispness that cut through the air. Amelia emerged from behind me and began walking toward Ana. Her face was as cold as her energy.

As she stepped into the creek, it froze solid. She walked across the surface until she was standing only a few feet from Ana where she fell onto her knees.

"I did pay," Amelia ground her teeth angrily. Her Russian accent made her sound intimidating, even on her knees. "I paid with the only thing I cared about in this world. The only thing keeping me alive now is the promise that his murderer will burn with us all, and that I will send him there." She unclipped her atom sword from her waist. Turned the blade end toward her chest and presented the hilt to Ana. "If you'll do it for me, then fine. Make me pay."

"Amelia!" I called out in shock. I didn't run to her. There was nothing I could do now. I prayed Ana would show mercy.

"Go on!" Amelia demanded, "I have nothing left to live for."

I watched her icy tears fall and bounce off the ground.

Ana extended a hand and placed it on the hilt. The two women stared into one another's souls. Their eyes each burning with hatred.

"Ana?" Blake questioned, losing sight of the woman he loved.

Hunter stood on the road behind them. He had been getting something out of the car. Surprise filled his expression when he realized what was happening. He watched in fear.

I watched as well, waiting to sense something change in Ana, waiting to see her expression soften. It didn't. She looked as though she might do it.

The ice Amelia had walked across was now covered with the water from up stream. The banks of the creek expanded a bit and the water had to find a new path to flow. It tried to wash around the two women, but Amelia's energy field froze it. Before long, there was a ring of ice around them. Even they seemed to be frozen.

I watched a tear slip down Ana's cheek. Blake was standing just outside the icy ring. Water was begging to run over his feet. When he saw the tear, he stepped in.

He placed his hand on top of hers. He lowered the sword and pulled it out of both of their hands. He put his other arm around Ana. She began to cry and hid her face in his shoulder. He tossed the sword into the creek and wrapped her in a full embrace.

The hilt landed in a part of the creek that had been frozen. It sank in the water, but slid across the ice sheet underneath. It was carried down the river and out of sight.

I finally let out a sigh of relief. Everyone did.

As my gaze turned down the creek, I saw Ryder walking up to me. "You're some strange people," he commented.

"Thanks," I half-laughed.

"If I was her, I would have done it," he continued. I could tell he was genuinely surprised that Ana hadn't killed her. For a moment, I was too. I don't think he had experienced that sort of thing before. I sensed he was calloused.

"I guess it's a good thing you weren't her," I pointed out, hoping to offset the tension.

"I don't know what makes you people so…"

"Different," I finished for him.

"Yea," he agreed, "You're not like The Organization. You're not really like the Ekklesia. You're…weird. Why?"

I thought about it for a moment. There was only one real answer. Or maybe a few. We loved each other. We loved the people and the world that we fought for. We didn't fight for power or control. I hadn't experienced that anywhere else in his war other than our little Protectorate.

The other thing was our God. We all loved him. We all tried to serve him. We all prayed. I summed it up with something I had heard Pastor say.

“We don’t get everything right,” I admitted, “But we just love God and love people. Obviously that’s hard sometimes. But we do our best.”

Ryder narrowed his eyebrows. He looked like he was going to try and say something, but the words escaped him. He looked genuinely puzzled. Off guard.

Finally, he just shook his head and walked off.

I looked at my team, broken and strown about the creek. I realized that we couldn’t stay here any longer than we had. The Onyx bearer was still here, probably trying to find us. Even if he wasn’t, there was a battle about to take place.

They had succeeded in their goal. The Bearers were out of the game for now. That meant that they would be moving quickly to attack The Organization’s capitol base: Jericho. We had information that would sway that battle's outcome. We needed to be there.

I also wasn’t sure how long the peace between our two sides would last. It seemed to me like Amelia and Ryder were ready to join us. Maybe not The Ekklesia, but us. That wouldn’t keep there from being tension. We needed to act now.

I walked down the stream, past the ice, and crossed over. Ana and Blake were having a conversation near a few large boulders (there were quite a few lining the creek). Bailey was now standing up at the car with Amelia. They were talking as well. Hunter was up stream skipping rocks, not to have fun, but as a distraction from all the crazy events happening. I didn’t see Brady anywhere. Ryder was down stream, staring into the water.

“Alright everybody,” I announced, "It's time to go.” Everyone looked at me, but no one moved. “We have a war to win.” There was limited movement in my direction. Hunter was the only one making an active effort to get to me. Everyone else was awaiting some sort of plan.

"We all have something we want," I offered, "I would say that because of what we want, we can all agree that The Organization needs to fall. The Ekklesia will be attacking Jericho soon. We need to get out of here, play nice, and make sure that attack is successful. After that, we can deal with The Ekklesia and put the world back to the way it's supposed to be."

Everyone seemed to agree. Everyone was standing now. "We don't all have jetpacks, so we'll have to dive out of here. I know how to get us to Gatlinburg from here. Once we get there, we can find a spot to lay low. If we can get back in communication with the Mountain base, maybe we can get a feel for what's going on."

"You ever think that the Mountain Base cut off our communications?" Ana suggested.

Our comms ran though El Dorado. Obviously, they couldn't do that now. ALI ran through the servers at the Mountain base. It was suspicious that he was cut off from us.

"There's only one way to find out," I offered, "I need to find an old cell tower or something to boost our signal though."

When our comms are connected to a base or our ship, they have nearly infinite range because of their boosters. We were cut off from that. I needed something tall and metal to get a signal out.

Everyone agreed. At least, no one disagreed. We all walked to the SUV. It had eight seats. There were eight of us. I could tell this was about to be a very awkward ride.

Ryder reached the car first and acted like he was going to get in the driver seat. "What do you think you're doing?" I tried to make it sound light, but it came off a bit snooty.

"I drove us this far," Ryder said, "Don't trust me to take us the rest of the way?"

I hated I missed that. Everything I learned about the night before made it sound more interesting.

"It's not that," I started.

"Been a getaway driver since I was seven," Ryder boasted, "Drove around the biggest gangsters in L.A."

"I just know these roads," I defended, even though that was kind of impressive. "I know how to get us where we're going."

"Fine," Ryder agreed, "Never been one to ride in the back seat. You better be a good driver."

Everyone reluctantly piled in. Bailey offered to sit with Ryder and Amelia in the back. I could tell she was in a lot of pain, but she was forcing herself through it. She was trying to help Amelia.

Ana refused to let the former Organization bearers sit behind her, so Blake, Ana, and Brady ended up in the back. Amelia, Hunter, and Bailey sat in the middle section, and Ryder sat in the passenger seat.

I was starting to realize that Amelia and Ryder, despite being on the same team, didn't really have much of a relationship. I think Ryder might have been closer with Lucas, but that was just a guess.

We traveled down the winding mountain roads in silence. Thankfully, the scenery was nice. We all had a good view out our windows to simmer in our thoughts.

I tried not to think much. I just kept my eyes on the road. We went through the mountains, coming up one side and going down the other, driving over ridge tops and down through valleys. We passed many spots and creeks and overlooks that I remembered visiting with my dad. It brought back good memories - the best memories. Things were so much more simple back then. For me anyway. I realize now they must have been overwhelmingly complicated for him, leading a double life, a superspy of sorts trying to raise a young boy. He was the best at both.

I noticed the sun was completing its arc across the sky. That means I was out for half of the day. It took about an hour before we reached the town of Gatlinburg. This is where my father and I would stay when we came on vacation. It was a strip of connected buildings, shops, arcades, and restaurants. Outside the strip were hotels, put-put golf courses, and hiking trails. The streets were always packed.

As we drove in, that was the first thing I noticed. There wasn't another car or human in sight. I leaned forward in my chair and stared at the deserted streets.

The windows of the storefronts were boarded up. Their merchandise was still hanging on the racks, visible though the missing or open doors. Trash was strown about. The buildings were dirty and long deserted. Leaves littered the street and piled up in the alleyways. I slowed our vehicle to a crawl.

"Some town you've found for us," Ryder commented, looking out his side window.

"Where is everybody?" Blake asked, remembering how lively the streets had once been.

"I don't know," I admitted. I almost asked ALI if he knew before realizing he wasn't there.

The fountains in the old-timey nooks were corroded. Shrubs had overgrown their planters. Weeds and small trees were beginning to grow through cracks in the sidewalks.

A building on the corner of the street had a sign that read "RIPLEY'S BELIEVE IT OR NOT". A few of the red letters were missing. The rest were covered in black corrosion. The building itself had once depicted a scene from the woods. It had columns that were meant to look like tree trunks and fake animals rested in its fake branches.

I remembered coming here when I was little. It was a museum filled with funny things to look at and world records. Out in front was a giant marble, the world's largest (or so they claimed). It used to be suspended in a fountain that made it so kids could come up and roll it around. The Marble was still there, but the water was off and its once polished surface was beginning to wear.

Just beyond this building was what we called the "Space Needle". It was a tall metal tower that stood above all the buildings. It used to be an attraction. You could ride to the top of the colorfully lit tower and look down at the city. I had never done it. I was too scared to ride the elevator.

I would be even more against it now. It was rusted and appeared to be missing pieces. There was a precarious looking staircase that led to the top. Ryder peered at it though the windshield.

"I think we could wire that up and boost your coms" he suggested.

"Yea, should," I agreed. "Let's find a hotel to set up shop at and then we'll come give it a look."

I drove down headed for the hotel we would always stay at when I was little. It was at the end of the strip (so it would be a bit of a walk back here), but I knew my way around it in case we were attacked.

All the way down, the scene never changed. We never saw a person. Everything looked like it had been deserted in one night. Everything was left behind just the way it was.

Finally we reached the hotel. It was next to what used to be a put-put golf course. Most of the playful statues still stood. There was a racoon with a shot gun, a bear with a fishing pole, and a vulture wearing a top hat. One of the wooden towers had rotted and collapsed.

As I looked at the golf course and reminisced, Blake spoke up, "Is that a light on in there?"

I looked and, sure enough, there was a light on in the lobby of the hotel. The hotel itself looked just as run down as everything else, but I did notice that the parking lot was kept clean. It looked like the lower windows had been washed too.

I pulled our car into the parking lot, and everyone piled out. Skeptically, our group eased toward the lobby. Naturally, we fanned out and stood at different distances away. The Onyx bearer couldn't have beat us here could he?

I led the way. I could see the lobby through the glass front door. It was tidy and clean. Past the reception desk, there was a fluffy red couch and a wooden rocking chair facing a fireplace. They were on a tan woven rug. A bearskin was laid under a rickety looking coffee table. It looked exactly like I remembered it.

Hunter stayed by my side as we got closer. I could feel him tensing up. I didn't sense any danger. I walked up to the front door, pushed it open, and walked in.

"Hello!" I called, "Anybody here?"

Out of the corner of my eye, I saw something move. I turned. Peeking around the corner of a hallway was a young boy, probably Hunter's age. When he realized I saw him, he ducked behind the corner and ran down the hall.

"Wait!" I called, "Come back!"

I took a few quick steps forward, so I could see down the hall. He had made it past all the room and was disappearing up the fire escape.

"You want me to go get him?" Hunter offered.

"Nah," I replied, "He's gotta have parents around here somewhere."

"Unless he's the last one," Hunter pointed out.

"He has to come down here to get out," I remembered, "We'll see him again."

"You'll have to excuse the boy," a new voice said. Hunter and I both jumped. Impressive, since it's hard to sneak up on us.

A shaggy looking man in overalls and a short sleeve button up shirt was standing in a doorway behind the reception desk. He had a long brown beard and a bald head. His voice was gruff and his southern accent was much thicker than mine, "Been a while since he's seen other people. 'Specially young'ins like yourselves." His eyes fell on our tattered uniforms. "Little young to be fightin' in the war aren't ya?"

"Didn't have much of a say in it," I replied. I looked out onto the deserted streets. "What happened here?"

"Seems people don't take vacations when the world's endin'" the man said in his gruff voice. "Seein' this town's built on tourism, most people made for the cities when the spaceships started flyin' 'round."

"Looks like they went in a hurry," I pointed out. Hunter was walking around the lobby checking things out. My friends were pressing toward the door.

"Most of 'em panicked when the power and cell went out," the man explained, "When no one came to turn it all back on, that's when the rest left."

"No one came to help you?" I asked, knowing I had sent aid everywhere in the U.S. I thought I had anyway.

"I think the closest help ever got was Maryville," he said, "Mountains get a little too dangerous and there wasn't enough people here to make it worth it."

"I'm sorry," I consoled. I never realized just how much was happening, or wasn't happening, under my watch.

The man put his hands on his hips and started past me. "Our ancestors lived off these hills. 'Spose we'n do it again." He slapped me on the shoulder, "Now, enough of that, what brings you here?"

He was really strong. I might have gone flying across the room without the strength of my crystal. "Well… The war, unfortunately."

The man's eyes turned wild, "You didn't bring it here did you?"

"I hope not," I continued, "We just need a place to camp out until we get our comms up and going again."

The man returned to normal, "Well, you came to the right place! We're the only place for miles with electricity."

As if to mock him, the lights shut off. The man looked around in disgust. "Dern generator!" I looked back into the room he had just come out of, "Ethel! Get Ricky to start 'er up again."

"Yes, dear!" a soft woman's voice called.

"Tell you what," I offered, "You fix us up a couple rooms, I'll fix your generator for good."

"If you can fix that generator, I'll let you stay here as long as you like," the man promised, "I'll even have Ethel fix you som' good to eat."

"Deal," I held out my hand, "I'm Dylan by the way. That's Hunter," I shrugged my head toward him, who was rocking in the rocking chair. He stood up when I said his name.

"Rodney," the man replied, "Make yourselves at home. How many of you are there?"

"Eight," I replied.

"Best we'n do is probably three rooms by sundown. That work for y'all?" He offered.

"Should," I replied, without thinking too much into it.

Bailey led the rest of the group inside. The only one missing was Ana. I instantly realized it and looked at Blake. He just shrugged his shoulders. I started trying to divide rooms and jobs.

"Bailey, you and Ana get a room. Brady, Blake, Hunter can be with me. Ryder and Amelia, umm" I scratched my head. I didn't know how to divide this up.

"I'll sleep down here if you don't mind," Ryder saved me, "I like to keep my eye on the door."

"Then, I'll let the ladies figure out the other two," I decided. I didn't really think Bailey would want Amelia to be alone. Then again, Ana didn't need to be alone. Bailey might want to be alone because of her migraine, but we definitely couldn't put Ana and Amelia together. I would just leave all that up to them.

"Now, I've got to fix these nice peoples' generator. Somebody, or a few somebodies, need to go to the Space Needle and run a wire from the base to the top of the spire and hook that wire into the comms link."

"I can," Ryder offered, "If Bailey will let me use her energy so that I can fly."

"You've never had to ask before," Bailey joked sluggishly. She allowed her arm to turn white. Ryder's grey foggy energy flowed from the stone on his chest to her arm. The fog and his stone turned white.

"You'll need help," I said, "Blake?"

"Sure," he agreed. I could tell by his voice that his mind was heavy.

"Take Brady along too," I suggested, "He's a good help and he needs to learn." "Girls, why don't you help Ethel get the rooms ready."

"Awe, now they don't have to do that," Rodney butted in. I only now realized that he was still standing there. I was shocked he didn't speak up when Bailey used her energy. Maybe word of there being crystal bearers was becoming wide spread.

"I don't mind," Bailey replied. Amelia nodded. I was glad the two were hitting it off. Amelia needed a friend and we needed her partnership. When the time was right, she and Ryder would be able to help us with their knowledge about The Organization. I hoped some of that might come out during their tasks.

"Alirghty then," Rodney agreed, "I'll show you the way."

"Can we get rooms on the top floor?" I requested, "And a way to access the roof."

"I guess you can," Rodney agreed. I knew he didn't understand why. That was okay. He didn't need to. I hoped we would be gone in the morning.

Ryder headed for the door he had just entered through. I walked over to Blake. "Is Ana good?" I asked.

"No," he sighed, "But who can blame her. She lost a lot more than we did."

"And we lost a lot," I pointed out.

"I think she just needed a little time alone," Blake concluded, "Keep an eye out for her."

"I will," I patted him on the shoulder. He and Brady followed Ryder out. I walked to Hunter. He had turned his rocking chair toward the meeting.

"What do you want me to do?" Hunter asked.

"Go find the boy," I suggested. "We've got everything else covered, and he might need a friend. You might also be able to find out a little more of what happened here." I sensed the room to make sure everyone else was gone. I didn't want Rodney thinking I didn't believe him. "It doesn't make sense that The Ekklesia aid just didn't make it here. Clearly it didn't, but I want to know why. I want to know if there was something here… someone, wanted to slip under the radar."

"On it," Hunter jumped up, "What was his name again? Richard?"

"Ricky," I corrected.

Hunter nodded and headed toward the last place we'd seen him. I headed out the back door and found the generator. It was large and gas powered. I assumed that they just robbed gas from the surrounding gas stations. There were still quite a few up here. The tourism meant more gas engines made it this way. Those people were probably glad they hadn't swapped over when all the quantum batteries stopped working.

The generator itself was about the same size as I was. I think it was an old fashioned emergency generator. I thought they were just for hurricanes and such. I bet these people were glad they had it.

I took off the side panel and began to tinker with it. I didn't have tools, but I could use my energy to undo the screws, nuts, and bolts. It actually worked better than tools.

After a while, I had a plan. I made my way to the car we had driven here and began to remove one of its quantum batteries. It would be more than enough to power the hotel.

The tag on the car said that it was from New York. That was a long way to travel to the Smokies, but it wasn't surprising. This used to be THE vacation spot. The reason it was working now was because we had the power facilities in New York back up and running. I wondered if the owners ever made it back home. By now, surely they had.

I got the battery and walked it back to the generator. I rerouted wires and removed the gas engine. They wouldn't be needing it anymore. I fashioned a new housing for the battery and slipped it in.

As I tinkered, I couldn't stop my mind from dwelling on the events of the past 24 hours. They were heavy. I'd gotten used to heavy things. They didn't effect me like they used to. They used to crush me. Now, what was a little mountain?

I was better at looking and assessing what came next. I wondered what my new breaking point was now. I quickly decided not to consider that.

El Dorado was gone. We couldn't go back. We had to press forward to The Mountain base. I could expose Sparks and maybe take back over the Ekklesia. I wouldn't want to stay there, but if I could end the war, I would do that, and then leave it to someone else to figure out what came next.

I hoped the Onyx bearer had counted his losses and gone home. The other option was that he called for backup and was headed our way. Someone would need to keep look out on the roof tonight. I wouldn't mind a little time with Blake. I knew he was struggling with the way Ana was taking everything.

I clipped the last wire together and the lights in the hotel behind me lit up. I heard a cheer come from inside. It sounded like Hunter and probably Ricky.

I smiled at a job well done and walked in. I had finished just in time. It was getting dark.

Hunter was sitting back in the rocking chair, rocking playfully back and forth, much further than the chair was intended to rock. Ricky was laying on the red couch, his head on the arm rest. He raised up and looked over the back when I walked in.

"Hey! Thanks for fixing the lights," Ricky said. He talked a bit more properly than his dad, "I was gettin' tired of fixin' it."

"Well, you shouldn't have to fix it anymore," I informed him, "I hooked you up to a quantum battery."

Ricky looked puzzled, "I thought all of them were dead?"

"Not all of them," I smiled. "You and Hunter getting along?"

"He's cool!" Ricky exclaimed, "Hunter, show him that thing you can do."

Hunter laughed, "He taught me all the things I can do."

I held my hand out and took a slight bow, "What can I say? I'm awesome."

Ricky rolled off the couch onto his feet. He looked like he was about to talk, but he was distracted by the opening of the front door. It was Blake and his group.

"Comms are loading, now all we do is wait," Blake announced.

Brady walked over to Hunter and Ricky.

"Great!" I congratulated, "Shouldn't be long now." I turned to the boys, "Ricky, can you get us up to the roof? We need to set up a look out."

Ricky's eyes grew wide. He was excited that he got to help us. "Yea!" he beamed, "Follow me."

"You guys can handle that," Ryder shoved, "I'm going to follow that smell."

The smell of home cooking had filled the lobby. I was looking forward to a hot meal, but I would wait for the dinner bell. The rest of us headed for the fire escape.

We clanked up ten flights of concrete and metal stairs. When we reached the top, there was a door that led out onto the tenth floor. Above it was a hatch with a ladder and a bold black sign that read "**ROOF ACCESS**".

Ricky took a key from his front pocket and jumped up on the ladder. He unlocked the hatch, flipped it open, and climbed out on top. We followed out behind him.

It was pitch black now. There was still no moon. The stars however, were putting on a show. There was no light pollution out here. The milky way was the only light: a milky could of light, billions of stars flowing together. There were so many stars visible that it was hard to make out any constellations. I admired the sky.

"So how do we establish a look out?" Ricky asked, hopping on top of one of the air units.

I stopped my star gazing and placed my hand above my eyes. I scanned the area dramatically, leaning in the direction I was looking. Then, I pulled my arms to my chest, summoned my purple energy, and threw my arms out to the side. A harmless disk of purple light expanded out from me. It went out from the roof and traveled a ways before dissipating.

"Lookout established," I said seriously.

Ricky's jaw dragged the ground, "Woah."

"He's just messing with you," Hunter laughed. He looked at me, "Can we go swimming?"

"Do they keep the pool running?" I asked. I didn't think they would be wasting so much energy for something like that.

"It takes more gas, but we have plenty, so I keep it going," Ricky said.

"Can we?" Brady begged. He hadn't moved far from the hatch.

"Sure," I agreed.

"Yes!" the three boys pumped their fists and scurried back down the hatch. It slammed behind them, and Blake and I were left in silence. Or, no human noises. The bugs and birds of the night sang and hooted. A gentle mountain breeze shook dry, late summer leaves. Really, it was anything but quiet.

Blake was leaning against one of the air units. I leaned next to him. "Kids," I laughed.

"I'm glad they get to enjoy it for a little bit," Blake said sentimentally.

We sat, letting the noises of the night sooth us. It was a while before either of us said anything else.

"How are you holding up seeing, well, everything?" I finally asked.

"I'm doing alright," Blake said, "It's Ana I'm worried about. She's so… angry."

"So was I," I remembered, "You helped me. Bailey helped me. We'll help Ana too." I let it sit for a minute. "Did the Chief make it out?"

"When the pillar collapsed, I grabbed him. I got him out," Blake explained, "I couldn't save the elders." He stared at the sky. "I flew the chief down after the pillar collapsed. He was supposed to be taking an escape tunnel the last I saw him."

"So he could be alive," I concluded.

"It's possible," Blake agreed, "But there's no way to contact him." He shook his head, "And that bothers Ana, but I think she knows in her heart that he's alive. The part that's getting to her is that she lost her people. The bearer, in their culture, she's their..."

"Their guardian,"

"Right!" Blake agreed, "Their guardian. She feels that she failed at that task. What makes it worse is that her brother was supposed to be the guardian, but he died a while back and that was pushed off on her. She feels like she's always been trying to live up to that, and she failed her brother too."

"That's a lot to carry," I stated.

"Too much to carry," Blake corrected, "She doesn't have to carry all that. It wasn't her fault."

"You couldn't have convinced me of that when I failed my dad," I pointed out, "Things like this, they only heal with God and time."

"I know," Blake sighed, "It's just hard to sit through."

"Well, if it makes it any better, I'll sit through it with you," I put my arm around him. Blake returned the favor.

"Thanks, Dylan. Really"

"Anytime."

We sat looking out at the stars for probably half the night. I'm sure the others had dinner and were in bed. The boys were likely still swimming. I was sure Bailey had come up to get us and realized we were better off up here. I had sensed her earlier.

I extended my senses through the building and found her asleep quite early. She was in a lot of pain. More pain than I could recently remember. I said a prayer for her. Finally, Blake spoke again.

"So, when are you gonna teach me to use those powers you gave me.?" he asked.

"Do you have powers?" I asked. I hadn't seen him use them. I only assumed the other half of the crystal was his.

He pulled the shard out of his pocket and gripped it in his hand. The purple energy spread across his body and a huge grin spread across his face. "I paid attention to a few of your lessons," Blake revealed.

"This is so cool," I laughed. I allowed my energy to spread across my body as well.

However, the second I connected with my crystal, a torrent of thoughts, not my own, filled my mind. One moment, I was looking at Blake. The next, I was looking at myself. My vision flip flopped back and forth between the two perspectives.

I felt Blake's pain. I felt his love for Ana. I felt his worry. I felt his fear. I felt his brotherly love for me. I felt that he missed his family back in Tullahoma. I felt that he feared we had lost more than we realized.

Finally, I stopped using my power and the sensation stopped. We each stared at each other. "Well, that was weird," we said in sync.

I scrunched my eyebrows. A quote from my dad came to mind and I said it out loud, "Only one person can be connected to a crystal at a time."

Blake looked back at me, "But we both have one," he questioned.

"Same energy though," I pointed out, "Maybe that's why we can both connect, but since it is connected to our consciousness, somehow it's blending the two."

"English?" Blake requested. "You sound like ALI."

"I think we may be connected to each other just like we're connected to our crystals," I explained.

"See," Blake laughed, "I told you you're a nerd."

"What?"

"You just figured that out in like two seconds," Blake leaned back on his air unit, "You're a nerd."

He disarmed me. I thought this was a much more monumental moment. One that didn't warrant a joke. But, I couldn't help but smile at the jab. So much had happened today, I think he just wanted to wait until the morning to deal with this. I agreed.

I leaned back on the unit myself. "Well, that's pretty cool," I commented, "Although, it might get annoying."

"Nah," Blake brushed off, "I already know what goes on in your head."

Suddenly, the hatch to the roof burst open with such force I thought I might fly off. Blake nearly fell off the unit he was startled so badly.

Hunter's head popped up. He was soaking wet and in the undercloths of his tactical suit. He was out of breath, rare for him.

"What's wrong?" I asked as I jumped off my seat.

"It's Bailey," Hunter panted, "Come quick!"

Chapter 31

We sprinted from the roof, down the hatch, and down the stairs. I leapt down the flights, skipping all the individual stairs.

"Eighth floor!" Hunter called after me. Thankfully, I only had to go down two flights.

I burst through the firedoor, nearly knocking it off its hinges. I saw Ryder standing outside of an open door about half way down the hall. I ran to him. He gestured with his head, confirming that she was inside. I ran in.

Inside, there were two queen beds side by side. The only light in the room came from a lamp on the night stand between the two. Ana stood between the two beds. Amelia had pressed herself against the floor-to-ceiling window on the far side of the room. Brady was standing between the bed and the wall.

Bailey was lying on the bed closest to the door. She was on top of the blankets. It looked like she had cleaned herself up. She was in loose fitting pants and a tank top. She must have been getting ready for bed.

I pushed myself in front of Ana and took Bailey's hand. I pressed my other hand on her neck. She had a slow, faint pulse.

"Bailey," I called, squeezing her hand. There was no response. I turned to the girls behind me. "What happened?" I demanded.

"She was getting into bed and passed out," Amelia replied.

"They were alone," Ana detested, "I came in and found that snake leaning over her. Bailey was on the floor."

"I swear to you, she fell down climbing into bed," Amelia defended, "Her headache was getting worse." Her voice trembled a bit.

I did my best to sense her intentions through my raging emotions. I felt she was being truthful. I looked out into the hallway. Blake and Hunter were standing between me and the door.

"Contact the Mountain Base," I commanded, "We need their medics."

"We can't," Ryder said from the hall.

"Why not?" I demanded, "The coms should be linked by now."

"Oh, they are," Ryder said, annoyed, "We're being jammed. I thought these people were your friends?"

"It's complicated," I admitted.

"No it's not," Ana growled. She turned toward the window and her powers surged over her body. The room turned pink.

"Ana! No!" Blake yelled.

Before I knew what was happening, a pink beam of energy formed and smashed through the window, continuing out into the darkness. Amelia was forced to dive out of the way.

All of the bearers' energies flared. Including mine and Blakes. My vision blurred, unable to focus between seeing Bailey on the bed and seeing Ana charging toward the window.

I felt Blake's fear and my own.

I gripped the sheets for bearing and tried to form a shield around Amelia. I couldn't focus on one thing long enough to be successful. Thankfully, I didn't have to.

I caught a glimpse of Ana just as she leapt out of the window. I saw the flash of her jetpack igniting. Then, she was gone. I stopped using my energy and found myself crouched beside the bed. I guess I had lost my balance. The experience was dizzying.

Blake ran to the opening in the wall where the window used to be. "Ana!" he called, "Come back!"

She wasn't coming back.

I looked back at Bailey. Her face was pale and all scrunched up. She was out, but she was still feeling all that pain. Her breathing was shallow. I began to rack my brain for ideas. I didn't know what was going on, but if she had passed out like this, she needed help soon.

I heard the smashing of another window followed by the attaching of a jetpack to someone's back. I turned back around. Blake was preparing to follow Ana.

"No," I pleaded, "Wait!"

He looked back at me with tears in his eyes. "She'll do something crazy."

"She can take care of herself," I reasoned, "You have the last jetpack."

Needless to say, we didn't all have time to get a jetpack when we left El Dorado. Somebody left theirs on the ship. Mine was damaged beyond repair back at El Dorado. Ryder could fly, but I didn't trust him enough with the errand I needed run. On top of that, they would probably try to blow him out of the sky as soon as they detected him, and Alex would never trust him.

He gritted his teeth and shook his head. I had to get him on my side before he took off again. "I need you to fly back to Tullahoma," I explained, "You need to get Alex. The two of you need to hayjack a ship and bring that doctor that's stationed there. She's trained on helping bearers." My lip began to quiver, "Ana will survive. Bailey needs our help if she's going to."

He shook his head and scowled, but he didn't jump. I knew he was angry that he was in this position. It didn't technically have to be him that went to Tullahoma, but he knew it would be best. This was our best option, and he knew it.

Knowing this, he turned, jumped out the window, and flew away.

Amelia was standing in the corner now. Hunter had made his way beside me. "Can I help?" he offered. His hand glowed green.

I nodded, and he placed it on Bailey's head. The second he did, Bailey let out a blood curdling scream. She writhed on top of the sheets. Hunter immediately yanked his hand off and stumbled backward. "I'm sorry! I'm sorry!," He stuttered, "I didn't - I don't"

I held my hand toward him to be quiet. I knew he didn't mean to. I put both hands on Bailey to keep her from falling off the bed. "Bailey, Bailey, it's okay," I whispered. She finally calmed down.

I guess since he speeds up what the body does, if the body is causing the problem, his energy makes it worse. Hunter fell back onto the bed behind me and buried his face in his hands. I turned to him.

"Hey, everything's gonna be alright," I asserted, "We just need to get her to a doctor. Blake will be back soon."

I noticed Bailey's crystal sitting on the night stand under the lamp. Its glow was burning brighter than the light bulb.

I was wishing she had finished her treatments at El Dorado. She was going once a week for something. I wasn't sure what it was exactly. She didn't like to talk about it, but it was supposed to help her migraines. I was wishing I had pressed a little harder for answers now.

I looked around the room. Amelia looked scared and weak. Even in the forest, I had never thought that. I made her make eye contact with me. "I know it's not your fault." I looked at the rest of the room. "Get some sleep," I suggested, "I'll stay here. We leave as soon as Blake gets back."

Ryder didn't protest. He went down the hall to his room. Amelia began to walk out, but as she passed Bailey, she took hold of her foot. "Thank you for your kindness, Bailey," she whispered emotionally. Then, she walked out.

I looked and Hunter behind me, then at Brady in front, "Boys, I know it's hard, but you need to try and get some sleep too," I suggested. Hunter never looked up. Brady just looked at Hunter.

"Come on," I prompted, "We don't know what tomorrow holds. If Bailey's out for a little bit, I need you two strong and alert."

Brady seemed to agree. He walked around the bed and said something to Hunter. After a minute, they were both on the other bed, laying on top of the sheets in their still damp clothes.

"We'll sleep here if that's alright," Brady suggested.

"Perfectly alright with me," I smiled. A smile felt sort of strange, but my love for those two forced it out of me. They were like brothers to each other. Though the age gap was relatively small, they were like sons to Bailey and I. We had filled the role of parents for them since we had come into each other's lives.

I climbed up into Bailey's bed and carefully made my way to the opposite side of her. I gently pulled one of the sheets out from under her and covered us both. I probed my back up on the headboard. I placed her head on a pillow. I leaned down and kissed her forehead. "Hold on for me," I requested.

I heard Bailey's voice in my mind. It was more quiet than usual and difficult to hear over my other thoughts. "I love you."

I nodded. "I love you too."

I stroked her blonde hair with my hand, and I prayed for her. I prayed for Ana and Blake too. I prayed for Hunter and Brady. I found that we all need a lot of prayer.

My worry never allowed me to sleep, but I was thankful to see Brady and Hunter had dozed off.

It was about four hours before I saw the lights of a transport in the distance. It flew just over the top of the mountain that hid Gatlinburg. It flew low and was headed straight for our destroyed window.

"Boys," I called gently. They both jumped as they woke up, "Go get Ana and Ryder. We're leaving."

They both looked out the window. When they saw the transport, they rolled out onto opposite sides of the bed.

"How is she?" Hunter asked as he walked by.

"She's still holding on," I said.

This was enough for him. The two left the room to fetch the others. I watched as the transport neared. It pulled right up to our window. The side door of the transport turned toward us, and the door slid open. Alex was standing on the other side, the wind of the engines lofting his thick dark hair. He was back in his old black Taken uniform. "Need a lift?" he offered. His words were meant to lighten the mood. His face and tone were serious.

I smiled painfully. It was good to see him. I scooped Bailey up and headed for the ship. I jumped out and over the small gap that was between the floor and the ship. Alex grabbed my arm to steady me as we landed. In the center of the cabin was a hospital bed bolted to the floor. An I.V. rack stood behind it, as did a myriad of monitors.

One either side was a woman in a white uniform and a red patch on her sleeve. One was a taller than average woman, the same one that had come out of the football field in my first battle with Lucas. The other was Bailey's mom.

I rushed her over to the bed and laid her down. I gave Ms. Boone a quick, tight hug. Then, she was focused solely on her daughter. "This is no migraine," she said, "Do you know anything else, anything at all that was going on?" she asked.

"No," I replied, "Not that I know of."

Ms. Boone nodded. Then, she and the other Doctor got right to work. They started to hook up I.V.s, draw blood, give shots, and hook up monitors.

"We'll get a better feel for what's going on when we get back to Tullahoma," the other lady said.

I saw Hunter and the rest enter from the hallway. One by one they hopped on board. Once everyone was on, the door closed, and we took off toward Tullahoma.

"Was it hard to get the ship?" I asked Alex.

"How many ships have I stolen?" he reminded me, "This was nothing. The Doc just said there was an emergency. Which was true, and we took it."

"Thank you for coming," I held out my hand.

He ignored my hand and gave me a hug. "I would have come sooner if you called me."

"You said to call you if someone was dying," I joked. Then, the joke punched me in the gut. I felt tears coming on, but I refused to let them flow. She wasn't dying. She was going to be just fine. There was no sense in blubbering. I pulled away. "Did Blake tell you everything?"

"A little," Alex said, "He seems a bit…off."

"Then, he didn't tell you everything," I sighed. "Hunter, Brady"

They walked from Bailey's bedside. "Yea,"

"Fill Alex in on everything that's happened, please," I requested, "I need to talk to the pilot."

"I'll try," Hunter agreed. I knew the story would probably take longer than the flight. That's okay. It would keep the boys' minds occupied and Alex needed to know.

I walked to the cockpit and closed the door behind me. Blake was flying solo. I sat in the copilot's chair.

"Impressive to be flying one of these without a co-pilot," I commented as I sat down.

"Alex flew most of the way here," he admitted quietly. I could tell he didn't want to talk.

"Thank you for doing this," I said, "I'll do everything I can to find Ana as soon as we get Bailey back."

"Don't have to look very far," Blake's voice was solemn. It held almost no tone. He grimly pointed to a flashing red button on the dash. It was the urgent alert channel for the Ekklesia. I clicked it.

My screen changed from the various buttons and dials and displayed two messages. The first was from two days ago, the day El Dorado fell. It was Sparks sitting at my father's old desk in the office behind the War Room. I clicked it, and a hologram projected up from the console.

"I'm calling all available Ekklesia forces to report to the Mountain base for re-assignment,"

"Not that one," Blake interrupted.

I was interested, but I obeyed and swiped to the next one. It was the same scene, but the time stamp was from one hour ago.

"All Ekklesia forces, be advised, The Organization has destroyed El Dorado, and the Mayans have turned on the Ekklesia. They blame us. A group of rogue insurgents have attacked the mountain base. Detain all Mayans on site. Use of lethal force is authorized."

Another man appeared in the frame. It was one of Sparks old alleys on the council. He whispered something in his ear.

"She's here?" I heard Sparks whisper back. The transmission turned off and the hologram retreated into the console.

"Found her," Blake said with saddened sarcasm.

She attacked the mountain base? That was bold, even for her.

"I doubt they'll win," I said, "Even if they do, they wouldn't kill her." I hoped they wouldn't anyway. "We can get this with Bailey sorted out, and then we'll go get her."

"I'm dropping you off, and then I'm going," Blake stated.

"Blake, you won't do much good without the rest of us," I pointed out, "We just need to make a plan."

"You can make a plan," Blake smarted, "I understand why you have to stay, but you have to understand why I have to go. I'm dropping you off. Then, I'm leaving."

I hung my head. This was a bad idea. He was right, but it was a bad idea. I didn't say anything. I just slouched back in my chair. My mind spiraled ever downward in the silence. Blake only glared straight ahead.

Everyone was breaking our rule of not splitting up. Everything was going wrong, and there seemed to be nothing I could do to stop it. The flight was long and dreary.

Hope finally sparked in my soul when I saw the lights of Tullahoma. Just as I spotted the shimmering lake, we turned away, headed for Arnold base. It was good to be home at least.

As we landed, I heard commotion in the back. I decided I would get up and check it out. When I returned, everyone was standing. The nurses were unlatching Bailey's bed. It detached from the floor and wheels lowered from the sides, lifting the base up.

We landed and the doors opened. They wheeled Bailey out. Hunter and Brady followed closely.

"Where will they take her?" I asked Alex.

"There's a medical center on the base," Alex told me, "Doctors are waiting there."

"Do you trust them?" I asked. I knew we weren't welcomed here anymore.

"Hard to tell who you can trust," Alex admitted, "But I think these guys are solid."

"That's all I need," I said. I looked at Ryder and Ana who were propped against the wall of the ship.

"Blake is about to go to our base," I informed them, "Can you help him?"

"Help him what?" Ryder asked.

"Yes," Amelia agreed, needing no further explanation. Ryder gave her a skeptical look. Amelia looked tired. Not physically. Like the rest of us, she was just tired of this.

"Thank you," I said, "Blake will fill you in on the way."

I motioned for Alex to follow me. We hopped out of the ship as Blake began to take off. He wasn't wasting any time. The doors closed and he sped off toward the base.

"What are they doing?" Alex asked.

"Whatever Blake needs them to," I said. I didn't know what his plan was, but I hoped they could protect him.

"You trust them?" he asked.

"Hard to tell who to trust," I repeated, "But I think they're pretty solid."

"That's good enough for me."

We walked across the complex to a one story building, not much bigger than a large house. It was the medical center. We walked in. There was a small waiting room with a few chairs, a T.V., and a couch. The boys sat on the couch, but stood up when we walked in.

"Wait here," I instructed, holding out my hand. They listened begrudgingly.

There was an empty receptionist's desk. Past it, a narrow hall. Everything was dark except for the light escaping from a room at the far end. I heard the chatter of busy doctors. We walked toward the room.

"She needs an MRI as soon as we can get it going," one said.

"Give her something to make her comfortable," said another.

"Get those X-Rays developed," one commanded, "and see if any records from El Dorado survived."

"Nothing survived," I informed them as I walked in. Bailey's mom sat by her daughter's side stroking her hair. Two nurses (one from the transport) and a doctor gave me their attention.

"Has this ever happened before?" the doctor asked.

"Not this," I said calmly, "She was receiving treatments for migraines back at the city."

"What kind?"

"I don't know," I admitted, "But she didn't have very many."

"We'll be starting from scratch, but we'll do our best," the doctor promised, and everyone went back to work.

There was a chair on the other side of the bed, opposite Ms. Boone. I sat there. I could tell Bailey was in less pain. I took her hand, and when I did, I heard her voice in my mind again.

"I have cancer," she said.

"What?" I said out loud. Everyone looked at me, but I ignored them. "Since when?" I thought back.

"They found it in El Dorado," Bailey told me, "It's why my headaches came back so strongly. They said my crystal did it."

"How?"

"They said I don't absorb all the energy, and it radiated my body every time I used it," she communicated.

"Well, that's good," I thought, "we can treat that."

"They were trying," Bailey sent. These sort of communications didn't have a tone most of the time, but I could sense her regret. "This cancer is...different. It's everywhere."

"Bailey," I breathed. Alex and Ms. Boone looked at me more intensely, "Why didn't you tell me."

"I'm sorry," she replied, "I didn't want to add stress if they were going to be able to fix it."

"Were they?" I asked.

There was a long pause.

"What is it?" Alex asked.

I held up my hand for him to wait.

"Were they going to be able to fix it?" I asked again.

"At my last visit, they told me my only chance was to give up my connection to the crystal and undergo surgery," Bailey explained, "They said it would be risky, but with Hunter's powers, they thought they could try removing it, followed by focused radiation, and have Hunter heal it up as they went." I watched a tear slip down Bailey's cheek. "I was going to tell you, I just..."

I stroked her cheek, wiping away the tear. "It's alright," I said out loud. "Rest. I'm going to fix this."

I stood up, grabbed Alex's shoulder, and pulled him out of the room. I felt Bailey calling after me, but I ignored her for now.

The breath left my lungs. I felt dizzy. I thought I would pass out. I stumbled out of the room. My mind was spinning, grasping for a way forward - a way out. I frantically accessed my father's files on my vanguard's tiny screen. I scrolled through the endless catacombs of information like a madman.

"No. No, No. Not it. No." I scrolled looking for one topic. "There!"

The Breastplate of Aaron. "My travels took me to the farthest reaches of the middle east, ultimately leading back to Israel," I spouted off my father's words. Alex looked at me as if I had gone insane.

"Dylan?" he questioned, "Is everything okay?"

"It will be," I snapped. I continued through my father's entry. "The mount of Olives!" I exclaimed, "That's where it's at."

"What?" Alex asked, growing annoyed and worried.

I took a deep breath and calmed myself. "My father found an artifact that could harness the power of all the crystals. Since only one person can harness a crystal at a time, that means it severs the connection with the previous bearer."

Alex stared blankly at me. "Dylan, what does that have to do with this?"

"Bailey's crystal is killing her," I said. My voice quivered.

"Dyaln, I-" Alex started.

"I need one more favor." I cut him off. "I don't have a lot of friends left. I need you to call in a few of yours."

"For you," he looked at Bailey, "And her - I think they'll gladly come out of retirement."

"Good," I said, "Tell them to meet us at the Mountain base. We'll converge on my personal fleet at 0-800"

"That's not a lot of time," Alex pointed out.

"They can handle it," I trusted.

"They'll want to know a plan," Alex added.

"We're going to steal back my personal fleet, recover the Breastplate, save Bailey, and save the world," I shrugged, "All in one day."

Chapter 32

I walked back into the room, but stopped just inside the door. “We'll be back soon,” I told Bailey and her mom. I turned around and prepared to walk out, but a feeling stopped me.

“Dylan,” Bailey's internal voice echoed, “Please stay.”

“I'm going to fix this,” I promised, “And I'll be back before lunch.”

“You can't fix this,” she communicated.

“You don't know that.” I felt tears threatening to fall, but I didn't let them win. I walked across the room to her side.

“I do,” she replied. I could sense her surety and her sadness, but also a peace. “Please stay. I need to talk to you.”

“We'll talk when I get back,” I countered, placing my hand on hers, “After I fix this.”

I leaned down and kissed her on the forehead. Bailey gently squeezed my hand. I squeezed back. I thought she might send me another message, but she didn't. The sounds of the beeping monitors and the buzzing lights flooded my consciousness again. It was time to go.

I marched out of the room. Alex fell in behind me. I walked down the hallway, my stride growing wider and faster as I went. When we came back by the waiting room, Hunter and Brady were already standing. They started to follow us.

“Stay here,” I commanded, not slowing up, “Protect Bailey until we get back.”

“Where are you going?” Hunter asked.

I didn't answer. Doing so would have required me to stop, and I didn't have a second to waist. I stormed out through the glass door and sprinted across the base.

My power gave me strength as I ran faster than any human could. I forgot Alex was even following me. All I was thinking about was the next thing I had to do. There was an airfield on the opposite side of the base. It housed our fastest ships, there to protect the city if it ever fell under attack. I reached it in only a few minutes.

The area was sparsely protected. There were only a few soldiers. I already had a Sting Ray before the alarm even sounded. Alex flew in on a jetpack and landed just before I took off.

"You forgot something," he quipped, as he climbed into the gunner seat.

"Sorry," I stated. I closed the glass canopy over us and we took off. Alex got to work on contacting the Taken.

I focused solely on flying as fast as I could to the base. Once we were about halfway there, Alex told me he had gotten together a group that could be there in time.

"They want to know what we're doing though," Alex said.

"Start a private transmission." A green light appeared on my vanguard and I began explaining in a cold, calculated voice. "Taken, sorry to interrupt your retirement," I began. "The Ekklesia is under the influence of a traitor, Jeremiah Sparks. As you know, Bailey is unwell. We need to recover an artifact to save her. We will be stealing back my personal fleet and going to Israel. My father attempted to recover this once, but he ran into a band of highly trained Zealots protecting it. Then, the war started. We'll be using the fleet to retrieve the artifact." I ended the transmission.

"You didn't tell me about the Zealots," Alex jumped in.

"Would it have stopped you?" I asked.

"No," Alex replied, "Now I'm excited."

We flew for about another fifteen minutes before the base came into view. With it came the first notes of sunrise. The moon still shown as well. The combined light fell on the mountain range, specifically highlighting the glistening memorial bridge over Broken Valley in the distance.

As we neared the base, I realized the shield was deactivated. This concerned me. The shield hadn't been off since the day my father turned it on. I slowed up and looked for anything that might be going on.

The ships that were usually stationed above the base were gone. The traffic of maneuvering fighters and transports was absent as well. I circled the base at a distance. Every hangar was sealed shut with its thick blast door. All except for one.

On the far side of the base, one blast door had a gaping, smoldering hole blown in the side. Hangar five was on the opposite end of the base. We would have to walk across.

I took the ship in, noticing some transports forming up behind me. They were the only ships in sight. Alex confirmed that they were The Taken.

The hole in the door was just big enough for us to fly through. Our Stingray squeezed through the opening. The inside of the hangar was scorched. Burn marks from energy guns and bearer's attacks scared the walls, floors, and ships.

Some ships had been destroyed. Some were turned over. Bodies littered the hangar. There had been a shoot out between the Ekklesia and El Dorado. Young men in both uniforms lay all around. My heart sank. What had this come to?

I sat the ship down where I could find a clear spot. Once we had landed, I jumped out and began to observe the damage. I checked some of the closest soldiers to see if they were stunned or if it was worse. It was worse.

Their armor was marked with blasts it had protected its wearer from. The fatal blows seemed to have come from atom swords that made their way between the armored plates.

"I'll scout ahead," I told Alex. "When most of The Taken are here, follow me."

I ran through the destroyed room and into the hall. All the while, I prayed I wouldn't spot any of my friends' more unique uniforms. I spotted some high ranking officers, but thankfully, none of my friends. I followed the path of destruction but it veered off from my path. I heard shooting and yelling coming from the hall. I turned to run toward it but stopped. I didn't have time. I had to get to my fleet.

I ran away from the ensuing fight and sprinted toward my hangar. I pushed my senses down the hall ahead of me to check for danger. I sensed troops, about twelve of them, running toward me. I kept my pace and prepared to fight.

They came into view as I rounded a loose turn. They were running two by two with their weapons drawn. I was about to attack, but I sensed that I was not their target. They weren't even paying me any attention. We ran past each other without them giving me a second look. These Ekklesia troops didn't even realize who I was. They just thought I was a fellow soldier. Even with my unique uniform. I was probably so dirty they couldn't tell it was different. I'm not sure how they didn't notice the crystal. Maybe they just chose not to fight me.

"Twelve soldiers headed your way," I informed Alex, "Act like you belong and they'll probably walk right past you."

"Copy," Alex replied.

I continued running until I finally reached the hangar. It looked like I was getting here just in time. The fleet was returning. The first ships were beginning to land in the hangar. Troops were filing out of the transports ready to attack. They were here to reinforce the Ekklesia. I would make sure their mission failed.

I waited in the entrance to the rest of the base as a large group of soldiers formed. I saw Cashner was leading the charge.

"ALI, shut the main hangar door on my command," I requested.

There was no response.

"Crap," I said to myself. I forgot that he had disappeared. I would have to do this one on my own.

It was protocol for a few fighters to circle the base while the strike team infiltrated. I waited until most of the ships were in the hangar. There were two exits in the hangar. The one I was standing in and one on the opposite end of the same wall. The instant Cashner noticed me, I conjured a beam to seal off the exit.

I didn't get to see it hit the mark. Instead, my head throbbed. I felt fear. I felt anger. I saw through Blake's eyes a sign that read "WAR ROOM". I saw a magenta flash. I heard a voice, "There he is!" and another, "Blake, what's wrong?"

I let go of my powers and realized I was on the ground. My entrance turned out to not be as intimidating as I had hoped. When I looked up, I realized I hadn't even conjured the beam. My connection with Blake had crippeled my focus.

I looked up to see a maniacal grin spread across Cashner's face. The corners of his mouth turned up. His eyebrows narrowed. His nose scrunched. His lip snarled, and the grin turned to a scowl. He pulled the atom sword from his hip and ignited it. The blade slipped out, and he began to walk toward me.

I drew my staff and stood up, careful not to draw on my crystal's power. Cashner's troops lined up behind him and aimed their own weapons at me. Cashner stopped about 20 feet away from me and his men stood about the same distance from him.

I stood firm, ready to face them all.

I gripped my staff, held it out in front of me, and slammed it into the ground. A blue ring spread out from the tip. Then, I drew it back and held it with both hands, lifting it up in a ready position. Without saying a word, I was challenging him. I was challenging all of them. I dared them to stand in my way.

Sparks took a few confident steps forward, but stopped. I noticed his eyes looking past me. I heard footsteps running up behind me. I sensed it was Alex and the Taken.

Alex flanked my right side. The rest of the Taken soldiers formed up behind me, just as my former strike team was behind Cashner. There were about as many on both sides.

Cashner analyzed the room. I remained stoic. Alex drew a pistol phaser off of each hip. The rest of the Taken followed suit by drawing their own weapons.

"I once fought alongside all of you," I announced. "I considered you friends." I paused, thinking about the faces under the helmets in front of me. The men who had fought at my side. "I'm taking this fleet. This is your only chance to stay out of my way."

No one moved.

"I'm sorry," I told them. I really was sorry, for all of it.

I lunged forward as the hanger erupted into a ferocious battle. Yellow phaser blasts flew back and forth between the two groups, clanking on the armor of their targets. The Taken were scrambling to gain cover behind the various ships – an advantage that Cashner's men already had.

Cashner and I ran at each other and clashed between the two groups of soldiers. My Unitum staff met his atomising blade with a horrible screech. I knocked it to the side and swiped at his head. He dodged and swung the blade at my chest. It narrowly missed the unarmored area. (My breastplate had been lost somewhere along the way)

I leapt back and returned with a jab. Cashner grabbed onto the staff. I yanked him forward, dodging a flailing swing of his blade as he passed by. He stumbled but quickly gained his balance. We exchanged a few more blows before he gained an opening.

He swung his blade at my neck. I let go of my staff with one hand, using the vanguard to knock his attack away. I brought the staff around to knock his blade away from me which I succeeded in, but this left him another opening. He kicked his foot out, landing the blow to my gut. The breath was forced out of me and I stumbled backward.

"You're not nearly as impressive without your powers," Cashner taunted.

I didn't respond. I used his seconds spent talking to catch my breath. I sensed a stray blast coming from behind me and tilted the back of my staff up to intercept it.

I took what must have only been micro seconds to observe what was happening around me. It didn't seem like either side was winning yet. We were wasting time. I could see Bailey lying in that hospital bet. I could see the hourglass running out. We didn't have time to waste.

I lunged back at Cashner. My attacks were forceful, fast, and aggressive. I overwhelmed what he could block with just one blade and was able to deliver a blow to his leg, then his side, but I never got an opening to jab.

An explosion rocked the hanger, but I didn't let it distract me. I kept pushing Cashner back. I could tell he was getting tired and desperate. Finally, he swung. I could tell he expected me to deflect it with my staff, but I didn't. Instead, I ducked and grabbed his arm. I dropped my staff and wrapped my arm around his neck.

Cashner was bigger and taller than I was, but the crystal made me strong.He used his one freed arm to elbow me in the chest, but it wasn't enough to break through my adrenaline. I squeezed his wrist. The longer he refused to drop his sword, the tiger my grip became. I could feel his arm begging to crush.

Cashner screamed and finally let go. The sword retracted as it fell, and I launched Cashner into the wall on the hanger (which we were very close to now). He slammed into it and fell to the ground. I kicked the hilt of his sword away, picked up my staff, and pointed it at his chest. I kept it just far enough away that I could react in time if he tried to grab it.

Cashner scooted away and propped himself up against the metal wall. His breathing was heavy and he coddled his wrist.

"Well, I guess I really am a traitor now," I snarled. I slammed the butt of the staff into his chest. A blue wave of energy spread over his body as he was shoved back into the wall. His body went limp.

I turned back to the rest of the hanger. The shooting had stopped. The Taken were already securing the ships. Alex was jogging over to me.

"I'll give 'em this," Alex said, "The Organization's training is better than whatever these guys had."

"How many casualties?" I asked.

"On our side, none," Alex said.

"We're all on the same side," I frowned.

"Not today," Alex corrected, "Anything else you need to do before we leave?"

"Just one," I replied, "I'm gonna find Blake. Get ready to leave. Send a few out to take down the security outside."

"On it," Alex saluted and ran back toward the fancy ships. I ran off down the hall.

As I was running, I saw a man running toward me from the opposite direction, a highly decorated officer in a grey Ekklesia uniform. I recognized his silhouette.

"Raddick?" I called.

"Dylan!" he called back. He seemed happy to see me. I couldn't say the same. I was still trying to figure out if he was on my side or not.

"Have you seen Blake?" I asked.

"Yes," he replied, "He's not far behind me. He said you were here. I came to find you."

"We'll have to talk later," I brushed him off and continued toward where Raddick had been coming from.

"No wait!" he placed his hand on my chest as I walked by. I looked at him angerly. "You need to hear what I have to say."

I gave him my attention.

"Sparks sent our navy to attack Jericho," he informed me, "Our seagoing navy."

"That's seuicide," I scoffed, "They'll see them coming days in advance."

"Well, they won't see them," Reddick replied. I stepped back and he took his hand off of me, "He's using Mayan technology to cloak the fleet."

"Then, they'll be destroyed by airships when they arrive," I countered.

"Sparks has sent our entire army to attack different known Organization outposts and cities," Raddick said, "He's diverting their support from Jericho."

I mulled this over. It was actually a decent plan. With one exception. Sparks probably thought that all of the bearers, on both sides, were dead after the Battle of El Dorado. If the Onyx bearer were at Jericho, it wouldn't matter how good his sinister plan was. He was also missing the information that we had gathered about Jericho. As much as I hated him, as much as he had taken from me, he had to win this battle.

"I need to speak to Sparks," my nose curled at the thought of even hearing his voice.

"You can't," Raddick stated.

"Why not?" I demanded.

The conversation was interrupted as our attention quickly turned to footsteps coming from behind the General. As they rounded the corner, my guard lowered. I recognized the brown Mayan uniforms and the people wearing them.

"Chief!" I exclaimed. I walked away from Raddick and greeted him with a firm handshake. "Good to see you in piece."

He nodded. Flaking him were two of the guards from theHall of Elders. They sported their flowing capes and Unitum spears. Behind them was a company of regular Mayan soldiers. They parted to reveal Ana and Blake.

My face melted and an uncontrollable sigh of relief escaped. I hugged Blake. We let go quickly, not to look weak in front of the other soldiers. And if we had held on any longer, we might have broken down right there.

Ana wore a sickened, hate filled expression. I sensed her grief, but I also sensed her relief having found her father.

"How's Bailey?" Blake asked me.

"She'll be fine," I promised us both, "Alex and I are on our way to get something that will save her." I noticed blood on Ana's uniform. It stood out, spattered across her shiny armor. "Are y'all alright?"

Ana stared at her father. I don't think she even heard me. Blake looked at the blood, then at me. "We will be."

Everyone certainly didn't look alright, but since they were upright, I decided to leave that there. We were fighting the clock. I looked back at Raddick. "Where's Sparks?"

Everyone looked at each other. Anyone but me. From some I sensed resolve, from others uncertainty. From Raddick I sensed accomplishment. I looked from person to person, seeking someone who would answer my question.

"He's dead," a voice grumbled. It was Ana. "I killed him."

"What?" I blurted uncontrollably.

"He killed my people and destroyed my home," Ana nearly yelled. "He died for it."

My mouth gaped open. I knew she was angry, but I didn't expect this. I didn't blame her for it though. I forced myself to move forward. "So whose leading the Ekklesia?" I asked.

"I am," Raddick spoke up.

It all fit together now. Raddick was after that position from the second I began to fall away from it. He knew I couldn't hold it. He knew Sparks would do something rash. He played the politics, and he won. I was angry, but I had to keep pressing on. "Then let's talk business," I proposed to the group.

We formed a small circle. "You have to recall the attack," I told Raddick. "The Onyx bearer survived. If he's there–"

"We can't," he cut me off, "It's already begun." He pressed a button on his vanguard that projected a hologram into the center of our huddle. It marked both the fleet and Jericho in the Mediterranean sea. The fleet was off the coast of Italy. Jericho was near Greece. The map zoomed out to reveal other dots. They were red, indicating that they were active battles. They filled Europe and Africa. "The fleet will engage Jericho in two hours."

"They'll be crushed," the chief shook his head.

"Sparks clearly thought all the bearers were dead," Raddick agreed, "He hoped to take the final stones, ending all the battles around the globe at once."

"It almost worked," Blake admitted.

"We need you to go there and support our attack," Raddick requested.

"I can't," I said, "Not yet. Not for at least six hours. I have to save Bailey first."

I expected him to complain, but he didn't. I silently thanked him for it. "Does El Dorado have any forces left?" I asked.

"We still have all of our cruisers," the chief replied. This made sense; none of them were at El Dorado when it fell.

"Send them to support the Ekklesia's attack," I told him.

"You want us to fight alongside the same people who destroyed our civilization," Ana skoffed.

"You killed the man who gave the order," I defended, "The Organization carried it out. The Ekklesia had nothing to do with it."

"You give them too much credit," Ana growled.

"Look," I addressed the whole group, "Sparks has forced all of our hands. If the Organization doesn't die today, it never will. If Bailey dies today," my voice shook, "I can't bring her back." I looked around the circle, "We get once chance at this."

Everyone seemed to agree. "Then tell us what to do," Raddick said firmly.

"We need to get as many bearers to Jericho as we can," I looked around. "Where are Ryder and Amelia?"

"They're protecting the ships we came here on," the chief told me.

"Take them and everyone you have left to Jericho. I'll retrieve the breastplate, save Bailey, and return to the battle." I looked at Raddick. "When I do, all twelve stones will be in the same place."

"Except for the one that's here," Blake pointed out.

"No, I need that one too," I said, "We'll use the mayan's remote entanglement tech to remove it from the generator and transport it there."

"Why would we take it there?" Raddick asked, "It would be safer to keep at least one away. Just in case."

"We won't get a second chance," I said, "Not like this one."

"What are you going to do with it," Raddick pressed.

"I'm going to wield it," I said, "I'm going to wield all twelve and defeat the Onyx bearer."

Chapter 33

The group disbursed, understanding their assignments. The Chief took his men to the Hangar. Ana was to break off and retrieve the yellow crystal from the generator. Raddick was to oversee the battle at Jericho. There was one more thing that needed to be done.

"Blake, come with me," I told him. He had already turned to go with the Mayans. We walked to me reluctantly.

"I would go with you, but I need to be with Ana," Blake said, before I even told him what I needed, "She's hurting."

I could tell this was not going to be easy, but the urgency of Bailey's sickness sat over our conversation. It filled my thoughts like a thick fog.

"Blake, this artifact is protected," I explained, "I don't know what exactly I'm walking into, but I know they were able to turn my father away, which was not easy. If I'm going to get it, I need my powers."

Blake's eyebrows scrunched. He looked at the crystal seated in his chest. "I don't know how to give them back," he said. I could tell he was hurt that I had asked.

"You can't," I frowned, "But if you're sedated, I can wield them freely."

"I just won't use them," he offered, "As long as I don't use them, you're good."

"What if you accidently do?" I pointed out, "We can't risk it... Bailey can't afford us to."

"Dylan, I can't be sedated right now. Ana needs me," he argued.

I was beginning to grow frustrated. Did he not see the urgency of the moment? Ana was still walking. Bailey was barely holding on. After all this, after always having my back, how could he possibly be doing this now?

I stepped toward him. "Blake, I-"

He stepped away from me and looked as though he might be ready for a fight. My lip quivered as my heart broke. I could see the hurt in his eyes as well.

"I promise you I won't use them," Blake demanded, "That's the best I can do."

"That's not good enough," I raised my voice, "We get one chance at this! One! Not everyone gets brought back to life."

"You didn't see what I just saw!" Blake yelled. His voice echoed down the now empty corridor. He pointed his finger in my face. A tear escaped his eye. His body trembled.

"Fine," shook my head, "Go."

He looked at me for a second longer. Shook his head, and walked away. As he walked, I couldn't see him. I could only see a small room with a grey wall and a white bed. I could only see a young girl with the most beautiful blonde hair. I saw her pale face. I saw her closed eyes. I saw the tear sliding off her cheek.

Then, I remembered it. The small vials of sedative the medic had given me on the football field those few months ago. I didn't use them all on Lucas. I still had two. That could buy me enough time. I slipped my hand into the small pouch hooked on my waist. I pulled out the syringe and bit off the cap.

Blake was only a few steps away. I lunged forward. I wrapped one arm around his neck. Before he could even struggle I had jabbed the needle into his neck and administered the drug. I let go of him.

Blake stumbled away. He turned around toward me. His hand was placed over his neck. He knew exactly what I had done. He tried to say something, but the drug wouldn't let him. His eyes closed, and he fell backwards.

All of it had been less of a thought and more of a reaction. I stared down at the deed I had done, the unconscious body of my best friend laying before me. My breathing became labored. I wiped my hand across my sweating forehead. I took a deep breath and knelt down beside my friend. I put my hand on his shoulder.

"I'm sorry," I said, knowing he was seeing through my eyes, just as I had my father's, "But this is the only way to save all of us."

I left Blake where he was. He would be safe there. I forced myself to bury my emotions. Of course I wanted to cry. I wanted to break down. I wanted to freeze, but I knew that would mean death. I sprinted back to the hanger, running toward Bailey just as much as I was running toward a ship.

As soon as I entered, I saw that the convoy was beginning to take off. The command ship was in the center of the hangar. Alex was standing in its open door waiting for me. I forced my eyes to focus on him, for bodies of fallen Ekklesia soldiers dotted the hanger's floor. I couldn't bring myself to look at them. I tried to tell myself that they had a choice, that they had chosen this. I told myself that about Blake too. It didn't help.

I leapt into the ship, and the door closed behind me. I felt us lifting off the ground.

"You found Blake?" Alex asked, naively.

"Huh?' I asked. I heard him, but my thoughts were too crowded to answer. I must have looked as bad as I felt.

"Is everything okay?" he pivoted.

"Yea," I assured him, but I don't think I sounded very assureling. I forced myself to think on the mission instead of all the things surrounding it. "Tell the convoy to get above the atmosphere and engage the emergency thrusters. I'll upload the strike point to everyone's HUD."

"Okay," Alex nodded. He didn't sound convinced, but he wasn't one to pry. Not like Blake. Blake always knew when something was wrong. He would press until I let him help me. Did I do the same for him? Maybe I was a terrible friend. I certainly was right now.

"Focus," I told myself. I sat at one of the control stations and began to upload the details of the mission. The Taken would have the short flight to review them. When I was done, I lowered my head into my hands and began to pray. I was reaching the end of my rope. Actually, I may have exceeded the end. My strength was waning.

"You've brought us this far," I prayed, "Don't let this tear us apart."

"Begining descent into strike zone," the pilots voice called.

"And let this be the last day of the war," I added firmly. I stood up and walked into the cockpit. Alex was sitting in the co-pilots chair. I stood between him and the pilot, steadying myself on each of their seats.

I could see the black void of outer space above us and the blue expanse of the Earth below us. The sun was behind us. It illuminated the ground and water below. It could see the edge of sunset and shadow far beyond where we were now.

The nose of the ship turned down and we began to plummet to the Earth. A red glow appeared on the other side of the windshield as our ship turned into a fireball, crashing through the atmosphere. A thin purple shield separated us and it. The red glow became brighter as we increased in speed until it was too bright to look at directly.

We finally picked up so much speed that my feet lifted off the ground. All of the dust on the ship began to float up. I wasn't just weightless, I was being pulled upward.

"You might want to sit down," the pilot suggested, "I'm about to put on the breaks."

I acknowledged him and pushed myself back into the cabin. I floated until I reached one of the seats. I grabbed it, pulled myself in, and strapped myself down. The ship shook. The roar of the passing air filled my ears. I gripped the arm rests. I heard the engines begin to wine.

Suddenly, my whole body was slammed forward. If I hadn't been strapped in, there is no doubt I would have died right then. It wasn't just a single jolt forward. I kept being pulled by the invisible G-force. This continued for a few minutes.

"Entering Organization Air Space," the pilot's shaking voice informed me. Then, as suddenly as I had been thrown forward, I was thrown back in my seat. "Two minutes from drop point."

"Can I stand up now?" I asked.

The opening side doors of the cabin answered my question. I unstrapped and stood up. The wind blowing in was dry and mild. Alex walked out of the cockpit. The door slid shut behind him.

"How long till The Organization crashes the party?" Alex yelled over the wind.

"Depends on how busy they are with everything else," I called back.

I looked down over the brown desert landscape. There was very little vegetation. Almost everything was just bare brown rocks. I held one of the handles on the ceiling and leaned out of the door. We were about to fly over the Holy City. It sat atop a hill. Its unique religious sites made it stand out. I could see, just beyond the temple mount, another taller hill. It was the Mount of Olives. The Breastple was within.

"The entrance is at the base of the second summit," I advised, referring to my father's notes. The pilot adjusted his course as the other ships fell into formation behind us.

We swung wide and circled around Jeweruslem. It wasn't difficult to find where we would need to land. In the valley, between the city and the mount, was a small army of men. They must have seen us coming. They were dressed in brown clothing. That was all I could tell from here.

I took a breath, focused my mind on the moment, and let go of the handle above me. I ignited my jetpack, and I fell out of the ship. My pilot pulled away and I flew toward the Zealots. The Taken filed in behind me.

As we flew, one man, dressed differently from the rest, walked from the base of the mount to the front of the group which fanned out in a battle array behind him. I flew and landed a few yards away from him. A dust cloud blew up as I landed. An even greater one formed as the Taken landed behind me.

The man leading the Zealots wore a red tunic. It was held together with a leader belt around his mid section. It came halfway down his thigh. Under this he wore brown breeches that cinched tight around his ankles. He wore no shoes. He was tall and fit. Around his neck was a golden necklace. Attached to it was a brown stone. Orange energy swirled faintly around it. He eyed the crystal on my chest.

"I've come for the breastplate of Aaron," I announced.

"You will fail, just as your father and all the ones before him," the Zealot promised. His Arabic accent was thick. His words were difficult to make out.

"This doesn't have to be a fight," I offered, "But if I don't take it now, one who bears the Onyx stone will come for it."

"Then we will defend it from him as well," he countered.

"If -" I started to continue reasoning with him, but I was out of time and patience. I took a sharp breath. My energy appeared across my body. The Zealots drew golden swords from their hips. The leader held his hands out to his sides. The brown-orange energy flowed in jagged lines to them.

The ground beneath me began to shake. Small rocks around the leader began to float up, endued with the dark orange energy. The Taken drew their weapons, and the fight began.

Huge pillars of rock exploded from the ground below my men. Many were launched into the air. I immediately turned my attention away from the bearer and did my best to catch them. The ones who remained conscious used their jetpacks to return to the ground safely.

As I lowered them, another pillar exploded from below me. My legs took a hard hit. I worried they were broken. I wailed as my concentration broke, and I was thrown into the air.

I ignited my own jetpack and returned blasts of my energy to the Zealot. Pillars of rock emerged from the Earth to protect him. They were shattered by the blasts but the Zealot was unscathed. I charged at him from the sky. As I did, two Stingrays formed up behind me and unloaded their missiles onto the battlefield. Dust, smoke and ash were kicked up. I was sure they had hit some of the other Zealots.

I used my senses to locate the leader in the dust cloud. As I flew down, I took the crystal from my chest and gripped it in my right hand. I charged up its energy and landed a clean blow to the leader.

I came to the ground faster than I could catch myself. The leader was blasted across the battlefield and smashed into the side of the mount. I rolled to a stop, still a good distance away. I quickly stood up, placed the crystal back on my chest, and readied to follow up with another attack, but I couldn't locate him. How had I lost him? I had kept my senses focused on him every second. It was like he had just disappeared.

I hardly had time to note a low rumble before the ground beneath me gave way. I sunk down a bit before a hand latched onto my neck. I was picked up and slammed back down onto the rocky earth. The leader's amulet hung in my face, and he punched me over and over. Rocky restraints formed around my hands and feet.

I could hardly bring my senses about me. It was probably about the fifth hit to the face before my struggle to get away turned to boiling anger. The energy across my body surged into a blinding purple light. I screamed as a purple shockwave exploded out from me in every direction. The bearer and his restraints were blown off of me.

I immediately sprang to my feet. I peered through the dusty haze that had settled over the area. The leader came into view.

"The Zealots have protected this artifact for 3,000 years," he snarled, "Today will be no different." Two chunks of rocks broke through the surface of the ground and flooded up on either side of him.

I wiped my mouth and spit blood onto the dry ground as though I were spitting it on his words.

The two rocks flew toward me. I destroyed each of them with my energy. As more came, I drew my staff and used it to break through them. I inched forward as the frequency of the rocks turned from one at a time to a full avalanche. I held my staff in front of me and formed a shield that came to a point. The rocks hit it and were pushed to either side.

As they continued coming, I was slowly able to tilt my staff toward the source of the rocks. Once it was in line, I pushed it forward, propelling it with my energy. It shot up the flow and hit its mark. I lunged forward, pushed by concussive blasts and grabbed hold of the bearer.

I picked him up and slammed him down into the cassem that had formed behind him (the source of the rocks he was throwing at me. We slid to the bottom. The ground shook. I felt the rock beneath us moving, attempting to swallow up its master. As the rock pulled him away, I ripped him up from the ground like a weed being pulled by the roots. I lifted him over my head and slammed him back down.

I began to pummel his face. Over and over again. When the ground would try and swallow him, I would rip him up and slam him down in a new spot. Finally, his struggling stopped. He was unconscious.

With blood on my hands, I sprang up and sprinted toward the base of the mountain. There was a small opening, just tall enough to walk through. I sensed that it was a straight, narrow passageway. There was a round room at the end. I also sensed struggling Taken soldiers nearby, but I stayed focused on the breastplate. I ran in the cavern. The second I stepped inside, I sensed the trap.

I looked back the instant the narrow opening sealed shut. In the last bit of light, I could see the leader crawling out of the crater and lifting his hand in my direction.

The walls began to crumple like cardboard. I had milliseconds to choose whether I lunged for the breastplate, or broke through the opening to the outside. It was hardly a choice.

I launched myself toward the end of the passage. My jetpack boosted me. In the center of a round room was an obelisk. On it was a small golden square. The Obelisk was retreating into the Earth.

I landed on the ground, ripped the artifact from its place and formed a shield to protect myself. The passage collapsed. The bearer pressed the rock in on me, but this was nothing compared to holding up an entire mountain.

My shield held strong, so I took a second to breathe and looked at my prize. I was on my hands and knees. In my right hand was a small golden square, smaller than I expected. It was divided into twelve smaller squares arrayed in four rows of three. There was an empty seat in each square for its crystal.

I felt a weight lift only to be instantly replaced by determination. I had it in my hand. I held the key to saving my love and saving the world. I had to get it out of here.

My eyes narrowed and my muscles tensed. The glow of my crystal intensified as I expanded my shield outward. I stood up. I turned back to where the entrance had been. I tucked the golden plate between my armored chestplate and my suit. Then, I held out my arm and opened my hand. With that motion I forced the rock to reform and expand outward. My purple energy pressed against the orange and dominated it. The harder it pushed in, the easier I pushed it back until light finally appeared.

I looked out of the swirling vortex of energy back out onto the dusty battlefield. The leader of the Zealots was standing at the mouth of the passageway, trying his best to seal it. He tried pushing up new rocks from below and pulling down rock from the side of the mountain, but I used my energy to hold the entire mountainside in place.

I noticed my control and focus was more keen than usual. My typically swirling thoughts were concentrated into laser focus, bound by one word reverberating through every corner of my mind: "Bailey".

I walked forward at a steady pace and emerged into the scorching desert sunlight. The Zealot's leader took a few nervous steps backward. He winced as he prepared to give his life in this fight. He wouldn't have to.

"You're relieved of your duties, Zealot," I stated firmly.

The leader balled his fists and raised them. His dirty orange energy drowned them, as did tiny particles of dust and rock. "We will fight until our dying breath to protect the breastplate of Aaron," he breathed.

"That won't be necessary," I told him. I ignited my jetpack and lifted off the ground. I turned on my coms, "We've got-"

A pillar of stone hit me from below. Then, another boulder crashed into me from above. I plummeted to the ground. I tried to cushion my fall, but there wasn't enough time. I crashed into the stony earth.

"Ugh," I groaned as I rolled onto my back. I felt the rock beneath me shifting as it prepared to pull me into the ground.

I had the wind knocked out of me and was forced to lay there for a second. As I did, I noticed my crystal behaving strangely. The energy that usually flowed from it was being pulled. It appeared that it was being sucked into my chestplate. The crystal vibrated. The puck beneath it suddenly shattered and the crystal lodged itself into the Unitum plating below. I was worried, but only until I realized what was tucked beneath that chestplate.

I reached into the space where I had tucked the golden square, intending to examine what was happening. I pulled it out. Once it was in my hand, my crystal flew across my chest and connected to it. I felt the energy flowing through my body cease. My heightened senses turned off.

"No!" I yelled uncontrollably. The Earth began to swallow me.

I clawed at the breastplate. The crystal was seated in one of the smaller segments of the plate. As I was taken into the earth, I pulled the breastplate into my chest and wrapped both arms around it. I couldn't lose it. I was too close. My only hope was that one of the Taken would see what was happening and defeat the leader.

The light faded. It became impossible to breathe. The rock began to crush me. I couldn't move. I couldn't fight. I couldn't think.

Then, a warm sensation filled my veins. A strength filled my muscles. A purple glow lit the back of my eyelids. My powers were back. Where they had gone, I didn't know, but they were here now.

I forced a concussive blast out from my body in every direction. Light instantly flooded my eyes. I leapt out of the crater before it could close in on me again. I held onto the breastplate, but I soon realized that my suit had misinterpreted it for a puck. The tan mist had secured it to my white metal breastplate. The crystal was still seated within it.

I landed on the edge of the hole I had just created and called my energy across my body once again. It felt pure - new - fresh. It was like a static that I never knew was there had been removed by the golden plate. The leader stood only a few feet away. His eyes were wide and his mouth hung open.

"You just don't know when to quit, do you?" I insulted.

He didn't respond. Instead, a great look of fear spread across his face. He looked from side to side frantically. "Stop!" he cried. At first I thought he was talking to me. Stop what? What was I doing? "Zealots! Stop fighting!" He looked back at me, pressed his hands together, and got on one knee. He bowed his face toward the ground.

I didn't slack up on my fighting stance. I thought this was a trap of some sort. I did notice, as the dust settled, that the other Zealots had laid down their swords. Their hands were raised, and the Taken held them at gunpoint. The sounds of the battle were replaced by a gentle rustling wind.

"Only a true descendant of Aaron's firstborn lineage, pure in heart and just in his convictions, can wield the breastplate," the Zealot said, refusing to lift his face from the ground. "It is returned to its rightful owner."

I let my guard down now. I sensed that he was telling the truth. I sensed a completeness in his mission. Now it was time to complete mine.

I bowed slightly toward him. "Thank you," I said, unsure if that was the proper thing to say at the moment. What do you say to that? All I knew was that the clock was ticking for both Bailey and humanity. I eyed the crystal around his neck. "Now I need your crystal," I commanded. I wasn't sure if he was obligated to obey me now or not, but I just went for it, "The fate of the world depends on it."

He seemed hurt that I had asked this of him, but he didn't object. He reluctantly pulled it from his neck. I sensed a torrent of emotion welling up within him.

"Yes, my lord," he quivered, "It will serve you well."

"I'll give it back," I promised, "I just need it today."

This seemed to satisfy him. He looked away, turning back toward the ground.

"Taken," I announced, "Head to Jericho. I'll meet you there."

Chapter 34

I blasted myself off the ground, and my jetpack ignited. I spied a stingray and flew toward it. They were the fastest ships I had in my personal fleet. I flew alongside it. The pilot and his gunner realized I was requesting it.

The canopy slid open. The two men jumped out, using their jetpacks to fly to another ship. I rolled into the pilot's seat in a seamless transition. I took hold of the controls, closed the canopy, and began to climb out of the Earth's atmosphere.

The ships weren't made to do this, especially twice in less than half an hour, but it was the fastest way to travel long distances. We could leave behind the limiting factor of air resistance and fly at speeds surpassing that of satellites.

I performed the same maneuver we had done to get to Israel. I despised every second of the short flight. For every one of those seconds, I could think of nothing but Bailey. This was going to work. It had to. Of course it would.

The ship shook and the engines wined as I climbed.

I had prayed, I had done everything in my power to make it work. God would meet me there just like he always did. I had reached the end of myself. I trusted none but him. He would make it work. He always made it work.

I prayed. Every second that passed, I prayed.

As I began my re-entry into the atmosphere, I felt something change. I felt a tremor in my crystal connection. It was Blake waking up. While I still had his consciousness looking through my eyes, I spoke to him.

"Blake, I'm sorry. It was the only thing I knew to do."

"You…should have…trusted me," His groggy voice played in my mind.

"I do trust you," I defended. I began to feel his anger and his hurt. The needle that had jabbed his neck had cut a deep wound into his heart. "You just didn't have enough experience to control."

He didn't say anything, so I continued, "I couldn't risk it. You know what's at stake." I wanted him to say something back, but he didn't. We would have to fix this later, I told myself. "Meet me at Jericho," I told him, "This all ends today."

Red streaks from the angry atmosphere surrounded my Stingray. The little ship shook violently. I could hear bits of the outer shell begin to rip off. The shields were failing to protect it from the intense heat. Sensors were screaming at me. Shields 15%. Hull integrity, 25%. Heat shielding failure. The outer metal began to glow red and the cockpit began to heat up.

I nodded, forming my helmet over my head. The suit responded to the temperature by activating its cooling system. I threw the thrusters into full reverse and extended the drag flaps. The G-force pulled my body forward. It stretched my skin and churned my stomach. I wasn't sure if this ship or my body would be able to handle another one of these maneuvers today, but we would have to find out.

Finally, the ship slowed to normal speeds as Arnold Base came into focus. A long trail of smoke followed me as I sat the ship down on the lawn in front of the medical building. The ship clanked as pieces fell off and it dropped to a stop. Hunter and Brady were standing outside the doors. They must have seen me coming.

I landed and jumped out of the ship. Heat poured off of the ship. The air itself sizzled on the hot metal. Smoke poured from the tired engines.

Hunter greeted me first. "Did you get it?"

I smiled, "Was there ever a doubt?" I gestured to the golden plate on my chest.

"That's so cool," Brady commented.

"It is pretty awesome," I agreed. We walked through the glass doors of the facility. "How's Bailey?' I asked.

"About the same," Hunter said.

"Has she said anything to you?" I asked. That would be the best marker for her state.

"She's communicated with us in our minds," Hunter said, "But she's still asleep."

I nodded and walked briskly to her room. Her mother was still sitting in a chair beside her bed. Wires and tubes came from nearly every part of Bailey's body. Thankfully they hadn't put anything on her face though. I hated to see people like that.

I walked over. Bailey's crystal was sitting on a table against the wall, near the door. I went to Bailey first. I took her hand and then bent down to kiss her head. "I got it," I whispered. I nearly cried with joy, "We can fix this now."

She didn't communicate, but I sensed her love swelling in her heart, so I knew she heard me. I got up, placed her hand down gently, and walked over to the little table. All that was on it was a glass of water and the white crystal. Its glow was as soft and pure as ever. I picked it up and raised it to the golden plate on my chest. As it got closer, its energy began to seep from it. The breastplate pulled it in. I felt my crystal begin to connect to it. I let go and it seated itself next to mine, in the upper left corner.

The energy swept across the breastplate and then across my body. The purple followed it and the two combined. Their glow overpowered the sterile white lighting of the room. Hunter and Brady watched anxiously from the door.

The initial wave of energy subsided, and I contained the power within myself. Nothing felt all that new. I was used to wielding her powers. I did feel stronger, lighter. Most of all, I felt free. I had done it. I turned back to the bed. To my thrill, Bailey's eyes were open. She smiled at me through her tears. For the first time in a while, I allowed my own to fall.

"Bailey," I said through a relieved sigh. I ran to her and scooped her up into my arms, "I told you we could fix this."

"I love you," she cried. She was nearly weeping. "I love you so much."

"I love you too," I said. I heard another sniffling. It was Bailey's mom. I motioned for her to join the hug. Hunter ran up and joined in too. We held on for a good while. The warmth of our love coursed through us and surrounded us just as tangible and real as the power that came from the crystals. The echoing urgency that had bound my mind fell off of me. Everything became clear again. It was as if the world was finally on an upward turn. Slowly, people began to pull away until it was just Bailey and I.

I finally backed off enough so that we could talk to each other, but I didn't let go. Bailey's eyes were tired, red, and full of pain. I could sense a deep sadness within her. I didn't understand why. We'd won.

"You're going to be fine," I assured her.

"It's not me I'm worried about," she whispered with all her strength. She began to cry again. I pulled her back into my arms. "Promise me…" she whimpered, "Promise me you won't change. Promise you'll keep everyone together… Promise you'll stay the man I love…Promise"

"I promise," I replied, puzzled. I wasn't sure what had brought this new wave of emotions on. "I'm not going anywhere."

Her sobs began to cease, but it wasn't because she felt assured. She was losing consciousness. She had expelled the last bit of her strength and her body demanded sleep. I laid her down gently as she continued to whisper "Promise…Promise…"

When she was out of my arms, I spied the Doctor in the hall, "Prep her for surgery," I commanded.

"About that," he said, "I don't know what the Mayan doctors were planning to do, but I have no idea where to even start. The damage is-"

"Just do your best," I cut him off, "It will be enough."

He nodded, but he had no confidence. I didn't care. I had confidence. That's what mattered. Maybe I could find one of those doctors with the Mayans at Jericho and bring him back. I decided to keep that in the back of my mind. For now, it was time to save the world. Leaving her felt like tearing myself in half, but the only way to save her was to win this war. If I failed here, she wouldn't survive the next day anyway.

I looked at Hunter who was standing behind me, "I need you to come with me," I said. I turned to Brady, "You'll stay here. Look after things. I should be back in a few hours."

"Don't you need me to stay and help with the surgery?" Hunter questioned.

"I need you and your crystal at Jericho," I said, "I'll add it to the breastplate there, and I'll be the one to help with the surgery when we get back." I looked at Bailey, "You don't need to see her like that anyway."

I gave Mrs. Boone a hug and assured her this would work. As I turned to leave, a team of nurses entered to retrieve Bailey. I knew it would take them a few hours to prepare for such a large surgery. They should've finished by the time I got back. "Don't start without me doc," I greeted as I walked out of the room.

"Yea," he said in a bit of a daze.

I ignored his unbelief and walked out of the building with a sense of optimism. This contrasted the sinking feeling in the pit of my stomach. I told myself to ignore it and chose optimism.

Hunter and I ran up to the Stingray. It was looking a bit worse for wear, but everything had had enough time to cool off.

Let's see if I can get one more trip out of her," I hoped as we climbed in.

"I'm not sure she's even gonna start the trip," Hunter reasoned.

"Have faith," I said optimistically.

"Oh, she's definitely going to make it," Hunter said sarcastically.

"That's more like it!" I smiled as I started the engines. They sputtered, but soon their low hum filled the air. I gave the thrusters a bit of a test, and then fired the anti-gravity repulsers. Everything sounded good. The cockpit closed over us and we took off.

I had to focus a lot on flying, but with my mind less distracted than before, I began to make a plan.

Of course, there was still a sense of urgency that hung over all of this. Bailey's clock was still ticking. I needed to be back as soon as I could so that we could perform the surgery and get her on the mind. On the flip side, I didn't feel like this would be an in and out mission. I wanted to call ahead and see what I was flying into at Jericho, but at this altitude, the coms wouldn't connect to any of the relays. I could only pray that the bearers who were there had been able to keep the Onyx bearer at bay. I would need to collect the rest of the stones as quickly as I could upon my arrival.

I took inventory one more time, just to be certain that a miscalculation had not led to one of the crystals being absent. Blake had one. I had mine, Bailey's, and the Earth stone. Hunter had the life crystal. Amelia wielded the ice crystal and still carried her brother's fire stone. Ana wielded the Mayan crystal and was supposed to have the Ekklesia one as well. Ryder had the moonstone. The remaining two were within Jericho to power the beacon. That's twelve. Then, of course, there was the onyx stone.

"This is so cool," Hunter exclaimed. I could sense his awe.

We had just exited the Atmosphere. The Earth and its continents were below. We were still on the sunlit side of Earth, though our destination was near the line of the sunset. As we flew, the dark side came into view, as did the moon. Looking up, we could even make out a few stars. It was beautiful. The weightlessness of our freefall orbit added a sense of peace to the beauty.

For a moment, I closed my eyes and allowed the unfiltered sunlight to warm my cheek. I was exhausted and nearly fell asleep. But sleep would have to wait. There was a war that needed ending and a world that needed rebuilding. I had a future ahead of me that finally began to shine with the parts of life that were worth living.

I thought of the war we had all endured. I thought of what it had taken from me. I thought of what I had found in it. I started it living in a broken down apartment with my fake, dead beat mother, who was implanted by The Organization to keep me from discovering who my father was. It had been a long broken road, but just past this battle ground I saw an open field. I could finally just live.

I opened my eyes with a fury of determination. "Let's end this," I commented as I slammed the controls forward. The stingray nosedived. The closer we got to Earth, the further back we were pushed into our seats. The ship began to heat up, and I instructed Hunter to dawn his helmet.

"Are you sure this thing can survive *another* re-entry?" Hunter asked nervously.

"Nope!" I admitted enthusiastically, "It just has to slow us down. Be ready to jump."

"Great," Hunter groaned.

The Earth grew until its round sides became four corners. As we plummeted, less and less of the continent came into view, until it was mostly just the expanse of the Mediterranean sea. I could see, through the red streaks outside the ship, bits of color coming from the ocean. Then, there was a bright flash. I peered though the tinted windshield. It looked like it was getting brighter…or closer…

There was a loud swoosh. My entire field of vision became consumed by a blinding white light. Every sensor on the dash began to scream at me. The ship shook violently.

"Are we gonna blow up?" Hunter cried.

I wildly pressed buttons, trying to steady the ship. What was happening? "I really wish ALI was here," I complained. Finding him would be at the top of my list when I actually had time to look.

Finally, I just decided to slam the thrusters into full reverse. I used the Anti-gravity repulsers to hit the breaks even harder. The metal winced as the ship began to break apart. I was being pulled forward so violently that I thought my eyeballs might pop out. The blood rushed to my face and my stomach attempted to get rid of everything inside. Thankfully, I hadn't eaten anything.

There was an ear-piercing screech. The ship shook even more. I noticed the right hand wing beginning to wobble. It was being ripped off.

"Time to bail," I announced. I pressed the button that opened the cockpit. The canopy flew off. I unclipped my restraints and used my jetpack to thrust me out of the decaying ship. Hunter followed closely. We were still falling at faster than free fall speed. I pointed my feet to the ground and turned my jetpack on full force to slow my fall.

I realized now that the blinding light was consolidated to a relatively narrow column of energy. It sliced through the air from the ground below. From this angle it appeared to be coming out of the ocean. It sucked air into it and we had to be sure not to let it pull us in as well. The pilotless ship was not so lucky. Only a few seconds after we ejected, the wing ripped off. It was sucked into the vortex immediately. The rest of the Stingray continued for a ways, but ultimately met the same fate.

As we fell a small island came into view. The beam originated from there. I should have known sooner, but there was just too much chaos from me to put it together. This beam was the beacon of Jericho. They had activated it. I prayed we weren't too late.

It wasn't long before ships came into view. They were staying a good distance away from the island. Tiny flashes of light passed in the open space between as the two forces exchanged fire.

Hunter and I were finally slowing down. He was just above me. I began to scan the ships for a good place to land. I eventually was able to spot a Mayan command cruiser in the back of the fleet. I aimed for it and Hunter followed.

"All bearers," I said over the coms, "All bearers report to the Mayan command cruiser with all of your crystals."

A few seconds later, I landed on the deck of the ship. I cushioned my fall with concussive purple blasts, more for show than anything. I forgot I could fly now, since I wielded Bailey's crystal. Hunter landed a bit sloppier beside me. I turned to the nose of the ship and assessed the battle.

The ships looked like they had performed an initial attack run on the closest side of the walls of Jericho. I could tell they were damaged, but it didn't look like they had done much good. Of course, they knew they wouldn't. Any attack on the walls should have been a cover for a team to get inside. Clearly that had failed. Now, it seemed as though the armada fired hopelessly at the indestructible walls as the walls themselves returned fire with massive guns. I could see many ships on the front lines taking heavy damage, and I could tell where some had already sank.

As I observed the battle, I saw people on jetpacks coming from every direction. Ana and Blake came from the bridge of the ship I was standing on. Amelia and Ryder came from the battle. They all landed at about the same time. We formed a circle.

Most of us had our helmets on, so we retracted them to see each other's faces. We looked…tired.

I looked at Blake. I instantly felt the weight of what I had done to him. I felt sick. He refused to make eye contact with me. It was like he wanted to. He was angry, but sympathetic. "I can't," I heard his voice echo. At first I thought he said something. It even sounded like it came from his direction. However, I quickly realized that I was using Bailey's crystal to look in his mind. It felt wrong.

"I got the breastplate," I said, forcing myself to break my concentration, "How have things been here?"

"He's just standing in there," Amelia snarled. "He's guarding the beacon."

"Has anyone tried to fight him?" I asked. Everyone shook their heads 'no'. "Has he tried to fight?"

"He hasn't moved an inch," Ryder replied.

"Well, let's change that," I offered.

"Are you sure this will work?" Amelia questioned.

"It's the best we've got," I said, "Unless anyone else has a better idea." No one made a suggestion. Everyone nodded. I don't think anyone liked the idea of giving up their crystals. I planned to give them back. I think they knew that. I don't even think that's why they were so reluctant.

The crystals all carried parts of us. Some of us our heritage, our legacy. For others, the crystal had been all they had, the only thing that they could trust, the only thing that protected them. Amelia was the first to offer hers up.

Though her crystal was on her chest still, she held out her closed fist. I extended my hand. He placed her fist inside my open palm and placed her other hand below mine. She opened her fist and pressed a warm object into my hand. A single tear escaped each of her eyes.

"Avenge him," she whispered in a quivering voice. She took her hand off the top of mine, revealing the fire-stone. She detached the ice crystal from her chest and placed it beside her brother's gently. Then, she closed my hand around them both. "Avenge us."

Pulled my hand back to myself and nodded firmly. I felt the weight of these siblings as I held their lives in my hand. I held it close to the golden breastplate. Before I opened my hand, I felt them being pulled toward it. The fiery red/orange and icy blue energy escaped through the gaps in my fingers. They danced elegantly around one another, and they traveled to their respective spots on the breastplate. Fittingly, they were right beside one another.

Their energy spread out over the golden square and surged through my body. I felt the searing heat in my veins become instantly cooled by a teal icy wave. I winced at first, but as quickly as it came the, pain was gone.

Ryder offered his next. "I expect to get this back," he threatened. Not that he could do anything about it if I decided I want to keep it. I nodded and accepted it. I held it to my chest. It chose the spot just above Amelia's crystal. This one didn't make me feel much different.

I turned to Ana and extended my hand to her next. She looked angry. She hadn't stopped looking angry. She deserved to be. She harshly handed me the yellow crystal that powered the Ekklesia's weapons (and everything else too). I placed it on my chest.

This time, a bright wave of volatile, yellow-white energy surged across my body in zig-zagging patterns. It made me feel fidgety. My mind ran at twice the speed it normally did and the world seemed to move twice as slow. It was disorienting and made me feel sick. My head ached. I expected it to subside, but it didn't. I staggered backward a bit. I heard my heart in my ears. I felt every particle of air that entered my lungs. I honed in one every sound: the blast of the cannons, the roar of the mechanics that operated the ship we were standing on, the sloshing of the waves. Then, slowly, everything sped back up. Everything returned to its normal volume. I blinked a few times to adjust my vision.

"Are you okay?" Hunter asked, grabbing my shoulder.

"Yea," I nodded. I instantly put my focus back on Ana. She was clutching the pink stone on her chest, its light escaped her fingers. Her face shriveled up.

"I can't do it," she demanded. Blake rubbed her back.

"Come on," he whispered to her, still refusing to even look in my direction. I felt my stomach in my throat. I wasn't sure if that was guilt, my three orbital re-entries, or the excess of energy surging through my body. Probably all three.

"No," she demanded, "This is all I have left of my home. It was given to me, trusted to me." She was crying now.

Blake looked in my direction, but not at me. He eyed the breastplate I wore and whispered something I couldn't hear. I made it a point not to use my powers to decipher it. Ana cut her eyes toward me. Sniffling, she took my hand and placed her crystal in it.

"You wear this with the pride of all the Mayan people who lived and died for this moment," she commanded with zeal and deep seated hurt.

"I will," I nodded and placed it on the breastplate. Its magenta energy spread across my body. It was a much more pleasant sensation than the others had been.

I took the Earth stone out of the pouch on my hip and added it to the growing collection. It completed the row with Amelia's crystals. I didn't feel a whole lot different with this one, except I did feel a certain intensity endow the fire and ice energies.

I looked at Hunter next. He promptly handed his crystal over. I held his in my hand for a moment. I couldn't help but be taken back to that scared boy, cowing in the corner of a cold Organization cell. Instead, this time, he was handing the crystal to me. He'd come so far. He meant so much to me. I was truly proud of him. Before I placed his crystal in his spot, I put my hand on his shoulder. We didn't say anything, but I think he knew exactly what I was wanting to say.

I allowed the life crystal to jump to its spot. It completed the row with mine and Bailey's. It felt my power grow. It felt my senses expand. I felt my focus narrow. I turned it onto Blake. He held the last crystal we had.

I tried to smile at him, but when I did, I nearly cried, so I attempted to keep my stoic expression. That didn't work very well either. He held out his crystal before I could extend my hand to ask for it.

I wanted to put this whole battle on hold to fix things with him. I wanted to explain why I did what I did. I wanted to tell him how much I hated that I did it.

"Blake I-"

"Take it," he demanded coldly.

I winced. It felt like a knife was being twisted into a fresh wound. Even worse, I had no choice but to leave it there. I held out my hand and took hold of the crystal.

"How is she?" he asked, struggling to add much emotion to his voice.

"She's gonna be fine" I affirmed. We held our gaze for a bit. Then, a blast rocked the cruiser we were standing on. "Talk about it later?" I proposed.

"Yea," Blake agreed. "Go put this all behind us."

I felt direction. I felt power. I felt the will of all those who had fought and lost in this war. I saw the evil of the Organization personified and standing before me. I saw the end of the war finally within my grasp.

No politics. Just one more fight.

Chapter 35

I clinched my fists. I searched my new array of powers for the ones that could make me fly. The glow of all the crystals intensified. The two remaining slots ached to be united with their crystals. I couldn't help but agree.

"Time to put an end to all of this," I proclaimed. Then, I opened my hands and launched off of the deck. I propelled myself through the air of my own accord. I wove through a tangle of fighters and bombers and soared toward the Circular walled fortress.

I shed my jetpack as I flew toward the massive beam shooting up from inside the ring of walls. I gained enough altitude that I could see into the capital. Everything looked just as the hologram had predicted. I immediately spotted the two units that housed the crystals. I targeted the one on the right.

Every gun in every section of the wall turned to fire on me, but none of the blasts even came close. I was moving too fast and was too small for them to lock on. I held my hands out in front of me and used Hunter's, Bailey's, and by own crystal to from a beam of energy that destroyed a section of the wall. A gaping hole was blown right in the center and I whizzed through.

I felt an anti-energy blast hit me, and my powers of flight flickered. Still, my momentum carried me toward the silver box that housed one of the crystals. I crashed into it. I could sense the crystal and made sure my hand was in the exact place to grab it. I rolled across the ground and came to a stop at the base of the massive energy beam.

The whole ground shook with the power of the machine. The light was so bright that I could hardly see anything now that I was inside the walls. I formed my helmet around my head and the visor dimmed to protect my eyes. I looked down at my prize. In my hand was a small dark green crystal. Its energy was flowing out of it and falling off the sides of my palm. As I admired it for only a second, my senses warned me of an incoming danger. I looked up just in time to see the Onyx bearer walking menacingly toward me. He launched another ball of his black energy in my direction.

I slammed the new crystal into my chest where it fused with the breastplate while I raised a shield to block the anti-energy. The anti-energy destroyed it, so I used the power of a different crystal to make a new one. He made quick work of it as well. Pink, green, purple, yellow, the shield changed color. Each time the energy would strike, the glow of the corresponding crystal would dim.

Thinking of what I knew the crystals could do, I connected to the earth stone. I sought out a large rock from below the pavement we were standing on and yanked it up between the Onyx bearer and myself. It handled one blast. Then another. This tiny break was enough time for me to summon a blast from the big three. I held the rock up with my left hand. Then, I held out my right. A beam of purple, white, and green formed. It smashed through the rock and caught the Onyx bearer off guard. It hit him and knocked him across the courtyard inside the walls. I ran toward the other housing unit.

It was about 100 yards away. I sprinted as fast as I could. All the while, the roar of the beacon seemed to grow louder. I guess it only needed one crystal to run. I didn't know who they were contacting, but I knew I needed to stop it as soon as possible.

I made it about half way across when the Onyx bearer reached me again. He opted for close combat this time. He punched me in the face, leaving behind a field of his black energy. I fought back, but his energy contaminated the hands that touched him. I used the powers of all the crystals to replenish the affected areas, but even all ten of them together were becoming overwhelmed after only a few seconds of fighting. Still, I continued to fight.

The pillar of white light served as our backdrop. My colorful fists contrasted his pulsating black ones. At one point, I tried to fly up. I knew he couldn't fly. I thought I was clever, but he grabbed my foot and slammed me back down into the ground. He attempted to reach for the breastplate, but I caused a pillar of fire to shoot out from Lucas' crystal, just as Lucas had used it to penetrate my shield. His hand took the full force of the focused beam.

"Guaaahh!" the onyx bearer screamed with hatred as he yanked his hand away.

I leapt up and sprinted for the final crystal. If I could just disconnect it, The Organization would lose power to all their ships and weapons.

My feet left the ground, and I flew toward it. Just as my hand reached it, a black blast engulfed it. It was extremely powerful, strengthened by the Onyx bearer's rage. My muscles in the hand withered, and I yelped in pain. I slammed into the box and bounced off of it. I coddled my hand, feeding it the healing energy of Hunter's crystal.

The void silhouette of the Onyx bearer marched angrily toward me. I knew he was expecting it, but I summoned another beam of purple, green and white. He lifted his hand and shielded himself from it as he continued forward.

The box was only a few feet away. I could sense the crystal inside. I stood up and lunged for it. The Onyx bearer lunged toward me. I called Lucas' energy to my hand as it instantly melted through the hardware. I felt the last crystal on my finger tips. Then, the Onyx bearer tackled me. We rolled across the pavement until I was hanging over the edge of the massive gun in the center.

I could feel the air rushing around us. My helmet heated up. The Onyx bearer gripped his hands around my neck and squeezed with all his might. I choked and gagged. White light was all that filled my vision. I clawed at the bearer's hands, but it was no use. Just before his black energy could consume me, I used all the crystals at once to form a beam that came from the breastplate, and finally threw him off of me. He left behind the sickness of his own energy on my crystals.

I immediately rolled away from the chasm from which the beacon came. I coughed as my airway opened back up. I forced myself to stand. Surprisingly, I noticed an eerie quiet. The cannons had stopped firing. The ground had stopped shaking. The blinding white light of the beacon was gone, replaced by an orange and yellow sunset. The walls of Jericho cast a shadow over the interior. The barrel of the beacon was now just a steaming hole in the ground. I looked around and quickly spotted the cause. In our scuffling, we had destroyed the housing for the crystal. It was now a steaming pile of scrap. An orange glow shown up through the rubble.

The Onyx bearer had landed a few yards away. Between us was a glowing orange crystal. The shadowy silhouette lunged for it, but I used the earth stone to shift the ground beneath it. A column of rocks lifted it up and delivered it to my hand. I plucked it from the stones and allowed the rock to crumble.

I smiled at the bearer. It was over. He'd lost. He wasn't ready to accept that though. He screamed in anger and used all of his might to push a tsunami of the black energy toward me. I turned away and raised a shield. It didn't hold. I was shoved to the ground as the darkness overtook me.

I immediately placed the last stone in its place. The instant that it was seated in the gold, I felt the energy in my body intensify to a magnitude I had never experienced. With all twelve united, their power was increased a hundred fold. I fell to my hands and knees as I began to radiate with a golden light. Energy escaped me in violent white bolts. My veins surged with a searing heat. I tried to contain it, but I couldn't. A colossal explosion erupted from me with the breastplate as its epicenter. It swept across the complex and slammed into the armored walls.

This offered me temporary relief, but I felt the energy building up again. I looked around. The paved area surrounding the beacon had been turned to gravel. The area directly around me was turned to dust. The impenetrable walls of Jericho were now crumbling as massive sections collapsed to the ground. As they fell, the golden light of the sunset broke through. The colors reflected off of the sea in nearly every shade that was on my chest. From the opposite direction, I sensed fear and darkness. I turned.

The Onyx bearer had withstood the blast. He was lucky that he wasn't disintegrated. I guess his powers had protected him. Powerful bolts of energy continued to leap off of my body onto the ground around me. Each one rumbled like thunder and dented the ground.

In one final effort, the Onyx bearer ran at me, charging up all of the might he could muster. He leapt into the air and drew back his fist endowed with energy so dark it absorbed the light around it as though it were a black hole. As he neared, it was as though time itself began to slow. There was a rushing sound in my ears. I observed the Onyx bearer as he hung in midair. I was overtaken by the unsettling sense that I had lived this before. It was like I had seen it somewhere. Maybe in a dream.

I began to hear the haunting voices of both people I knew, and ones I couldn't place. I even heard my own. They all played at once, echoing over one another.

"Promise me."
"It's not your fault."
"I'm giving it to you."
"I'm staying."

I almost ignored the voices. I was hearing them, but it was almost like I couldn't respond to them. Instead, my attention was captured elsewhere. I looked down and noticed that the two fragments of my crystal had migrated to the same seat. This left one open spot in the center of the plate on the second row. I looked at the open seat and then at the bearer, inching his way through the air. I spied the shiny black stone on his chest.

My perception of time began to move at its normal pace once again. I caught the bearer's fist in my left hand. This time, the golden energy of all the crystals began to contaminate his. We made eye contact. I could see fear in his eyes, but he wasn't afraid of me. It was on something more distant. He tried to pull away, but I wouldn't let him. He swung with his other fist, but I caught it as well. I forced my energy up his arms. He began to become frantic and enraged.

He kicked wildly at my legs, but I couldn't even feel it. My energy kept him from touching me. More bolts of energy discharged from my body as I continued to tame his anti-energy.

When the two forces met, they fought, but as mine pushed back, what was left was a refined version of the glitching golden energy. When it made it to his elbows, I shoved him backwards. As he stumbled, I grabbed the stone off of his chest. He fell to the ground at my feet. He looked up with disgust.

"You have no idea what you've done today," his evil voice grumbled. "You'll wish The Organization had won."

"I doubt it," I smarted.

I held the final crystal to my chest. It leapt from my hand and seated itself in the last open spot. This time, instead of the new energy surging across my body, the golden energy tightened. It was refined. The messey, glitching discharges ceased, and I glowed with a radiant gold. I felt the uncontainable build up become tamed. I was in full control now. I told all of the energies to return to their stones.

Now, feeling quite normal, I allowed myself to fall to the ground. I leaned back on my hands and looked at the setting sun. I couldn't stop the huge smile that spread across my face. We won.

I began to laugh. I threw my hands up in the air and fell onto my back. "Ha, Ha! We won!" I yelled.

I sensed the Onyx bearer standing a few feet away. He was walking away from me. I wasn't worried. He was powerless and had nowhere to go. I let him walk off. As he did, he grumbled, "You've won nothing."

I ignored him. I just took a second to look at the beauty of the sky. The clouds were a luminescent orange. The sky itself was a radiant red. Purple clouds sat lower in the sky. Some cast long shadows onto others. A white glow outlined the edges of the clouds. Then, a speck appeared. A boy on a jetpack. It was Hunter.

I sat up as he landed a few feet away and ran over.

"Are you okay?" he asked, concerned. He extended a hand to me. I took it and stood up.

"I think okay would be an understatement," I chuckled.

"The chief said that all of the Organization ships are down!" he exclaimed. "Does that mean we won?"

I smiled, "We didn't just win," I said, "I think this can be considered a victory."

He hugged me. I hugged him back. Then, I kept one arm around him as we peered out at the sunset. Some of the Ekklesia Naval ships had drifted in front of it. Mayan cruisers followed. They were on back-up power and were heading for land, since I was using the crystal that had powered them. I could see the soldiers on the decks celebrating. They were jumping and hugging and running.

After a few minutes my mind turned to the next pressing matter. Bailey. I opened a com channel to the room where she had been staying in the medical facility.

"Hey, Mrs Boone! Hey, if Bailey's asleep, you're gonna want to wake her up for this," I almost laughed; I was so full of excitement.

There was a long pause of silence. Then, uncontrolled sobbing.

"Mrs. Boone!" my voice took on a sympathetic tone. Was she just overcome with joy?

"What is it?" Hunter asked, innocently.

The sobbing continued. This wasn't a joyful cry. My heart sank. "No," I whispered.

I launched from where I was standing, forgetting anything else existed. I broke the sound barrier and every law of physics in milliseconds. I pushed myself as hard as I could. More energy coursed through me now than ever before. What had been tamed by the Onyx stone was unleashed with its full force and fury. My senses guided me to the source of my aching heart.

The world moved past in a blur of blue. I came over land and in just a few seconds, I sensed Tullahoma was near. I slowed almost instantly. I had no tailwind, but a sonic boom erupted from me. I saw it burst the windows of the buildings on Arnold base. I landed in front of the medical building and ran through the shattered glass door. I saw a bit of energy escape me and blow out a section of the wall. I ripped the golden breastplate off my chest and tossed it aside without slowing up. My connection with it ceased. I burst into the room where Bailey had been.

Mrs. Boone was at her side, sobbing and holding her hand. She didn't even have enough of her senses about her to be surprised to see me. I ran over.

"Bailey!" I called, taking her other hand. Her mother moved away.

Her face was pale. Her eyes were closed. Her hands were cold. I stroked her frigid face.

"Bailey," I said, as tears escaped my eyes, "Bailey, we won. It's over." I cried now, "Bailey, we can fix everything now." I rocked back and forth. "Come back." I looked up, "Bring her Back!" I screamed.

It was no use. She wasn't coming back. Bailey was dead.

Chapter 36

I laid over her dead body and wept until I was out of tears. Everything faded into a gripping blackness, a suffocating void. There was nothing here but death. I became completely detached from the world. I drifted through that void as it pulled me apart.

Words never escaped my mouth. They were consumed by the void. They only appeared as flickering thoughts. Some came as memories. Every one of them made it worse, but none was worse than "Why?".

Every time it surfaced, it felt as though another piece of my heart was sliced away. Any time a good memory surfaced, we had so many, that question "Why" turned into pain. Every time a thought of the future came, that word tainted it an ugly shade of black.

I eventually found myself in a heap on the floor. I made no sound. I just stared at the white tile. I felt sick. I felt empty. I felt alone.

I felt betrayed by God. I had done everything right. I had fought with integrity. I had refused to kill. I had trusted him. I had done everything he told me to do. Was this my reward? Here, at the end of myself, where I had no power to save her, the one who could, didn't. Why?

This time, the question brought with it a burning anger. I felt the blood rush to my face. My eyes burned and my eyebrows narrowed with fury. My fists clenched so tightly they might have broken. I screamed in emotional agony and slammed my fist into the ground.

The next scream was in physical agony as the tile refused to give. My powerless fist bounced off, but it only intensified my anger. I came up from the ground in a whirlwind of emotion. It felt like the walls of the room were closing in. It was as if all the air had been sucked out of the room. I was being crushed and suffocated. I had to get out.

I stormed toward the hall. The small table by the door was the next thing to catch my anger. I kicked the leg out from under it as I left.

The air was not better in the hall, and those walls were closing in faster than the ones in the room. My walk turned into a sprint. I made it down the hall and through the broken double door. One fell off of its hinges as I broke through. Even outside, I was still dying.

My breathing was heavy and uncontrolled. I coughed and gagged. I put my hands on my knees. It felt as though death were coming for me now, which might have been welcomed, but somehow, I knew it wouldn't touch me. It would only torment me.

I did feel someone's hand on my shoulder though. "Dylan! Breath," It was Brady, "Please breathe." His voice shook.

"Jetpack," I choked out, "Bring me your jetpack."

He must have had it on, because it was almost immediately fastened onto my back. The instant it was secure, I pressed the button and blasted off.

As I flew, the rushing air actually helped me catch my breath. I was still running from the vacuum. It was pursuing me. I knew that if I slowed up, it would crush my lungs again. So I flew. I flew to the one place I thought I could escape it. The one place I had escaped it before.

I didn't feel relief when I saw Tullahoma come into view, nor when I saw my subdivision. I didn't even feel relief when I saw the lake, or when I saw the Vale's house. Still, I flew. I was almost there.

Finally, I set foot on the dock. I pressed the button to detach my jetpack, but I missed and all of my armor fell off with it. It was the emergency release, so it all just clanged to the wooden floor of the dock. I took a deep breath, fell to my knees, and began to cry. The difference now was that I could breathe. Slowly, very slowly, the breathing replaced the crying, until I was just looking out over the lake. That terrible question still running through every corner of my mind: "Why?"

"Why her?"
"Why not me?"
"Why anyone at all?"
"Why not just let me live out my happy life with her?"
"Why not just let her live?"

I stood on that dock for hours as the questions continued. Some brought tears. Some devolved into anger, but they all just led back to "Why".

I stood until I began to watch the same sunset I had seen at Jericho a few hours ago. It had finally caught up with me. Yet I don't think the events of the day had. Somewhere over the course of standing on that dock, I just began to feel numb.

I stood, hands firmly behind my back, and stared at the sunset. I couldn't see its beauty. I couldn't feel peace. It was as though everything on the inside of me had been compressed into a tiny ball and then locked away behind fortified walls. All that was left was the pain.

I heard footsteps approaching behind me. I couldn't sense who it was, but I didn't turn around. I heard a bit of sniffing. Then the clack of boots on the wooden boards, which squeaked with the visitor's weight. They stopped behind me. After a few seconds of silence, I built up the energy to look at them. I turned, only moving far enough that I could cut my dry, red eyes and see them. It was Blake.

The second I saw him and his red eyes, I lost it. That tiny compressed ball of emotions exploded. I fell into his arms. "Blake," I sobbed. I thought of what I had done to him. I thought of every time I had taken him for granted through this war.

"It's okay," he said. His forgiveness hit me even harder. It began to squeeze all of the aching things inside me to the surface.

"Blake, she's gone," I cried. He was crying too. "I couldn't…I couldn't fix it…I couldn't…" I sobbed and squeezed him as tightly as I could. I felt that if I let go I might float away and be lost to the void forever.

Every attack that had come against me, whether it was from the High Council or The Organization had been unable to touch me, but this had destroyed me. I was powerless against it. The storm in my mind had formed a ravaging cyclone. All that was left behind was a desolate wasteland.

Finally, as my tears ran dry the crying gradually subsided. I still didn't let go. My eyes burned, and I sniffled. I didn't feel good. The storm was still there, but at least I felt safe. I let go.

We sat down on the edge of the dock, and the sunset turned to twilight. We didn't say anything. I'm not even sure that I really thought about anything for a while. We just sat there and grieved together.

I had lost my love, and Blake had lost a dear friend. We all had. The stars appeared above, and the cicadas began to sing. It was just the two of us. Just the way it started. Only I wasn't the same. I don't think Blake was either. The war had taken its toll. This was the final blow - its last act of vengeance toward its victors.

I kept expecting Blake to stand up, to suggest that we should go in or move on, but he didn't. He sat with me in silence. The celestial bodies moved overhead and the critters of the night sang their sad songs. Eventually, the dawn returned, but the darkness stayed. The morning birds sang their song, but the darkness stayed. Tears came and went, but the darkness stayed. So did Blake.

When the sun was well up and the long shadows of the morning had grown short, there was a sound of more footsteps approaching. This time, I turned around sooner. It was Mr. James. He stopped at the edge of the dock.

"Long night, huh," he said sorrowfully. I looked away. I was standing. Blake was sitting beside me. Mr. James walked over and put his hand on my shoulder. "Blake, would you mind checking on Hunter?" he requested.

Blake nodded and stood up. He looked at me. Then, he walked back to the house. I felt the pit in my stomach deepening. Mr. James stood there for a moment. I could tell he was biting his lip, trying to think of the right words. I hoped he wouldn't think of any.

"Son," he started. His voice quivered a bit. He cleared his throat and composed himself, "I don't have the words to say." He paused again. I wanted nothing more than for him to go away. "I went through this with your father once. I never dreamed we would be here again, but it seems that's the way life would have it."

I trembled as the word creeped its way up from my soul. My breathing quivered. I ground my teeth, but it escaped anyway. "Why?"

"I don't know," Mr James admitted. "I've wondered the same thing many times, but that never made things any better." He looked down and tilted his head back and forth as he recalled his memories. "I just keep reminding myself of what I do know." He pulled me in so that I was looking at his face. I was still shaking. Tears ran down my cheeks. "What I do know is that you can't stay on this dock forever."

"Why not?" was the first thing that came to mind, but that thought made me realize my hysteria. I knew why not. I knew I had lost the most important person to me, but I still had a lot of important people to be there for. I knew there was a world that I couldn't allow to devolve into the same chaos I had. I couldn't admit it right then, but Mr. James was right.

He gave me a hug. I hugged him back. I would have cried but I hadn't the strength or the tears to do it. This time, I felt a release. It wasn't relief, but some things had at least rearranged. He let go, and left me on the dock.

I a few tears managed to build up and slip down my cheeks as I looked out over the lake again. The Sunlight reflected off of the glassy surface giving the entire slue a radiant glow. Every once in a while, I built up the courage to look behind me.

I looked at the edge of the dock where the wood became well kept grass. I followed the grass up to the large glass doors on the back of the house. Then, I turned back to the lake. I couldn't go yet.

I balled my fists. I clenched them tighter and tighter until my arms began to shake. Why wasn't she standing beside me? Why wasn't I rewarded for what I had done for the world? Why didn't you save her? Why…

Then, a different set of words echoed through my mind. "What do you know?"

It didn't come immediately, but my mind started to chase those words instead of the other one. The shaking stopped and my grip loosened. What did I know?

I knew that the war was over. I knew that I was back home. I looked around my home. I looked at the sun and the water, the trees and the sky, the fish swimming around the dock.

I knew, deep down inside me, somewhere that was covered up for now, I knew that God is good. I had been told so many times, but I also just knew.

I began to shake again, but for a different reason this time. I began to take small steps toward the edge of the dock. I moved one board at a time. Each step was harder than the last. The closer I grew, the heavier I became. Every crack between the board was like a huge canyon that I had to cross. Each board was a mountain top. I ascended and descended through the perilous range.

The mountain tops brought good memories. The valleys reminded me that we wouldn't share any more. Each memory played through my mind as a tribute to her. The further I went, the more I felt myself being pulled back toward the water.

I thought of the day we met. When I saved her. Then, after we crashed, when she saved me. I thought of ascending the mountain together and finding my father. I remember him showing us that we could combine our powers.

I remembered defending Tullahoma against The Organization in this very spot. I remembered seeing her fly for the first time - how her long blonde hair would trail behind her.

I remembered defeating the parasite. I remembered going on missions together. I remembered our plans. I remembered our first kiss. I remembered the ones that followed. I remembered her comforting presence. I remembered her strong silence. I remembered her struggles - our struggles. I remembered how she never let it get to her.

Each good memory brought painful smiles, followed by tears. I cried until I heaved. I coughed bile onto the wooden boards. With every memory I tumbled down into the valley and then clawed my way back up the mountain side. Then, I stumbled onto the last plank and everything quieted. I looked out onto the peaceful prairie that lay before me. I looked back at the mountain range I had traversed. I couldn't go back, but a part of me didn't want to go forward. I didn't want to know what the world was like without her. Even if I could, would I want to survive in it? Why would…

I stopped. I wouldn't entertain that word anymore. Not today at least. I took a deep breath, lifted my foot, and mumbled, "God is good."

Then, I stepped off the dock.

Chapter 37

It was a gloomy day. The sun refused to peek out from behind the black clouds. The same overcast filled my mind. It was a proper day for a funeral.

I had made sure to arrive late. I didn't want to talk to anyone. I hadn't in days. I didn't even want to come, but I wouldn't be able to forgive myself if I didn't. I found a place behind the crowd to stand. I had a clear view of the pulpit and the casket underneath the green tent in front of me. I looked everywhere but there.

The graveyard was small and green. It was an older yard not far from where I lived. There were no flowers on the grave stones. Any relatives of these people had long been buried themselves. All of the people were dressed in black. I spotted Hunter and Brady standing between Blake and Ana. They stood near the front. In the back, General Raddick greeted Amelia and Ryder. Chief Cantun and his wife stood off to the side. Mixed among them were plenty of other familiar faces. Mrs. Boone sat directly in front of the casket. Mr. and Mrs. Vale sat beside her. She was crying as a woman sang.

"When I've run my race, and I see your face."

I turned her out.

Try as I might, my eyes ultimately fixated upon the closed coffin. The forbidden word broke from its cell and began to play over and over again. Why? Why? Why?

I gritted my teeth as silent tears slid down my cheeks.

"I'll worship you forever in that holy place."

I wanted nothing more than to be in that place. I just wanted to leave this place. I had spent so long trying to save it. There was no saving it. There was just surviving in it.

Finally, the woman finished and Pastor approached the podium. Before he began to speak, a trumpet played. It was the song Taps. A fallen warrior's tribute. Two soldiers of the Ekklesia approached the casket and draped a flag over it. It was a quilt, made of all the flags of Earth's nations. Overlaying them was the Ekklesia's dove. The soldiers saluted the casket and walked to the side.

"How fitting for someone who gave so much to this world, to be wrapped in its arms," Pastor began. "Bailey was someone I am blessed to have the privilege to have met..."

I began to zone out again. The trivial, usual things to say at a funeral always annoyed me. They had never annoyed me more than they did right now. Pastor knew her. Why wasn't he...

"And that's everything you're supposed to say at a funeral like this," he caught my attention slightly. "Like many of you, I too wondered 'Why her, God?' Why take such a pure soul? A soul who gave everything for her God and her people." A whimper spread through the crowd like a virus. "Well, the Lord answered me, and I wanted to relay the answer to all of you —That's exactly why he took her."

There was silence as the grieving crowd listened intently. I began to shake with anger. That was a terrable answer.

"She was pure of heart. She ran a good race and fought the good fight. God gave her an assignment, and she carried it out with honor," Pastor paused. He scanned the crowd until he found me. He looked into my bloodshot eyes and tormented soul. "Now, her assignment is complete, and God has called her home."

The crowd sniffled as they accepted his wisdom. Everyone but me. I wasn't ready to hear it. I certainly wasn't going to accept it. Pastor continued his graveside sermon, but I was forced to walk off. I cried tears of anger. I kicked one of the random grave stones, but all I achieved was stubbing my powerless toe.

God may have called her home, but I wasn't ready to let her go. We still had a home to build together here. We still had children to raise together. We still had a life to live together. I sauntered through the graveyard until the green tent was out of sight. I weaved my way through the garden crying, grumbling, and arguing with God. Eventually, I found an old oak tree on a hill that overlooked the site. The service had ended and people were beginning to leave.

I watched Blake make his way through the crowd. He hugged all of our friends. Then, he took Hunter and began walking him through the graveyard. I could tell Hunter was crying. Ana stayed behind with Brady. Amelia came up to talk to them. Ryder watched from a distance. My family spotted me, but Mr. James ushered them away, back to their car. Mrs. Boone stayed for a while, sitting in her seat.

As the crowd disbursed, I began to look at the coffin. My emotions stirred again. Any progress I had made appeared to be lost. My numbness turned back into anger. Any disbelief that this was happening was crushed as I failed to wake up from the nightmare. I stood under the tree until everyone was gone. Then, I made my way back to the casket and fell down in front of it.

"You can do it," I sobbed, "You can bring her back." I slid my hand under the flag and gripped the polished wood. "Please bring her back," I pleaded, "I know you can bring her back… I know…"

My words trailed off into further sobbing. I tried to form words, a prayer of last hope, but the words refused to form. They just sounded like the groanings of a man who had gone mad. Perhaps I had.

I was there for a while. I'm not sure how long, but I eventually heard something behind me. A chair scooting. It was a long time still before I looked to see who it was. It was Pastor. I didn't look at him

"I just want him to give her back," I told Paster with a shaking voice, "I have faith." There was silence as I awaited his response.

"Suppose God were to answer that prayer. Think of what you'd be taking her from," He proposed tinderly, "Doesn't she deserve Heaven?"

He disarmed me. I felt like there was nothing he could say to prevent an explosion of emotion, but he proved me wrong. I thought about what he said. What would I take her from? I didn't know, but I would be taking her to me. Then, I felt bad. I knew what I was taking her from. I would be taking her from God.

I reasoned that it would be selfish to take her from Heaven. She had finished her assignment and was headed to a reward greater than here. Greater than a life with me.

I turned toward him, still on my knees. “Then why won’t he take me too?” I quivered.

It was the only reasonable next step. I would rather us have died together in the war, than to be in a world without her afterwards. Didn’t I deserve a reward for saving the world? What more could God want me to do on Earth more than what I had already done?

“If He hasn’t taken you yet, that means your assignment isn’t complete,” Pastor guided, “There must still be something in this world that only you can do.” He took his finger and placed it on my chest. Perhaps unintentionally, he caused me to think about the breastplate of Aaron, and subsequently the war that came with it.

He then turned my attention to the graveyard. Blake and Hunter were just getting back from their walk. I could only make out their silhouettes in the distance. “There are people here who need you,” Pastor said. “There’s a world that still needs a hero.”

I looked up at him painfully. Bailey had made being there for people, and being there for the world easy because she was there for me, and I was there for her. The rest came naturally. A new question arose in my mind, “How?”

“I don’t know,” Pastor admitted. He stood up, “But there’s only one way to find out.” He patted me on the shoulder and walked off. I stayed on my knees and turned back to the casket. I looked over my shoulder at Blake and Hunter, then looked away.

“I don’t know how,” I cried to both Bailey and God. “I don’t know how to move on. I don’t know how to do what you asked.”

I hung my head. I was overcome with a sense of purpose. I clenched my jaw in determination. “But I’m going to try,” I promised. A tear slipped down my face. I stood up and placed my hand on top of the flag. A ran my fingers over the white dove.

“For the nations, Bailey Boone,” I smiled tearfully. I looked over my shoulder once again. Blake had his arm around Hunter. They were both looking at me. I looked back at the flag draped casket. “Don’t worry,” I promised, “I’ll keep us together.”

I took a deep breath and looked back at my friends. They waited patiently. "I'll see you soon," I whispered. Then, I lifted my heavy hand off of the casket. When I did, I felt regret. I wanted to look back, but I knew Bailey wouldn't want me to right now.

I put my hands at my side, closed my burning eyes, and stepped toward my friends. They waited for me to make my way to them with my slow steps. When I reached them, their arms were open and waiting for me. I fell into their embrace.

I closed my eyes and leaned in. As their arms surrounded me, it was almost as if Bailey joined the embrace.

Chapter 38

They say grief is the price you pay for loving someone. If that's true, then it is a heavy price to pay. For a while, I wasn't sure if it was worth the cost. The cost was a deep gash in my heart. A piece of me ripped away. It couldn't be healed or replaced. However, in the grief, I found something else.

The other pieces of my heart moved in to hold me together. The days were hard, and I threatened so many times to give up, but those other special pieces helped me navigate my way through the mountains and valleys. They ran with me as we all ran away from the ever encroaching void. We grew together, and they grew around the piece of my heart that was broken.

Though it never went away, the hurt became less noticeable. Always there, but growing subtle. Some things would make it hurt worse, some things less. At first, the bad far outweighed the good. There were flickers of hope in a sea of darkness. A hug, a laugh, new good memory. But after a while, as is the way of things, the sun began to rise again on the dark sea, and the darkness was confined to the inward parts of the ship.

You would think that since the war was over, everything would have returned to normal, but that was far from the case. I knew normal would never come back to me. It would probably never return to the world now. But in that, I began to find a new course - a purpose.

When I took on all of the crystals at Jericho, Everyone's technology that ran off of a connection to them went dark. Even the Ekklesia. I didn't realize it, but I had left everyone's ships of battery backup. Blake and Hunter barley made it back here. The world had gone back to the way it was before the crystals made their debut. All of the wearing powers were now powerless.

For a while, I think everyone was scared to ask me to give the crystals back. It didn't take long for them to get over that. Raddick found me the day after the funeral and filled me in on what happened. To say I lost my temper would be an understatement. The short answer was "No".

Though I refused to wield them, I kept them protected. I kept them close. I knew no one would be foolish enough to try and steal them.

Ryder and Amelia stayed in Tullahoma. I had become some what of a recluse, but my friends saw them often. Hunter refused to leave my side for weeks. He wasn't just there because he thought I needed him (which I did), he needed me. Blake stayed close too, but he had a lot to deal with. He was taking up the slack in my absence.

Ana and her people probably would have gone to war with the Ekklesia after the battle of Jericho if any of their technology worked. I knew Ana was mad at me for not giving the crystal back, but Blake didn't let her get to me.

Though defeated, certain sects of The Organization still held on to power. The Ekklesia was struggling to liberate some European cities. Some countries and their citizens had widely united behind The Organization and fully stuck with them even after their loss at Jericho. They also held onto some of their stronger bases. I reasoned that we hadn't even found them all yet.

As I began to venture out of my reclusive state, I began to see more problems in the world. At first, everyone was united behind our victory. There were celebrations. People literally danced in the streets. But soon the initial high faded. As countries began to work out the details of rebuilding and redrawing boundaries in this new world, people started being people again. As time went on, more problems occurred. Really, it was falling apart. There was no common cause or force holding everything together. The world was spiraling into chaos.

Raddick was in full control of the Ekklesia. They did their best to govern the world and keep the peace without their fancy cruisers. It was hard work putting the world back together. There were daily border skirmishes and other conflicts. I had gotten word that the council of nations was on the verge of dissolving. When these people had united to defeat the Organization, I thought that regional differences would end. I thought war would end. I thought we would finally learn to accept each other and work together. I was wrong. Everything went right back to the way it was before. I guess The Organization didn't cause all of the chaos in the world.

For a time, I had convinced myself that I had done my part. I only ever got involved to save my family. Now, my family was safe. I had defeated every enemy that was too strong for humanity to overcome. I had removed the crystals that created the imbalance of power in the world. If they destroyed each other, then that wasn't my fault. Until, one day, that changed.

***

I sauntered down the stairs of the Vale's house. It was early, but Mrs. Cassie was already getting the kitchen ready to cook breakfast.

"Goodmorning, sweetheart," she called as she placed a skillet on the stovetop.

"Goodmorning," I replied in a tired tone. I wished I had slept in, but sleeping was difficult these days. Everytime I let my mind rest, I would think of all the memories I had - good and bad. They weren't always so painful now. My mind was just so busy that I couldn't get it to shut down. When I did sleep, it was in short bursts. And it was probably worse than being awake.

I would have dreams that I was back in the war. It had been months since I heard a gunshot or an explosion in real life, but I experienced them again and again every night. I hadn't seen someone die in months, but I witnessed it every time I closed my eyes. Every night I would be fighting to protect my family or my troops… or Bailey. And every night I would fail. Then, I would wake up. If I fell back asleep, then I would fail again. And again. And again. Every night, I failed.

I think I was starting to get used to it by now. Some nights I would scream, and Blake would come in and check on me. I wasn't the only one who had such vivid dreams though.

There were many nights were the terrors would visit Hunter. Sometimes they would visit us at the same time. We often ended up on the couch together before the morning came. How could you sleep through that?

They were so real. They were disorienting. Some more than others. We talked about them sometimes. When we could, it helped. Some were in places we didn't recognize. Some were places we had been before. Sometimes we knew the people in them, and other times there faces weren't familiar. Some meant the end of a life, and others concluded with the end of the world. But every time, we failed.

I entered the living room and sat down on the couch. Hunter was already there. His eyes were red and sleepless. He held the remote in his hand, but the T.V. wasn't on. It looked like he had grabbed it and then got lost somewhere along the way.

"What happened in yours last night?" I asked him. Talking about the dreams always neemed to help.

"I was on a cruiser," Hunter said. He stared at the remote and ran his fingers over the rubber buttons. "There was a girl... I don't know who she was, but in the dream I knew her." He flipped the remote over and messed with the battery port. "We were fighting these crazy looking ships. They were coming from space."

"Aliens?" I asked.

"I don't think so," Hunter replied, "Their fighters still kind of looked like ours." He continued his sotry. "There were so many of them. There was no way we could win." He popped out the battery, and then popped it back in. "We fought anyway. They bombed our cruiser. It was like our shields weren't even there. Then, we crashed. And I woke up."

I nodded. That one had been a recurring one for him. Sometimes the details were fuzzy. I think he had slowly stitched the whole story together.

"Was she pretty?" I asked. I instantly regretted it. I felt my stomach turn as I thought about Bailey standing on the bridge of one of our cruisers. Her long blond hair covering her back. Her arms crossed in front of her. I had to take a deep breath and focus on the goodness of the memory. Thankfully, Hunter answered and pulled me out of it.

"I don't know," he said, "I still can't really see her." He stared ahead blankly as he tried to summon the image to his mind. "I think she might have been wearing a crystal though," he remembered. "I don't know which one though." He looked at me, "What about you."

"Just the usual," I evaded.

"No it wasn't," Hunter observed. He was right. I just didn't want to talk about it. Hunter realized it and decided not to press. I was glad. I didn't want to relive this one right now. Hunter turned the T.V. on.

It was already on the news. That usually warranted an immediate change of the channel. However, my tired fingers fumbled over the remote's buttons long enough for something to catch my attention.

A young lady, brown haired and tan skinned, was standing in the ruins of a city. Smoke still rose from the pile of rubble behind her. That's not what caught my attention though. Standing a short distance behind her was a man that I recognized. He was an older man with salt and pepper hair. He wore jeans and a button up shirt, with the sleeves rolled two rungs up toward his elbows. It was the man who had given us the schematics for Jericho - one of the main reasons we were able to win the war.

I recognized bits of the rubble as well - specifically the one thing still standing: an old church. It was Horo, Spain, the place where we had met this man and received the plans. What was he thinking? He was probably right next to me at the top of The Organization's hit list. There were too many cells still active for him to risk being out in the open. And in such an obvious place? And now he was on T.V! It was as if he were inviting a hit.

"With the Ekklesia stretched so thin, attacks like these have left the world wondering where the heroes that protected us during the war have disappeared to," the reporter read off a prompter. "While some attacks, like this one, seem like random acts of terror, some fear that The Organization may regain power. Without our heroes, it would seem as though they may have the means to achieve this."

I mostly tuned out the reporter after a moment. My focus became fully trained on the man in the distance. He wasn't looking at the camera. He was looking off into the sky. He raised his hand to block the sun from his eyes. Sunrise here was sunset there. A low familiar rumble made its way into the broadcast. The reporter's attention slowly turned in the same direction the man was looking. As she turned to look away, he turned to look at the camera. It was as though we made eye contact through the lens. He smiled.

Immediately, the camera shook. An explosion rang out. The reporter could be heard screaming. Flashes of light filled the shaky images coming from the camera as its owner ran for cover. Then, the broadcast cut off and an error screen displayed the message “we’ll be right back”.

I turned the T.V. off and tossed the remote onto the coffee table as I quickly stood up. I felt sick to my stomach. My breathing was uncontrolled and fast. I headed for the door, intending to hastily walk to the lake to calm down. I wanted nothing to do with violence. I was done. That chapter was closed for me, and I never wanted to see it again.

I didn’t make it more than two steps before Hunter called out after me. “You have to help them,” he pleaded.

I stopped, frozen. I ground my teeth. I had been able to keep these world events at a distance since I couldn’t see them. Now that I was seeing it, I was experiencing in real life what had been confined to my dreams. I could wake up from those, but I was trapped in this reality.

“You can’t just let him die,” Hunter added.

I shook my head. I knew he was right. I commanded my body to turn back, but it wouldn’t. I told myself that time was running out, but still I reached for the door. My fatal flaw told me I had to help them, that I was their only hope, that is was my responsibility. I used all my might to fight it, to tell it no. “Guah!” I grunted as I finally had no choice but to give in.

I sprinted, for fear that moving any slower would result in me stopping. I bounded up he stairs, ran down the hallway, and slid onto my side as I entered my room.

My arm slid under my bed and I grabbed onto the breastplate. I stood up and rolled over my bed. As I did, I pressed the golden plate to my chest. There was a puck attached underneath. My suit had spread over my body before my feet touched the floor on the opposite side of my bed. The golden energy raced over my body. Heat surged through my veins as the crystals’ power welled up within me.

I held out my hand and raised up my window. It shattered as it rose. I leapt through the opening and instantly used my powers to propel myself through the air.

I did my best not to think. I only focused on my destination as the Earth moved beneath me. I couldn't think about those who had owned these crystals. I couldn't think about all the battles I had fought before. I could think about what it took to win the war.

Sadness and anger fought for space in my mind. A single tear escaped my eye. The red heat of the atmosphere surrounded the golden dome that encapsulated me. In a matter of seconds, I reached my destination

I slowed myself down, but not enough to keep from crashing into the ground. I did have enough control that I landed on my feet. A crater formed around me and dust filled the air. I couldn't see much, but I could sense everything for miles. One troop transport had just landed in the field below the city hill. Three fighter jets were circling the area. It looked like they were prepared to bomb the city again. Everyone who was still alive was inside the circular part of the church. All except for one.

I ran over to a pile of rubble. One of the buildings had fallen during the first bombing run. A man was pinned under one of the larger sections of the broken wall. I lifted it up. It was so light to me that it felt as though it were made out of styrofoam. I tossed it to the side, revealing the wounded man underneath.

His body was facing away from me. He had a large gash of his forehead that was bleeding profusely. His legs looked as though they had been completely crushed. His eyes slowly opened, and he cut them upward toward me. I walked to face him and knelt down beside him. He used all his strength to smile.

"What were you thinking?" I asked him, "You should have been hiding."

"Hiding never saved anyone," he whispered, "The world needs its heroes."

I knew then that he had been caught on camera on purpose. He wanted them to attack, and he wanted me to see it.

"That was stupid," I insulted, angry that he would do something like that. "How did you know I would see you?"

The man raised his shaky hand and took hold of mine. He looked deep into my eyes. Hope filled his soul. "Faith, boy…Faith."

His head dipped to one side and he trailed off. "Hey, stay with me," I commanded as I gave him a bit of green energy from Hunter's crystal. I had to be careful not to give him too much. He looked back up at me.

Gunfire rang out, but I ignored it. "The world needs you…" he took a deep breath before finishing his thought, "not to save it… but to keep it…safe." He closed his eyes, but he used his hand to point at the church. A group of soldiers was closing in on it. "They need you…to protect them" he whispered.

I stood up and took a step back from my friend. I used the earth stone to form a protective, rock shell around him. Then, I turned my attention to the soldiers. I sensed ten, each of them moving at the church from a different angle. They had to have known I was here, but they were trying to complete their mission.

I planned to run at them, but somehow I nearly teleported. I zipped across the surface of the ground and moved so fast that the shockwave following me thrust my target into a section of a stone wall. He bounced off of it and landed on the ground.

I was surprised for a moment, long enough for some of the others to begin firing at me. They were using old fashioned bullets and machine guns. Their repeating blasts rang through the air. The bullets came faster than the speed of sound, but my mind processed it in slow motion. I could have moved out of their way, but instead I allowed them to bounce off of the thin golden vale that covered my body.

I held my right hand out slightly and caused the Earth to open up underneath the four soldiers that were firing at me. They fell in, and I closed the ground over top of them.

I made my way around the church, taking out the rest of the soldiers one at a time. I took each one down a different way. I wasn't exactly testing my powers. It was more like instinct. I just knew what I could do and how to do it. Some I electrocuted, others I pushed into walls. It only took about a minute to clear the area.

I finished near the south end of the church, furthest away from the door. My senses alerted me that the jets were closing in. They had formed up, and I could sense that their missiles were primed and locked. They were all aimed at me.

I flew up to their altitude. I expected the area around me to suffer from the force of my takeoff, but the energy was instead directed up with me. Once we were even, the jets released every missile they carried. I didn't move.

They sliced through the air at supersonic speeds before colliding with me. I didn't budge. I hardly even noticed that they had detonated. The only tell was the ball of flames and smoke that engulfed me.

I used my energy to dissipate the smoke. I looked through the cleared air and locked eyes with the lead pilot. The three jets pulled up and split up. I chased the wing men first. I chased down the first one and conjured a beam of energy that destroyed the back half of the jet. As the cockpit fell, the pilot ejected. I took down the other wing man with a similar beam which hit its mark even though the jet had already flown a few miles.

I chased down the lead jet now. I was there in an instant. I latched onto the top of the jet just behind the cockpit. The pilot began to spin as he tried to shake me off. The G-force didn't effect me. I shoved my hand into the metal hull like it was butter. I grabbed onto the edge of the canopy covering the cockpit and ripped it off. This immediately caused the pilot's seat to eject. I let go and allowed the ship to crash into the vacant plain below.

I hung in the air for a moment, observing my work. Smoke rose from the city and the three crash sites of the jets. I didn't sense any more enemies. I spotted Ekklesia ships on the horizon coming to give aid to Horo. I decided that I needed to check on my friend.

I gently floated back to the city. I found the bubble of rock that was hiding Manuel and caused it to recede back into the Earth. He was unconscious, but he was breathing. I placed my hand on his chest and gave him a bit more of the green energy. I could sense his thoughts. I wasn't trying to, but the phrase was so near the front of his mind it was hard not to. "The world needs its heroes."

I looked around. He was right. These people would have died if I hadn't arrived. Many had already died because I stayed away. As much as I wanted it to be, my work was not done.

Dirt began to swirl around us as the Ekklesia medical transport landed in the nearby open space. I made eye contact with the pilot through the front glass, communicating that I was standing over a survivor. Manuel would be safe now.

Knowing this, I stood up and flew away. With the sunset ahead of me, I flew as fast as I could, until sunset became sunrise and ocean became mountain. In no time at all, the mountain base came into view. I flew in without any trouble. The yellow shield was down and the main hangar bay was open. I flew in and landed with a booming thud. It echoed through the hangar and the rest of the base. The metal floor dented under my feet. Every eye in the hangar turned fearfully in my direction. The sun shown in behind me, turning me into nothing but a glowing silhouette to the soldiers.

"I need to speak with Director Raddick," I announced.

Chapter 39

I stood on the edge of the hangar door. Below me was a cliff that fell about a hundred feet before turning back into forrest. The sun was up now. Its white light illuminated the mountain side as well as a haze that limited visibility. The rolling green mountains faded into a blue haze in the distance as white puffy clouds cast their shadows upon them.

I stood with my feed apart and my hands pressed firmly behind my back. I fidgeted with my fingers as my mind mulled over what I was doing here. I only had a few seconds to think on my flight here, but even that was enough for my decision to be made.

Manuel was right. The world needs heroes. I didn't want to be a hero. I didn't feel like one either. But I had hid long enough. It was time to move. The world needed protecting.

I thought about standing in this hangar, those months ago, when time stopped and I looked at Bailey. When we crossed the threshold, and there was no turning back. "I wish you were here," I whispered. I couldn't be confident without her guidance, but I knew it was what she would have wanted. It's what I promised.

I thought back further to when Bailey and I had talked to my father in this same hangar. This is where he had showed us that our powers could combine with each other. I smiled as I remembered our innocence.

The hangar was silent with the exception of the cool mountain breeze blowing across the opening of the hangar. Every soldier in the room had stopped their busy tasks. Some had left. Others were waiting to see what I would do. No one trusted me, and no one was happy to see me. I didn't expect either to be different. I did expect something different from Raddick, but I didn't receive it.

"Dylan. It's good to see you," Raddick announced. His voice echoed through the hangar.

I didn't really hear his words. Instead, I felt what was underneath them. He was afraid. For a moment, it felt good. I had been looked down on for so long that being feared almost felt like respect. Almost.

The thought soured as soon as it formed. I looked over my shoulder at him, turning my body, but not my feet.

"You don't have to be afraid of me," I told him gently and turned back toward the mountains.

Raddick was quiet as he approached me. He stopped a few paces behind me. He ran through a few options of what to say. 'How are you doing?' 'Why are you here?' 'What do you want?' 'Did you come to give us the crystals?'

I decided to answer his questions so that he didn't have to ask him. "I'm not giving you your crystal back." I felt his heart sink. I turned around to him fully now.

"Then why did you come?" he asked.

"Because I'm tired of hiding," I alluded.

I was going to explain, but Raddick's fear interrupted me, "You know I had to play the politics to get Sparks out of office," he explained, "I never meant to-"

"I don't want to be Director," I cut him off, "You'll do it better than I ever could." Raddick looked stunned. "I do have a proposition."

"Of course," Raddick held out his hands, "Tell me."

"The crystals are too powerful for any institution to hold," I explained, "They're also too powerful for any one person," I looked down at the glistening golden breastplate. The energies of the crystals radiated around it in a rainbow of colors. Then, I looked out toward the sun, toward Manuel, "But the word needs heroes." I paused, "It won't survive without them."

Raddick listened intently. I sensed his question, but I let him ask it, "So what are you proposing?"

"A Protectorate," I explained, "A team that works with the resources of the Ekklesia, but does not answer to it. You handle the politics. We'll put the world back together."

Raddick stroked his chin, "Im...I'm not sure I can make that work under the rule of the High Council."

"Then, I'll do it without you," I presented.

"I know you will," Raddick admitted, "I'll see what I can do."

"I'll assemble my team," I told him.

He held out his hand, "It was good seeing you," he smiled. I sensed that he meant it. He saw something in me that he admired but didn't understand.

I shook his hand. "For the Nations, Director," I smiled.

"For the Nations," he replied sentimentally. He turned to walk off. As he did, I remembered another order of business that I had been putting off.

"Director," I called after him. He turned back. "One last thing." He listened. "My access to ALI was blocked during the craziness. I would appreciate it if you could fix that."

Raddick scrunched his eyebrows and clenched his hands. I sensed unease. My first instinct was to search his mind for the source, but he presented it before I could look. "You haven't heard?" he asked sadly and nervously.

"Heard what?" I asked back, a bit snappy. What could possibly be the problem with this request?

"He was destroyed."

The words didn't land at first. ALI wasn't something you just destroyed. And whoever had done it was suddenly very lucky I didn't yet know their name.

"What?" I demanded. "By who?"

Raddick winced as my energy intensified. Sweat beaded up on his lip.

"It wasn't us," he stammered, "We came under a cyber attack," I clenched my jaw as he explained. I worked hard to restrain my energy. "ALI fought it off from our main servers, but he was destroyed in the process."

"What were they after?" I asked.

"That's classified," Raddick shut down.

"Not anymore," I growled.

I held out my hand and used the power of the crystals to search his mind. Our conversation had brought the story to the forefront of his thoughts. The virus had attacked. It was never meant to cripple the Ekklesia. It was after information: classified sciences. Specifically, it stole everything we knew about the crystals and their bearers.

As I searched through his thoughts, I found an image, a memory burned into the active regions of his mind. A blinking screen - a message from ALI in plain text , "The Overseers are coming."

I exited Raddick's mind without him ever knowing I had entered. The extracted image hung in my own thoughts. Surrounding it were the images from my dreams: ships descending from the skies, strange soldiers attacking all of Earth's cities: flames - death - ashes. My anger melted away into fear. Then, it quickly turned to purpose and focus.

I blinked to clear my mind. When I opened my eyes, I was no longer standing in the hanger. I was in a tiny concrete room. In front of me was a metal bench, and on it was a man in an orange jumpsuit. He cut his eyes up at me through his long shaggy hair. He spoke, but his lips weren't visible under his scruffy beard. I didn't hear what he said. I was disoriented.

I looked behind me. The steel door was shut. There were no openings. I looked down. All of the crystals' lights had intensified. A bright golden light came from the breastplate and illuminated the dimly lit room with a heavenly glow. I realized my subconscious thoughts had taken over my powers through my emotions. I knew exactly why I was here.

"That's quite the trophy," Darren's words finally broke through my daze. I looked up at him, then down at the breastplate again. I took hold of one corner and peeled it off my chest. Arcs of energy leapt between me and it until it was away from my body. I tossed it to Darren.

I knew he couldn't use it, and I didn't want to lose control again. The power left my body and the plate left my hand. Darren caught it. He gave a sly smile from under his beard, then he began to examine the breastplate.

"You know I-"

"Who are the overseers?" I demanded, ending his anecdote before it started.

"It's always business with you, isn't it?" Darren scoffed.

"They're coming," I informed him (as if he cared) "How do we stop them?"

"Ha!" Darren laughed, "Stop them? You can't stop them."

I felt my chin quivering as the images from my dreams filled my mind. Every battle, no matter how hard we fought, ended in ashes. I felt tears well up at the edges of my mind. I fought them off, but I couldn't fight of the shake in my voice, "They haunt my dreams," I confessed, "Every night I fight them."

"And every night you lose," Darren grumbled. There was a note of empathy in his voice. "Every dream ends with ashes falling from the sky like snow."

I swallowed hard. Darren stood up and sat the breastplate on the bench beside him. He took an ominous step toward me. His shadow covered my body.

"Why do you think I built such a large fleet?" he proposed, "You think I needed *all* those ships to take over the world? I could have done it with three if your father hadn't meddled with my plan."

"Then why build the beacon?" I questioned. I couldn't tell if he was toying with me. I didn't think he was.

"I did what they told me," Darren defended, "But I planned to turn on them if they ever invaded. My men would have followed me." He paused and stared past me. "Then, I got my powers…and the dreams started."

"They're just dreams," I pointed out, trying to give myself some sense of security.

"You don't believe that," he shook his head.

There was a long pause. He was right. I didn't believe that. I did my best to push past it.

"We can change it," I reasoned, "We just have to prepare."

"I used to think the same thing," Darren sighed. This was the most normal I had ever seen him. "I know that's foolish now." He walked back toward his seat. "You can't defeat them."

"You don't know that!" I protested.

Darren spun around and pointed his finger at me. "I'm the only one that knows that!" he yelled. His eyes were full of rage and fear. I didn't have to have powers to sense that.

"The world is unified now," I told him. That was mostly true. "We can change this, but we have to work together. You have to tell me what you know."

Darren slouched into his bench. He looked at the breastplate. Then, as if it spoke to him, he looked at me and asked, "Did they light the beacon?"

"Yes"

His face sank, "Then it's too late."

"How much time do we have?" I asked.

"Five, maybe six years," he sulked.

"That's plenty of time!" I elated. I was expecting weeks, not years.

"You could prepare a lifetime, and it still wouldn't be enough," Darren contested.

Now, I was annoyed with him. I could understand feeling defeated, especially in his position, but now he had the chance to actually do something good - not that he wanted to do something good. He at least had the chance to save himself.

I walked toward him and stood until he looked at me. "When you die, say the Overseers kill you, when you look in their eyes, do you want to have rotted in this cell having done nothing to fight them, or do you want to at least take a few of them with you?"

Darren sat still for a moment, then chuckled. "You always surprise me," he said, shaking his head. "I'll tell you what I know."

"Good," I smiled. I leaned down and picked up the breastplate. I pressed it back to my chest. The suit latched onto it and the energy ran back across my body. I tamed it down until it was no more than a few flickers of light racing around my body. "I'll be back shortly."

I turned and used just the right amount of energy to trick the mechanisms in the door to Darren's cell. It opened, and I walked out. I made my way down the hallway until I came to the station at the front. Raddick and Benjamin were standing next to one another. It looked as though Raddick had run the entire way down here.

"Good to see you Benjamin," I greeted. I looked at Raddick "Director, summon the Council of Nations."

Chapter 40

My whole life, I had been wading through a river, the banks too tall to escape. I had no choice but to make my way through the current. These past two years, the water had grown deeper and stronger than ever before. I had a choice then: I could pick up my feet, float down the river, and react as I came to things, or I could dig in my heels, fight the current, and make my own path upstream. I thought fighting the current was the same as surviving, but for the longest, I had only reacted. Now, I felt like that was changing. Now I was fighting the current, less with my actions and more with my choices. The battle now wasn't between peoples and powers, it was between ideas. Choosing right, choosing peace, choosing independence from the world and dependence on God and family - that was fighting the current.

The Council of Nations was summoned. I - and Darren - told them everything we knew about The Overseers. Raddick proved his loyalty by backing my claims. I vowed to help rebuild the world, but in return, they had to vow to build it better. We had to be ready when the Overseers arrived.

In the months that followed, I assembled my team. Some members were obvious, others had to be sought after. The process was rigorous.

There were only a small number of people in the world who had inherited the gene allowing them to wield the crystals. Thanks to The Organization, we had a large data base of candidates. The hard part was finding someone worthy, someone who was pure of heart, incorruptable, and complemented the team.

In the meantime, the bearers I had selected were helping me run missions all around the world. We settled border disputes, freed cities from gangs, locked up criminals, and chased the remaining loyal members of The Organization to the ends of the Earth. With the help and resources of the Ekklesia, we purged their influence from society.

In time, scientists used my fathers research to create fusion reactors. The absence of the crystals forced innovation forward. Essentially, they created tiny suns to power the technology that once could only be supplied by the energy of a crystal.

The survivors from El Dorado traveled to Boulder, Colorado. Hunter led them to their lost temple in the Rocky mountains. There, I used the Earth stone to expand and repair the small cavern. It didn't look like much when I was done, but I knew the Mayans could rebuild. I also returned their crystal to Ana. Thankfully, time and trust healed the wounds that had formed between us. It was good to have her back.

El Dorado became acknowledged as an independent country and the Mayans were given the entire rocky mountain territory by the United States as a thank you for their service and sacrifice in the war.

The lines and borders that defined countries were redrawn as a new age of brotherhood and cooperation took hold of the world. It might not have lasted if it weren't for the Protectorate holding it together. In that, we found our purpose.

Ekklesia and Mayan ships patrolled the world, searching out and destroying every last Organization hid out. The flaming dove made its way onto every flag pole. The symbol dominated the skies, the airwaves, and T-shirts around the world. Though I knew their sins better than most, I also knew that the idea my father had fostered was pure, as was the cause. The image of the Ekklesia that the world saw was the one I wanted to remember.

Perhaps one of my favorite things to come from the war were the stunning monuments that were set up all around the world, for every generation after us to see. On many, were the names of the millions of lives that were lost. Others stood tall, hoisting the flaming dove high above the landscape, as a tombstone for all those lost without a grave. Some marked the locations of battles, others the locations of destroyed or deserted bases. All of them stood as a bridge between the past and future: honoring the sacrifice of my generation and warning future generations not to make the same mistakes.

As for me, I never found "normal", and I was finally okay with that. I wasn't meant for normal. God had something better than normal for me. Looking back, I couldn't help but see the hand of God writing my story and guiding my every step. He gave and he took, he built up, and he tore down. He refined me into the man I was. I didn't always believe in that man, but I did believe in the God who is making him - forging him.

In that vein, I finally got back to church. Every Sunday, without compromise, I walked through those sanctuary doors and thanked the God that kept me this far. He was the center of my life, and at his direction, I made him the center of the Protectorate. We were his force for good, fighting for the future of the world and endowed with his divine protection.

*** 16 Months Later ***

"What do you think?" I asked Hunter. He was standing on the dock behind our headquarters at Tullahoma lake. I had just walked down behind him.

"Me?" he asked. His breath materialized in the sharp winter's air.

"Yea," I assured, "We've seen a lot of candidates. What do you think?"

Hunter looked out over the lake. His face shifted slightly with every thought that crossed his mind. He squirmed a bit as he adjusted his new uniform. A brisk wind grabbed his white cape and pulled it out behind him. Mine followed suit.

"Honestly," Hunter started, "None of them feel right to me."

He looked at me over his shoulder, causing his breastplate to catch the light of the white sun. The reflection highlighted our creed "FOR THE NATIONS" that was engraved above the green crystal seated in the center of his chest.

I had to agree with him. The candidates had undergone scrutinous vetting before they ever got to meet with us, but even the ones that made it here, despite their resumes, just didn't feel like a fit.

"Good," I sighed, "I was hoping it wasn't just me."

I walked up beside him and placed my hands behind my back, tucked firmly under my cape. I shifted as the Ekklesia dove on my shoulder pushed down uncomfortably. The suit immediately morphed to fix it. The pure white material reflected the light of the sun in a way that almost made my eyes water. Even my half of the purple crystal shined a bit brighter.

"We get a new round of candidates tomorrow," I informed Hunter, "Amelia and Ryder should be back from their mission in Thailand by then." I looked out over the water, "I told them they could sit in and help us decide."

Hunter's eyes glistened, "Amelia's coming!" he smiled, "I feel like I haven't seen her in forever."

It wasn't that they hadn't been around, but with Hunter's work at New Dorado and in the field, I guess their schedules hadn't lined up for a while.

"It'll feel good to have the whole gang back together," I smiled sentimentally. Of course, there would be one member missing, but something told me she would be watching… and proud.

We both looked out toward the dam. Between gusts of wind, I could hear the water crashing down the stream below. A school of fish surfaced near the dock, some jumping up to avoid the bigger predators down below.

My mind drifted over the events of my life and my time with Hunter, never sitting on one specific memory, but seeing broadly how far I had come, and how far I had seen him come. At this rate, he would far surpass me in every way.

I put my arm around him and pulled him close, "I proud of you, you know"

Hunter smiled and put his arm back around me, "I know," He said.

"Bailey would be too," I added.

"I know," he repeated.

We didn't stand there for much longer before a voice called from behind us, "Dylan! Hunter," It was Blake. I turned around. He was standing at the back door of my old house. The entire thing had been renovated to house our new team. The glass door behind him was open wide, and Ana stood with her arms around him from behind, her head barely resting on his shoulder.

"Yea?" I called back, not yet letting go of Hunter.

"Amelia and Ryder just got here!" he called, "They just landed at Arnold Base."

"They're here already!" Hunter exclaimed.

"I guess they're early," I grinned.

He smiled, but didn't let go of me. I nodded, giving him permission to let go. He did, and bounded up to Blake and Ana. His white cape spread out behind him as he ran. He leapt into their arms, almost knocking them down, then continued inside. I was sure he would be waiting at the door when Amelia and Ryder arrived.

Blake and Ana chuckled. He kissed Ana on the cheek as they entered the house. When he turned to close the door, he looked at me to ask "are you coming?". I nodded. He grinned, and shut the door.

As I started off the dock, I turned my attention back to the lake once more. The water sparkled as a gust of wind troubled the surface. That same sparkle filled my eye as a proud, hopeful tear formed. A purple glow swelled across the white uniform as the energy reacted to my emotions.

I looked up at the sky. The dreams still hadn't stopped, but they didn't haunt me anymore. The Overseers would come - let them. What they would find here would be far more than they could handle.

They would find a world united against them, and a team prepared to protect it. While the sun was up, we would prepare, and when it fell, we would be ready to fight. For now, our love, and our God would carry us.

I gave the lake one last look and surrendered to the icy tear that was fighting to fall. I smiled, wiped my tear, and walked back to the house.

The wind caught my cape, and hope caught my heart. My tall white boots crunched through the frozen grass. As I neared the house, I could see through the glass door.

Amelia and Ryder were walking through the front door. Hunter had sprang up from the couch and was already hugging a reluctant Ryder. He smiled nervously. Amelia embraced him next. Ana and Blake were walking up to them from the kitchen.

As I neared the door, the sun revealed my own reflection in the glass. My hand reached for the handle, but my eyes became locked on their reflected gaze. I looked deep into my own green eyes. Tinges of purple danced through my irises.

After all this time, I finally saw myself. I saw a leader. I saw a unifier. I saw myself through the lens God looked through. On the other side of the glass, I saw the future. I saw the hand of God writing stories just as complex and beautiful as my own. And for this season, he had allowed our stories to merge.

I took one last look at myself. I gave myself a resolute and hopeful nod, and my reflection nodded back.

Then, I opened the door.

Hello reader!

I hope you enjoyed this second installment of “The Crystal” Series. This book was a long one and it helped me explore a lot of complex topics. I would encourage you to go back and give the other books in the series as well as the “Legends” books so that you can appreciate the vast amount of foreshadowing and connections.

Speaking of that, there will be one more book in this series, The Crystal, Parts 7-9. This will conclude the trilogy (but I do plan to make more “Legends” books).

Coming soon will be The Legend of Daniel Sons where we will explore the story of Dylan’s father and his original vision for the Ekklesia. It will also explore how The Organization rose to power.

Keep an eye out, and until then, happy reading! I hope you got something out of this work. Please share it with a friend!

For The Nations,

J. A. Daniel

www.ingramcontent.com/pod-product-compliance
Lightning Source LLC
LaVergne TN
LVHW090544110826
845146LV00001B/18

* 9 7 9 8 9 9 1 9 0 8 9 4 8 *